Shadows of the Dark Realm

The Dark Realm
Book 1

Tyler Edwards

Copyright © 2023 by Tyler Edwards

All rights reserved.

No part of this book may be reproduced in any form or by any electronic or mechanical means, including information storage and retrieval systems, without written permission from the author, except for the use of brief quotations in a book review.

To my son Rowan, my little dragon,

for all the dreams I have of what you will grow up to be, my greatest desire is that whatever you do, you will know that you are loved.

Prologue

Worlds, like kingdoms, rise and fall. Some fade into decay. Others are brought to ruin.

Long ago, the Mortal Realm, the Dark Realm, and the Spirit Realm were connected; three worlds linked by shared borders. Tensions rose as beings from each realm crossed freely into the others. To avert war, the lords of each realm formed an agreement, and a fragile peace was forged. But one day Praetor Rath, the King of Shadows and ruler of the Dark Realm, broke the agreement and invaded, seeking to conquer the other realms for himself. And conquer them he nearly did. His monsters wreaked havoc on the other worlds, slaughtering and pillaging in the name of their king.

The Lord of the Mortal Realm and the god of Spirits joined forces to resist the advancing forces of the Dark Realm. But Praetor Rath was not so easily contained. His seemingly endless armies overwhelmed the other two realms. Darkness spread across the lands. It was then, when all hope seemed lost, the Lord of the Mortal Realm sacrificed himself to create the Darkstone: a magical stone powerful enough to seal away Praetor Rath and the Dark Realm.

The monsters trapped in the other realms went into hiding, living in shadows and biding their time. One day the Shadow King will return. His armies will cover the world in darkness. This will be the day of doom. This will be the fall of men.

—Barenthu the Seer, Visions of the Three Realms

The idyllic kingdom of Parisia sat nestled securely in a secluded basin in the Great Emerald Mountains. Ruled by the noble family of the Vila Delaluche, Parisia was a kingdom like no other. With an abundance of natural resources, Parisia enjoyed generations of peace and prosperity that made her the envy of all the other kingdoms. For Parisia housed the Darkstone, a magical gem the size of a bowl that was rumored to grant the greatest desire of whoever held it in their possession. The Darkstone blessed the land, protected the kingdom, and turned the kingdom into a paradise filled with comfort and pleasures beyond measure.

But comfort often leads to complacency, complacency to apathy, entitlement, and ruin. Nothing brews weakness as effectively as abundance. Over the years, the people of Parisia had grown accustomed to their wealth; they wanted for nothing and worked for nothing.

They believed themselves untouchable until their greatest treasure was taken from them by Draka Mors, an ancient Elder Dragon. For the first time in centuries, the great kingdom of Parisia was vulnerable.

Chapter 1

Missing Children

Lightning danced across the sky as a storm rumbled in the distance. Thick, billowing clouds made dusk look like midnight. A knight in pure black armor with a black cape wrapped around his shoulders and down the right side of his back stood at the edge of town. Standing before him was the frantic village elder.

"You have to help us," the elderly man's voice cracked as he fought back his tears. "It took him."

The Black Swordsman looked past the elder at a crowd of gathered townsfolk all eyeing him suspiciously.

"How long?" his voice rumbled.

"Two nights ago. His mother sent him to get some logs and said he never came home. Everyone's been searching, but . . . nothing. His mother's worried sick something terrible has happened to him."

"Anyone else see him?"

"Oh, aye, couple of the youngsters saw him heading out of town with someone. They couldn't rightly say who. I can show you where they seen him going. Come on." His tone was urgent, almost panicked, as he waved for the black knight to follow.

The Black Swordsman didn't move. He stared intently at the elder. "You think it was a Swapling?"

The elder looked away. "Don't rightly know what it was. Just that little Brexiton went with him. Could be a . . . Swapling, you say?"

"Swaplings are known for taking children."

"R-r-r-ight. So let me show you the tracks, and you can go find it."

"Why?"

The elder's stammering grew more pronounced. "T-t-that's why you're here, ign't? To track whatever 'tis that took the missing child?"

"Children."

"What's that?"

"Children. Oakton is missing two children."

"Two?"

"Yes. A child went missing from here three months ago. Strange that you would forget something like that."

The elder's eyes widened. His lip quivered as he struggled to push the words out. "Forgive me, sir knight. A child is missing, taken from his family not two nights ago. We are all so worried. I have hardly slept. I am not thinking clearly. Please, help us. Let me take you to where the boy was last seen. Maybe you will be able to see something we missed? I am happy to answer any questions you have after that. Please, just . . . come with me."

The knight's eyes narrowed. "Ever since I arrived, you have been trying to lead me away. What is it you don't want me to see?"

"What? I'm sorry. I don't follow."

"There are twelve towns like Oakton around the capital. A child has gone missing from every one of them."

"That's . . . terrible. Y-you think this Swapling . . . is responsible?" the elder asked.

"No. Swaplings are impulsive—never heard of one following a pattern."

"A pattern?"

"The children were taken almost exactly one month apart. Your town is an anomaly. Yours is the only town to have a second child go missing."

"Forgive my directness, sir knight, but I fail to see how this helps us find Brexiton. The light is fading quickly. Every passing moment the boy could be getting farther away. Yet you're just standing here. What are you waiting for?" the elder pressed.

A bolt of lightning flashed in the sky, illuminating the area for the briefest of moments.

"That." The Black Swordsman tilted his head toward the sky.

The elder looked up. "Lightning? Why?"

"Swaplings are extremely talented shapeshifters; they are a near-perfect replica of the person they model. There's just one thing they can't get right . . ."

"Sir knight?"

"Their eyes—a quick burst of light turns them gold."

The elder gasped as the sharp blade pierced his chest, skewering him. He coughed and blood painted his lips. He tried to speak, but his words were gargled and indecipherable.

"Human eyes don't do that. But yours did." The Black Swordsman pulled his blade free and the elder dropped to the ground.

A woman screamed from behind the elder. A group of men rushed over holding torches.

"What have you done?" one shouted, charging toward the knight.

"Wait—" The Black Swordsman held up his hands, but the villager wasn't listening. He swung his fist at the swordsman's face. The knight stepped back, moving out of the man's path. Another charged at him, swinging a club he had been carrying. The swordsman ducked out of the way. He clutched his sword as he moved, dodging the punches, swings, and thrusts of four different villagers. He kept his sword away from them as he moved.

"Wait!" he called out again but to no avail.

"What is that?!" a woman's voice cried out from behind them, stopping the villagers short. One looked over and stopped.

"Gods below," he muttered. The others hesitantly turned to see what was going on.

Lying on the ground was not the body of the old man they'd known their entire lives. Rather, they saw a lanky, wire-haired creature with large eyes and skin that looked like smooth clay.

"What—" one of the men asked, unable to even finish his thought.

"A Swapling—a shapeshifter that preys on children," the Black Swordsman answered.

One of the men who had been attacking the knight was now leaning over the body of the creature. "This is what took our children?"

"Child. Just the one from yesterday. Is there a cave nearby?"

The man nodded. "There's a stream near the other side of town. Past the stream is a hilly forest. There are a few caves there."

The Black Swordsman nodded. "You will find your missing child and the village elder in one of those caves." The knight turned to leave.

"Wait—you're going? Y-you just . . . at least stay the night. We can get you a warm meal and place to rest."

"Very well," the swordsman said.

One of the villagers smiled. "I'll get you taken care of."

The swordsman followed the villager down the dirt road into town.

"I'm Josh Turner. I run the stables. What's your name?"

"Vale Lox," the swordsman replied.

Josh winced. "That's unfortunate. Having to share a name with the disgraced knight; that can't be easy."

The Black Swordsman grunted.

"I remember hearing the stories of Vale when I was growing up. The legendary hero who fearlessly defended Parisia from all her enemies. I even wanted to be a knight because of him. Then to find out what he did . . . How does someone do that? How do they live with themselves afterward?"

The Black Swordsman shrugged. "Everyone has their reasons."

"Yeah, I can't imagine what could possibly justify that. If I were the king, I'd have given him a long, slow public execution to make an example. Letting him live after what he did—where's the justice in that?"

The Black Swordsman grunted.

Shadows of the Dark Realm

"I can't even imagine a more shameful and villainous thing to do. I wonder—"

"Where's the inn?" Vale interrupted.

Josh pointed to a two-story wooden building. The second floor was wider than the first, creating a covered walkway in front of the building's entrance. A sudden rush of color and movement caught Vale's eye. A man who had been standing out of view rushed away. He was wearing an exceptionally bright blue hood that was lined with ornate silver designs. Vale had seen something like this before in one of the other villages.

"Who is that?" Vale asked.

Josh followed Vale's gaze. "Oh, that's Havaron. He's a priest of the . . . umm . . . what are they called?"

"The Regilum?"

"That's the one. Don't know much about it—said he wanted to set a temple for worship. He mostly keeps to himself. Weird, right? What kind of priest shows up, starts a temple, and then doesn't try to convert anyone?" Josh chuckled.

"They worship the Royal family as if they are gods," Vale answered.

"Oh, well, that's different. He seems like a nice enough guy —little weird maybe."

"Where is this temple?"

"Not built yet. He's still gathering the materials needed."

Vale turned, his voice suddenly urgent, "Not finished? When did he arrive?"

"Oh, a while back. Can't remember exactly. A year? No, less. Maybe two seasons ago."

Vale's eyes widened, and he turned around and headed back out of town.

"Where are you going? Room's this way," Josh called out.

"Another time," Vale called back.

Vale's mind outpaced his legs as he started trying to put the pieces together. He'd first heard the story when he was sitting at a tavern in Olia Village. Some of the locals were theorizing what may have happened. At the next town, a pair of grieving parents offered him a purse of silver if he could find their missing son. He'd rejected the coin but promised to look into it. Their son was the same age. Same details as the town before. Vale moved from one village to the next. In each he heard the same story.

A local boy under the age of ten had gone missing. The circumstances around it were peculiar. There were no signs of abduction, monsters, or even indications that the child was unhappy and may have run away from home. There was no trail to follow, and no body was ever discovered. It was like the boy just vanished.

He hadn't realized it until he saw the priest in Oakton, but he'd seen a priest of the Regium in several of the other towns. It could be a coincidence. The Regium were usually aggressively evangelistic. Maybe they were involved somehow. But what would a group of religious fanatics who worshiped the royal family want with a bunch of children? What were they doing with them? Why? The more he thought, the less sense it made.

He was missing something, that one piece of the puzzle that brings the image into focus. Vale was so lost in thought that by the time he stopped to see where he'd wandered, he was already at Silver Lake. To his surprise, it was already morning.

Like all the towns and villages in Parisia, Silver Lake was pristine. The grass was vibrant, the crops bountiful, the houses well-decorated. Silver Lake was named after the small lake that it was set along. At the back of the lake there was a little waterfall where the rocks were veined with thin strips of silver, making the whole lake glisten and appear to shine in the light. It was a mesmerizing sight as the water looked almost magical.

Vale wasn't interested in taking in the scenery, though. He made his way to the local town hall—a wide, two-story, gray, stone building with a blue shingled roof. Flowers of blue and yellow filled the decorative beds that hung from each of the oak-framed windows, adding splashes of color and life. Vale pushed his way through the doors.

The hall was a large, open room with a long table on the back wall. The town council used it to host meetings for the community when needed. A small group of half a dozen villagers, most of them council members, sat around the table talking.

"You have returned?" one of the villagers said, looking up from his seat at the table. "Any news?"

Shadows of the Dark Realm

"The order of Regilum," Vale replied.

"What about it?"

"Are they here?"

"What do you mean?" another of the villagers asked. "Are you suggesting they had something to do with these missing children?"

"I'm asking a question. Are there any priests from the cult of Regilum that live in Silver Lake?" Vale pressed.

"No. There are no members of the cult that live here or near here. Even if there were, the cult could never do something so vile. They are the pious servants who have devoted their lives to showing the kindness and love of the great royal family to all of Parisia. They are the hands and feet of our king's benevolence and mercy," one of the townsfolk objected.

"The Royals are our champions, our protectors. It's the blood of their family that keeps us safe and prosperous. It's the Royals who keep the outside world at bay. How could you even suggest their followers would be involved in something like this?" an older woman questioned.

"The king rescued me when I was a child. He saved me from a life of violence and death. He took care of me, helped me. He was like a father to me. I served him for years. I am not making accusations. I have to chase down every lead. I don't think the Regilum would be involved, but it wouldn't be hard to pretend—for someone to put on the robes and act the part. If they haven't been here, then that's not it either." Vale couldn't tell if he was more frustrated or relieved. He turned to leave. This had been a waste of time.

"Hold on," a voice called out from behind him. "None of the Regilum live here, but they have been here."

Vale turned around, his heart thumping rapidly in his chest. "They have? When?"

The man leaned back and rubbed his chin. "Pair of 'em came through town about four or five months ago. Stayed for about a week, then left."

"Yeah, I members that," another villager added. "T'was weird. I'd always thought they were the preachy type, but the two of 'em came, stayed awhile, and didn't try to convert nobody."

"That was odd. What were they even doing?" another added.

"How long ago did the boy go missing from here?" Vale asked.

The room fell silent. Tension built in the air as one by one the villagers came to the same conclusion—an answer not a single one wanted to voice.

"Gods below—five months, almost exactly," an older man in the back of the room finally said.

Confirmation. He was on the right track. Before he could respond, the doors to the town hall burst open. Heavy, metal boots clanged in unison against the wooden floor as a small detachment of soldiers marched in.

The soldiers wore elaborate silver armor that glimmered, unblemished by battle or the elements. Each had a well-crafted, ornate sword in a blue sheath at their hip and carried a long halberd in their hand. A blue cape that carried the two crescent moons turned together with a thin flame in the middle signified they were the pride of Parisia—royal knights. Not just any royal knights—these were the king's personal detachment of knights.

They moved in unison, twelve knights as one. Their boots shook the floor as they paraded into the middle of the room. Just as they stopped, another man entered behind them. His armor and cape were of a similar style, but, unlike the others, he wore no helmet. He walked past them, assessing the room, his short, dark hair holding the same perfect attention as his men. He turned to face Vale and stood at attention.

"Disgraced knight Vale, you have been summoned to the palace of Parisia by order of his majesty, King Alistar." The man didn't look Vale in his eyes; his gaze was above Vale's head, a deliberate insult.

"I am in the middle of something important. I will answer the king's call as soon as I have—"

"You are to come with us immediately, desisting of any previous commitment at the request of the king himself. Delay will not be tolerated," the man said.

"Children are being taken. His majesty's knights have not responded to the requests of his people to investigate. I can't just leave this," Vale protested.

"The king knows of your work. He commanded you be brought to him immediately. You can come willingly, or I am authorized to bring you by force."

Vale grinned. "You know who I am?"

"I do." A note of disdain hung on the captain's response as his hand fell to the hilt of his sword.

Every instinct in Vale's body burned with a need to respond. Years of experience and instinct made his hand pull toward his own sword. It would be so easy. Vale closed his eyes and took a deep breath, keeping his hand far from his own weapon. The last thing he needed was a group of overly eager soldiers forcing him to defend himself. Defeating them would not be difficult. Even the way they stood betrayed their lack of experience. These knights had never ventured outside the wall. All their training was for show in the safety of a courtyard. But if he resisted, he'd be forced to kill them. Vale sighed, and his shoulders slumped.

"Lead the way."

Chapter 2

Seekers

King Alistar sat at the war table in his palace listening to his generals and advisors argue about what to do.

"My king, without the Darkstone we are vulnerable. Our mages are working to hold the veil in place, but they won't be able to sustain it. If we don't get the Stone back, the veil will fall, and the gates to the Dark Realm will re-open. If that—"

"Stop your fearmongering, Urthal. We are not children to be scared by bedtime stories," one of the generals snapped.

"We are already receiving reports of monsters in our realm. It's only going to get worse," Urthal countered.

"He's right," a voice echoed around the room as the doors opened. An old man in flowing white robes hemmed with gold hobbled in. He was hunched forward, leaning his weight on a gnarled staff. He wore a white hood that was pulled up, hiding all but the massive white beard that stretched halfway down his stomach.

"Master Gonway, thank you for joining us. As the Master of Scrolls you know more about the prophesies and histories than anyone. I was told you have something pressing to share with us." King Alistar gestured for the old man to take the floor.

"My king, my lords. It is grave news that I bring to you. I believe the loss of the Darkstone has set in motion the grimmest of prophesies."

"The days of doom?" No one paid attention to who asked the question as all eyes were fixed on Master Gonway.

The old man gave a smug smile in response before nodding slowly. "Always nice to see a fellow scholar. Yes. The days of doom. I believe they are upon us."

"Based on what?" one of the advisors challenged.

"In the words of the great seer Barenthu who wrote in the ancient scroll:

I saw the king seated on his throne of smoke, shadows all around him. Destruction reigns in his heart. Death follows in his wake. For so long, he has been denied his desire. For so long, he has been kept at bay.

When the land is at peace, and trials are all but forgotten, this will be the beginning of the end. When the source is taken, the wall between realms will grow weak. The King of Shadows will rise, and ruin will befall the race of men."

"We don't know that the Darkstone is this source; that's just one interpretation," an advisor challenged, his objection sending the room into an uproar.

With everyone speaking at the same time, making sense of anything being said became near impossible. The king banged his fist on the table, making it shake and quieting the chaos.

"Gentlemen, this is not a productive approach." His voice was stern as he scolded the council. "One at a time if you please."

It took a moment for anyone to work up the courage to speak after that.

The Master of Commerce finally broke the silence, "Master Gonway, am I correct in understanding that you are suggesting the source referenced in the prophecy is the Darkstone?"

Master Gonway replied with a nod.

"And that the loss of the Darkstone is an indication that the days of doom are now upon us?" he continued.

Master Gonway nodded again. Quiet murmurs started to boil up around the room, silenced quickly by a glare from the king.

Master Gonway continued, "There is yet hope, my lords. The prophesy ends:

By the mercy of the gods below, when the day of doom is at hand, a deliverer shall rise and bring hope unto the land. An heir of royal blood who could never wear the crown shall bring salvation to the world of man."

The Master of Law spoke up, "If these are the Days of Doom, we need to find this man and—"

"Woman."

Everyone turned to look at the speaker, a man standing in the back corner of the room. He was wearing a unique and elaborate blue cloak that gave him the look of nobility, an appearance contrasted by his disheveled black hair and seeming lack of concern for his appearance. The man was tall with dark skin. Little was known about him before he arrived in Parisia many years ago, Rumor had it, he was a mage from Arcani the kingdom to the south.

"What?"

"The deliverer mentioned in the prophesy; it is not a man. It is a woman," the man in blue explained.

"Honestly, Dante, do you hear yourself? A woman? The gods below would never send a woman. There is simply no way," the Master of Law grunted, his face turning red.

"Difficult as it may be for your feeble mind to process, not only can it be a woman, it can only be a woman."

"Have you taken leave of your senses?"

"An heir who could never wear the crown," Dante repeated, cutting off the noble. "Tradition is for the oldest son to inherit the throne. The Law of Succession states that the king may select any of his sons to inherit his crown if he believes them to be the most fit to rule. Royal Law prohibits a woman from sitting on the throne. Hence, an heir who cannot wear the crown must be a woman of royal blood."

The room went quiet. No one, general or advisor, wanted to speak aloud what they were all thinking.

"Prophesy or no, it changes nothing!" Zamor, General of the

Shadows of the Dark Realm

First Army's voice boomed as he stood, leaning forward on the ornate marble table for effect. "We hunt and kill the dragon and take back the Stone. The First Army would be honored to take up this mission, my king!"

"Aye! Of course, the First Army wants to hog all the glory for themselves. My king, give us all the opportunity to show our quality. Let each of your armies take up the call and reward whomever successfully reclaims the Darkstone," Briga, General of the Second Army contended.

"And who will protect the king and kingdom should all our soldiers go chasing after a dragon?" The Master of Treasury challenged.

The room descended into a cacophony of shouting, bickering, and boasting, with everyone agreeing something needed to be done and no one agreeing on how to do it.

King Alistar rubbed his head, fighting off the throbbing drum pounding inside it.

"This is fruitless. You're advisors to the king. Where is your dignity?" the commander of the Lion Legion shouted, silencing the room. "My king, if you will allow my men to—"

"If the king entrusts this mission to you, or to any other general, the only thing the he will get is a bunch of dead soldiers and a kingdom that is even more vulnerable," Dante interrupted.

"You are not a military man. You have no right to speak here!" the general of the First Army snapped. This was the first statement all the generals agreed on.

"Think for a moment," Dante replied. "Reaching the Dragon Lands requires traveling through Taggoron, Rag'amor, and Baronia. That's just to reach the Fang Coast. You know what all those places have in common?" He paused for effect, then continued before anyone could answer, "They all hate us. What do you think those kingdoms will do when they see our armies marching through their lands?" Another pause for effect. "I'll tell you! They will attack. First our armies and then Parisia. Without the Darkstone, we'll be powerless to stop them. If the army leaves—if any large force leaves—we will be inviting an invasion and death."

"So, what's your plan, alchemist? Make a potion and hope it

lures the dragon to return the Stone?" The generals around the table chuckled at the challenge.

The king sat up and motioned for Dante to come to the table. "Tell me what you would suggest."

"Where an army draws attention, hunting parties could go unnoticed. Put out a call for heroes, warriors, champions—anyone willing to take up the king's quest. Your generals can form them into teams, train them, and send them out."

"Hunting parties—that's your solution? Train commoners to journey across the land, fight a dragon, and retrieve the most important and powerful magical object in the world? You really are bat gwar crazy," the commander of the Lion Legion chuckled.

"Why do they need to fight the dragon? All we need is the Stone. They can steal it," Dante replied.

"My apologies. That plan is so much better. Just send some townsfolk to sneak into the lair of a dragon and steal its treasure? This will be easy."

"Without the Stone, we are doomed. Everyone in Parisia will die. We are not asking people to risk their lives on some errand. We are calling on them to help save not just the kingdom but the entire realm of men. You are calling for townsfolk. You are calling for the King's Seekers. That will draw plenty. For the rest, offer a reward. Land. Title. Fame. Fortune. You'll have more volunteers than you'll know what to do with."

"You think that will work?" the king asked.

"This is too important to entrust to commoners. The Stone is the only thing that keeps the Shadow Lord locked away."

"Do you have another option?" King Alistar turned to his general.

The general shrank back in his chair, avoiding the king's gaze.

King Alistar rose to his feet, and the sneering among the generals quieted.

"These are challenging times we find ourselves in. We face a threat beyond anything we've experienced before. It is important for the sake of the kingdom that we work together. Dante is right.

I trust you will listen to his plan and carry it out without complication, understood?"

The table of advisors and generals nodded dutifully.

"Dante, tell them what you would have them do."

"General Zamor, General Briga, gather your best soldiers and put them in civilian clothing. Each one will lead a team of Seekers. Their purpose is to keep the team on task, and should they succeed, ensure the team returns with the Darkstone. Keep the teams small but not less than five."

The generals grunted in approval. In Parisia, five was considered the holiest number and a good omen. Though a silly superstition believed only by fools, Dante knew this would make them more cooperative moving forward.

"Spend a few days training and equipping each team to increase their odds of success," he continued. "Space out their departures over a week or so to keep them from drawing too much attention."

"Put out the call," King Alistar added. "Let it be known that anyone who undergoes this quest will have their families taken care of and offer a reward too tempting to be turned down."

The generals and advisors quickly filed out of the room to carry out the king's instructions. Master Gonway remained, examining a scroll he'd laid out across the table as everyone was leaving. Dante was at the back of the line, keeping a little distance from the others. Before he could reach the door, the king caught his arm and motioned for him to stay.

Dante waited until the others had disappeared down the hall. The king pushed the door closed and smiled warmly. Dante knew that look, the look of someone who was about to ask for a ridiculous favor.

"Dante, you have been an advisor to my family for as long as I can remember. My father trusted you, as do I. Parisia needs you."

"Needs me to what?"

"Become a Seeker."

"No, my work is here. Send one of your generals. Send all of them; they are desperate to prove themselves."

King Alistar put his hand on Dante's shoulder. "Taking up a king's quest is a great honor."

Dante shook his head. "Honor is the currency of fools. I care not."

"Of course, you don't. You care only about your books."

"Make it sound cold if you want. Knowledge is our future. It is our hope and our deliverance. When the Red Empress burned the Royal Library, centuries of tomes containing wisdom, machines, and recipes for potions of healing and restoration were destroyed."

"Yes, and, fortunate for us, you have them memorized."

"That is why I must refuse you. My work is not complete. This knowledge is too important to risk. If I die before documenting it, it will be lost forever."

"I understand, Dante, I do. But what good is it to compile all the knowledge in the world if there is no one left to learn from it?"

"You cannot ask this of me," Dante protested.

"I must. My kingdom stands on the brink of ruin. You are one of the most gifted wizards I've ever seen. You're smart. You think on your feet, and you can problem solve. This is your plan. You bring the greatest chance of success."

Dante shook his head. "I am not a hero."

"I don't need you to be. I have a hero already, a knight who will accompany you. The rest of your team, you can select as you see fit."

Dante rubbed his chin as he thought it over.

"Do this—bring me back the Darkstone, and I will grant you any request you ask of me," the king vowed.

Dante's eyes lit up. "When we return, you give me three days with the Stone to use it as I see fit, unencumbered by your wizards."

"Three days? Have you lost all sense of yourself?" The king's face flushed, and his eyes narrowed. He caught himself, took a slow deep breath, and forced a smile. "Very well."

The king departed a few moments later with a pair of guards in his wake, leaving Dante alone with the Master of Scrolls humming idly.

"He certainly thinks very highly of you," Master Gonway snickered.

Dante turned to face the old scholar. "I am curious, Master of Scrolls and advisor to the king, why did you withhold information from the council?"

Master Gonway turned from his scroll and faced Dante with a look of agitation growing on his face. "Withhold? And what, pray tell, did I withhold?"

Dante shrugged, "You told them the heir who could never wear the crown would bring salvation."

"Yes, that is what the prophesy states."

"It does. But the word that is used for salvation also means destruction."

Master Gonway stared deep into Dante's eyes. "That's an odd thing for you to know."

"That is an odd thing to leave out of your report."

* * *

Heralds shouted all throughout the kingdom: "Hear ye, hear ye, Parisia needs you! The king is calling for men and women of great courage and character to become his Seekers. Any who take up the king's quest will, upon their return, have all of their debts and crimes forgiven. For the Seekers who successfully retrieve the Stone, they will be given land, title, and wealth from the royal treasury. A statue will be built in their honor, and they will be named heroes of Parisia!"

The king's call was answered en masse. Citizens from all over Parisia flocked to the castle, lured by both the promised reward and the rumors of the Darkstone's special magic: that it gives the one who possesses it the greatest desire of their heart. The royal family had denied this vehemently for generations, which only seemed to fuel the people's belief.

Dante watched their training from the palace walls, looking for promising candidates. While some stood out more than others, no one really caught his attention. How was he supposed to pick a team? He had never done anything like this before.

The crowds came in waves. The generals spent several days

training the groups before they were divided into teams. Each was equipped with supplies, weapons, and coin to make purchases along the way. They were given an enchanted writ authorizing their travel in and out of Parisia. The process was efficient. Once a team was ready, they were sent out to make room for the next batch of eager adventurers to be trained. Thousands of parties of various sizes departed on the king's quest to save Parisia.

After three weeks of waiting, the king summoned Dante for an audience.

"The knight I have chosen for you has arrived. Are you ready to meet him?" King Alistar asked as he sat comfortably on his elevated throne.

"Who is he?"

"Vale Lox, the Century Slayer and hero of Parisia."

"You mean, Vale the disgraced knight? Was he not one of your commanders before you stripped him of all titles and honor?" Dante questioned.

"He was."

"I am not sure that is a good fit. I will keep searching."

"Vale provides your best chance of success. He will be joining you."

"I am sure there are plenty of knights who are just as capable but whose names draw less attention."

"This is not a request. Vale will be joining you."

Dante raised an eyebrow. "Why do I get the sense that you are keeping things from me? What am I missing?"

The king smiled. "Nothing. Dante, you are an asset and a friend. I need you on this quest and, just as importantly, I need you to return. Vale can make that happen. He is relentless. His will is unrivaled. Never in all his years of service did he ever fail to complete a mission he was given. I wish it weren't so. After what he did, he's lucky I allowed him to live. But now we need him. Before his fall, he was the most trustworthy and reliable knight in Parisia. He is one of the greatest warriors I've ever seen and a natural-born leader. You couldn't ask for better."

Dante stared. Secrets do not build trust. He could fill a canyon with what the king wasn't telling him. Fighting it was of no benefit. "I suppose you do not acquire as many nicknames as he has without cause. Very well, I will meet him."

"Good."

King Alistar smiled and lifted his hand; a side door opened, and two guards stepped into the room, then stood at attention on either side of the door . A man in pure black armor with a black cape entered the room. He moved with confidence and authority. He walked past Dante without so much as a glance and bowed to the king.

"Dante, this is Vale. He will be your sword and your shield on this quest. I am certain he will serve you well." The king grimaced at the remark.

The black knight turned, acknowledging Dante for the first time. Dante extended his hand.

"Dante Cres. Seems we will be traveling together."

Vale replied with a grunt as he shook Dante's hand. Dante winced under the knight's grip. He waited expectantly, but the knight offered no other words.

"Now for the rest of your team. I trust they are ready?" the king asked.

"No. I have found only one suitable candidate, my king," Dante answered.

"One? You've had weeks, and you've only selected one? You test my patience, Dante. Who is it?"

"You are not going to like my answer," Dante replied.

The king leaned forward. "Tell me."

Dante smiled. "The witch your men caught in the treasury."

The king slammed his hand down on the armrest of his chair. "No!"

Dante shrugged. "Shapeshifting is a rare and very useful magic."

"We are investigating her connection to the Kinspira."

"Does it matter? Did you not say the fate of the kingdom, nay the world, hangs in the balance?"

The king spoke through gritted teeth. "How do you know she would agree?"

"I am certain she will require a royal pardon. I will take care of the rest," Dante smiled.

The king grunted, "Very well. Find the last two and quickly."

"I presume your majesty would prefer success to expedience?" Dante said flatly.

"Careful," the king warned. "If you are playing at a game or stalling for time, you will not like what comes next. Friend or not, I will grant you one more week. If you cannot make up your mind, General Briga will make it up for you."

"I will be back in three days. If I have not found anyone else, I will suffer whatever fools Briga offers." Dante bowed.

"Vale and the witch will be ready when you return," the king said.

Dante made his way out of the palace and down to the streets below. Lush gardens perfectly trimmed lined the sides of every building in sight. The walls were pure white and unblemished by dirt or decay. An artist couldn't paint so perfect a picture. While all the capital city was overflowing with beauty and luxury, the palace itself was near overwhelming. Dante had lived in Parisia for much of his life, but he remembered the kingdom he came from, the poverty, the struggle. A single brick for the impeccable street would be enough to feed an entire village outside of Parisia for a year, maybe longer. It was almost an embarrassment.

He stopped on the wide street staring off at the sky, getting lost in his own thoughts. How had it come to this? His work was not near finished. The thought of being away from it for so long was almost painful. Why was the king forcing him to do this? His mind flowed with scenarios, objections, opportunities to talk his way out of being involved. He knew the king well-enough to know it would only make things worse to try.

Dante was examining the writ the king had given him as he walked. As he read, he heard little footsteps growing closer at a rapid pace. He looked up to see a young woman sprinting toward him. She crashed into him, and they toppled to the ground.

"I'm so sorry; I'm such a fool," the girl said, standing up and dusting herself off. She was dressed as a cook, probably one for a noble family based on the quality of her clothing. She was young with dark hair and pristine, unblemished skin. She stood over

Shadows of the Dark Realm

Dante and grinned, seeming more amused by the accident than apologetic —strange for a servant girl who could be flogged for such an offense. Stranger still, she offered her hand to help him up. Most servants would cower and avoid eye contact, trembling in hopes to appeal to mercy. Perhaps her masters were lax in training proper etiquette? When she saw the writ lying on the ground, she pulled her hand back, forcing Dante to get up on his own.

"Y-you are going on the king's quest! You're a Seeker!" Her words were more an excited accusation than a question.

Dante picked the writ up and tucked it into his cloak. "Yes."

Her eyes lit up and her mouth dropped. "Gods below! What very good luck! I wanted to answer the king's call, but I . . . I was unable to get away from my duties until now."

"You wish to become a Seeker?"

"More than anything, yes."

"What are these duties that kept you?"

The girl shifted her weight nervously. "I'm a cook for the Vila Delaluche family."

Dante's eyes narrowed. "Why would the Vila Delaluches allow a cook to become a Seeker?"

She averted her gaze.

"I see. You are trying to escape. Go home, girl. I will grant you the mercy of not reporting this." He turned to walk away. Before he could move, she caught his arm.

"Please. I can't go back to that place. Take me with you. Let me prove myself," she pleaded.

"This is not a leisure trip nor a means to escape your station."

"No, it's the most important thing to happen in Parisia since the banishing of the Red Empress. This is my chance to show the world who I really am!"

"I wish you luck, but I can't help you," Dante replied.

"You don't understand. All my life I've dreamed of adventure. I've wanted to do something great, to be something great. I know I was meant for more than to be . . . than to be a cook. I can feel it in my soul. I want to make a difference in this world. Like the heroes of old, I will leave my mark on this world. Give me a chance," she pleaded. There was an intensity to her voice, a desperate desire and conviction that dripped from every word.

"Many fantasize about being a hero. Becoming a Seeker seems glamorous until you encounter the danger. No amount of dreaming will prepare you to stand in the presence of monsters. I'm saving your life, girl—go home," he stated.

"I can fight!" Before he could protest, the girl drew a sword from her hip. It was a long, thin blade but well crafted. She lunged and swung it around, moving and twirling with it. She sliced, thrusted, and struck pose after pose. She moved well. She was quick and graceful.

"See?" She smiled, posing like a dancer with one leg in the air and her sword extended toward Dante.

"Unlike the wind, real enemies tend to fight back. Knowing how to wield a blade is a far cry from knowing how to fight. Now, if you will excuse me, I must take my leave."

"Don't walk away from me!" she glared, teeth gritted.

"You are persistent, I will give you that. I don't need your blood on my conscience. This quest is no place for a cook."

"My blood will be on your hands if you don't take me."

"Excuse me?"

"If you say no, I'll find someone else. If they say no, I'll go by myself."

"Don't be dim; you'll die."

"You're right. Alone, I'll die. With you, I may live. It seems my life is in your hands."

Dante glared. "Counter—I inform the Vila Delaluches of your plans. They lock you up. Problem solved."

"And if you do, your quest will fail."

Dante snickered, "And just how is that?"

"According to the Academy of Antiquities, eight out of ten quests fail for the same reason. It's not a lack of skill. It's a lack of heart."

"Where did you read studies from the Academy of Antiquities?"

"The Delaluches have a secret library with all sorts of scrolls. I may not have experience, but I have something you need."

Dante folded his arms. "And what is that?"

"Conviction."

"Plenty of people have conviction."

"Not like I do. I know what happens if the Darkstone isn't returned. I will not fail. I will not quit. There is no length I will not go to, no bridge I will not cross. I will travel to the ends of the earth. I will bleed, suffer, go hungry. If the quest demands my life, I will lay it down. I will sacrifice everything if it means saving my . . . if it means saving the kingdom."

Dante raised an eyebrow. "What is your name, girl?"

"Celeste."

Dante sighed. Better to have an overeager girl than an extra goon from General Briga. "Ok. Two days. Meet me here at the entrance to the palace. Come ready. I will give you a chance. If you cannot keep up, we will leave you behind."

Tears welled in her eyes as she grabbed his hand and held it in hers. "Thank you! Thank you! You won't regret this. I swear." She rushed off, practically skipping away.

Chapter 3

The Bounty

"I understand that your majesty wishes to send me on a quest. I am here to humbly request that you reconsider." Vale spoke loudly to ensure he could be heard, with his gaze facing the ground.

"You would deny your king?" Alistar glared.

"Not deny, my king. I was merely hoping that one of your many capable commanders could undertake this quest in my stead."

"The knight dares question the judgment of his sovereign? Is that it? You know better, do you? Perhaps you should wear the crown?"

Vale lowered his head farther. "No, my king. It is just—I am in the middle of an investigation."

"What investigation is this?"

"Missing children, my king."

King Alistar raised an eyebrow. "Sounds like a matter for the village marshal. Why are you involved?"

"It is not just one village. I have found twelve, so far; each one has had a child around the age of ten disappear without a trace."

"I have heard nothing of this."

"I am not surprised. They are small, remote villages. There is not a lot of travel to or from them."

"You believe something is taking these children—like a monster?"

"Something or someone. I would like to request your permission to continue my investigation."

"Denied."

"My king?"

"You will become a Seeker and take up the quest to retrieve the Darkstone."

"My king, a child goes missing every month. I gave the families my oath. I will not break it."

"Your oath?"

"It is all I have left, my king."

"And whose fault is that?" King Alistar slammed his hand on the armrest of his throne. His face was red, his words flowed like fire from his tongue. "You dare blame me for the consequences of your actions?"

"No, your highness, forgive me."

"Do you know what happens if the Darkstone is not returned? Every child in the kingdom will be at risk. You are to forget about these missing children. I will have my guard look into it, I assure you."

"My king, have you not a thousand men as capable as I who could do this? I do not understand why it must be me."

"I need you to lead this team."

"Lead? I thought Dante was the leader, and I was to be his sword and shield?"

"Dante needs to believe it so. He is brilliant. He's a powerful wizard and an even more impressive alchemist. He is one of Parisia's greatest assets. He is not a leader. You were once a great commander and a loyal knight in my service. Before your fall, you were the one man I knew I could count on. No matter how great the odds or how dangerous the task, I knew you would see it done. I need that man. Parisia needs that man. For if this quest fails, it does so to the ruin of us all."

"My king, you honor me with your words but—"

"Need I remind you, Vale, that it is this obsessiveness of yours that led to your downfall? It cost you your honor, title, position, and your legacy. I am giving you a chance to redeem yourself. You would question me for it?" The king's voice grew louder as he spoke.

"No, my king, forgive me. I—"

"Then the matter is settled. Be gone."

Vale bowed his head deeper before departing the throne room.

* * *

When Dante returned to the palace, he'd had no luck finding another suitable candidate. Celeste was waiting and practically bouncing on her heels with a sack over her shoulder when he arrived. He instructed her to wait before he was escorted by guards in to see the king.

The witch, Azalea, was standing near the entrance, looking annoyed. Her striking red hair was long and flowing, looking almost like a fire. As he passed by, the guards removed the chains from her wrists.

"There are four here, yet five are needed. Have you one more?"

Dante shook his head.

"General Briga," the king called out.

The general stepped forward and presented a young, strong-looking man with a clean-cut face and the sort of air of superiority that comes only from nobility. Dante took one look at him and knew this was the son of some wealthy lord. Dante groaned.

"This is Sir Brevioar. He will be your fifth."

Those in attendance chanted, "By five may your journey thrive. By five may you return alive."

Dante bowed, "My king."

Since the training had begun, the king would address all the groups leaving that day. He offered them a benediction of encouragement and support to send the Seekers off with high morale. The departures were staggered over the course of the day and, one by one, the Seekers made their way for the Great Wall to begin their quest.

Dante's group would receive a private benediction just for

them. King Alistar stood, pacing back and forth. He stopped and extended his arms out dramatically.

"The Darkstone has been stolen. The power that keeps our kingdom safe and prosperous is gone. I call upon you to undertake a king's quest to get it back. The path before you is of the utmost importance. It is no exaggeration to say that the fate of a kingdom, perhaps even the realm of mortals, goes with you. Succeed, and you will be heroes. Songs will be written in your honor. Your names will go down in history as the saviors of the realm. Fail to the ruin of us all. I name you: Seekers of the Stone. The hopes, dreams, and prayers of Parisia go with you. May the blessings of the gods below go before you." King Alistar bowed his head and closed his eyes in a silent prayer.

Azalea clapped her hands together slowly as she glared at the king. "I have a question, your great majesty of highness and lordship and all . . . The Stone grants wishes, right? So what's to stop us from getting it and keeping it for ourselves?"

King Alistar forced a smile. "The promise of wealth, titles, land, and favor are not enough for you, witch?"

Azalea sneered, "Hardly. I could wish for all that, couldn't I?"

King Alistar grit his teeth. "Perhaps, if you could actually use the Stone."

"I'm sure I can figure it out."

"My family has spent the last two hundred years adding layers upon layers of enchantment to the Darkstone, binding it to our bloodline. Only those who have my blood in their veins can wield its power. Without me, the Darkstone is just a pretty rock. That reason enough?"

"A royal using all his power to ensure that everyone will know how important he is? Why am I not surprised? You gershwa!" Azalea rolled her eyes.

"I don't expect a witch like you to understand the responsibilities of a king. The Darkstone is one of the most powerful objects in the mortal realm. My family has possessed it and used its power for the good of our people. If it fell into the wrong hands, the Darkstone could be used for unspeakable horrors. My family did what we always do—we used our power to protect the realm from people like you. People who would use the Stone for their own selfish agenda without any thought as to the cost of others. Guards!"

"Your Majesty," Dante interrupted. "Forgive her impertinence. I'm sure she's just agitated from being locked in a prison cell for days. But she is still part of my team, one that I have chosen for this quest."

Azalea put her hands on her hips. "Oh, lamera, no, you did not just apologize for me!"

"I will not tolerate her insubordination."

"My king, I understand. It is not her personality that makes her useful. Once we are gone from here, you will have to suffer her no more."

"Oh, you'll suffer me . . . " A purple flame started to pulse from Azalea's hands.

Before the guards could react, Vale's sword rang as he pulled it from its sheath and placed the edge against Azalea's throat.

"Put your magic away."

"Or what?" Azalea ignored the sword at her throat.

Vale placed himself between Azalea and the king, glaring into her eyes. "Or I'll have your head before you lift a finger."

Azalea scoffed and squeezed her fists, the purple flame dying out. "I have no interest in helping some self-important royal from Parisia. You can count me out."

"Despite my better judgment, witch, Dante suggests you may be helpful. I will make you this offer once. Return with the Darkstone, and I will facilitate your wish, within reason."

Azalea raised an eyebrow. "What does a pompous royal define as reasonable?"

"Quiet your tongue, witch, lest I have it removed from your mouth."

"Your majesty, if you will permit, I think it best we take our leave," Dante interrupted.

King Alistar nodded. "Very well. A warning before you go." The king turned his attention away from the red-haired witch. "We have reports of Aligari and other monsters roaming the countryside. I have dispatched troops to put them down, but you may encounter some opposition before you reach the wall."

"How would they be getting into Parisia without being detected?" Dante asked.

The king grunted, "Without the Darkstone, the veil cannot hold. Now go, complete your quest in service to king and country."

They made their way out of the throne room, doors being pushed open for them by the palace guard and the light of the midday sun suddenly filling the room.

"I was thinking, perhaps we should stop at a tavern on the way out. Have a drink, share some stories, get to know each other better before we leave," Brevioar suggested.

"Oh, I like that," Azalea smiles. "Then maybe we can braid each other's hair and stay up late sharing our deepest, darkest secrets."

"We are about to put our lives in each other's hands. You don't think it's a good idea we get to know each other first?" Brevioar countered.

Her expression turned to an amused sneer. "Pretty boy like you, there isn't anything worth knowing."

Vale felt someone brush past him as they made their way into the town below the palace. Out of the corner of his eye, he saw a man in brown leather armor, which was mostly covered by a green cloak, with the hood pulled up and a bow slung behind his back.

"I have an idea for what we could do," Celeste offered, her voice excited and peppy. "We could—"

Azalea rolled her eyes. "No one asked you, fancy girl. Just stand there and be quiet."

"Enough!" Vale interrupted. "We've got bigger problems."

"Oh, please, Sir Gloomy, what are these great problems we have?" Azalea challenged.

Vale turned in the direction the cloaked man had been headed. "The writ of passage, as well as all our pouches . . . were just stolen."

Azalea laughed, "Well, isn't that just the perfect way to start. What's that, Mr. King man? Did we get your Stone? No! We got robbed instead."

Celeste turned to face her. "Who do you think you are, talking about the king like that?"

Azalea rolled her eyes. "Putting a man in fancy robes and dropping a metal circle on his head doesn't make him better than anyone else."

Vale wiped his hand over his face.

"I hate thieves," he muttered to himself. "Come on." Commanding others came as natural to Vale as breathing, a byproduct of his time as a captain in the Phoenix Legion. He chased after the thief, dashing down the immaculate, cobblestone streets.

The thief had already disappeared from sight, but Vale could sense the direction he'd gone, feel it in the murmurs of people passing by. A man running in a crowd will always create a disturbance. You can track him if you know what to listen for.

Vale darted around one corner and another, weaving between the streets, as the others struggled to keep pace. He heard a preternatural sound, and a hawk flew over him, oddly close to the ground for a hawk. The bird of prey lifted up and moved as if chasing the same quarry Vale was.

On instinct, he followed where the bird led. He turned down one street and into a dead-end alley. Vale pulled free his shining silver blade and slid to a stop, cutting off any exit. Standing at the end of the alley was the man in the green cloak. The wizard and wannabe adventurer came huffing behind him. The witch was missing. That was going to be a problem.

"Hey, it looks like we got off on the wrong foot. Let's talk, get to know each other. Maybe grab a drink at the—" the man in the green cloak says. Hearing his voice made Vale hate him more. He spoke with the smooth, easy charm of man who can never be trusted.

Vale stepped forward, stretching his sword toward the man.

"You have something of ours. Return it, and I will consider sparing your life."

The man seemed oddly unphased by the threat. Vale was not used to that. But it had been a long time since he threatened someone who didn't recognize him.

"Consider? That is mighty generous of you. I think, if my

options are to give up and maybe live or don't give up, I'm going to go with the one that leaks you off the most. Nothing personal. I'd just prefer to make the person who kills me work for it, you know? Principle and all that."

"Do as you wish. You won't live an instant longer." Vale warns.

"Um . . . Mr. Swordman?" Celeste called out. "Do you think you could help us?"

Vale turned around to see a dozen thugs armed with various blades. Celeste and Dante were both being held with a knife to each of their throats as the others moved in a half circle around them. Brevioar was sprawled out on the ground, unconscious. Two of the thugs on the ends had crossbows aimed right at him.

"Didn't think we'd find you here," one of the thugs jeered at the thief. "But what luck. The bounty on your head is so high we could swim in the reward."

Vale looked over his shoulder and then back at the thug. "You want him, you can have him. I need to retrieve several items he stole from us. Once that is done, we will be on our way, and he will be all yours. No need for trouble."

"No need for trouble, he says, lads," the thug cackled. His minions laughed with him. "Trouble is what you find yourself in. Now, be a good lad and die quickly for us."

A screech echoed from overhead as the hawk Vale had seen earlier flew down and clawed one of the thugs holding a crossbow. The man screamed and fell back. Vale tensed as he heard the unmistakable sound of an arrow whistling through the air.

A gust of wind from the arrow moved past him. Did he miss? The second thug—the one holding a crossbow—fell to the ground with an arrow in his head. Vale turned around to see the man in the green cloak holding a short bow. In the time it took Vale to turn, he'd fired and reloaded. His movement was so quick, Vale hardly saw it happen. Another arrow whisked by his head. In the blink of an eye, the thugs that were holding Celeste and Dante lay dead.

The initial shock faded, and the thugs roared to life. Dante reached into his cloak and pulled out a small, blue vial, tossing it to the ground in front of one of the thugs. The vial shattered, and a blue smoke filled the air. The thug spasmed and dropped his sword as he fell convulsing to the ground.

Celeste managed to dodge her attacker. She moved with grace and precision to side-step and slide away from the thug's attacks. She was faster than Vale expected. Her form and technique were well practiced. Her movement betrayed formal training with a complete lack of practical experience. She smiled smugly as she danced around the thug's attacks. With each move, the expression on the thug's face grew more and more frustrated. She was toying with him, so confident in her ability that she hadn't even drawn her sword. Vale winced as the thug's fist crashed into her face.

Celeste yelped as she toppled back, her hand covering her face as blood poured from her nose. She hit the ground and froze as the thug lifted his long, curved knife and stepped toward her.

One of the thugs rushed Vale. The ruffian was wielding a long sword. He was the opposite of Celeste. No refinement, no form, just considerable raw experience. The attacker's movements were sloppy and obvious. Vale leaned right to avoid the clumsy thrust of the man's blade then dashed forward like a flash of light, cutting the thug down. Two more rushed at Vale, and he darted left, then right. With each step, another thug fell as he closed the gap between himself and Celeste.

Two more thugs, two more steps, two more bodies hit the ground. In a near instant, five thugs had fallen to his blade. The seventh drove his knife toward Celeste's chest. Vale swung his black blade, deflecting the knife away from her. He spun and thrust so fast that the thug's body was pierced by his sword before he was able to take a step.

The thug choked on his breath as Vale pulled the sword free and watched the thug collapse to the ground. Glancing over, Vale saw the hawk transform into a person, her sudden mass knocking the thug she'd been clawing at to the ground as she drove a knife into his chest.

Interesting, he thought. The witch could shift into the form of a bird. An arrow flew just past Celeste, missing her hair by an inch, piercing the chest of the thug leader who was rushing toward them.

Shadows of the Dark Realm

That left one—a single thug in the back—holding a small, curved blade. "I . . . I . . . let me go!" the thug pleaded. He held his hands out and dropped his blade before turning and running away. He ran fast and made it most of the way down the street before a swift whistling sound pierced the air. An arrow struck his back, and he fell dead.

The man in green walked up next to Vale. He smiled and extended his hand. "I'm Caelan; nice to meet you."

Chapter 4

The Fifth Man

Caelan stepped forward only to find the edge of a blade pressing against his neck. "Come on, and after everything we've been through, this is the thanks I get?" he protested.

"You have something of ours, thief." Vale extended his hand, his gaze icy.

Caelan smiled and grabbed his extended hand, shaking it. Vale pressed his blade more firmly against his neck, drawing a little blood. Caelan tilted his head back and curled his lip.

"You have something of ours!" Caelan mocked the swordsman's low voice. "Anyone ever tell you that you have the personality of a constipated golem?"

The pressure of steel against his neck grew.

"Alright, alright. So serious. Gods below, you need to lighten up." Caelan reached into his cloak and tossed the pouches back to their original owners.

"It better all be here," Vale growled.

"Alright, well, this was fun. Let's do it again never."

Vale moved in front of Caelan, blocking his exit.

Caelan shook his head. "For ralk's sake, man. Just let me go."

"You're a criminal with a bounty on your head. It would be irresponsible to let you leave," Vale replied.

"We should bring him with us!" Celeste suggested, her voice high-pitched and energetic. "He's good in a fight."

"No," Vale replied.

"Having a bowman could be helpful. Plus, he's a thief. Considering our quest, that's a useful skillset," Dante added.

"Aww, guys, you're making me have all the feelings. But, you know, hard pass." Caelan smiled and tilted his head.

"You're not leaving," Vale stated flatly, as if that had already been decided.

Caelan narrowed his eyes and peered at the swordsman in black armor. He looked strong and was almost a full head taller than Caelan. He certainly knew how to use that blade.

"I wasn't asking, chief."

Caelan leaned back and extended his leg, kicking Vale in the chest and knocking the knight back a step. Vale planted his foot and lunged forward, swinging his black blade. Caelan ducked under the sword and drew a long dagger from his hip. He spun and was barely able to deflect a second strike aimed for his chest. Vale seemed surprised. He stared at his blade for a moment, as if confused at how it could have failed to find its mark.

Caelan charged at Vale, swinging his knife. Vale dodged. Caelan pressed his attack—lunging, diving, spinning. Vale turned and twisted, his movement minimal as he blocked and parried Caelan's blade. The two went back and forth—one dodging and deflecting, then the other. Caelan's movements were erratic and unpredictable. There was no technique or form to his attacks, and yet there was a remarkable experience and skill to them. Most fighters got sloppy within a few strikes and left openings that could be exploited. Everything about Caelan's style seemed like an opening, but when Vale tried to take advantage of it, the archer would just dodge or parry at the last moment. He wasted so much energy in his undisciplined style that he should have worn himself out by now.

Vale, on the other hand, was precise and efficient; not a single motion was wasted. He dodged a seemingly sloppy attack from Caelan and then pressed his own, each swing perfect in both form and technique. Vale grew more and more frustrated as they fought. Why was this witless fool so hard to kill?

Glass shattered at their feet. Caelan and Vale jumped back, creating a space between them as a haze of yellow smoke rose from the broken vial.

"That's enough!" Dante stepped between them, standing in the yellow smoke. He turned to face Vale. "You should consider this."

Vale grunted and glared.

"Be reasonable," Dante pressed.

Vale scowled.

"How many fighters have you encountered who could hold their own against you for so long?" Dante let the question sit for a moment.

Vale growled but eventually sheathed his sword. "How could you even suggest such a thing? He's a thief and a criminal. We could never trust someone like that."

"You know how important our mission is, what happens if we fail," Dante started. "Are you telling me that you'd rather trust the pompous son of a noble who is so inept he was knocked out by a common thug?"

Vale pursed his lips and let out a long, slow breath, his frustration rumbling with it.

"I like him; I say we bring him along," Azalea smiled.

"Are you just saying that because Vale doesn't?" Dante asked.

"Yup," Azalea smiled and blew a kiss in Vale's direction.

"Who's the red head, I like her," Caelan grinned.

"You don't know? I'm the witch who tried to steal from the king and therefore must be a Kinspira, pleasure to meet you." Azalea bowed in a mocking motion.

"Vale," Dante urged.

"I hate thieves," Vale protested.

"You do realize, if we are successful, you will be one."

Caelan cleared his throat. "As confusing as all this has been, I'm just gonna get going."

"We are retrieving it. Not stealing it," Vale protested.

"Semantics. Draka Mors has the Darkstone. He's not going to give the Darkstone back. So, we are going to have to steal it."

Caelan turned around. "Did you say Darkstone?"

Shadows of the Dark Realm

"Yes, our mission is to seek out and retrieve the Darkstone from an elder dragon and to return it to Parisia before the veil between the Mortal Realm and the Dark Realm fails."

Caelan smiled warmly. "Well, gwar, why didn't you just say so? I'm in."

Vale grunted. "Excuse me?"

"When do we leave?"

"There is no we; you are a criminal."

"And a good one. You want to steal from a dragon's lair, you're going to need me. Lucky for you, my services are available, for a price."

"I'm going to remove your head and deliver it to the royal guard for a price," Vale countered.

Dante turned his attention from Caelan to Vale. "You don't have to like it. We need a thief."

Vale turned and glared at Caelan. "You wanted nothing to do with this; why the sudden change of heart?"

"Well, it seems I've overstayed my welcome in Parisia. As you can see, there are some unsavory people who are looking for me. Ever since that dragon showed up, the kingdom is on lock down. Only way in or out is with one of those fancy writs you've got in your pouch there."

"So, we get you out of the city—then what? What's to stop you from just leaving once you're free?"

"Well, nothing really. Except I'm incredibly bored. Petty thieving doesn't really satisfy the way it used to. I need some adventure, some excitement," Caelan answered.

"You want to travel across hostile lands, face elements and untold monsters, and risk your life to try to steal one of the most powerful objects in the world from one of the most powerful dragons, because you are . . . bored?" Dante asked.

The perplexed expression on his face made Azalea burst out laughing.

"Not because he's bored. He wants the money. The reward would be more than enough to remove the bounty from his head," Vale said.

"Yeah, but I worked really hard to get that bounty. I'd rather not just waste it, you know?"

"Then tell me why you would risk your life for this," Vale insisted.

"Why are you? Why would any of you? This was not a draft. You volunteered. Everyone has a reason. We can stand here and talk about our deepest desires or—and this option gets my vote—we leave before more bounty hunters show up."

"How am I supposed to trust you?"

"Well, when the thugs showed up, I could have shot you in the back first, but I didn't. Yay me. That's got to count for something right?" Caelan smiled an insufferably irritating smile.

"We good?" Dante asked.

Vale closed his eyes and begrudgingly nodded.

Dante shook Brevioar awake. The young knight groaned and rubbed his head.

"What happened?" he asked.

"You got knocked out," Dante said.

"And replaced," Caelan waved.

"What?" Brevioar looked confused.

"Go back to the palace. Tell the king I found a fifth."

"No, it's been decided. I am your fifth, man. My father arranged it with the king."

Caelan lifted his bow. "We could just kill him here."

Vale glared at him in response.

"What? Everyone will just assume the thugs did it."

Brevioar started sweating as he looked around.

Celeste knelt down in front of him. "Brevioar, you could have been killed, and we haven't even left the capital yet. Do you really think you'll have what it takes outside the walls?"

"The king is not going to be happy," Brevioar said.

"No, but he will survive. Unlike you, if you come with us," Dante said.

Brevioar nodded, and after regaining his composure, he started back to the palace.

Vale shoved past Caelan and started walking. "Let's go!" he shouted.

"Oh, he's a real bossy barrel of sunshine, isn't he?" Caelan commented as he followed, making sure to lag well behind.

Shadows of the Dark Realm

* * *

Perched on the roof of one of the buildings, watching them as they fought and bickered, was a tall man with dark hair and a triangle-shaped scar on his right hand. He wore black and red armor with a thick, fur collar.

A second man in a long, black cloak with the hood pulled over his face stood behind the first, keeping himself well out of view from the street below.

"These Seeker teams are going to complicate things," the man in the black cloak said.

"We will need to deal with them quickly."

"How?"

"With your help."

"To do what?"

The man with the triangle scar smiled. "The Seekers pose a threat to our shared interest. They must be destroyed. As soon as they get outside the walls, kill them."

"There are many."

"Use the Demoa."

"If they refuse it?"

The man with the triangle scar laughed. "These savages would never turn down a free drink. But if they do, use your sword. I will send you to the wall. You'll need to move quickly."

"Me? What about you?"

The man with the triangle scar turned his attention to the direction the group had headed. "I have found the Vas Noomi."

"You're sure?" he asked.

The man with the triangle scar smiled. "She's the one. I am certain of it."

* * *

They hadn't made it far before Caelan and Vale started squabbling again. Azalea watched silently as the two men argued back and forth like children. *Men are such idiots*, she thought to herself. *Always fighting to prove they are the toughest, meanest fool around.* Worse, she was stuck with them. Azalea folded her arms and turned her gaze upward, trying to look as disinterested as possible. This was going to be a real pain in the owa. What choice did she have? There were not a lot of prospects for a witch like her.

Growing up in extreme poverty, even the clothes she wore she had stitched together herself. She'd devised a way to change all that, but her plan failed epically. However, that failure had turned into an even greater opportunity. If she could get her hands on the Darkstone, she could change everything.

Sadly, her best chance at that seemed to be to hitch her cart to these buffoons who were still squabbling. It was like watching oil and water in human form. The two men couldn't have been more different. The one in black was disciplined, practiced, and precise. The one in the green cloak, the yin to his yang. He was erratic, unpredictable, and wild. It was almost comical watching them go back and forth. For all their stupidity, they did both have some skill, which would come in handy.

When their fight finally quieted, she pushed past the opposing idiots toward the edge of the city. "Now that you're finished measuring your swords, perhaps we can focus? We do have some place to be, right?" she shouted back as she walked.

The band made their way down the cobblestone streets toward the center of the capital city, passing homes and other buildings until they reached the market.

"It's going to be a long journey. We need to get packs with food, sleeping supplies, medicines, and other materials for the journey. Let's divide up, gather what you need, and meet back at the gate at midday," Vale instructed.

Who put the tall, dark, and handsome idiot in charge anyway? Azalea thought. Though she had to admit, when a man looked like he did, she was much more willing to tolerate his leading on account of the view.

They each went their separate ways—checking out shops, gathering supplies. The king had decreed that all shopkeepers were to offer goods to Seekers of the Darkstone at highly discounted prices. Azalea managed to use that to negotiate several things for free. She didn't need them for the quest, but they didn't know that. It wasn't her fault they had porridge for brains. Anyone foolish enough to get taken advantage of deserved to have their things taken. She was doing them a service.

She even got herself a nice dress that would suit a witch of her skill. She found a place to change into it, out of view of the main streets. At midday she was ready, but she waited on principle. What kind of message would it send if she showed up right when he told her to? After about an hour, she made her way to the gate, and, as she'd hoped, the others had already arrived. The cook girl, Celeste, looked particularly annoyed.

Even at a quick glance Azalea could tell that her bag was far larger than any of the others. She walked right up to the group, slung her pack off her shoulder and handed it to Vale. "Here you go, big guy."

Vale looked at her, confused, but she just kept walking. By the time she looked back, he was toting not only his own bag but also hers.

The capital city was fortified by a large stone wall lined with hanging vines, flowers set on shelves, and other decorations that made it seem more cosmetic than functional. The massive gate leading out was made of pure white stone trimmed with gold and adorned with precious jewels. The gate itself was a rare white metal that glistened in the light of the sun. Azalea felt her stomach turn. Just one of the gems from the gate wall could have fed her entire community for life. Disgusting. She could feel her blood boiling just thinking about it. She was so lost in thought she practically crashed into the two guards who stepped in front of them.

"Papers," one said.

Vale handed the guard their writ of passage.

"Seems in order. Check in at the stables to get your mounts. Best of luck to you. The thoughts and prayers of the kingdom go with you as we long for your triumphant return. By five may your journey thrive. By five may you return alive." The guard's tone contrasted his words, betraying his lack of sincerity. He must have recited this for every Seeker party that left the gates.

At the stables, the variety of mounts to choose from was impressive. Vale claimed a tall black stallion. Caelan, a lean gray and brown speckled horse. Dante and Celeste both selected white horses. For all the horses in the stables, there was only one for Azalea—a strong, red mare.

With their bags filled and supplies fully stocked, their journey began. Parisia was a large kingdom, and the capital was at the far southern edge. The only way out was a lone gate on the northern wall. The journey to reach it would take some time.

"I got a question," Caelan announced loud enough for everyone to hear.

"I can't wait to hear it," Vale practically groaned in response.

"Does anyone have any idea how we are supposed to find this Darkstone?"

There was a long, drawn-out silence.

"We know Draka Mors will have taken it to the Dragon Lands," Dante answered.

"Yeah, that's great and all, but that's a big area, isn't it? How are we supposed to find it once we get there? It's not like we can go door-to-door til we find Draka Mors' roost now, is it?" Caelan replied.

"We know which direction we are headed. That's enough for now. When we reach the Dragon Lands, we can figure things out from there," Vale answered.

"Oh, the old shoot first, aim later tactic. I like it. Sets the expectation real low," Caelan snapped.

"You're more than welcome to leave," Vale countered. That brought silence back to the journey.

Bright green grasses, lush trees, harvest fields ripe for the picking stretched as far as the eye could see. Parisia looked more like something from a painting than a real place. Even the farmhouses and sheds scattered across the countryside screamed of wealth and affluence. The farther they got from the capital, it was more of the same. It was a land blessed by the gods in every way. Its only blemishes were hidden on the edges, out of view of the masses. The ride through the country was tranquil and peaceful. Even at a steady pace, it felt like a relaxing journey to some paradise getaway.

Soon the open fields and grasslands gave way to the thick, dense tree line of Phoenixwood Forest in the distance. As they approached the great wall of lush trees Azalea sat up, her ear twitching. She sniffed the wind. Something was off. There was a scent in the air she couldn't place. She felt a tingle on the back of her neck.

"Get down now!" She closed her eyes. Her body felt warm, and a moment later she was flying weightlessly into the air. Her view enhanced as she soared up, up, up . . . The wind caught her feathers as her avian body lifted on the breeze. It took her a moment to adjust to her new form. Then she saw them, a band of Aligari. How could so many of them have made it into Parisia?

They were already drawing back their spears as they charged her unsuspecting companions. *Great*, she thought. *These idiots are going to die before we even reach the wall.*

Chapter 5
Tension Rising

Azalea dove as fast as she could, snapping her claws in front of Celeste's horse. The stallion reared up and tossed the girl from its back. She screamed and thudded onto the ground as the spear flew harmlessly by.

Vale quickly shot back, moving his body out of the path of another spear. He reflexively snatched the spear as it flew by. Impressive. Caelan slid off his horse and ducked behind it, using his mount as a shield while Dante's foot got caught in the stirrup, causing him to fall forward off his horse, hitting the ground with a thud. *At least that was something*, she told herself.

Azalea surged her magical energy through her body, transforming herself again. As her talons turned to claws, she landed on the ground in the form of a large bear. She roared and charged toward the attacking lizard men. The Aligari pack was large, maybe twenty in number. Each carried a long, hooked, scimitar blade. They were going to be trouble.

Aligari were a wild race of lizard men and remnants of the Dark Realm. They were part of the Shadow King's invasion of the Mortal Realm. When the Shadow King was pushed back, many of the Aligari scattered, remaining in the Mortal Realm even after the gates were closed. They tended to keep to themselves and avoid areas with lots of people but, if approached, they were highly aggressive and territorial. They were fast, cunning, and resourceful, making them a very dangerous foe.

Arrows flew over her as Caelan, the green-cloaked archer, began firing at the approaching Aligari. Each arrow hit its mark and bounced harmlessly off the Aligari's scaly skin.

"Aim for their necks; it's their soft spot!" Vale shouted.

The Black Swordsman hurled the Aligari spear back at the charging horde. It whistled past Azalea and buried into the neck of one of the Aligari warriors. It fell to the ground in a heap.

I like a man who knows how to kill his enemies, Azalea thought before focusing her attention on the issue at hand.

Azalea bounded ahead, raising her front paws and tackling one of the Aligari to the ground. She sank her teeth into his exposed neck and ripped as the cool, black blood oozed from the wound. It tasted like metallic licorice—disgusting. She tried to spit it out, but it was too late—the taste was already coating her tongue.

The rest of the pack was already rushing past her. She pounced on another, pinning it with its neck exposed. The lizard man squirmed under her. She turned her head, not wanting to taste gross lizard blood again. Steel cut at her arm as the Aligari sliced its scimitar over her fur. She roared in pain and instinctively bit the lizard's neck, snapping it with a jerk of her mighty jaw.

"Eww. Gross. Gross. Gross." She spit out the blood as fast as she could, trying to paw the rest off her tongue. She looked up to see Caelan smile and wink at her. *Why was he winking? What an idiot,* she thought.

Steel rang against steel as Vale engaged a few of the warriors. Caelan exchanged his bow for a pair of knives he held with a reverse grip. Vale and Caelan may have been capable fighters—impressive even—but facing off against the speed of the Aligari, they were outmatched.

Caelan was surrounded by six of the lizard warriors. He kept them at bay with his knives, but it was only a matter of time. They moved, trying to get past him as he turned, keeping the group in front of him. He was spending more energy trying to keep the group bunched together than he was actually trying to fight them.

A great ball of blue flame crashed into the group of lizard men like a meteor falling from the sky. Azalea looked over to see Dante laying on his stomach, stretching one hand out and swiping it through the air. The blue flame moved with his hand, engulfing the lizard men one at a time until it consumed them. The scent reminded her of roast turkey, and Azalea found herself suddenly very hungry.

She turned to see three Aligari corpses at Vale's feet as he fought two more, somehow matching their speed and holding his own. While surprising, it was not nearly as unexpected as what she saw when she looked at Celeste.

The girl was dancing to a silent song, her body moving and flowing effortlessly and elegantly. It wasn't the dance that was impressive but how each movement allowed her to dodge the lizard men's attacks. She seemed completely oblivious to their presence as she twirled and pranced about. In her hand was a beautiful sword, sleek and slender, and adorned with gems all around the hilt. Her weapon was not made for combat; it was a decoration, an accessory that some fancy lord or lady might carry to make themselves look more like a warrior. Despite the absurdity of her sword, Celeste handled it quite well. In no time, her dance of death left two lizard men lifeless at her feet.

A lizard head thumped and rolled along the ground as Vale's black blade separated it from the lizard man's body in a single slice. Two more fell to Caelan's daggers as he hurled them into their necks, leaving only one. He was moving toward Vale's back. Azalea transformed back into her human self and uttered the words of a magical incantation. She focused the energy and aimed it at the creature.

"Noooo!" Vale shouted, but it was too late. A purple light shot from Azalea's fingers. The moment it contacted the lizard man's skin the creature turned to a pile of ash.

"Cursed witch! We needed that one alive!" Vale growled.

"You got a funny way of saying thank you," Azalea snapped back.

"Thank you?"

"For saving your life before that thing could stab you in the back."

"I was letting it get close!" Vale grunted.

Azalea shrugged. "How was I supposed to know that?"

"That Aligari may have had invaluable information."

Azalea interrupted him with a slow, deliberate yawn.

Vale exhaled. "I knew teaming up with a cursed witch was a mistake."

Azalea lifted her hand and a purple flame rose from it. "Call me that again, and you can ask the Aligari all the questions you want in the afterlife."

"Hey, whoa, whoa, let's all just take a minute." Celeste stepped between them, looking ever the naïve child.

Azalea glared at her, eyeing her sword. "Get out of my way, servant girl; this has nothing to do with you!"

Celeste put her hands on her hips and planted her feet. "I am not a servant girl!" Her words were as hot as the flame in Azalea's hand.

"Oh, yeah? Tell me how does a cook, or whatever you claim to be, afford a fancy sword like that?" Azalea snapped. "You steal it from your royal masters?"

Celeste gasped. "How dare you! I am no thief! What does my sword have to do with anything?"

"You're not a cook. You don't even smell like a cook. You're a noble, aren't you? Just another entitled brat trying to cure the boredom of your posh little life by pretending to be an adventurer."

She heard the pop before she felt it. Her head jerked violently to the side, and she stumbled, nearly falling over. *Did that little, rich brat punch me? Did it really hurt?*

"You spoiled little Naiflo!" Azalea screamed and dove at Celeste.

Celeste moved quickly out of her path. Azalea crashed into the ground. She shrieked, pushing herself off the ground and whirling around, and for a moment she looked more beast than human. Cursing wildly, Azalea squeezed her hands into fists and purple flames engulfed her arms.

"You're going to regret coming here, slag!"

"What exactly have I done to you that made you hate me so?" Celeste snapped back, her face flush and her defensive posture starting to slip.

"You exist. You nobles are all the same. You think your money and your titles make you better than everyone else. You live your whole life in a fancy castle where everyone does everything for you and caters to your every whim, but then you start thinking you can do anything. Well, you're not inside your fancy castle anymore, sweetheart. This is the real world. There's pain and ugliness out here. Now you've stepped in it."

"You don't know the first thing about me, you wild, old shrew."

Purple flame blasted into the sky as Caelan pulled Azalea's arm up, keeping it away from Celeste.

"Get off me, goraum!"

"And that's enough of that." Dante's voice was calm and even.

Azalea started to speak, but her words faded into a slurred, soft groan as green smoke floated into her nostrils from an open vial in Dante's hand. Her eyes grew heavy, and her body went limp. Dante caught her as she collapsed and guided her slowly down, laying her on the soft green grass below.

"We should leave her here," Celeste snapped.

"Don't be ridiculous. We are not leaving someone behind because they are rough around the edges," Dante said.

"Rough? Girl's pricklier than a cactus forest," Caelan chuckled.

"The guards at the wall will be expecting five of us. We need her to get through," Dante reminded her.

"We can find someone else." Celeste folded her arms.

"This is getting us nowhere." Vale sheathed his sword and then picked up the limp body of Azalea. He walked over to her horse and slung her over the side, draping her across the saddle like she was a rolled-up rug. "I don't care how volatile she is, I am not leaving a woman alone, unconscious, in the middle of nowhere." Vale's tone was firm and unwavering.

Celeste stomped her foot in protest. She huffed and turned away from the group.

"Before we reach Phoenixwood, there is a town called Greensleaf. We will stop there. We can decide what to do with her then."

Celeste groaned in annoyance but could see she was not going to change his mind. Vale was too stubborn for that. Vale rode next to Azalea's horse, guiding it as Caelan took the lead.

Greensleaf was a pleasant looking town. The main stone street ran right through the middle. It was sizeable, with its own specialty shops for apothecaries, soldiers, farmers, even mages. It had a blacksmith, stable, armory, two inns, and a large tavern.

When they reached the stables, Vale dismounted and tied his horse to a post of one of the open stalls before doing the same for Azalea's.

"Now what? We duke it out on the streets, winner gets to decide what we do with the redhead?" Caelan grinned, sliding casually off his horse.

"No, we should find a place to sit down and discuss it. We can each make our case and then decide which is the best course of action," Celeste suggested.

"And what happens when we inevitably fail to come to an agreement? None of us agree on what to do with the witch. She could help us, hurt us, get us all killed, or anything in between. There is no way to know."

"There's one way," Dante interrupted.

Vale shook his head. "No, not that . . . "

"What?" Celeste asked. "Not what?"

Dante shrugged. "Greensleaf has a seer of particular skill. She once worked in the royal court."

Caelan laughed. "Oh, you're serious? You want to base the decision that could determine whether we live or die on the word of a charlatan with a fancy bauble? I love this plan! Let's go."

Vale grunted. "Fine."

Vale carried Azalea in his arms as they followed Dante down a side street to a smaller building at the edge of town. A small wooden sign hung over the door with a single open eye carved into it. Inside, the room was even smaller than expected. The walls were lined with candles, vials, and other arcane ingredients and the floor littered with pillows and other objects, leaving very little open floorspace.

They filed in until they stood in a half circle around a short, round, wooden table with a translucent gray-blue pyramid set at its center. Sitting on a long, flat pillow with her legs crossed and her arms held out was an old woman. Her pure white hair looked more like hay than hair. The wrinkles on her face were so pronounced they created canyons. Her skin was like desert clay. The pupils in her eyes were offputtingly dim as she looked them over.

"Why have you come?" she squawked.

"Shouldn't you know that already? Isn't that your thing?" Caelan asked.

The woman smiled and turned her face toward him. "Ah, the witty archer who wears humor like a shield. Who pretends to care about nothing so that no one will see his pain. Welcome, Caelan, son of Glaine."

Caelan's eyes narrowed. "How do you know that name?"

"I am a seer, child. Touched by the goddess Isira herself. I gave up my sight in this world to see what others cannot. You seek the Darkstone to change your past. It will not. But it will change your future."

"Is that cryptic nonsense supposed to be impressive? If you're so all-seeing, why don't you tell us if we will succeed?"

The old woman smiled. "The future is not so fixed as if it were stone. Fate flows like a river, its course constantly changing. Your success will depend on the choices you make along the way."

"That has to be the most poetic and elegant load of gwar I have ever heard, and I've heard some things."

"Excuse me, Miss Seer?" Celeste interrupted.

"Ahh, Celeste," she smirked. "I see. You have such big dreams. Your ambition burns like the sun. All you desire can be yours and more. But obtaining them will not bring you happiness. For the cost of your dreams is grand. To see them realized, you will find you no longer recognize yourself. Your joy will turn to ash. Your hands will be stained with blood."

"What do you mean? Why?"

"Obtaining what you desire most will cost you more than you ever thought you would give."

Celeste stared with her mouth hanging open.

The seer turned her gaze toward Vale next.

"Don't."

She smiled wryly at Vale's word but did not speak, keeping whatever she knew of him to herself.

"Mislandri," Dante reached out. "I have need of your True Sight." He nudged Vale, who knelt down and laid Azalea in front of the seer.

"What is it you seek?" she asked.

"This girl—I believe she has a role to play in our quest. Others think she will cause trouble. We came to you to see if we should take her or leave her."

Mislandri nodded and stood up. She grabbed a candle from a shelf next to her and slowly moved it in a little path around Azalea's body. She returned the candle to the shelf and stretched her arms out, tilting her head back to the ceiling. The flames in the room danced as an unnatural breeze seemed to whirl around them. Mislandri's milky eyes started to glow. Her body began to shake. Her eyes closed, and she collapsed to the ground.

Dante rushed around and helped her up. She groaned and rubbed her temple with her hand.

"What did you see?" he asked.

"I saw a world covered in darkness, and a light shining in the distance. I saw the King of Shadows sitting on his throne and a woman bathed in flame. Take her on your quest, and she will bring you great trouble and pain."

Celeste clapped her hands together. "I knew it!"

"Take her not on your quest and you will fail, and the world will fall to shadow." Mislandri's voice trembled as she spoke.

"What about the other Seekers?" Vale asked.

"None of them will reach the Dragon Lands alive. You are Parisia's only hope." She held up her hand. "Please leave me. I need rest."

When they stepped outside, Caelan turned and looked at

the still-unconscious woman in Vale's arms. "That was foreboding. What now?"

"Were you not listening? We take her with us, or the Realm falls to the Shadow King," Dante answered.

"Great. No pressure then."

Chapter 6
The Memora

Phoenixwood Forest was a massive thicket of densely packed trees that stretched the entire width of the canyon. The forest itself was enchanted by some unknown ancient magic; whenever a tree was cut down, it would regrow in a matter of moments, creating an endless supply of quality wood for the kingdom. The trees were tall and sturdy, casting a long shadow on those who approached.

A group of wizards had managed to clear a central path through the woods, preventing the trees in one area from growing back. They paved the path with a beautiful, pure white cobblestone with a stone knee-wall on either side to keep carriages on the path. Enchatorches, which ignited at dusk and burned until dawn with a soft blue flame without ever going out, were built onto stone columns set periodically along the road.

The sun was starting to set when they reached the forest edge.

Celeste rode up next to Vale as Caelan began pestering Dante, which only seemed to irritate him into a deeper and deeper silence.

"Excuse me, Mr . . . umm —" Celeste started.

"Vale."

Celeste nodded. "Vale. May I ask you something?"

"I'd rather you didn't," he replied.

Celeste ignored his response. "You were once a great commander, were you not?"

"I was a commander, yes."

"That's a high honor—a position worthy of respect, even after your service to the kingdom has ended."

Vale grunted.

"So why do they call you the disgraced knight?"

Vale grunted again.

"What could you have done to earn such a title?" Celeste pressed.

Vale ignored her question and kept riding.

When it was clear that he wasn't going to answer, Celeste sighed. "Well, I was wondering, you're very good with a sword. Perhaps you could teach me?"

"No." Vale's reply was as cold as the deep winter's wind.

"No? Why not?"

The man in black armor turned and looked at her, his gaze like stormy winds. She felt simultaneously terrified and at peace as she gazed into his sapphire eyes. Time fell away. The world around her fell away. There was only the strange tension of his stare. *Why wasn't he answering? Was she supposed to see it in his eyes?*

"I don't take students," he finally said dismissively.

"You should. We are on a quest together. Helping me helps you."

"No."

"Can you at least tell me why not?"

Vale glared at her, his stare once again filling her with terror and calm. Then his piercing blue eyes changed. A great fog seemed to cover them. His body swayed slowly.

"Are you ok? Vale? What's going on?"

She moved her horse closer and reached out. She was too late. His body slumped over and slid off the far side of his horse, landing on the ground with a thump.

Dante watched it happen. From the way his body fell and the sound it made, Dante suspected the Black Swordsman's shoulder was dislocated. He slid from his horse and walked over. Celeste was shaking him vigorously, yelling in his ear, trying to get him to move. Even as he approached, Dante could see that Vale was as frozen as a stone. His body was unnaturally rigid. *Perplexing.*

Without a word, he pushed a frantic Celeste back. Caelan moved behind him, looking over his shoulder, appearing more confused than worried. Dante reached back, pushing at the air in front of Caelan.

"Space, please. Give him some room."

He knelt down over the Black Swordsman and rolled him onto his back. He was heavier than Dante expected; it took quite a deal of force to roll the man over. Either his armor was heavier, or he was even more muscular than Dante accounted for. Once the knight was finally on his back, Dante moved over the man, inspecting and searching. It was strange. There should be some indication of what happened.

His armor was intact and there was no visible damage to his skin. His nostrils showed no signs of discoloration. It could be his heart. Maybe he'd been poisoned. But that usually caused discoloration around the lips or eyes. It was hard to say with any real certainty. What he did know was that if he didn't do something, Vale would not survive the night. Blue-gray veining began to run up the knight's temple and down toward his neck.

"What is happening to him?" Caelan asked.

"Is he ok? Can you fix him? Is he dying?" Celeste asked louder and with greater exigence.

Dante ignored them both as a groaning Azalea added her chaos to the mix. She was still draped over her horse, but now she was starting to wake. Dante pulled two vials from his cloak and opened them, wafting them under Vale's nose. The vapor flowed in, but the spread of the bizarre, discolored veining didn't stop or even slow down. Vale's skin started draining of color, fading into a pale gray.

This doesn't make sense. That shouldn't have made things worse. He rubbed his chin.

"Hmm." Dante paced back and forth, thinking of what could cause a reaction like this.

"Hmm? That's all you have to say? How can you be so calm?" Celeste grabbed Dante, her eyes frantic.

"Take a breath," he said, his voice completely devoid of feeling.

"Don't you care?"

"Is your caring helping you identify the problem?"

"No . . . " Celeste released her grip on him but maintained her stare, a look of confusion on her face. She probably felt that way a lot.

"Does your caring slow the effect of whatever's happening to him?"

She shook her head.

"Not much use, are they, these feelings of yours? You know what they are good for? Distracting me and delaying actually finding a solution. Thank you for that."

Celeste scoffed. "So what, you just suppress your feelings?"

"I don't feel. Not for many years." Dante shook his head. "Emotions cloud judgment. Feelings muddy thought. Here we are—you, all in your feelings—delaying me from actually doing something helpful. Do you want me to be emotional or helpful?"

Celeste blinked and blurted out, "Help him."

"Very well. I see no wound or any other indication for what could have caused this. I can't fix it without knowing what it is."

"We should take him back to Greensleaf. I'm sure they have a healer," Celeste suggested.

"Won't help. The healer in Greensleaf is an herbalist," Dante said.

"So?"

"Herbalists treat physical ailments. This is almost certainly magical."

"Magical? How can you tell?"

Dante ignored her question and instead handed her a small, soft, marble-like orb. "Go wake up your friend. We will need her for this."

Celeste returned a few minutes later with a groggy, confused Azalea who was rubbing her head and muttering incoherently under her breath.

"Good. Listen. To cure him, I must identify what is wrong with him. I will need your help," Dante stated flatly.

"Our help? What can we do?" Caelan asked.

"A Memora."

Azalea groaned in protest. "A what?"

Dante rolled his eyes. "A Memora is a spell that allows a person or group of people to enter the memories of another."

"Enter the memories? That's a thing? How does that even work?" Celeste asked.

"Once I cast the spell, we will enter Vale's mind. We will be able to see moments in his life and can search for anything that could lead us to what is happening to him now."

Caelan started pacing back and forth. "This sounds like a truly, marvelously, impressively, terrible idea. I can't even stand the guy. I sure as ralk am not going traipsing through his mind."

"There's no quest without him."

"Ralk!" Caelan shouted into the air. "Fine. How does it work?"

"It's going to feel a little strange for a moment, but once you adjust you will look and feel like yourself. Then we just search until we figure out what's causing it."

"Yeah, I feel like you're glossing over all the important bits. How are we supposed to do that, professor?"

"Inside his head, the spell will connect all his memories by a shimmering golden thread. Grab the thread, then follow it from one memory to the next until we find the right one."

"Ralking wizard. You mean we have to watch every memory in his life until we find the right one?"

"No. The spell will serve as a filter. When you hold the thread, your thought will guide which memories it leads you to. We are looking for magical encounters or instances where his skin has this gray veining," Dante explained.

"And say we do find it?" Caelan asked.

"If you find the right memory, or one that could explain what's happening, all you need to do is walk over and make contact with Vale. When that happens, it will draw the rest of us to the memory you are in."

"Is it dangerous?" Celeste asked.

"Only for his mind. But he has bigger problems."

"Fine. Let's get this over with," Caelan replied.

Dante drew a vial from his coat. The liquid inside swirled in every color of the rainbow, each one moving and flowing but never blending with the other colors. He poured the liquid into four small tubes and offered one to each of them.

"Drink this," he instructed. Each emptied the contents of the vial down their throats.

"One last thing—the mind naturally resists intruders. You may encounter something called a Shade. It will look like Vale but be made of black fog. If you see one, run. They will attack you."

Celeste looked suddenly worried. "What happens if they get us?"

Dante shrugs. "On occasion, it can cause permanent psychosis. If they kill you in his mind, you will be expelled from his memory. It's very painful, but typically not deadly."

"Ralk you . . . typically?" Caelan's tone was agitated.

Dante shrugged.

"Oh, you goraum piece of gwar!" Caelan's words were cut off as his body slumped to the ground.

* * *

-CAELAN-

Caelan looked around. The group appeared to be standing in the same place. The hills, road, and trees all looked the same. It felt different. The others were standing in a circle. Vale's body was gone. *Well, this is going to be great*, Caelan thought.

"Sometimes it helps to squeeze your eyes closed for a moment. It lets the mind adjust to being in someone else's head," Dante offers.

"Oh, look! A field of fairies!" Azalea exclaimed, sounding uncharacteristically jovial as she frolicked off.

"Should she be doing that?" Caelan asked.

Dante covered his face with his hands. "That's not ideal."

At least he had a firm grasp on the obvious.

"Care to explain? Or do you just prefer being vague and unhelpful?" Caelan asked.

"Mixing magics can have side effects. Sometimes the chemicals that make the Memora work can react with other potions. Sleeping potions in particular can cause a hallucinogenic state." Dante explained this as if the information should have been common knowledge.

"You mean to tell me she's tripping on some sort of magical high while we are touristing someone else's brain? You goraum!" Before Caelan could finish his thought, a glowing golden thread moving like a thin stream through the air appeared in front of him.

"We should make haste. The less time we spend in his mind, the less risk we have of messing something up," Dante said.

"What about her? Gonna be a bit tricky to navigate all this with her chasing fairies," Caelan pointed out.

"Smartest thing to do is leave her here. Mind Shades are protectors. They are less likely to bother her as her presence is not venturing into anything significant. Be warned—the more emotional or impacting a memory may be, the more likely you are to encounter a Shade and the more aggressive it will be if you do. Don't linger in sensitive memories unless you have to."

"Just grab the thread and walk?" Caelan asked.

Dante nodded. "The thread will respond to your thoughts. Try to focus on things that could cause an injury."

"Alright, let's get this over with." Caelan grabbed hold of the thread and closed his eyes. He focused on an idea: fighting. That should be general enough. His body suddenly felt light, airy. The scene around him faded as he heard Dante say, "Wait! Before you go . . . " *Too late for that.*

All around him, metal crashed and clanged. He opened his eyes, focusing on the chaos around him. He was on a battlefield. Bodies lay strewn around him, and the ground below his feet was stained in blood. Soldiers were fighting, slicing, screaming. The air tasted of copper and smelled of rotten cabbage. The sky itself seemed gray.

Caelan looked, and there he was. Vale. Not the grizzled warrior of a man that he knew. This wasn't even Vale as a young man. He was just a boy dressed in oversized armor and holding a sword he could barely lift. He couldn't have been more than ten. *Who lets a child fight in a battle?*

The boy looked terrified as men two and three times his size charged at him. He fought with desperation, deflecting a blade from an attacker and getting knocked back in the process. He was crawling away, pleading for help, but the soldier kept approaching. Caelan reached for his knife. The thought that a grown man could attack a child made his skin crawl. The scene was so vivid, so real, he'd forgotten he was in a memory. There was nothing he could do here but watch. No, he didn't want to see this. Besides, this was far too long ago to be relevant. He grabbed the shimmering thread and took a step. The battle fizzled in golden sparks and was replaced by another. Different field, armors, and flags but the same carnage. He pulled the thread again. Another battle and another and another. So many battles and Vale was still no more than boy.

He pulled a little harder and finally was whisked onto a non-battlefield. A slightly older Vale was fighting a large rock troll. No wound. He pulled the thread again. Vale fighting a golem. No wound. He pulled the thread. Vale fighting bandits, ghouls, werewolves, vampires, all without anything that could explain his condition. *I need a new thought*, Caelan realized, and he focused on a different word. *Pain.*

Caelan found himself standing in the middle of a village on fire. Screams roared into the open air. Smoke filled his lungs—or rather it felt like it did. These memories were so real he had to remind himself again and again what it was.

Something about this place was familiar. The blacksmith shop on the right, next to the oddly-designed stable. The inn with the extra tall point on the roof. The streets, the houses—Caelan knew this place. He had tried to forget it, but it was burned into his mind. This was Oakwood Village. This was his home, before it was destroyed by knights from Parisia who had taken everything from him, wretches who bore the symbol of the phoenix, men he vowed to kill if ever he saw them. *Why did Vale have a memory of this place?*

No, it was worse. Vale didn't just have a memory of his former home. He had a memory of *that* night. Soldiers in black armor charged up and down the streets, slaughtering innocent, defenseless civilians. Screams of pain and loss filled the night as those who pleaded for mercy found none. It was a massacre. Caelan remembered it. He hadn't seen it happen, but he'd heard it, and he'd seen the aftermath many years ago. The carnage was far more brutal than he'd imagined. The soldiers weren't just killing, they were butchering, and they were enjoying it. They were laughing and cheering like it was some sick game. Maybe it was just the memory, but their eyes seemed to shine with a red haze.

"Kill them all! Bathe in their blood!" Caelan turned to see a man with gray hair atop a black steed. His armor was fancier than the others. This was the knight commander of the Phoenix Legion. The seasoned soldier was pointing a gold dagger with a ruby hilt into the sky. It seemed odd that he chose to wield a ceremonial dagger instead of the large sword still at his side.

Caelan's eyes went wide as he saw Vale rush around the corner. Vale was no longer a boy but a man, maybe ten years younger than he was today. Vale was rushing after another knight. He was wearing black plate armor with a great, golden phoenix on the breastplate. Caelan's pulse quickened. His heart thudded so loud in his chest he was certain It would burst. His teeth gritted, hands clenched into fists. Sweat formed on his brow as rage consumed him.

When he was rejected and discarded by his own family, these were the people that took Caelan in. They gave him a home, food, and loved him like he was their own son. They were his family—not by blood but by choice. This was the night they died, killed in their home for the crime of being an inconvenience to Parisia. Vale wasn't just there, he was part of it.

Caelan drew his bow and started to follow the Black Swordsman. Before he could give chase, a pair of knights appeared in front of him. Unlike the others who were oblivious to his presence, these two moved toward him. As they stepped from the darkness into the light cast by one of the nearby burning buildings, Caelan realized they were not knights at all. Though shaped like men, they were made entirely of black smoke. *Shades.* They'd found him.

Chapter 7

Shades of the Mind

-Azalea-

Mountains of gold, fields of Baylock, streams flowing of pure mana lined with glowing elemental stones surrounded her. *This place is amazing.* Azalea could hardly contain her excitement as she chased a flock of glowing, neon butterflies through the sapphire sky. The air felt fresh and light. A rainbow-striped, winged unicorn passed through, prancing down the diamond-studded path, offering himself to her.

"Ohhh!" Azalea exclaimed with glee as she climbed aboard the mystic steed.

"Wherev'r doth thine dreams lie, speaketh thy wish and I shall thee fly; ov'r the seas of frothy foam, my magical wings can anywhere roam. So speaketh thy wish my glorious lass and let thine steed take thee there in a flash," the unicorn said.

"Take me yonder!" Azalea laughed and pointed. The horned steed reared back and started off, carrying her into the sky, flying over vast mountains, seas, and green forests. The wind was refreshingly cool as it washed over her. On the ground below she saw a waterfall, hidden by trees on all sides, pouring into a tranquil lake with an almost silver glimmer.

"Down there!" she pointed, and her unicorn carried her

down, landing so gently on the ground she didn't even feel the transition from flight.

The lake was even more beautiful up close.

"Oh, shiny!" Azalea reached out and grabbed a golden, shimmering thread. All of a sudden, she was standing outside a house at night. Her head was throbbing. *What fresh lamera was this? Hadn't she been riding a unicorn? How did she get here? Where was here?*

She could see three women in red cloaks chanting under their breath. She couldn't make out what they were saying but recognized clearly what they were doing. She covered her eyes with her palms and tried to rub away the loud ringing in her head. She groaned as she opened them again to get a better sense of what was going on.

On the ground, in front of the three witches in red cloaks, there were three people kneeling: a man, a woman, and a young girl. *What sort of dream is this?* she wondered.

She saw movement out of the corner of her eye and looked over to see Celeste exiting the house behind the three on their knees. *What was she doing here?*

* * *

-Celeste-

"Wait, before you go—" Dante called out, but Caelan had already disappeared.

Celeste paused, her hand hovering over the gold thread.

"It is important not to touch anything. Memories are fragile and formative things. Sometimes interacting with them can change them," Dante explained.

"That's bad?" Celeste asked.

"Yes. Our experiences are all interwoven like a tapestry that forms our understanding of ourselves and the world. Changing even one seemingly insignificant memory can have a ripple effect. Since we are in his mind, it's particularly dangerous for us."

"Why?"

"If you were in a memory that was changed, you'd be trapped there, forever unable to return to your own body." Dante's tone was plain, matter-of-fact, which felt odd, considering how terrifying that would be.

"And you didn't think you should share that with us before?"

Dante shrugged. "I tried to tell him, but he's too reckless and impatient. That's going to cause him problems."

"No, I meant when we were talking about the risks. If you'd told us that—" she started.

"Then you would have questioned whether or not you should come. We end up at the same place. We need Vale; it just would have wasted more time. Time that he may not have."

"So, you just decided to keep it from us?" Celeste snapped.

"I decided to do what was necessary, yes. Anyway, it's done now. No point in arguing. Let's get going." Dante grabbed the thread and disappeared in a burst of gold sparks.

"Don't touch anything," she gulped.

She glanced over to see Azalea rolling in the grass, yelling, "Whee! I've never slid down a Wyren tunnel before!"

Celeste exhaled and grabbed the thread. Suddenly, she was standing in the middle of a house. It was dark and it was quiet, eerily quiet. She looked around. The house was modest and unimpressive. The decorations were minimal. While it lacked the luxury of her upbringing, it was clearly well-maintained.

"Please, take me. You can do anything you want. I won't resist. Just please, don't . . . don't do this!"

She recognized the voice immediately. She rushed out of the house to see three people tied up on their knees on the grass just before the steps of the front porch. Vale was in the center with a woman to one side and a young child on the other. Across from him were three women in red cloaks. The two on the sides were chanting while the one in the middle paced back and forth, brandishing a hooked knife.

"Your pleas fall on deaf ears, murderer. Just as your ears were deaf to the cries of our sisters. Beg all you wish, but justice will be served." Hate oozed from the woman's voice.

"They aren't my crimes. I wasn't there. I left the legion long before what happened to your sisters. I tried to stop them!" Vale's voice sounded softer than Celeste was used to hearing.

"Lies. Excuses. You will say anything, but your words will change nothing. Your suffering will be endless. Your pain will power the stone for years."

Celeste watched in stunned silence, trying to figure out what was going on. She noticed the glowing red vines binding Vale's wrists together and wrapped around his neck, keeping him in place. These were not ordinary women; they were witches. In the background, well behind the three women, she saw someone else. *Was that Azalea?*

The witch with the knife walked over to the woman next to Vale. The witch in red put her hand on the back of the bound woman's head and dragged the blade across her neck. Vale screamed as the woman collapsed to the ground. He pulled and leaned, tugging against his restraints, trying to get to the woman to hold her, but the vines held his body in place. He didn't stop trying. He pulled and tugged, screaming in pain and desperation, as tears streamed down his face.

Celeste started toward him. She could help cut the vines and set him free. Dante appeared next to her and caught her arm, holding her back as he shook his head. "Let me go! They are going to kill him!" she shouted.

"You know they won't. Don't forget—this is a memory. What you are seeing has already happened. You can't change it. All you will do is put us at risk."

Celeste pushed past Dante, but it was too late. The witch had driven the knife into the young girl's chest.

"Daddy, it hurts!" the young girl cried out.

The sound of Vale's pain was drowned out by the witches' laughter. They released the vines that bound him, allowing Vale to pull his daughter into his arms, cradling her in his lap as the life drained from her. Vale lifted his head to the sky. The cry of his pain and rage ripped from the pits of despair, sending chills into Celeste's very soul. If heartbreak had a sound, this was it.

Vale clutched his daughter, his hands frantically running down her hair, pleading against fate itself for a miracle that wouldn't come. The witch leaned in behind him and whispered in his ear. Celeste stood, stunned, a tear rolling down her face. She was so caught up in the emotion of the moment that she didn't notice the circle of shades that had surrounded them, moving in on them like prey.

* * *

-CAELAN-

Caelan watched as his arrow passed through the black smoke of the Shade and clanged along the ground behind it. The Shade stopped for a moment as the smoke swirled where the arrow pierced and then returned to normal.

Oh, I know. I'll try to shoot a humanoid smoke monster. Great idea, Caelan. That'll definitely work, he said to himself. How was he supposed to fend off something that could phase through his weapons?

"What are you doing? Stop! Nooo!" Caelan looked past the shade to see a body fall to the ground, Vale standing over him. Caelan's blood boiled even more. Here he was, trapped in the head of the man who helped slaughter his family. He knew killing Vale in the memory wouldn't solve anything, but ralk if it wouldn't feel good.

Caelan fixed another arrow, this time not aiming for the Shades but for the man in black armor—the man who he'd foolishly come here to help. He fired and watched as his arrow soared through the air on its way to the Black Swordsman's back. As if sensing the arrow in the air Vale whirled around at the last moment, pulling his head to the side and dodging it. Caelan's mouth dropped open. *How did he do that? Did Vale know he was here?*

Vale turned away again and started off in the other direction.

"Bavaso!" Caelan cursed.

Vale's Mindshades were now upon him, forcing Caelan back. He ducked and dodged as they swung their smoke blades at him. They weren't quite as skillful as their real-life counterparts, but they were good nonetheless. Caelan kicked off the wall of the general store next to him and leapt over one of the attacking Shades. The three spun and jabbed their blades, cutting inches from Caelan's body. He dove back, creating some space between them. *That was too close.*

Ignoring the smoky foes, Caelan turned and chased after Vale. The Black Swordsman was coming out of a house, his sword dripping with fresh blood.

"You're gonna pay!" Caelan yelled.

Younger Vale looked at him, confused. Caelan fired three arrows in rapid succession. Vale deflected the first, dodged the second, but the third caught his side. Caelan grinned. Before he could celebrate his accomplishment, the ground underneath his feet began to shake. *What fresh lamera is this?*

He ignored it and charged. Vale had just tugged the arrow from his side. He lifted his blade, but Caelan was too fast. He lowered his shoulders and tackled Vale, knocking him back into the house from which he had just exited. The ground shook again, this time much harder. The walls of the house creaked as the whole frame trembled. Caelan raised his knife, preparing to bury it in Vale's chest, when it hit him. He froze just before his blade pierced Vale's armor. This night was etched into his brain with a clarity that rivaled the finest jewels in the palace. Every detail carved into memory. One thing he knew for certain—there was no earthquake, no tremor. *Why did Vale remember one?*

Vale's foot caught Caelan in the neck, knocking him back with great force. The Black Swordsman's blade whistled through the air toward Caelan's neck. He jumped back, but there wasn't enough room. His back was now pressed against the wall with nowhere to go. Vale had him pinned in and was advancing.

Out of the corner of his eyes, he saw the shimmering thread. On instinct, he reached out and grabbed it. As the scene around him turned to glittering gold, Vale said something.

"I'm not here to hurt . . . " The rest was lost, taken up in the glitter of gold dust.

* * *

-AZALEA-

Azalea's stomach lurched as she watched the witches murder the woman and girl with Vale. Her keen senses caught the words whispered in Vale's ear.

"I curse you, blackblade, that while living, you will be ever living without living. In dying, you will be ever dying without dying. I curse you that all you love will die because you love them, that suffering will overwhelm you until you long for a death that will forever escape you."

Azalea gasped. She recognized the energy feeding the curse. It was a dark and powerful magic, a forbidden magic. The shock of it sobered her mind, causing the haze she'd been in to dissipate. Perhaps the effect of the magic was wearing off, but Azalea was starting to think clearly again. The ground beneath her began to shake so hard it threw her off balance. She reached out and caught onto a golden thread and the scene before her faded away.

She blinked and found herself on a farm, inside an animal pen.

A mystifying feeling of euphoria crashed through her body like a wave. The sky was an eerie purple, the clouds a glittering gold. The air smelled like chestnuts. Perhaps her mind wasn't as clear as she thought.

Standing in front of her was a giant, three-headed boar. Each head had four eyes and seven tusks. Each of the heads moved separately, as if each was making their own assessment of her.

"Well, what do we have here? Looks like a wee lass has wandered into our pen." The right head's words sounded jovial and almost whimsical but with an odd accent.

"Oh aye, tis that what it looks like to ye? I swear if it weren't fer stating the plainly obvious, ye'd nev'r have a thing to say. Which would be an improvement, if ye ask me." the head on the left responded in the same peculiar accent.

"Ralk, I'm definitely hallucinating," Azalea muttered to herself.

"Sorry, lass, ignore me squabbling friends here. We dunna get a lot of visitors. These bavasos take after their lowborn mothers, ye see," the central head spoke.

Some part of her knew this should feel strange, but she couldn't figure out why.

"Their mothers? Aren't you all from the same . . . " she started.

All three heads laughed heartily. "The same mother? Come on now, we dunna even look alike. Me mother was a beautiful and noble swine," the right head said.

"Yer mother was a shameless naiflo and a drunkard, ye daft bavaso!" the left head said.

Azalea blinked at the talking pig heads. "What?"

"Ah, me thinks she's a bit a bit out of it."

"A bit? She's high as a dragon's roost."

"Enough. Have ye both forgotten our purpose here? Have some pride in yer sacred duties. Now tell me fair lass, what it is ye are seeking?"

Azalea blinked. *Why was she talking to pigs?* Flying above her, she saw a large, horned squirrel made of sprinkles, with great eagle wings. She rubbed her head, trying to focus her mind.

"I am . . . trying to find a memory, something that . . . something that caused . . . pain."

"Ye will have a hard time narrowing that down here, dearie. This man's mind is full of naught but pain, starting from his earliest memory. Ye will need more to go on." The three boar heads looked down and sighed collectively.

As the boars spoke, the fog that had surrounded Azalea's mind faded, carried off like a cloud in the wind. She was surprised that as her mind cleared the three-headed boar remained. This was not a hallucination, but what was it—a spirit guide perhaps?

Azalea focused her thoughts. "I'm looking for something with magic: —an item, spell, creature, or option that makes skin turn pale and gray." The three boar heads exchanged a glance.

"Aye, that is a particularly unpleasant one. Ye will want to focus on Sarah."

"Who is Sarah?" Azalea asked.

"She was his sister."

"Was?"

"Tis a long story. Made short, their da was a real mean

drunk. Vale tried ta look out fer his wee sis, tried to stop his da from abusing her. Da didn't like dat so he beat Vale real bad and then sold him to a group of mercenaries who forced him to fight. Vale was forged into a warrior. He fought battle after battle, trying ta get back to his wee sister. But by the time he did . . . "

"What happened?" Azalea asked.

"I haven't the stomach ta speak it aloud, sorry lass. If ye want to know, focus on Sarah and the wraith. But I'll warn ye, tis not easy ta watch," the tri-headed pig instructed.

The ground shook again, this time more violently.

Azalea looked around. The sky and clouds had returned to their normal colors, and her mind was clearing. Finally, the effects of that stupid potion were wearing off. For some reason the tri-headed boar remained.

"Go lass; this place is no longer safe. The ripples are coming."

Azalea grabbed the golden thread, and she focused her mind on Sarah and the wraith. When she opened her eyes she was in a dark, damp cave. The space felt eerie and unnerving, with an unnatural energy pulsing in the air. *This could not be good.*

* * *

-CELESTE-

"Don't let them touch you." Dante's tone carried all the urgency of a comment about the weather on a bleak day.

Celeste reached for her sword.

"Don't bother. Steel will not affect them." Dante reached into his coat and pulled out a series of blue marbles. He spun around, flinging them in all directions. Blue light burst from them like fire as they crashed into the ground. The Mindshades shrieked and stepped back.

Celeste had an idea. There was no time to question—she needed to act. This was a chance for her to prove her worth. Using the flame as a distraction, she dashed forward quickly and carefully. She grabbed and drew the blade from one of the shades, pulling it from its shadowy scabbard. The distraction had been just enough for her to get it but not enough for her to get away. The shades swarmed, encircling her. Their blades sliced and stabbed through the air.

Celeste felt her heart racing. She twirled and danced, bowed and ducked out of the way of the blades. She knew she couldn't keep this up for long. It was time to test her theory. She swung the shade's sword. To her great relief, it deflected the blade that was being thrust toward her heart. Excitement surged through her as she quickly countered, the blade cutting the shade that had attacked her. Wild energy surged through her veins. It was working—she was doing it!

She danced, blocked, countered, and dodged, twirling her lean body to avoid the attacks of the shades surrounding her. Most of her attacks missed their mark, but when they landed, the shades would shriek and disappear into a cloud of smoke. She cut two, then a third, and then a fourth. This was easier than she expected.

As if intending to prove her wrong, one of the shades began to rip the blade from her hands. She grasped for it as the shade pulled it from her, but it was too late. She was encircled completely with a dozen blades held inches from her neck. *This is not great.* She closed her eyes and waited. A vial crashed at her feet, and suddenly she found herself back on the porch, standing next to Dante.

"We need to reach the thread."

"Then what?"

"We will have to move quickly. Now that his mind is aware of our presence, these shades will hunt us," Dante said.

The ground beneath them shook so hard that Celeste grabbed onto the porch railing to keep herself up. By the time it stopped, the Mindshades had swarmed all around them, cutting off any path to the shimmering thread.

"How would you suggest we get to it?" she asked.

Chapter 8

Shadows of the Past

---Azalea---

The dark cave was dimly lit by a series of sporadically placed torches that burned with a greenish light. In the distance a slow *drip . . . drip . . . drip . . .* echoed with a maddening consistency. In the silence between drips, she thought she heard something like a faint sniffle.

For those attuned to it, magic and creatures who possess leave a trace, like an aura. Azalea shivered, her whole body repulsed by what she felt in the air. Like a deer sensing an approaching predator, her senses screamed in warning. This was a dark and potent aura.

It was the sob that caught her attention. Following the sound, Azalea rushed through the cave, down a rocky tunnel path, farther into the earth. The path was wide enough to move quickly, but it was uneven enough to make navigation tricky. She followed the path, winding down and curving back and forth until the tunnel opened to a lair of sorts.

There was a stone circle in the middle of the room with a wall behind it and an apparent living quarter on a small ledge to the side. Chained to the wall was a young woman. She looked frail, and her body was beaten and bruised. Her clothes were in shambles, her hair a disheveled, unkempt mess. Blood dripped from at least a dozen places.

She looked crushed, defeated, and hopeless as she hung limply on the wall.

"Sarah! Sarah!" a man's voice echoed through the rocky tunnels, as Azalea heard boots stomping on the ground.

A moment later, Vale rushed into view. He ran past Azalea like she wasn't even there. That's rude. The man in black armor held his sister's head up. She groaned softly, weakly.

"What has he done to you?" Vale set down his sword and started to remove her shackles.

Her body fell suddenly into him. He caught her as if she were weightless and gently lowered her to the ground.

"Brother?" Her voice was weak and faint. "Brother, is that really you?" the young girl asked, her eyes barely open. She lifted her hand to Vale's cheek and smiled weakly. "I . . . never thought . . . I'd see you again."

Vale chuckled as tears ran down his face. "I am sorry. If I had just gotten here sooner."

"Shhh, you're here now . . . "

Vale pulled her into his arms, hugging her tight. "I'm here. I promise I won't let anything hurt you again."

"HEAAAHEAAA HAAA HEE!" An eerie, unnatural cackle came from the entrance to the lair.

Azalea looked over to see a floating skeletal creature wearing tattered cloth. Its face was covered by long, white, wiry hair. Blue lines cracked through the semi-opaque skin and seemed to glow. Azalea felt her blood run cold. She knew what this was. There was no doubt—she had found the source of Vale's condition. Her mind scrambled to remember what Dante had said to do.

She rushed over as quick as she could and put her hand on Vale's arm. She looked around. The others didn't appear. Isn't that what Dante said to do? Touch the memory, and they would all be summoned? *Why wasn't it working?* She touched his arm again. Nothing.

"You should have stayed away, boy. Now you both are mine." Each chilling note hung on the air, long and drawn out as the creature floated closer.

Vale lowered his sister's head down gently and grabbed his

sword. Azalea realized that this was not the black blade she'd seen him wield on their quest together.

"You won't touch her again, fiend!" he warned.

"No! It's a wraith! You need an onyx blade!" Azalea cried out, trying to warn him. Of course, he couldn't hear her; she wasn't really there.

He swung at the creature, but his blade sliced through it, finding nothing. Azalea was so focused she didn't even notice the others standing beside her.

The wraith laughed and dove into Vale's chest. He seized and convulsed as the spirit phased through him. Vale collapsed to one knee, his body drained of color as he struggled to hold himself up. -

Dante gasped, causing Azalea to jump, surprised by his presence.

"He shouldn't even be conscious," Dante said in disbelief. "A wraith's touch drains life from whatever it touches. It would take an incredible force of will just to stay upright."

Azalea's jaw dropped as she watched Vale struggle to his feet. He faced the wraith, raising his sword in a challenge.

"That's not possible. The pain . . . " Dante shook his head. "No one could endure that."

Vale's feat, no matter how impressive, was not enough. The wraith lifted Sarah off the ground, holding her body in the air, and laughed its hideous, unnerving laugh.

"Wraith's touch—that explains his symptoms. I know how to treat this. We must go now." Dante readied a vial and handed one to each of them.

Caelan took his immediately and a moment later vanished while Azalea held onto hers. She couldn't stop watching the scene before her.

"You will not have her," Vale grunted through what had to have been unspeakable pain. He charged toward the creature.

"You are too late; she is already mine."

Sarah gasped harshly and opened her eyes wide as the wraith laughed and stuck its monstrous hand through Sarah's chest. Vale stumbled forward and collapsed to his knees, screaming as he watched the wraith pull out Sarah's heart and eat it.

"Gods below . . . no, I can't . . . " Celeste downed her vial and disappeared.

"Lingering here serves no purpose. Let us depart this place." Without waiting for any response, Dante took his vial and faded.

Curiosity had overtaken her. Azalea wanted to know what happened. How did he escape the wraith? She would wait to take the vial.

Suddenly, a swarm of Mindshades entered the wraith's lair.

"Seven bells from seven hells!" she exclaimed. Her curiosity would have to go unsatisfied as she downed the vial and felt her whole body tingle.

Whisked from the cave, she found herself back on the road where Vale had fallen. Dante was already pouring a vial of fluid into the Black Swordsman's mouth, but the veining was covering his whole body. His skin looked pale as stone. *Were they too late?*

The group crowded over Vale as Dante continued working. He blended a series of potions together into one larger flask. The fluid changed colors dramatically every time he mixed in something new: first blue, then green, then silver, and finally a purple with orange flakes. Celeste lifted Vale's head up, and Dante poured the fluid down his throat.

"Now what?" Caelan asked.

"We wait."

Minutes turned to hours, and there was no perceivable change. As the dying light faded completely, Vale appeared just as gray and lifeless as before.

The traveling companions built a fire and sat around it in silence. A heaviness hovered over them all like a thick fog. Their journey into Vale's mind had proven far more draining than expected.

One by one, they fell asleep. The next morning, as the sun began its ascent, Azalea awoke and immediately went to check on Vale. To her surprise, his color was back; the veining on his neck and body were gone. As she watched, he let out a groan and sat up, propping himself on his elbows.

"You're awake!" Azalea smirked, trying to stop herself from smiling too brightly. "How do you feel?"

Vale replied with a grunt.

"It appears the infection is contained. You should be fine." Dante leaned over and inspected Vale, checking his skin and his eyes.

"He's recovered, then?" Caelan asked.

Dante nodded.

"Good." Caelan pushed Azalea out of the way and leaned over Vale, holding a knife to Vale's throat.

"Get your toothpick out of my face before I make you swallow it," Vale said.

Caelan glared at him. "Oakwood village."

"That supposed to mean something to me?" Vale grunted as he pushed himself up a little more, completely unconcerned with the knife at his neck.

"You were there. I saw you." Caelan pressed the blade so tight against Vale's throat that blood started to coat it.

"And?" Vale winced.

"Is this a joke to you? You slaughtered an entire village of innocent people—women and children who didn't even have weapons to defend themselves—and you're going to pretend like you don't remember? Well, I do!"

"In all my life, I've never killed anyone who didn't have the means to defend themselves."

"Liar! I saw you! Blood dripping from your sword as you and your men massacred my—"

"Wait, Oakwood in Taggoron?" Vale asked.

"Yes."

"You're not Targgoronian," Vale questioned.

"Not by blood," Caelan answered.

"What does that mean?" Dante interjected. "No one wants to be Targgoronian. They are a bunch of lawless barbarians who—"

"Eat our own young? Sacrifice our elders to the gods? What was that—oh yeah, we are monsters who take the form of people so that we can sleep with them and steal their souls. I rather like that one. I'm familiar with all the things you think we are." Caelan turned his attention from the wizard back to the knight.

"Tell me, does convincing yourselves that we aren't human make slaughtering us more palatable? Or do you just like to do it for sport?"

"Caelan, there's no way Vale would do that. If you'd seen the memory I saw, you'd know!" Azalea wasn't sure why she felt the need to defend him, but she couldn't stop herself.

"That's why they call you the disgraced knight?" Celeste asked. "Because you slaughtered a Targgoronian village?"

"No," Vale's voice rumbled.

"Stop lying!" Caelan demanded.

"I'm not lying. You're right, I was there. I didn't know it was called Oakwood, but I was there," Vale said. His tone had shifted from dismissive to shameful.

"Finally, you admit the truth!" Caelan moved back, pointing his blade in accusation.

"Admit what? We didn't see what you saw," Celeste replied.

"What were you doing in a Targgoronian village?" Vale looked to Caelan.

Caelan moved farther back, pacing as he processed. "My father never wanted kids. Lazy bum didn't want anything that would require him to actually do something. But he loved my mother, and she wanted kids. So they had me. Then she got sick. Caring for her and for me was too much for him, so he took me on a ride outside of the wall and left me at the edge of the woods."

"Your father just abandoned you? How did you survive?" Celeste asked.

"A woodsman found me. He and his wife raised me as their own. The village became my home, the people my family. They were the kindest, most caring, gentle people you'd ever meet. Until the King's prized guard, the Phoenix Legion, showed up for the Harvest Festival under the guise of friendship. They waited for the party to start, and when the villagers were dancing in gleeful celebration, they slaughtered everyone."

"What does that have to do with Vale?" Celeste asked.

"Vale was a captain of the Phoenix Legion," Dante answered.

"Murderer!" Caelan grit his teeth, pointing his dagger at Vale once more. "I will have justice for my family."

Caelan started forward, but Dante caught his arm and pulled him back, stepping between them.

"Take a breath," Dante cautioned.

"I vowed to kill every last member of the Phoenix Legion. You don't want to get in my way!"

"Calm down," Azalea said, placing herself in Caelan's path as well. She faced the archer, her eyes as wild as a flame.

"Get out of my way, witch, or his won't be the only death today," Caelan warned.

"Lia viam borra ensnar lia viam borra imprim." Azalea's hands glowed as she extended them. Vines burst from the ground, coiling around Caelan's arms, binding them to his side.

Caelan struggled and tugged at the vines but was unable to move.

"I'll kill you for this," he cursed through gritted teeth.

"After what I saw in his head, he deserves a chance to explain. If his explanation is unsatisfactory, I will release you, and you can do as you please. Until then, be a good little rogue and keep your mouth shut?" she snapped.

Caelan growled and cursed before reluctantly nodding once in agreement. Azalea turned to Vale.

"I'm giving you a chance to explain. For your sake, I hope you have a good answer."

Vale exhaled. "The prosperity of Parisia has made her the envy of her neighbors. The three bordering kingdoms—Taggoron, Rag'amor, and Vargr—have been trying to infiltrate our borders for years. Parisia has unrivaled wealth but when it comes to military power, she wouldn't stand a chance. It is the wall that keeps the kingdom safe. King Alistar knew that if the other kingdoms were left unchecked, sooner or later they'd find a way in. The invaders would pillage and murder their way through the kingdom until they reached the palace, and we'd be powerless to stop them. So he created the Phoenix Legion—a group of elite soldiers who would operate outside the wall to serve and protect Parisia."

"Spare us the history lesson. It won't save you," Caelan argued, glaring.

"Tell us about that night," Dante said.

"The king had brokered peace talks with a village just outside the wall. He called it Bouldon River, not Oakwood. Our mission was to form an agreement for the village to build us a fortress to serve as a Parisian base of operations. It would effectively extend the king's reach and put pressure on the other kingdoms to play nice. As a gesture of our goodwill, the king gave us an ornate dagger the likes of which I have never seen. We were to present it to the village elder along with our offer."

"Why use Taggoronians?" Dante asked.

"If a group of Parisians left the wall and started construction, any or all of the three kingdoms would attack and slaughter them," Vale answered.

"But if Targgoronians were doing the building, it would look like an expansion project for their village, and no one would think anything of it," Dante added.

"Exactly. Once the fortress was complete, King Alistar could send his men in. We were told the goal was to ensure the lasting safety of Parisia and create a place to forge relationships that could lead to a lasting peace."

"And then, when they didn't agree to be your subjects and help your king conquer their own country, you slaughtered them!" Caelan shouted.

"No!" Vale protested.

"Oh, it was an accident? You didn't mean to ransack a defenseless village and butcher everyone there, that it? It was just a great big misunderstanding," Caelan jeered.

"I'm telling you, that's not what happened."

"I was there. I only survived because the woodsman who found me hid me in a secret compartment he'd built under the floor of his home. I saw the bodies. I heard the screams."

"You were there, but you did not see. I know what happened, but it wasn't supposed to . . . I can't explain it. I don't understand it myself. Everything was going fine and then—" Vale started.

"I don't care what you say. There is no excuse that makes murdering innocents acceptable."

"You're right. Those were my men. Their actions are my responsibility."

"See? Now let me go so I can kill him!" Caelan shouted, pulling against his restraints.

"Let him finish," Azalea stepped in. "Or should I coat those vines in ice to help cool you off?"

The ground beneath them began to shake so hard that most of the group struggled to remain on their feet. The ground shook again and again.

"Grab your things; load your horses. We need to leave, now!" Vale instructed.

"Well, that's convenient. Saved by an earthquake at your hour of reckoning," Caelan glared, continuing to strain against the vines.

Vale stared in the direction of the rumbling. "That was no earthquake."

Chapter 9
The Wall

Azalea released her spell, binding Caelan. Vale half expected the wild ranger to charge him immediately, so his restraint was a pleasant surprise. Vale winced, his head was throbbing, and his body was trembling. He was hardly fit to walk, not to mention fight.

"What is it?" Celeste asked as the ground shook again, this time a little harder.

"He's bluffing, trying to bide his time until he can think of a story to make himself sound better," Caelan criticized.

"Get your gwar together and get moving. Now!" Vale commanded.

The rumbling grew stronger, louder, and faster. The source was getting closer.

"This energy—it feels warm and powerful . . . but also filled with hate." Azalea walked from the path toward the thick forest as if being beckoned by the sound.

The trees began to shake and bend in the distance, moving and parting as whatever it was grew closer.

"Dante, get them on their horses, and get them moving now!" There was an urgency in Vale's voice that put to rest any further argument.

The stomping, thumping, and crashing continued to grow steadily closer. Vale rushed toward Azalea. His body felt heavy and stiff, and pain surged through his veins, but he pushed through it. The trees just inside the edge of the forest cracked and broke. At the same time, Vale dove, driving his body into Azalea's side, knocking her away just as an enormous creature broke through the brush. Its massive arm caught Vale in the chest, sending him flying.

The Black Swordsman flew through the air, crashing to the ground so hard he bounced off it and then crashed down again several times before rolling into a heap. His body went still.

"What the ralk is that?" Caelan shouted, as he notched and fired a pair of arrows.

The creature looked, in form, like an enormous, overweight person, standing at least twelve feet tall. Its skin was flesh-colored but looked tough, almost leathered, with dark cracks in it. Around its waist, a series of bear furs had been sewn together to make a crude loin cloth. Its mouth looked more like that of a shark, with three rows of razor-sharp teeth. In its massive hand was a thick club that appeared to be a pair of trees he'd ripped out of the ground and bound together.

"Yous in my space. Yous must pay! Me smash yous into bits. Make yous into stew!" the creature bellowed out, his voice deep and rumbling.

Caelan fired two more arrows. The creature's skin was so thick that the arrows pierced it but couldn't break through. They didn't even divert his attention. It was like putting needles into a pin cushion.

Vale groaned as his whole body surged with intense pain. He pushed through, forcing himself to stand.

"Arrows are of no use here. That is an ogre. Get on your horse and ride!" Vale shouted.

Caelan slung his bow over his shoulder and rushed over to his horse. Dante and Celeste were already mounted, but Azalea was still near the tree line. She'd have to get past the ogre to reach her horse.

"Azalea, can you do enchantments?" Vale called out.

The red haired witch stared at him. He'd been at death's door only moments before, and now he was hobbling toward her. Here she was, too stunned to move. Creatures like this rarely made it into Parisia. If they did, they never passed these woods. She was looking at a monster unlike anything she'd seen before. It was a hideous-looking but mesmerizing thing. Try as she might, she couldn't focus on anything else.

"Azalea!" Vale repeated. He'd already crossed most of the distance between them.

She nodded. "Y-y-yes, I can."

"Put a bright, colorful flame on my blade, then when I say, run to your horse and ride," he said, his voice firm and commanding.

Azalea nodded, uttering a few words and moving her hand over Vale's blade. Bright purple flames engulfed it. As soon as they did, the ogre turned to face them.

"Go, now!" Vale instructed.

"Puuuurrrpple prrreeeetty," the monstrous creature muttered, turning and thumping toward Vale. "Mes wants it! Gimmie!"

Azalea rushed past the ogre. It paid her no heed as it stomped toward Vale, its gaze completely fixed on the glowing purple flames. Celeste was already onto the paved stone path, moving toward the woods.

"Where are you going? We can't just leave him!" Caelan exclaimed.

"He knows what he's doing, right? He told us to go. We should go. Otherwise, we will just end up in his way," Celeste replied.

"He can't defeat that thing alone; we'd be leaving him to his death," Dante pointed out.

"Ralk that, I'm not going anywhere," Caelan said.

"Curious. Moments ago, you wanted to kill him. Why the change of heart?" Dante asked, sounding genuinely confused.

"Nothing has changed. I'm still going to kill him. Me. Not some goraum hulking meat sack," Caelan answers.

"What can you do? Your arrows have no effect," Dante retorted as Azalea reached them on her horse.

Caelan thought for a moment, and a grin slowly formed across his face.

"The trees—they are magic, right? They grow back fully formed after being cut down?" Caelan asked.

Dante nodded, "Yes, the trees are enchanted to always grow back."

"Do you have to cut them, or does any removal work?"

"Any removal, I suppose. Why?"

Caelan grinned. "How long does it take?"

Dante shrugged. "I have never seen it happen. From what I've heard, it is quick—maybe a few moments."

"Here's what I need you to do . . . " Caelan turned to Azalea.

Vale was struggling to dodge the large ogre's attempt to claim his sword. The creature had given up on trying to take it and was instead slamming his club into the ground trying to squash Vale under it. The Black Swordsman was barely able to avoid the creature's attacks in his condition.

Caelan rode his horse between the ogre and Vale, firing an arrow engulfed in purple flame over the creature's head.

"Preeetty . . . " The ogre whirled around to see the arrow land.

Celeste rode in front with Dante not far behind. As Dante rode, he lobbed a large vial into a thick patch of trees as he rode past. The vial shattered, covering the trees in a thick, blue liquid.

As the flame of Caelan's first arrow went out, he fired another, then another. His arrows created a glowing path, leading the ogre toward the trees. The blubbering oaf stomped and charged, trying to grab one of the arrows, only to have the flame go out before he could reach it. With each step, the ogre got closer.

Caelan notched a final arrow, leaning over the side of his horse for one last shot. This was the one that counted. He aimed carefully as he rode, releasing the arrow. It struck one of the trees covered in the liquid from Dante's vial, and a great burst of blue powder erupted from the vial, burning a giant hole in the patch of woods.

The ogre cheered gleefully, running into the blue cloud. He suddenly tripped over a rope Celeste had attached as a tripwire. The ogre's sprint was already clumsy, and the taut rope sent its hulking form crashing to the ground with a loud, earth-shaking

Shadows of the Dark Realm

thud. Sprawled out over the stumps of destroyed trees, the clumsy creature tried to get up.

"Ooowie . . . thaaat huuuurt," the ogre grumbled.

"Azalea, NOW!" Caelan shouted.

The witch chanted and thrust her hands forward, and thick strong vines wrapped around the creature's arms and legs, pinning it to the ground.

"Heeey! Nos fair. Lemme goooo," the ogre muttered. "Lemme crush and eats yous." It struggled and pulled against its magical restraints.

Sweat formed on Azalea's forehead as she strengthened the spell, pouring more magical energy into the vines to keep the monster down.

"He's too strong! I can't hold him!" she shouted.

"Don't let go! Hold him as long as you can!" Caelan called back.

A slow, creaking, crackling sound filled the air. The trees that had been destroyed grew back fully formed, sprouting up through the ogre's body and impaling the creature in a dozen places at once. The massive creature died instantly.

Vale rushed over. "You killed it, you fools! Ride hard, or we all die!"

Celeste spun around on her horse as the others walked past. *What is his problem? Why is he freaking out now that the monster is dead?*

"What are you so worried about? We just killed that ugly thing. We should be celebrating our victory! Let's enjoy it. Celebrate. Where's the rush?" Celeste said.

From the forest, a large puff of smoke rose into the air, dark as a thunder cloud. The smoke sparkled with tiny green specks as it billowed up from the ogre's body. The bark of the brand-new trees bubbled and melted, toppling the trees one after another as they liquefied into a pool on the ground. The grass beneath the cloud shriveled and charred before melting away completely. Everything the smoke touched began to boil and then break.

"What fresh lemara is this!?" Caelan asked as the smoke wafted closer and closer.

"Ride! Now!" Vale repeated, smacking the backs of their horses.

The horses charged fast and hard down the stone path, away from the smoke and through the forest, and they didn't stop until they reached the clearing on the other side.

As they came out of the forest, they saw rolling hills stretching for many miles, and in the distance, the silver wall rose into the sky, separating Parisia from its jealous neighbors.

Celeste was the first to stop, tugging on her reins to slow her mount to a gentle trot.

"What exactly was that?" she asked, her head cocked to the side, an expectant expression on her face.

"An example of what happens when you don't listen. You all could have been killed," Vale snapped.

"You really chug at saying thank you—anyone ever told you that?" Caelan replied.

"I did! I told him that!" Azalea agreed.

"I would have been fine. That smoke would have killed you all, painfully," Vale glared at them. "When I tell you to ride, you need to comply!"

Caelan rolled his eyes. "Spare me the lecture, boss man. I don't answer to you."

"Is someone going to answer my question? What exactly was that smoke?" Celeste huffed.

"Ogres were created by dark magic," Vale explained. "When they are killed, that dark magic releases in a toxic cloud. The cloud spreads and destroys any organic life in its path."

"How far does the smoke travel?" Dante asked.

"No way to know exactly. It varies, dependent on the creature."

"Are we safe here?" Celeste questioned.

"Yes."

"How did that thing get into Parisia?" Caelan asked.

"The veil between realms must be weakening," Vale replied.

"That's not good. It's already starting," Celeste said.

"The Order Arcana is working to patch and secure the veil. They will get the realm secure," Dante explained.

"But for how long?" Celeste questioned.

"Hard to say. We should make haste," Dante suggested.

"It's a long journey. We must pace ourselves. It does us no good if we reach the Dragon Lands sooner but are too weak to defend ourselves. Success is more important than speed," Vale countered.

"Well, standing here listening to you talk isn't helping anything, is it?" Caelan jabbed.

"There is a city near the gates; we should be able to reach it and take lodging by tomorrow night. From there we can restock our supplies, recover, and make our way to the wall," Vale said.

Without another word, the group rode through the hills, passing farm after farm, picturesque and flush with bountiful crops. Monsters were loose in the kingdom, and yet these farmers seemed completely unaffected. The cool breeze rolled over the hills, making the remainder of their journey to the wall feel like a leisurely stroll.

They made camp at the top of a hill. Far in the distance, at the edge of the horizon, they could see Parisia's great wall. Even from a distance the wall was massive, like a great mountain towering into the sky. Somewhere along that wall was Elysia, the largest city in Parisia outside of the capital, and their final place of rest before leaving the kingdom.

Vale took first watch, letting the others sleep around the campfire. The moon was a smile in the serene, starlit sky. The occasional puffy cloud drifted through the otherwise clear sky, creating a sort of hypnotic calm.

"You ever notice how much clearer your thoughts are at night?" Caelan asked quietly as he sat down next to Vale.

"It's easier to focus. Less distractions," Vale replied.

"Maybe that's it. Even when I get away from everyone and find a nice, secluded spot, I find my thoughts are still clearer at night than during the day. It's weird, right? Like during the day I'm always thinking about stuff, but it's functional, practical things—like what I have to do or what I should be doing. At night, my mind calms down, and I think more about the meaning of stuff—what really matters."

"Is there a purpose to this, or did you just come over to fill the silence?" Vale asked.

Before Caelan could answer, they heard a noise nearby. Vale's hand grasped the hilt of his sword. They crept over the hill and lay down to keep themselves out of view. They could see several shadowed figures approaching from below. Vale pointed. Caelan nodded and crawled over to the other side of the hill, sliding down to keep himself out of view.

Vale went the other way, staying out of view of the approaching group as he kept his eyes on them. He counted six in total. They wore long, flowing robes which meant they were likely monks or assassins. They moved straight for the fire, climbing the hill toward where the others were sleeping. Vale slowly, quietly pulled his blade from its sheath.

The group of cloaked figures marched straight up the hill. Vale watched as long as he could, trying to gauge their intent. He couldn't see any weapons, but that didn't mean they weren't carrying them. They were only a few paces from the others when Vale made his move. He sprang forward, tackling the man in the front and knocking him to the ground. He put his foot on the man's chest and held his sword against the man's neck.

"Heathen! You dare assault our chief deacon!" one of the men shouted.

His shout woke the others, but they were slow to respond. Each of the hooded figures moved in unison, each reaching one hand into the overly large sleeve of their other arm and pulling free a short, thick dagger.

"You might want to reconsider that," Caelan challenged, moving behind them, arrow drawn and ready.

The men in robes glanced back and lifted their hands, still holding their daggers.

"Do I really have to tell you to drop your knives?" Caelan asked.

One by one they tossed their weapons onto the ground and returned their hands above their heads. Dante, Celeste, and Azalea stood and moved next to Vale.

"What is going on?" Celeste asked.

"You will regret this. An attack on the holy servants of the gods is punishable by death," one of the men said.

In the light of the fire, Vale noticed that their robes were bright blue and lined with silver stitching.

He sighed, "You're Regilum?"

"We are. You have assaulted one of our leaders. You will answer to the king."

"We won't answer to anyone if I turn you all into piles of ash," Azalea smirked as flames erupted from the palms of her hands.

Most of the robed priests trembled, but the speaker let his hands drop down to his sides and stared her down.

"You wouldn't dare," he challenged.

"Dare? You're that weird cult that worships the Royals, right? It would be my genuine delight to remove your special brand of crazy from this world," Azalea replied.

"Azalea, stand down," Vale instructed. He removed his foot from the man he'd tackled and put his sword away.

"Perhaps we can chalk this up to a misunderstanding. You approached our camp at night without identifying yourselves. We had no way of knowing your intentions, so we had to assume you could be hostile and responded accordingly."

The man Vale had tackled dusted himself off, a scowl pressed on his face.

"You can't plead ignorance to assaulting a holy priest. You must pay for your insolence."

Vale shrugged. "Well, you can take the matter to the local magistrate if you wish. I am sure the king would love to hear how his priests delayed the departure of his Stone Seekers over this."

The priests gasped and murmured amongst themselves.

"You are Seekers, truly?" one asked, as a sort of nervous energy charged the air.

"We are," Dante answered.

The robed men fell to their knees and bowed.

"O great saviors of our people and servants of the gods, we humbly beg your forgiveness for our disturbing you."

"Well, that is unexpected." Caelan relaxed the tension in his bow as he stared in confusion at the robed men.

"You have stood in the presence of the gods. Please, tell us what they are like; impart on us a blessing, we beseech you," one spoke, and the others echoed in unison.

"This is officially creeping me out," Caelan shook his head.

"What are you doing wandering the lands at night?" Vale asked.

With their heads bowed to the ground, one answered, "Our order was blessed by the gods themselves to—"

"Wait, when he says gods, he means . . . " Caelan interrupted.

"The Royals. The Regilum believe the Royal family are the last remaining gods in our realm," Dante answered.

"We don't simply believe it. It is the truth," one of them said. Another nudged him with his elbow, and he stopped. "Forgive me, great Seekers, my zeal sometimes gets ahead of my sense."

"You were telling us what you are doing out here," Vale pressed.

"Yes, of course. The Regilum are the most faithful servants to the gods. We do whatever the gods ask of us."

"Stop evading the question," Vale grunted.

"Our Order is tasked to acquire . . . supplies . . . from around the realm and bring them to the Capital. Our service to the gods is to bring this great offering to them that they may be pleased with us and continue to grant Parisia their blessing."

"What supplies do you gather? I see none," Vale questioned.

"Quite right, great Seeker. The gods decreed a temporary cease to all offerings until further notice."

"If you weren't gathering supplies, what were you doing?" Vale asked.

"Preparing. The supplies are not always easy to come by. We do not wish to be lax in our responsibilities. Soon, we know the gods will tell us that it is time to bring our offerings once again. When that day comes, we, the faithful, will be ready."

"What do you gather?" Vale asked.

"We are forbidden to share that information with anyone outside of the Order."

"Not even with a Seeker?" Vale pressed.

"Not with anyone."

"What happens now?" Caelan asked.

"Perhaps the great Seekers would allow us to camp with them for the night?"

Caelan laughed, "A group of Regilum priests, a Taggorian, and a witch assassin set up camp together. Sounds like the start of a truly terrible joke."

"This . . . is the kinspira who tried to kill the king?" one of the priests said under his breath.

"Don't—" Vale warned.

"Death to the Antilyte!" they shouted, as they rushed toward Azalea, knives lifted.

Chapter 10

The Red Empress

Despite the sudden surprise of their attack, the priests were not trained fighters. Vale reacted on instinct, drawing his blade and cutting down the first priest before he could even attempt to use his knife. All six priests fell in a blink. Caelan shot two. Azalea burned one with her magical flames, and Vale dispatched the rest.

"What the ralk was that about?" Caelan shook his head.

"You are really emptos sometimes, you know that?" Dante glared.

"Do you not understand what you have done? We just had to kill a group of holy priests because of your big mouth!" Celeste snapped.

"Don't get leaked at me. They are the dim ones that attacked us for no reason," Caelan replied.

"No reason? You can't really be this ignorant," Celeste started.

"What's done is done. We don't have time for this. We need to move the bodies and be on our way," Vale interrupted.

"You want to hide the bodies of holy priests?" Celeste's jaw hung open in disbelief.

"Nothing can be done about them now. We bury them quickly and move on."

They spent the rest of the night digging shallow graves and

dragging the bodies to them for burial. Celeste protested and kept talking about how the priests deserved better until she realized no one was listening and gave up on the issue.

By the time they were finished, the sun was already peeking over the horizon. They gathered their supplies, mounted their horses, and started their journey. As the sun rose and fell in the sky, the city of Elysia came into view, growing steadily closer as they rode.

By the time they reached the city gates, the sun set on the horizon. Elysia could have been a royal resort. Each building was made of white stone and clay. Colorful flowers grew up the corners of most of the buildings. Little gardens lined the outside of shops and homes and grew across the flat roofs and balconies, as if the entire town had been designed by a single person. Colorful banners waved in the wind, and everything was in its proper place.

As the group rode into town, Vale slid off his horse and walked over to the noticeboard. His eyes drew immediately to a posting with bold letters, at the top which read: Missing Child

He put his hand on a different notice and pretended to read it so the others wouldn't know what had captured his attention. *The missing children had reached towns all the way to the wall?* It was worse than he expected. After staring for a moment, he turned around to face the group.

"I'll get us rooms at the inn. Get your horses set up at the stables, and meet me there when you are ready," Vale instructed.

Celeste was surprised that none of the others offered protest. The stables, like the rest of the town, were perfectly kept, and they reminded Celeste of home. She found herself feeling oddly uneasy at the sentiment. When she reached the inn, Dante guided her to her room. She looked in and saw Azalea laying sideways on one of the beds, with her hand and back hanging off the side.

"You're putting me in a room with her? No. I want my own." Celeste put her hands on her hips in protest.

"Only had the two rooms—unless you want to sleep in the room with us." It was unclear from his tone if Dante was aware of the suggestive nature of his comment.

Celeste rolled her eyes. "Where are the others?"

"Caelan went to the tavern. Vale left not long after, probably followed him."

"And you just let them? They will kill each other!" Celeste protested.

Dante crossed his arms. "No, those two have more in common than they want to admit."

Celeste exhaled dramatically and stormed out of the inn, making her way to the tavern down the street. She pushed the door open and stepped inside. There he was, standing in the center of the bar.

Caelan raised his glass. A foam-covered golden liquid spilled over the brim as his words slurred.

"Ladies, gentlemen, short and tall, hear me, hear me, one and all. You have the honor of drinking with the future hero of Parisia!"

Caelan held his hands high into the air. "That's right, you lucky ghouls! I have been tasked by the king himself to save the world from the evil Shadow King! In the morning, I will take my leave of your fine city and travel into the wilds outside the wall to save you all. So, drink up and sleep easy. You are in good hands . . . mine!"

The crowd cheered and raised their glasses, eating up his every word. Celeste made her way over to where Vale stood, leaning against a wall in the back of the tavern.

"What exactly does he think he's doing?"

Vale grunted. "Apart from making a bigger fool of himself than usual?"

"We need to stop him. Even here, it's not wise to share all that," Celeste started.

"He'll tire of his own voice eventually. Let the fool be," Vale replied.

"What if he finds trouble?"

"Get some rest, Celeste. I'll make sure he makes it back." Vale leaned his back against the wall, casually resting where he could see the whole room, watching to see if anyone showed unusual interest in Caelan's proclamations.

Shadows of the Dark Realm

After breakfast the next morning, the group gathered their supplies. Caelan seemed alert and focused, showing no signs of any side effects from his drunken bender the night before. Vale took their supplies to the stables to prepare the horses for departure.

After settling up at the inn, the others made their way to the stable.

"Celeste?!" A voice, familiar and high-pitched, came from behind them. "Celeste Vila Delaluche?"

Celeste froze as her heart lurched in her chest. Her body trembled as a strong ache rushed over her. She took a deep breath, closed her eyes, forced a smile, and turned around.

Standing behind her was an older couple, both small in stature, though the woman was slightly taller and broader than the man whose arm she held. They were dressed in fancy silk garments with oversized, gaudy jewelry around their necks and wrists. The jewelry looked as uncomfortable as it did absurd.

"Friends of yours?" Caelan asked.

Azalea made no effort to hide her disgust as she eyed the pair dressed in outlandish, lavish clothing with rampant disdain.

"Who is this ruffian who speaks to you so casually, my lady?" The scowl on the woman's face threatened to make her wrinkles even more pronounced.

"Oh, he's um . . . " Celeste chuckled. "He's my bodyguard." She smiled sweetly, trying to sell the lie.

"The ralk I am," Caelan objected.

Celeste elbowed him in the ribs. He grunted and shut his mouth.

"They both are. You know father, always so protective of his little girl. He wouldn't let me leave the grounds without a couple of expert escorts."

"I beg your pardon, my lady, but these scoundrels do not have the look of those employed by your father. If he wanted you protected, why did he not use his house guard?" the man asked.

"What the gwar?" Caelan started, but another elbow from Celeste cut him off.

"No, the proper guards are currently at the inn taking care of our accommodations. These two were hired as guides with a special knowledge of the area."

"Special knowledge?"

"Yes, my father thought it was time for me to really see Parisia. These two are guiding us around the wall."

"How odd." The man, whose face was covered by a bushy gray mustache that was styled to run down off his chin, raised an eyebrow. "I had heard rumors that you had run away or been kidnapped. It's been the talk of the palace for days."

"Oh, no, nothing like that," Celeste giggled, her pulse racing. *How could word have spread so fast?* She wasn't close with Lord Arginto and his wife Bealimi, but she knew them well enough to know they were nosy, well-informed, egotistical, and more ambitious than their station merited. If she couldn't calm their suspicions, things could get very tricky.

"My dear, go summon our guard; I want to get to the bottom of this. If the young lady has been captured and is being held against her will, it is our duty to the crown to rescue her," Lord Arginto said.

"My lord," Dante cut in with a bow. "I can assure you that will not be necessary. I presume you know who I am?"

Dante smiled and stood up straight, pulling down his collar to reveal a silver necklace lined with different colored gems. Lord Arginto held out his hand, and his wife stopped moving toward the guard.

"Of course, of course. You are Dante, the king's advisor and a mage from the king's royal court. The one they call the Blue Alchemist?"

Dante nodded. "I am. I am currently working on a very special project for the king. I requested an assistant for my work, and the king was gracious enough to provide me with Celeste. She's got quite the sharp mind and has been very helpful."

"I've not heard of any special project," Lord Arginto protested.

"No, I don't suspect you would. It's a surprise for the queen. Everything about it is secretive, including our departure. I'm sure that mystery has led to many rumors, but that is all they are."

This only resulted in the man's scowl growing deeper. "I

don't understand why a court mage would need a noble's daughter to help," Arginto began.

"Yes, I am sure there is quite a lot you don't understand. Nobility provides the opportunity for education; however, all the books in the world can't cure an addled mind," Dante responded.

"Excuse me?" The nobleman took a step back, as if to distance himself from the words.

"No, I don't think I will. I have informed you that we are about the king's business, and here you are questioning us and wasting my valuable time. Would you like me to inform the king that the reason his project was delayed was because you wanted to start an inquisition?" Dante retorted.

What was he doing? That is too bold. He shouldn't be talking to a noble like that. Celeste thought.

Arginto paused as he looked to his wife for direction. She provided none.

"Perhaps I should question what a noble lord like yourself is doing out here on the outskirts? I've heard rumors myself. Perhaps I should bring them to the king's attention." Dante stepped forward as if to push the man further back.

"No, that will not be needed. Please forgive my curiosity. I was merely surprised to see others from court this far from the palace." Arginto gulped and reached for his wife.

Dante smiled. "No more questions then?"

The noble held up his hands and walked away suddenly. "No, no, please. We are just out on a little getaway; no need to bother anyone about it."

Celeste blinked in shock as she watched Dante rob the lord and lady of all their power in a few sentences. Never before had she dreamed of someone speaking to a noble that way. It was exciting. All of a sudden, the odd wizard was more intriguing to her. *What was that necklace he had, anyway*, she wondered as the nobles rushed off.

"A kitchen girl was it? Any other lies we should know about?" Azalea's eyes narrowed in accusation.

"Mind your tongue when speaking to your betters, witch," Celeste met Azalea's ire.

"I knew it. You're a noble, I could smell it on you."

"That's called clean you beast," Celeste countered.

Azalea screamed and lunged forward, Dante caught her hand and pushed her back.

"That is enough. To be clear, she is not a noble. She is the Duchess Celeste Vila Delaluche, fourth in line to the crown and niece of the king. She's a royal."

"Ah, wonderful." Azalea chuckled, "Killing a royal brings us one step closer," purple flames engulfed Azalea's hands and forearms as magical energy surged through her body. This was not just her usual aggression; something was different about her.

Azalea felt her body surge with rage. A small voice in the back of her mind tried to calm her down but to no avail. She wasn't just traveling with some entitled noble, she was traveling with a relative of the king himself. The fire in her mind gave birth to a dark idea. *No.* She resisted, but the voice persisted. There was something inside her, something foreign that was clawing to get out, desperate to take control. She felt the anguish of unbearable tension as she tried to hold on to control. The soothing, calming voice promised release, satisfaction, vengeance.

"Let go," the woman's voice whispered in her mind. "I will make the false gods pay. I will purify the land of their disease. I will establish a new and better world."

Azalea felt the heat from the flames on her arms. Her eyes flashed as she pushed the voice down, releasing the flames as she forced herself to remain calm.

"Threatening a royal is punishable by death!" Celeste grabbed for her sword.

"Sorry, I hate to interrupt a good freak-out, but how is this news? Didn't we already know she was a noble because of the whole fancy sword thing?" Caelan asked.

"Don't be a goraum, fool," Azalea snapped. "A noble is a part of the wealthy, ruling elite that serve in the king's court. A royal is a member of the king's bloodline," Azalea winced as she felt that force clawing at her mind again. She closed her eyes and tried to focus on her breathing. Everything else was drowned out as she tried to hold back the tide.

"What's the difference? Aren't they all a bunch of pompous,

entitled, self-important bavasos who couldn't tie their own boots?" Caelan looked from side to side and gestured in confusion.

"I suppose since you did not grow up in Parisia, your impressive ignorance is understandable," Dante explained. "Though I would have thought in your time here you would have learned; perhaps I give you too much credit. The difference is in the blood. Anyone can become a noble be obtaining land and title. Only those with the blood of the Vila Delaluche are royals. The blood makes them special."

"Oh right, that's why them Regium rookis with their weird blue robes are always talking about how the king is some sort of god?" Caelan chuckled. "What a joke."

"It's not without basis," Dante challenged. "The Royal family has had exclusive access to the Darkstone for generations. It has given them supernatural powers which they have in turn used to bless the lands. Part of the reason Parisia is the prosperous jewel that it is, is because of their magic. There is a special power in the Royal bloodline that allows them to use the Darkstone in a way no one else can. This power has made the Royal family objects of worship and hate."

"That can't be it. Hating someone for being an entitled, rich snob—that's as natural as breathing. But hating someone because they use their power to make other people's lives better? No, I don't buy it," Caelan stated.

"Your knowledge of history is unsurprisingly lacking. Parisia was not always what it is today. This land was once ruled by a dark sorceress so powerful she was thought to be a Kanji from the Spirt Realm. Many considered her a god and worshipped her. The Red Empress, she was called, on account of the blood that flowed during her reign. She was a savage, cruel leader who ruled the kingdom with fear."

"You coming to a point anytime soon, professor?" Caelan asked. As they argued they failed to notice the change taking hold of Azalea.

Rage threatened to consume her as the two went back and forth. Azalea resisted. She'd felt this deep-seated hate inside her for as long as she could remember. She knew it well but had never felt it so strong, never so consuming.

"Let me in," the voice whispered again. The thought of letting go was as refreshing as a cool breeze on a sweltering day. She was tired of fighting. All she had to do was submit. Her resistance weakened, and her resolve faded. She felt herself losing control, her mind being drawn back and locked away.

"It's simple, so try to keep up. The Royals, using the power of the Darkstone, banished the Red Empress to the Spirit Realm, imprisoning her there in constant suffering. The Regilum worship the Royals as the heroes who saved the land from her. The Kinspira feel differently."

Caelan exhaled dramatically, "Ralk, what's a Kinspira?" he asked, as if the question caused him fatigue.

"The Kinspira are a coven of dark witches who drew power from the Red Empress. Her imprisonment nearly destroyed their order. They are radical disciples devoted to bringing about the Red Empress's return by slaughtering all Royals," Dante explained.

Azalea could not hold on any longer. Her mind blurred. Her own mental voice faded to a whisper and then was silenced. It felt good. It felt like freedom. All her life she'd been carrying this weight without even realizing it. Now she could finally let go and just rest.

"Deceiver! Destroyer! Impure! I will rid the world of you and all your kind!" Azalea's voice felt different, even to her. It sounded different. It was as if she was watching the world through the eyes of someone else. She tried to move her arms, but she couldn't. She watched in shock as flames covered her hands and ran up her arms. The flames weren't purple; they were red. Azalea realized then that she wasn't in control.

Celeste stepped back, her eyes wide as horror gripped her. Azalea's entire body pulsed with a dark red light that radiated from her like flames climbing to the sky. Her eyes, no longer their soft yellow-green, were now a bright crimson speckled with purple.

"W-w-what are you doing?" Celeste cried out.

"Death to all Royals! Destroy the imposters! Liberate the

true queen!" Azalea raised her hand, and a ball of fire shot from it.

Gasps rang out from passersby who turned and fled the streets in fear. Celeste covered her face with her arms as if that would deflect the magic. It did not. The absorption spell Dante cast did. It caught the ball of fire and the flames fizzled out inches before it consumed Celeste.

"Wait," Caelan interrupted, as if nothing had happened. "You're telling me some washed up old hag of an Empress wants her little goraum followers to kill a bunch of rich people so she can get out of her cage? Why would anyone be stupid enough to sign up for that?"

"Insolent cur!" Azalea growled, turning to face Caelan.

Dante groaned. The fool drew her attention. *For what? Perhaps Vale was right about this thief,* Dante thought. Caelan reached for his dagger more dramatically than necessary. He glanced at Dante and winked. *Clever.* He was frustrating her as a distraction. *Maybe not as dumb as he looks.* He bought Dante just enough time.

Before his hands could pull the blade free, vines wrapped around his arms, chest, and legs, binding him tight.

"Ralkin' vines again! Really?" he cursed before another vine wrapped around his mouth, muffling his words.

"That should shut you up." She waved her arm, and the vines dragged Caelan away, fastening him to the wall of a nearby building.

"You do not seem yourself, Azalea." Dante stepped between her and Celeste.

Azalea laughed. "You who possess the gift would stand in my way? You would protect these usurpers?"

"You threaten the life of a young girl who has done you no wrong. I cannot think of a better reason to stop you." Dante's hand reached subtly into his cloak.

"Then you shall die before ever lifting your curse. Such a shame to waste such talent." Flames burst from Azalea's hands and flew toward Dante.

Dante extended one hand, turning to the side. A translucent

blue wall appeared in front of him. The steaming flames broke and parted around it, funneled harmlessly away.

Azalea cackled. "That feeble construct will not protect you for long, Blue Alchemist. You disappoint me. We could have made a new world together. You could have ruled by my side. Instead, you will burn with the ashes of the old one."

"Interesting. So, you have chosen a Kinspira proselyte to be your vessel?" Dante asked.

Azalea laughed a sickening, twisted laugh. "You always were so very clever. The ties that bind me are loosening. The chains will not hold forever. Without the Darkstone to protect them, I will be free. The Royals will die, and I will return to my rightful place on the throne."

"Do you think killing one Royal will somehow free you from your prison?" Dante asked. "No. You chose a vessel that was actively moving away from the Royals. Why? What are you up to?"

"You cannot even comprehend the breadth of my plan. I will not be stopped."

The glowing blue protective barrier keeping the flames from consuming him grew lighter. He felt the heat of the flames as his defenses started to collapse.

"This is how you wish to spend your last moment in this world?" Azalea asked.

"This is not my last moment, Vespera, the Red Empress."

Chapter 11

The Blue Alchemist

Azalea laughed a sinister, otherworldly laugh. It sounded more like a wild animal than a person. Dante's barrier faded to near breaking. It was hardly holding back the flames. *This was less than ideal.* Dante stepped back, trying to create some distance between himself and the Red Empress, which would allow the potency of her magic to dissipate, buying him more time.

But the fire coming from Azalea was too strong. No simple witch could contain this power. It expanded too fast and was now surrounding her. What he was seeing didn't make sense. When a spirit possesses a mortal, the mortal host would experience an increase in power; however, it takes a toll on their body. If the spirit pushes too hard, the magical power they wield drains them, and they become too weak to maintain hold over their host. A spirit possessing a typical mortal host would not be able to sustain powerful magic for a long duration. There was something different happening here. The Red Empress was not losing her grip.

Azalea wasn't just pouring an endless stream of fire at Dante; her body was radiating flames that expanded around her. They practically covered the entire width of the street. What was more shocking is that she was also maintaining the vines binding Caelan. Wielding two types of magic simultaneously was something only the strongest magic-users could do and, even then, not for long. The flames grew closer and closer to Caelan as he struggled, pinned against the wall.

He was out of time. Dante needed to do something. If this continued, the entire city might be consumed in flame. He moved quickly, sliding his hand into his coat as he took a step back. Azalea followed. Her foot landed with a crunching sound as glass broke under her shoe. She looked down to see a blue burst of energy smashing into her stomach as it erupted from the vial below, launching her back. Her flames disappeared as her body hit the ground and bounced.

She managed to roll and plant her feet, sliding back on the ground. Her head lifted as a sneer formed upon her lips.

"Dimea vol selio," Dante exclaimed after he extended his arm.

A blue sphere expanded from his hand and covered the street and a few nearby houses in a giant dome, making everything inside appear a shade of slightly translucent blue. The sphere stopped just before it reached Caelan.

"What's this? Ah, the prism magic I've heard so much about. It's cute." Azalea looked around as if appreciating a rainbow.

Caelan, who was no longer bound by her vines, gasped. Without looking, Azalea sent a beam of lighting from her hands right at him. Caelan froze in place as he braced himself for the coming pain. The lightning crashed against the blue dome and fizzled out harmlessly.

"You will find affecting anything outside this dome quite impossible," Dante smirked.

Azalea tried again to no avail. She growled and grunted, trying again and again.

"Amusing parlor trick. You should have used it to contain me. All I have to do is kill you, and your little spell will fade," she cackled.

"You will find that feat quite difficult." Dante dropped in a stance that looked like he was preparing for a fistfight.

Azalea roared and cast spell after spell, shifting between shards of ice, balls of fire, bursts of lighting, and stone. Each cast hit the blue barrier and fizzled out before reaching Dante.

"Very clever. I see your reputation in our Realm is well earned. But you are a mortal. I am a god. All you are doing is delaying your fate."

"That is not entirely true. This prism doesn't just keep the magic inside from getting out. It prevents magic on the outside from getting in. Whatever link you are using to maintain your power is gone. Inside this prism, your hold on your host is limited. Once you have expelled your power, your grip will be lost, and she will be free," Dante replied.

Azalea's eyes widened and her sneer grew. "You can't cast me out; she is mine. I am bound to her and she to me. Even if you do expel me, I will return."

"Perhaps, but when I send you back, your power will be exhausted. It will take you time to grow strong enough to return. In that time, I will be preparing her to ensure that you can never take control of her again. You may be immortal, but time is not on your side," he answered.

"Curse you! I will destroy everything and everyone you love!" Azalea started.

"You cannot do anything my condition has not already done. Nor can you take anything from me that it has not already taken," Dante answered.

"We don't have to be enemies, Blue Alchemist. We could help each other. I know what you desire more than anything. I can give it to you. I can end your suffering. I can make you human again in all the ways you're not."

Everything about her changed. Her tone was seductive, with charm ringing from every note. Her demeanor was sweet and friendly.

She knew exactly how to tempt him. Ever since his accident, he had done everything he could think of to undo his mistake. Every trial, every spell, potion, and enchantment had failed. Here she was, offering it to him freely. This was no bluff. The Red Empress had the power to restore that which he lost. She could give him everything he desired. All he had to do was agree.

"Rookie wizard, don't be dim! She's playing you," Caelan shouted from outside the sphere.

"I know the burden you face. You struggle every day. In

every conversation, in every moment—but you suffer needlessly. I can help you. We can help each other. Free me, and all you desire will be yours. I can give you back your heart." Azalea's words flowed like honey.

Dante's mind salivated at the thought. *Was it so bad a thing?* After all he had lost, was it really so wrong? It's not like the Royals were perfect—Dante knew that better than anyone.

"We don't have to fight. I can be generous to those I find worthy."

"You can restore it?" Dante's resolve seemed to crumble under the weight of the choice she was giving him. Her appeal made sense. His work could continue; his impact on the world would be unrivaled. One choice, one moment and he could do so much good.

"I can, and I will. Release me. Pledge your loyalty to me, and I will give it all to you."

"Ok," Dante's shoulders slumped.

"There, there. You made the right choice. You won't regret it." She stepped closer and put her hand on his shoulder.

Dante lifted his gaze and grinned as he looked into her eyes. He brought his hand to his mouth and opened it in one quick motion. Azalea's eyes widened as she recognized the pile of glimmering dust. She screamed and tried to push away, but it was too late. Dante blew the powder into her face, the shimmering sands floating into her nose and mouth. She tried covering them with her hands, but it made no difference. She could feel it working. She gasped and choked, clutching her throat as she dropped to her knees. Her breaths grew so heavy, each one sounded like a groan.

"You . . . will pay . . . for this . . . B-Blue—" she warned before Azalea's body collapsed.

Dante released the spell that held the protective dome around them.

"Gods below, what was that?" As the blue light dissipated, Caelan stepped inside, looking around.

"That was a prism of holding, a containment spell of sorts," Dante explained.

"She did pose a good question. Why didn't you just cast it around her?" Caelan asked.

"It only works if I'm inside it," Dante answered.

"Well, that's useful in a dodgy sort of way, isn't it? What's her deal then? Is that a typical witch thing to do? Go all murdery without warning?" Caelan pressed.

Dante ignored him.

"Right, so you gonna explain what the ralk just happened?"

"I'm handling it," Dante answered.

"That's a far cry from what I asked, isn't it? What the actual . . ." Caelan persisted.

"Azalea is a Kinspira, a group of witches who draw their power from an ancient and evil spirit called the Red Empress," Dante started.

Caelan waved his hand in the air. "Right, I remember that bit from before her vines got all clingy. What does that have to do with Azalea trying to kill us?"

"That was not Azalea," Dante answered.

"You having a laugh?" Caelan pointed at the girl on the ground. "You telling me that is not the same person we've been traveling with all this time? What, she some sort of swapling? Just snuck in when we weren't looking?"

Dante groaned and shook his head. "No, that is Azalea."

Caelan's expression soured. "You can make me keep asking questions, or you can just explain it all. How big a plek you wanna be?"

"Azalea is a vessel either by her will or by offering. What you saw was Azalea, but she was being controlled by the Red Empress."

"What was that shiny dust then? Did it kill the Red Empress?" Caelan asked.

Dante chuckled. "No. That was silver dust. Silver is a conduit. It bonds to spirits and monsters of magic and dispels their power. The dust will keep the Red Empress dormant for a time. Then it will be up to Azalea to keep her at bay."

"That was the Red Empress?" Celeste stood, her jaw dropped in stunned disbelief.

"Celeste! Zular's crack, I forgot you were here." Caelan turned to look at her.

"The dust bound her, but she's still in there? Like she could come back?"

Dante nodded. "Yes, it is possible."

Caelan drew an arrow and notched it to his bow.

Dante stepped between them. "What are you doing?"

Caelan sighed. "Sorry, professor, if that *thing* is still insider her, she has to die."

"You can't just kill her!" Celeste moved over next to Dante, further blocking Caelan's path.

"No, I'm pretty sure I can."

"Heroes don't kill defenseless people!" Celeste put her hands on her hips.

"Oh, grow up princess. This isn't a bedtime story for children. She's a danger not just to us, but to anyone she comes across."

"You don't think I know that? She's a Kinspira; I'm a Royal. Her whole purpose in life is to kill me and my family simply because we were born. Even if she's not possessed, she's a danger to me. Yet here I am, standing between you and her."

"Then you should move, princess; letting her live is not a good idea."

"A good idea? Bringing a volatile witch on the most important quest in the last two centuries was never a good idea, but here we are. I'm not saying we bring her with us. I'm saying we can't just kill her."

Caelan glanced over Celeste's shoulder. "Not to interrupt your moral positioning, but we may have a problem."

"What is that?" Dante asked.

"It looks like we've got company," Caelan gestured.

Marching straight for them was Lord Arginto in all his gaudy glory. Behind him were two dozen armed soldiers, weapons ready. They marched until he stood a few yards from Celeste.

"Have no fear, my lady; your humble servant is here." The old noble's declaration dripped with the easy self-adulation that comes from regular practice. "I knew you needed rescue. When I bring you home, I'll be heralded as a hero, and my house will finally get the recognition it deserves—"

"Put the bow down, Caelan. This discussion is over." Celeste ignored the noble, cutting off his speech while using his presence to her advantage.

Caelan ignored her. "You outwitted her this time. Doubt you can play that card again. Tell me, professor, what happens if you aren't there to stop her next time? Or if we are in the middle of a fight when she reemerges? Have you thought about that?"

"I promise you, buffoon, there has never been a thought in your head that did not cross my mind first. I have considered the possibilities. My answer is unchanged."

"You saw what she is capable of, same as I. You think I want to do this? I don't like it either. Sometimes you have to make hard choices for the greater good. As long as she draws breath, she puts everyone around her at risk. If the Red Empress returns, you know the destruction she will cause," Caelan pressed.

"Better than you ever will," Dante replied.

"Step aside, professor. Let me do what needs done. Your hands will be clean of it."

"I will not." Dante stood resolute. "She can control it. I will help her."

"I don't even like her, but she just had her body taken from her and used against her will. Don't you think that deserves a modicum of sympathy? I understand what you're saying, Caelan, I do. You are weighing one life against the lives of an entire kingdom. It feels like there are no options. But killing someone who cannot defend themselves because of something they can't control? Could you really live with yourself after that?" Celeste asked.

"Heed my lady's word, fiend. Put down your bow or my men will put you down," Lord Arginto sneered.

Caelan chuckled but relaxed his bow. "Mind your dog, princess."

"What did you call me?" Arginto's face flushed red.

"Be silent," Celeste snapped at the noble.

"You really think this is a good idea?" Caelan turned to Dante.

"Killing her will not accomplish anything,"

Caelan's eyes narrowed. "How's that?"

"The Kinspira. It is an entire cult that worships the Red Empress. Any one of them would gladly offer their lives as a sacrifice to be used and possessed by the Red Empress. Killing Azalea does not hurt the Red Empress, nor does it hinder her. All you would be doing is killing an innocent victim of her possession. Once she was dead, The Red Empress would just select another host and keep going."

Caelan released more tension from his bowstring. "You're sure?"

Dante nodded.

Caelan let out a long, slow breath and returned his arrow to its quiver. "You better be right about this, professor. I'm trusting you."

"My lady, please, come with us. We will ensure these people can't hurt you anymore. I will take—" Lord Arginto interjected, completely oblivious to the conversation happening around them.

"No, it's ok. You can go," she said dismissively.

"My lady, you misunderstand me. I heard the crier announcing that you were missing. Your father wants you home. He will reward us very well for bringing you. If he doesn't, well, I'm sure your ransom will be quite large." Arginto motioned and his guards marched around Celeste, Caelan, Dante, and the incapacitated Azalea.

"Seize the duchess. If the others resist, kill them," Arginto declared.

Before they could even respond, twenty-one soldiers encircled the group, swords drawn and at the ready. Only three remained behind, one on either side of Arginto and one, the captain of his house guard, standing between him and the other soldiers.

Celeste's hand returned to the hilt of her blade, but she knew it was pointless. There was no way to fight her way out of this. If she resisted, her companions would be killed. She did not want that. Rather than resist, she held up her hands in surrender.

"Ok, ok. I'll go with you. Just don't hurt them," Celeste said.

Shadows of the Dark Realm

Arginto smiled. "As you wish, my lady."

Celeste turned and glared at the man. "Let me be clear. If your men so much as bump into them when they pass by, my father will hear a very different tale than you want him to."

The smug satisfaction painted on the noble's face washed away as he gulped nervously.

He sneered, "Do not threaten me—not if you know what's good for you."

Arginto was cut off by a gasping, choking sound from his right. The guard standing there slumped to the ground in a heap. Arginto looked quickly to his left, just in time to see the second guard clutch his throat and drop to his knees. Then Arginto's eyes went wide as the edge of a blade pressed lightly against his throat.

"You and your men are going to leave Elysia and return to your home now." Vale stood behind Arginto, holding the noble against his body like a shield. The noble's small stature was even more pronounced in contrast to the large swordsman in black.

"It is our sworn duty to protect the Royals. We will leave, with the duchess."

"You will leave empty handed, or you won't be leaving at all."

"If you kill me, my men will kill you." Arginto's voice was snide and condescending, even with a blade to his throat.

The captain of his house guard, who had been standing with most of Arginto's men in front of the noble, looked at Vale, then took a step back, face ashen.

The captain was visibly trembling as his skin went pale.

Arginto scowled at him. "Hathga, what are you doing? Get over here and kill him."

Hathga backed up again, almost stumbling over himself. "That armor . . . that look," he said quickly. "I'd know him anywhere. That's the Black Swordsman . . . the century slayer."

Murmurs echoed from the other guards as their weapons begin to shake.

"Foolish plebs, those are just stories! Stop being children, and do what I pay you to do! Kill them!" Arginto cried out.

Vale smirked and said to the guards, "You men are free to go, provided you drop your swords and leave now. Do it, and you'll live. Do it not, and—"

"And what? You'll kill us all before we can take a step?" Arginto sneered.

"There's a place between your ribs where a sword can run through your entire body without killing you. Twist the blade just right, and you will die but not for a while. It is a slow, agonizing death where every beat of your heart feels like torture. Stay, and I will show you exactly how it feels."

Chapter 12

The Rubicon

Metal clanged and bounced as swords fell like rain. Twenty-one men, twenty-one swords crashed to the ground in unison as the soldiers rushed off, scattering in the wind like fall leaves to a strong breeze. Vale released Lord Arginto and sheathed his sword. He turned to check on Azalea.

"You're going to pay!" Arginto pulled a small, ornate dagger from his hip and whirled around, lifting the blade and bringing it down at Vale's exposed back.

Down the blade went, bouncing off the ground like the swords before it as an arrow pierced his palm. Arginto screamed and clutched his wrist as blood dripped from the shaft of the arrow piercing it.

"Step away. Nobody kills him but me." Caelan glared as he notched another arrow.

"You . . . you will pay for this . . . you will all—"

"I'll give you a 15-second head start. Then, if you're still in my line of sight, this arrow is going to ruin more than your hand."

The little noble moved surprisingly fast, darting back and forth as he sprinted in a zigzag away from the group, crying out, "No no no no no no no!" while still clutching his hand.

"What happened here?" Vale asked, looking up at Dante.

"It's a long story. Perhaps we should find a more private location?" Dante suggested.

Vale nodded. "Let's head back to the inn. We can't leave with her like this."

The group started toward the inn, leaving Azalea on the ground with Caelan standing there alone.

"Oh no, don't worry about it, guys. I'll carry the witch all by myself. It's the least I could do after constantly saving everyone's life." Caelan put his bow away, talking to himself.

When he caught up with them, carrying Azalea over his shoulders the way a hunter carries a deer, Dante slowed to walk next to him.

"Why do you play the fool?" he asked coldly.

"I'm flattered you think I'm playing," Caelan chuckled.

Dante's eyes narrowed. "You are observant, even clever. Why do you pretend not to know what you know?"

"Professor, I'm sure I don't know what you're talking about. Or should I say Blue Alchemist?" Caelan grinned.

Dante grunted. "You know of me as well?"

Caelan chuckled at the question. "The wizard who created a simplified process for enchanting weapons; a famous inventor who designed more potion recipes than all the other apothecaries in the kingdom combined; and the one who defeated the entire wizard council of Rag'amor by himself. Yeah, I may have heard a thing or two about you."

Dante raised an eyebrow. "You are well-informed."

Caelan wagged his finger, cutting off Dante's response. "But my favorite bit is that you removed your ability to feel. What's that like?"

Dante frowned. "You've heard of that?"

Caelan laughed in response. "That's the kind of story that spreads quick, professor. I've always wondered—do you feel, like, numb all the time? Is it like sleepwalking but you're awake? How does it work?"

Dante turned his head away. "It is far worse than you can ever imagine."

Caelan shrugged. "Hmmm. Still, I bet there are times when it comes in handy, eh?"

"I did not do it to avoid pain, you cur!"

"Oh, such foul language from the dignified professor. I like it. So why did you do it?"

"I believe that the key to humanity's future will come not from magic but from knowledge. We have found ways to make pain bearable, prevent sickness, ward off spirits, and even heal wounds that would otherwise be fatal. We can make potions by combining naturally occurring elements that anyone can use. With knowledge, we can put an end to the divide between those who have magic and those who don't. Medicines are just the start. The possibilities of what we can do are endless. Knowledge is power. Knowledge is pure. The problem with obtaining knowledge is that we filter it through our feelings."

"Right . . . so the reason you destroyed your ability to feel is that you like learning stuff?" Caelan asked.

"Interpretation is the enemy of understanding. We are wired in such a way that all information gets filtered through our feelings. I watched so many of my colleagues lose objectivity, skew data, even reject obvious possibilities because of their feelings. Truth is not an emotional thing. It's clear. It's simple. Our feelings twist and conform it from what it is. My goal was to create a way for us to silence our emotions temporarily for the purpose of greater understanding and the advancement of knowledge."

"To each their own," Caelan said with a shrug. "Did it enhance your understanding?"

Dante's expression darkened further as he shook his head. "No, my goal was to cage the emotions. I unintentionally removed them completely. In their void, I faced the harsh reality that had escaped me prior. Emotions fuel drive, desire, ambition, and motivation. In losing them all, I could more clearly identify and interpret information, but I cared not to do so. I did not care about anything. Without feelings, life was an empty series of rituals that meant nothing. After I lost my . . . after, I made this." Dante reached into his cloak and lifted his necklace.

"What's that do?" Caelan appraised it.

Dante pointed to the colored gems that encircled his necklace. "These are enchanted stones, each one governing a separate emotion. When I need motivation or need to process what's happening, I activate the corresponding gem, and it allows me to feel what I am supposed to feel. It's a bit odd, but it helps."

"You made a necklace to magically feel for you?" Caelan asked, stifling a chuckle.

"Feeling nothing is more costly than I could have ever imagined. I used magic to try to stop myself from feeling. Now I use magic to try to feel again."

"Really? I mean, I get that it makes some things challenging but so what? A lot of people would love to have the power to not feel," Caelan replied.

"That's not the problem."

"Oh? What is it then?" Caelan said, teasingly.

Dante sighed. "Emotions don't just affect thought. It's not just happy or sad. It is all of them: concern, love, fear, sympathy, caution, urgency. The mind processes facts and can comprehend feelings. Without emotion there is no drive to act. If I had just been able to feel, she . . . "

"She?" Caelan's tone shifted from playful to almost sincere.

"My daughter."

"I didn't know you had a daughter."

"I did."

"What happened to her?"

"We were walking to the market for some supplies. I was thinking, processing an idea I had in my head. Now I cannot even remember what. She was laughing and skipping along. She let go of my hand. I warned her to be careful, but she perceived the lack of concern in my voice to mean my instruction was not important. I saw a cart break free from the horse pulling it. I saw it rushing toward her. My mind processed it, but I felt nothing. I knew I should do something. She was close enough. If I had reacted quickly, I could have . . . I watched it the way a bird might watch a worm crawling along the ground."

Caelan stared, unable to look away.

"I am no longer a man. I am a living shell. A golem of flesh and bone, doomed to walk this world knowing what I am without, being unable to restore that which is most precious."

"You want to feel, after all that? Wouldn't it break you?" Caelan asked.

"I watched it happen. I did not run or cry out. After, I did not even cry. Believe me, knowing it happened and feeling nothing is so much worse."

Caelan gulped. He looked at the wizard, not sure what to say. As his gaze moved down, he noticed an empty slot in the wizard's necklace.

"Looks like you're missing one."

"Not missing. That one I left out on purpose," Dante said.

"Why? What's that one for?"

"Happiness," Dante answered.

"Why would you leave that out? That's the best one."

"It's meaningless unless it is real."

Azalea was nearly comatose, lying on a small mat on the floor, her still, statuesque slumber broken only by occasional bouts of tossing and turning, as sweat poured down her face, soaking her hair. The Red Empress was clawing to get out. Dante's silver powder may have weakened her, but she had not yet lost her grip. He'd need to remedy that before they could leave. He spent an entire day weaving barriers and other protective magic around Azalea, as well as healing spells to help her recover.

She was not the only one who needed attention. The Black Swordsman protested and tried to refuse, but Dante insisted. They argued back and forth until finally, to put an end to the argument, Vale gave in. Dante instructed him to lift his shirt so he could assess the wounds. Vale's body bore many battle scars but no sign of anything recent. There were no bruises, gashes, or any other indication of injury.

"I do not understand." Dante scratched his head.

"I told you, I'm fine."

"You were hit by an ogre. You are lucky to be alive. You should have bruises, internal bleeding, broken bones at the very least."

"It's been a few days. I heal quickly."

"No one heals that quickly," Dante puzzled.

Two days later Azalea woke, appearing to be recovered. Dante performed several tests to make sure she was, in fact, herself. Azalea claimed to have no recollection of the event, but from time to time Celeste would catch a look in her eye—and not the spiteful disdain she had become used to from Azalea. The loathing was still there but was now mixed with a dose of shame.

Celeste was increasingly inquisitive about Parisia's history of the Red Empress. She had heard the stories; everyone in Parisia had. It was said that the Red Empress killed so many people that the sky turned red. All the greatest legends and folktales of heroes and champions were about those brave enough to stand and fight against the tyranny of the Red Empress. Most believed that they were just that—legends, fables told to children before bedtime.

Thanks to her station, Celeste had spent most of her days being tutored by scholars from all around Parisia. She studied in libraries that smelled of stale dust. She lived on the stories her teacher, Sir Bali Lamor, told her of the heroes of legend. When he wasn't around to calm her wanderlust, she was nose deep in stories of the adventures of others when all she wanted to do was go on an epic adventure of her own. Her readings of the histories of Parisia had confirmed that the Red Empress was, in fact, real. She was revered as the goddess of blood, and the whole kingdom was terrified of her fury.

According to the histories, it was her ancestors who, with the help of the Order Arcana, managed to defeat the Red Empress and banish her to the Spirit Realm, where she had been bound for over two hundred years. There were always rumors from the more rural areas of the kingdom—alleged Red Empress sightings —but none ever held merit.

"Tell me everything! I want to know all of it! How is she still alive? How did she escape the Spirit Realm?" Celeste's voice almost bubbled with excitement.

Dante sighed. "The Red Empress is an Ifrit."

Celeste cocked her head to one side in confusion.

Dante continued, "There are many realms, most unknown to us. We live in the Realm of Mortals. Long ago, our realm was connected to two others: the Dark Realm and the Spirit Realm. We were linked together like clover leaves. Thanks to the power of the Darkstone, we severed our connection to the Dark Realm.

Shadows of the Dark Realm

The Realm of Spirits and the Realm of Mortals remain closely linked. Some even suggest the two realms exist in the same space, separated by a thin veil. The Spirit Realm is the source of all magical energy and the place of origin for all magical creatures. While the veil typically prevents beings from crossing over, sometimes when the celestial bodies align that veil grows thinner, and things that were never meant for our world pass through. When a spirit being is born in the mortal realm, that creature is known as an Ifrit. They are immensely powerful creatures. Most choose to return to the Spirit Realm, while others find they enjoy having a corporal form."

"She was born in our world?" Celeste asked. "And then her body was destroyed, and her spirit cast back to hers? How was she able to take over Azalea's body like that?" The excitement in her voice made her words flow so rapidly they bled together, making her thoughts hard to follow.

Dante looked over at Azalea who looked up, suddenly more interested in the conversation. "Perhaps this is not the best place," he cautioned.

"It's fine. I'd rather hear it," Azalea stated.

"We should know what we are getting into. It affects us all equally," Vale added from his place in the corner of the room.

Dante took a deep breath before continuing. "How Vespera first came to the Mortal Realm, I do not know. Powerful spirits can cross over and seize control of a person to use them as a vessel."

"You mean to tell me she can just take control of anyone at any time?" Caelan interrupted, looking up from the new set of arrows he was fletching.

"No, not entirely. All living things have a certain degree of sensitivity to the Spirit Realm. It is why some can perform magic, and others cannot. Spirits need that sensitivity to take control. A typical person could only be possessed for a moment. Even then, the Spirit could do little more than use them as a voice box. The real threat are magic wielders," Dante replied.

"Great, so anyone with magical powers could get taken over without warning?" Caelan pressed.

Dante shook his head again. "There are wards and ways to

protect yourself from possession. Not all wizards use them, but most do. Either way, before a spirit can take hold of a mortal's body they would first have to overpower their will, which takes time."

"Azalea just got unlucky then?" Caelan asked.

Dante's brow furrowed. "It is hard to be sure. I have seen spirits take control of a people before, but this was different. It was not like Vespera appeared—it was like she was already there, beneath the surface, just waiting. Almost as if . . . " Dante shook his head. "No, that is not possible."

"Well, don't leave us guessing. What?" Caelan pressed.

"All we need to know is—can it happen again?" Vale interjected.

Dante shrugged. "In theory, yes. Sending her back to the Spirit Realm will have weakened her considerably. It should take her months, at least, to recover enough of her power to try again."

"Great, this is a fun talk," Azalea scoffed. "I'll just be here living the rest of my life with that little gem hanging over my head. It's just lovely."

"You are surprised? I was under the impression the Kinspira wanted to see the Red Empress return," Dante looked confused.

"See, yes. No one said anything to me about being the Red Empress. I rather like having control of my own body thank you."

"Interesting. That would explain why they did not teach you to ward yourself. You were the offering."

"What every girl dreams of," Azalea shook her head. "What do I do to make sure whatever that was, doesn't happen again?"

"While you were recovering, I layered a series of binding and barrier spells on you. Even when her strength returns, it will be very difficult for her to take control again," Dante said.

"Difficult . . . but not impossible?" Vale asked.

"Few things in this world are truly impossible," Dante replied.

"I hate to say it but, we should leave her," Celeste blurted out. Everyone turned to look at her in surprise. She held up her hands. There was a mournful determination in Celeste's eyes.

"We don't need her. On a good day, she's a witch with a bad attitude. On a bad one, she could lose control and kill us all."

"Bad attitude? Ralk you, I'm a delight!" Azalea crossed her arms and glared.

Celeste rolled her eyes. "Our mission is too important. She's a risk we can't afford and don't need to take."

"Take it easy, princess. Dante just told us he has it under control," Caelan challenged.

"Are you dim? That's not what he said at all," Celeste snapped.

"It is true, though. While nothing is impossible per se, she is at no more risk than anyone else of getting possessed by Vespera again."

Celeste's eyes narrowed. "That's not even the point. She's an unpredictable, unreliable, ill-tempered, volatile, witch whose presence on this quest could put us all in danger. That's not if she's possessed—that's if she's herself!"

"Naiflo, I'm sitting right here! Keep running your mouth, I'll be happy to shut it for you," Azalea protested.

"You see?" Celeste pointed as if Azalea had made her point for her. "She's Kinspira. I'm a Royal. She's as liable to kill me as she is look at me. You can't ask me to travel with her."

"No one is asking you to," Dante replied. "You begged to come—begged to be a part of this team of Seekers. I let you. Now, if your resolve has waned, you can go. Return home to your family. We will not think less of you."

"You'd choose her over me?" Celeste's eyes welled up. "Even though she possesses a threat to the mission given to you by the king himself?"

"If we do not take her, we do not succeed. That is what the seer told us. If you want to safeguard our quest, keeping her with us is the way to do it," Dante said.

"She's coming with us. You should make your peace with that. Now, if there's nothing else, get some rest," Vale interrupted, shutting down the conversation.

The next morning, they gathered their supplies and made their way out of the resort town. The road that led past the short, decorative fence surrounding the town was well-adorned with pristine cobblestone.

The road was short between the town and the great wall that separated Parisia from the other kingdoms. With each step, the wall seemed to grow taller, threatening to blot out the light of the sun as it towered over them, reaching impossible heights.

The wall was a breathtaking colossus of stone reaching a dozen times higher than even the walls around the palace. It was so tall even birds struggled to fly over it. The only thing left between the adventurers and their egress was a stone fort. Small only in comparison to the wall, it was a castle, complete with a battalion of soldiers, a blacksmith, stables, and training grounds.

"Papers?" a tall, lanky soldier barked out as the group walked toward the presently closed gate to leave the kingdom.

Vale retrieved the transit papers with the king's seal.

"State your purpose for leaving Parisia," the guard said as he inspected the form.

Vale spotted no less than twenty bows drawn on them and two dozen trained knights with hands on their hilts. Were they to try anything, Vale did not think they would get very far.

"We are Seekers on a quest to retrieve the Darkstone for the king," Vale answered.

The air around them seemed to shift. Soldiers tensed and looked at each other. The guard nodded.

"Another crew? What took you so long? Most of those that left on the king's quest did so days ago."

Vale shrugged. "We were delayed."

The guard chuckled. "Seems so. Well, everything is in order. You're free to pass."

Vale scanned the area. There was something suspicious going on. The soldiers had formed a human wall between where they were standing and a nook in the courtyard. It was exactly the kind of move designed to hide something without looking like you were trying to hide it.

"What's over there?" Vale pointed, his tone commanding.

"Oh, that. Don't think you want to know," the guard replied.

"I wouldn't have asked if I didn't," Vale confirmed.

"Well, mayhaps the delay brought you good luck, I think." The guard was forcing his voice to sound optimistic.

Odd. Vale walked toward them, and the soldiers who formed the wall of bodies parted. No wonder they were hiding it. Behind them was a small mound of corpses stacked up with a tarp over them next to an empty cart.

"What is this?" Vale asked.

"That's the good luck I was telling you about. These are Seekers, like yourselves—some of the others who left before you," the guard answered.

"What happened to them?" Vale pressed.

"That's the thing. We couldn't rightly tell you. Our scouts outside the wall found them all butchered to bits. No tracks coming in. No tracks going out. It's like whatever killed them just vanished into thin air."

"Well, that's foreboding," Caelan muttered under his breath.

Vale looked at Azalea.

She sighed and nodded. "I'll go take a look."

The guards opened the gate, and she walked forward ahead of the others. Her body was engulfed in purple mist disappearing for a moment before a giant eagle appeared out of it, soaring up into the sky.

Vale took a step forward.

"You're not going to wait for her to come back?" the guard asked.

"Whatever she finds, it won't change what needs to be done," Vale replied.

"Well, you're brave. May the gods below bless you on your quest," one guard said.

"By five may your journey thrive. By five may you return alive," the other recited.

Vale led the others out, and the gate closed behind them. As it locked, Celeste realized there was no going back. She was outside the walls that kept her safe her whole life. She was on her very own adventure.

"Are we not going to talk about what we just saw?" Celeste asked, her voice shaking as she looked around, scanning the area before her.

"What's there to talk about?" Vale replied.

"There were at least a hundred bodies in there!" Caelan answered. "And did you see what was done to them? I've never seen anything like that.

"We knew this would be dangerous. It changes nothing," Vale said.

"It changes one thing," Dante countered. "Now we know someone, or something, is hunting us."

Chapter 13
Encounter

Celeste looked around at the vast, open sky. It was weird enough being outside of the capital. Now, for the first time in her life, she was standing on foreign soil. Home had never been so far away. She couldn't tell if that was more exhilarating or terrifying.

Everything about the land outside the wall felt different. The grass was sparser and more yellowed, the ground was harder, the trees less flush. The air didn't smell as sweet, and even the sky was a paler blue.

Vale led them away from the wall but stopped before they reached the woods.

"Why are we stopping?" Celeste asked.

"We will wait here for Azalea," Vale replied.

"Wouldn't it be better to continue until we reach the forest, where we can stay out of sight?" Celeste questioned.

"If something is hunting us, I want to see it coming from a long way off," Vale answered.

Azalea descended from her flight, transforming smoothly back into her human form as she gracefully landed on top of her mount.

"No sign of anything for miles," Azalea said, answering the question no one asked aloud.

"Well, that's good. So, how do we get to the Dragon Lands from here?" Celeste asked.

"Best path is northwest," Dante answered.

Vale groaned.

"What? What's wrong with that?" Celeste asked, trying to picture the maps of the kingdoms outside the Parisia.

"It means we have to go through Rag'amor," Dante explained.

"Rag'amor is fine. They just don't care for Parisians much," Caelan grinned.

"We are Parisians," Celeste replied.

Caelan shook his head and looked away.

"Rag'amorians are a tough people. They are fierce warriors, always looking for a fight. They view death on the battlefield as the greatest victory in life. They are wild, barbaric, unpredictable, and extremely territorial," Vale explained.

"Gods below, that sounds horrible. There's no other path to avoid it?" Celeste gasped.

Caelan smirked. "Why would you want to avoid such a wonderful place? They are great."

Celeste could not tell if he was joking.

"We could go around, travel easterly and take a route through Taggoron."

Vale laughed and shook his head.

"It's not a joke. I have contacts in Taggoron. They could help us out," Caelan replied.

Vale glared. "Taggoron is a kingdom of thieves and murderers run by thieves and murderers. I'd sooner throw myself in a pit of Murmucks than travel there. They are as likely to poison you as look at you."

"I'm just curious—does that come from your extensive experience in wiping out defenseless villages there?"

Vale grit his teeth. "Careful."

"Or what? You'll finish what you started? It's got to bother you, right? Like a real blemish on your perfect record. Butchered all but one of an entire village just doesn't have the same ring to it, does it?"

Vale's hand grasped the hilt of his sword.

"We are not going to get anywhere if we turn on each other," Dante interjected, stepping between them. "We have a job to do. Like it or not, we need to work together. Let us leave the past where it belongs—behind us, at least until the Darkstone is returned. Once that is done, you two can kill each other all you want."

Vale released his blade. "We travel through Rag'amor to Baronia until we reach Stomdale on the Fang Coast."

They rode to the north and west for three days.

Celeste pestered Caelan and Dante for as much information about the world outside the wall as she could. Her knowledge was inconsistent. She knew a plethora of facts, mostly the sorts of things found in reports, but had no understanding of the cultures or attitudes of any group outside the capital. Her complete lack of practical understanding made her seem like a child, much to Dante's annoyance.

"You are... a powerful mage..." it was difficult to tell from her tone if Celeste was making a statement or asking a question.

"I am."

"Um...how does that work? Could you teach me to wield it?"

Dante raised an eyebrow, "you wish to learn magic?"

Celeste smiled sheepishly and nodded.

"Why?"

"Why?" The question caught her off guard. "Magic is power. It's control. To have the ability to influence, to shape, who wouldn't want that?"

"I have nothing to offer you."

"Nothing? I've heard the stories of what you can do. Yet you choose to spend your time with books. Why did the gods below give you all this ability if you aren't even going to use it?"

"Perhaps it is because I am reluctant to use it."

"How is having it and not using it anything but a waste of potential?"

"Power is a dangerous thing. The more you use it, even for good reasons, the easier it becomes to give in to it. Power yearns for control. If not held in check, it can consume even the best of intentions."

"It's also freedom. Hope. The ability to-"

"You speak of power like it is the end. That is a dangerous view. Power is a means; a tool, not a prize."

"Spoken like someone who has always had it," Celeste shook her head, disappointment on her face.

"It matters not. Magic comes from a connection to the spirit realm. Some are born with it. Others are not."

"Anyone who has the link can become a great mage?"

Dante shook his head, "Was this not in your books?"

Celeste frowned, "The writings talk about great mages who did great things, not how they became great mages. It's like they just assume everyone already knows."

"Why some are born with a connection to the spirit realm and others are not, is uncertain. Those who have the link can be trained to use their magical powers more effectively, but they will never be able to overcome their limits."

"Magic has limits?"

"Yes. In the same way our bodies have limits."

"But how does it work?"

"Magic is energy. Take Vale for example. He is a strong warrior. He is well-trained and capable. Despite all his skill, the longer he fights, the more he is drained by it. Over time, his body will tire, get weaker, move slower until he rests and recovers his strength. Magic works the same way. Those with a strong connection to the spirit realm, like the Red Empress, can obtain an almost godlike power. Like physical strength, it wears out. Unlike physical strength, it takes more than rest to replenish it. At least that is how it is for humans. There are creatures, like dragons, that do not seem to have limits to their power."

"How do you know if you have the link?"

Dante stroked his chin as he processed the question. "Intuition. Almost like love. It is hard to explain. When you have it, you know. Those who have it can sense it. Also, like love, it takes some longer than others."

Celeste nodded, "Why is your magic different than Azalea's?"

Dante grinned, "I have seen wizards who could wield only a single kind of magic. I have seen wizards who were adept at many different styles. There are some magics that are common.

Others, like Azalea's shapeshifting, that are rare. Magic is as diverse as those who wield it. Only the gods know why and how. At least, for now. This is why my work is so important. If I can discover how these things work, imagine, if we could find ways to teach it, to open things up to those who do not have an innate link."

Celeste continued to ask questions until Dante grew weary and forced her to go to sleep. As they traveled, Azalea seemed to be more and more herself. Dante crafted her a necklace with a blue and silver stone. He said it would ward off any attempt of the Red Empress to take over her body so long as she wore it.

When they made camp, Caelan spent his time fletching new arrows. He fashioned most with silver arrowheads, which were better suited for bringing down monsters.

At night, when the others had gone to sleep, Azalea would wander away from the camp to sit alone, looking up at the stars. She was leaning back on her hands enjoying some time to reflect.

"None of us should wander alone, especially now." Vale sat down next to her and followed her gaze to the stars.

"Does this look like wandering to you?" Her words were playful with a bit of an edge.

"How are you holding up?"

"Oh, I'm dandy as a lion, aren't I? I'm just trying to figure out what my favorite part of this little adventure has been—getting my body taken over and used by an Ifrit or knowing that she could try again at any time? Or having to go on this gods' forsaken quest to save a kingdom I can't stand? Or wait, no, the best part is having to travel with a naiflo Royal," Azalea replied.

Vale smiled. "You really hate Royals, don't you?"

"Nothing gets past you."

"Any particular reason? Or are you one of those people who hates something just because they had something you didn't?"

Azalea glared. "I got more reasons than you can shake a stick at. I could tell you stories of the abuses my people faced."

"Abuses?"

"Yeah, abuses. We were a community that chose an alternative lifestyle."

"You mean a community of covens and cults," Vale challenged.

"I mean free-thinking people who don't just drink whatever cup of horse gwar the nobles hand them and call it fine wine. We were different. Every time something happened, we got blamed. Crops don't produce well, dog goes missing, crickets chirp too loud—must be the witches. We never did anything to anybody, and all we ever got was accusations and dirty looks and whispers behind our backs."

"People don't do well with different. What does that have to do with Royals?"

"When I was a girl, we lived in a poor village. Yes, there are a few, even in Parisia. I remember one day this family of Royals came. They looked so elegant, so beautiful. Their skin, hair, clothes, everything was clean and perfect. I'd never seen someone who wasn't covered in mud and didn't smell like a stable. They smelled like flowers in a fresh garden. They wore these shiny robes with patterns unlike anything I'd ever seen. I'd have sworn they weren't people at all, but the gods below come up to grace us with their presence. Gods they were not; monsters they were. All their beautiful attire was nothing more than a mask to hide the ugliness of their hearts."

"I take it the visit didn't go well?"

"At first it did. They stayed in our village, ate all of our food. Everyone rushed around, serving their every need. They said that they wanted to change the attitude the people had about us. It was exciting; we thought there was hope that we might be accepted into Parisian culture. Maybe we wouldn't have to live as pariahs anymore."

"What happened?"

"They Royals had a son with them—golden hair, blue eyes, looked like a doll. One of the boys in town, Daavey, took a liking to him. He just wanted to be friends. Daavey was a sweet boy, just overly excitable, clumsy. He made a gift for the young royal. Nothing fancy, just a piece of metal he'd shaped to look like two kids holding hands. In his excitement to give his gift, he slipped. The toy flew from his hands and struck the royal boy in the head. Not hard, but it drew blood. As punishment, they beat Daavey's father so bad he never walked again. Then they took Daavey, told us that he was gone, and that was it. We weren't to speak of it to anyone. If we did, they would come take all the children and burn our village to the ground."

Vale's hands gripped tightly into fists as he listened. After a long moment of silence, he asked, "How old was Daavey?"

"Maybe ten or so. Why?"

Vale shook his head.

"Every month after that, at the new moon, a man would come, sent by the Royals to collect a tax. Our village barely had enough food to eat. Once a month, they took what little we had. We were starving. One time, I followed him—thought I might try to appeal to his better nature, see if he'd give us back some of the food. Before I could catch up to him, I saw him dump out most of the cart. He piled it up, called it rubbish, and burned it. They weren't taking our food because they needed it for soldiers. They took it because they could, to remind us we were nothing to them. That's what Royals do. From the clothing they wear to the titles they hold, it's all about reminding the rest of us our place, under them."

Vale shook his head. "That isn't right."

"Thank you for that unnecessary and unrequested validation. I'm glad my struggle meets your standard for sympathy. Now, if you don't mind, I came out here to get away from you lot, so kindly ralk off."

Vale granted her request and headed back to camp to sleep.

On the seventh day of their journey outside the wall, Celeste was starting to feel more at ease. Perhaps it was because they hadn't encountered any dangers in their travels, but the tension she had carried since they left Parisia was starting to fade.

They had stopped for lunch near a riverbed. The gentle waters rippled along under the steady current. From behind the trees on the other side of the water, they could hear the noise of a town. From the sound of it, the community was small but energetic. Laughter and revelry, even in the middle of the day? This was not the sound of a group of bloodthirsty barbarians.

"You know, you really had me going. All that talk about

Rag'amorians being savages—this place doesn't seem nearly as—" Celeste stopped mid-thought.

A shadow passed overhead. It was quick—too quick to be a cloud. Something in the air changed, like the rolling in of a storm, but this was no storm. This was something far, far worse. Birds became silent. The temperature dropped noticeably as a chill washed over the area. The trees stopped swaying. The wind itself dared not move. It felt like a heavy, wet cloak had suddenly landed on her shoulders. Her knees wobbled. Her body trembled. This was a sensation she was utterly unfamiliar with.

That's when she heard it: a loud, earth-shaking, heart-piercing screech. Celeste looked around. Vale's blade was in his hands; Caelan had already drawn his bow. There was no question what it was. The shadow in the sky dove down, descending closer and closer into view. It landed just out of sight and disappeared behind rows of trees.

Screams followed. Flames lit the sky. Metal crashing against scales. A roar and more flames.

Caelan started across the water, but Dante stepped in front of him.

"What are you doing?" Caelan protested.

"What are *you* doing?" Dante repeated the question back to him.

"Oh, me, I'm going for a swim. Water just looked so refreshing, I couldn't resist. What's it look like I'm doing?" Caelan snapped.

"Nothing will be gained by this. We are not prepared to battle a dragon in the open, not like this. You'd be throwing your life away," Dante cautioned.

"If we can't defeat a dragon, what are we doing out here?"

"He's got a point Caelan," Celeste added. "We are Seekers not dragon hunters. Maybe we should stay focused."

Vale stepped into the river and pushed past Caelan and Dante.

"You agree with Caelan?" Azalea asked.

Vale grunted and kept walking.

Azalea laughed. "Well, if he's going . . ."

Caelan smirked and walked past Dante. The three forged

across the river while Dante and Celeste stared for a moment in surprise.

"Is this a good idea?" Celeste asked. "Should we stop them?"

Dante shook his head. "Some battles cannot be won. There is no point in expending effort where victory cannot be obtained," he said before reluctantly following the others.

The village was on the other side of a thick patch of trees, allowing the group to move quickly without being detected until they reached the end of the tree line, where they stopped to assess the situation.

"We need to be careful," Dante whispered.

"Careful? Fighting a dragon? Any other words of wisdom, professor?" Caelan retorted.

Dante rolled his eyes. "Goraum, listen. Dragons are not just powerful beasts. They are highly intelligent creatures born of raw magical power. They are nearly impervious to most weapons. This task is beyond us."

"Good pep talk. I feel very encouraged," Caelan replied.

"Give me one of your arrows," Dante instructed.

Caelan pulled one free and offered it to him. Dante pulled a vial from his cloak and poured it over the tip. He muttered something no one but he understood and handed the arrow back.

"What did you do to it?" Caelan looked at the arrow, which now seemed to emanate a blue mist.

"I enchanted it; the magic should allow the arrow to pierce the dragon's scales and then explode with a torrent of ice magic. It will not kill the beast, but it might hurt it enough to scare it off," Dante explained.

He worked a similar spell onto Celeste's sword. When he reached for Vale's blade, the Black Swordsman brushed him off.

"No need; it's made of Nightstone." Vale tapped the edge of his blade.

In a roaring flash, the dragon burst into view, stalking out from behind two tall houses that had hidden it from the travelers' view. The creature was massive, terrifying, beautiful, wondrous, and awful all at the same time. Its scales were a glimmering, polished silver. Its claws and long maw were stained red with blood that trailed behind it. The buildings were ablaze as the dragon turned its head from side to side. The fierceness and raw power of the creature seemed to pulse through the air.

A few villagers were scattering and screaming, trying to escape the creature as it approached. The dragon reared back, but before it could project its deadly flame, an arrow pierced its shoulder. The dragon screamed in rage as the arrow pierced its scale and erupted in a burst of blue light that sent the dragon toppling to the side. Before the others could clear the tree line, a mysterious man in a brown cloak rushed the dragon. He held a large bastard sword over his head as he ran.

The dragon rolled and swung its tail at the charging man. The man slid, ducking under the swiping tail. As soon as the tail passed harmlessly by, he was back on his feet. After two more steps, he leapt into the air, his blade arching toward the long neck of the dragon. A blur of silver moved impossibly fast as the dragon caught the man in mid-leap. With a roar, it flapped its massive silver wings and flew up and away from the town.

Vale and the others gave chase. Caelan fired a series of arrows, all of which the dragon skillfully dodged. It flew higher and higher, making it hard to see what was going on, but they could barely see that the man in the dragon's clutches was struggling. A moment later he fell, released from the dragon's grip. His body hurtled toward the ground before crashing through the treetops on the other side of the village. The dragon gave chase, a plume of flame erupting from its silver jaws as it hovered over the place the man had fallen. The flame continued for a long-drawn breath before the dragon stopped, reared back, and roared. With a flap of its mighty wings, the dragon disappeared into the sky in a burst of silver light as it flew up and out of view.

"Where did it go?" Azalea asked.

"I lost sight of him over the tree line," Caelan replied. Vale and Celeste were already moving to the other side of the village in the direction of the man who had fallen.

"Surely he couldn't have survived that," Azalea remarked.

A rustling sound came from the woods. Celeste and Vale dropped into fighting stances, swords ready. Caelan notched an arrow. Azalea stood next to them, completely unconcerned. The sound grew closer, slowly moving through the woods toward them.

The man stumbled into the clearing. He was wearing silver armor and dragging a massive bastard sword behind his arm that clung to his side. He hobbled slowly, dragging his leg even more than his sword. Blood dripped from his head, neck, and side. A blue cape draped over his back, partially hidden by the tattered remains of a burned, charred brown cloak.

His hair was silver, his eyes bright blue. He was well-built, taller than average, and looked like a refined warrior. Apart from the muck and blood, Azalea found herself entranced by his appearance. The man looked at them, opened his mouth as if to speak, and collapsed to the ground in a heap.

"Is he dead?" Azalea blurted out.

Chapter 14

Dragons, Knights, and Kings

"They want to what?" Vale's voice dripped with disbelief.

"Join us," Dante replied.

"Join us as in . . . " Vale let his words hang on the air.

"They want vengeance. The dragon destroyed their home, killed their friends and families. I don't blame them," Caelan answered.

"We could use some extra blades for the journey ahead," Azalea interjected.

"And from what I've seen, the ones who would be joining us know how to use them," Caelan added.

Vale sighed. "It's not a question of blades or skill but agenda and trust. Rag'amorians are violent and unpredictable. While we might share an enemy, we do not share a mission. Our interests do not align. What happens when our quest demands one approach and their rage another? Or worse, when we do reclaim the Darkstone, they decide they'd rather keep it for themselves?"

"Would it help if we said we have no interest in the Darkstone?" a man said as he stepped in through the open door.

He was tall and lean but muscular. His face was clean-shaven, his sandy brown hair was short and messy. He was clearly young, but he carried himself in a way that made him seem more experienced and mature. He was wearing an unusual

Shadows of the Dark Realm

looking green and brown leather armor with a dark green cape draped over his shoulders.

"My apologies for interrupting. My name is Rivik. I'd like to make a proposal, if you'd be willing to consider it." His voice had a natural grace to it, the smooth, easy confidence that many long for but few achieve.

Vale folded his arms across his chest and faced the man. "Speak your piece."

Rivik smiled, his perfect white teeth adding to his casual, easy charm. "Your journey to the Fang Coast—to get there, you must pass through Rag'amor, which can be very dangerous for outsiders. But I know all the lands from here to the Fang Coast. Let us join you. A local guide could make things much easier."

"Perhaps. What do you get out of this arrangement?"

"You do not know our customs. Here, it is a great shame to let your home be destroyed. The only way to restore our honor is to hunt down the creature and bury its head under our village gate. Until then, we are no longer Rag'amorian. We are Vagra, wanderers, outcasts with no right to a place to lay our heads. Our own people will not acknowledge us, accept us, or trade with us lest our shame fall upon them. This is our way."

"We aren't dragon hunters. We seek the stone. Our best chance of success is to steal the stone without having to fight dragons at all," Vale countered.

Rivik nodded. "Your chances of reaching the Fang Coast alive, without our help, may be smaller than you think. I am proposing that we work together. We help you reclaim your stone; you help us kill the dragon."

"Even if we wanted to agree, we could not," Dante said. "We have no way of tracking the dragon that attacked you. Even if we got lucky and found it, we would not know it was the right one. What you are asking is impossible. We would have to hunt down every dragon, or at least every silver dragon, in the Dragon Lands just to honor our end of it. Our chances are better of reaching the Fang Coast on our own."

"Sygenis for sygenis," Rivik replied.

"Is that supposed to mean something, or were you just clearing your throat?" Caelan asked.

"It means kin for kin. Under Elder Law, if it is impossible for a Vagra to reclaim their honor by killing the one who stole it, killing a close kin or connection is considered an acceptable alternative."

"You are saying it does not have to be the same dragon but that any dragon will suffice?" Dante confirmed.

"As long as a Vagra deals the death blow, yes."

"Why do you need us for this?" Vale asked.

"We are but simple warriors. We aren't equipped to kill a dragon on our own. You hurt it so bad that it fled. Our best chance to bring down a dragon is with your help," Rivik said.

Before Vale could speak, Rivik straightened his hand and held it to his nose as if tracing a line between his eyes and bowed. "I make you this oath, on the name of my father and his father and all our ancestors—if you allow us to come with you, we will follow your instructions; we will fight by your side. Your enemies will be our enemies. Your mission will be our mission. We will be brothers until the stone is yours, and a dragon lies dead at our hands."

"And what happens then?" Dante questioned.

"Then, when our oath is fulfilled, we guide you back to your wall and return to our home."

"The others? Will they swear this same oath?" Vale asked.

Rivik nodded. "They will."

Vale thought in silence, his mind weighing the choice before him.

Rivik grinned confidently, assuming the silence meant agreement. "Also, the other one is awake."

Vale and the others followed Rivik out of the charred hut they had been gathered in and through the shambles that remained of the town of Wellar. Sitting on a bench outside one of the blackened buildings was the man in silver armor with silver hair. He saw them approaching and stood up, his legs appearing a little shaky, but he seemed otherwise unharmed.

"You're the ones who attacked it?" he said, before anyone from the group could get a word in.

Vale nodded.

"You are not from here." His brow furrowed.

"We are Seekers from Parisia. Judging from your armor you are not Rag'amorian either. Who are you and what are you doing here?" Vale asked.

"My name is Spiro Bakoni Garris, and I am a dragon knight from the Mystic Keep at Calladun. As to my purpose, I was to hunt down and kill a dragon reported to be roaming these parts. I did not expect it to be a ralking silver-scale Elder Dragon."

"What in the lamera is an elder dragon?" Azalea asked.

Spiro looked confused by the question. "You do not know of Elder dragons?"

"Elder dragons are among the most powerful and dangerous types of dragons. They are fierce, possessive, and territorial," Dante explained.

"They are much more than that," Spiro interjected.

Vale sighed. "That will make our job considerably more difficult."

Spiro raised an eyebrow. "What is your purpose here, friend?"

Vale stared at the man, pondering for a moment how to respond.

"A dragon stole the Darkstone from Parisia. We are the Seekers, called upon by the king to retrieve it," Celeste blurted out.

Vale grunted in displeasure.

"Interesting. Any idea what type of dragon it was?"

"Not just a type. It was . . . " Celeste started. Vale grunted louder this time, nudging her. " . . . an Elder Dragon," she finished.

"I assume, since you are here, that this stone is of some particular value?"

"You might say that. It contains the power that keeps our world separated from the Dark Realm. Without it, the Shadow King returns with his army of monsters." Caelan smiled like he was heralding a royal wedding. "Unless we get it back, everyone in this realm is going to die."

Spiro's face wrinkled in concern. "Well, I have bad news. If you want to take back this Darkstone, you will have to kill the dragon that took it."

Dante cocked his head. "Explain."

Spiro shrugged. "You'll have two problems. The first will be trying to steal it. Elder dragons are extremely intelligent."

Celeste scoffed, "Intelligent for a monster. I have no doubt that we can handle it."

Spiro shook his head. "I wouldn't be so sure. You think of dragons as beasts because you've only heard tales of the lesser dragons. Dragons don't just kill, they consume. When they consume, they absorb some of the knowledge of the person. The more they consume, the smarter they get. Elder dragons have consumed enough humans to be smarter than any one person. They know how we think, how we feel, and what drives us. They understand us in a way we often fail to understand ourselves."

"Gods below." Celeste stood, arms limp at her side, jaw hanging open.

"You said there were two problems?" Vale pressed.

"The second is that an elder dragon will never let you take something that belongs to him. Even if you were to steal the stone and get away, which would be impressive, he would hunt you down. He would track you to the ends of the earth. If you were able to get the stone back to Parisia, he'd not only take it again, but this time he'd leave the palace in ash and ruin." There was a peculiar sense of admiration as he spoke.

"How do you know all this?" Caelan asked, peering intently at Spiro.

"The libraries in Calladun are filled with the collected knowledge of the Dragon Knights. Generations of hunters have recorded every known weakness, theory, and observation in their hall. All dragon knights must study these works before being sent into the field. Otherwise, how could we hope to defeat them?"

"How do you defeat a dragon?" Dante asked.

"It's not easy. Dragons share two primary weaknesses: Spirit magic, which is all but gone from this realm since the banishing of the Sidhe a thousand years ago, and other dragons."

"That's it?" Vale asked.

"There are certain things that can hurt them, and they do

have other weaknesses, but those vary from dragon to dragon and type to type," Spiro answered.

Azalea looked confused. "Types of dragons? They have types?"

Spiro chuckled. "You set out on a quest to hunt a dragon, and you understand so little of them?" Something about his tone was incredibly condescending. Azalea wondered if he would seem so smug and superior with his handsome face half-burned by fire.

"Yes, dragons have types. They are identified by their color. Most dragons are elemental creatures. The most common of the elementals are the red fire dragons. Ice dragons are blue. Earth dragons are brown and are nearly impenetrable, and their tails have a hammer-like boulder they use as a smashing weapon. Mist dragons are green. They can vanish into mist and reappear somewhere else, so long as it's in their line of sight. They don't breathe fire, but their eyes emit a green burst of energy that cuts through anything in its path. Thunder dragons are yellow and exceptionally aggressive. Those are your basic types."

"And the elder dragons?" Vale asks.

"When a dragon of any type grows strong enough, it sheds its scales and grows larger and more powerful. It becomes known as an Elder Dragon. Elder dragons are only ever two colors: gold or silver. Gold elder dragons are the strongest and most common of the two. Silver elder dragons, which we call silver-scales, are the rarest and most elusive of all dragons. They are also by far the deadliest."

"Wonderful!" Caelan exclaimed. "Well, this has just been a delight. Any other good news you have for us?"

Spiro smiled. "You fought an elder dragon and lived. Very few can make such a claim."

"You should come with us!" Celeste nearly shouted.

"Apologies, my lady, but I am a dragon knight. I need to return to Calladun and report back my findings."

"Very well. May the gods below bless your journey," Vale started.

"She's right. You should come," Dante added.

Vale grunted and raised an eyebrow in response.

"Think about it. We are going to the Dragon Lands to steal

from and possibly kill a dragon. It would be handy to have a knight trained to kill dragons with us," Dante explained.

Spiro bowed. "I am flattered by the offer. But I have a job to do."

"Your job is to kill dragons, right?" Caelan asked.

Spiro nodded. "Yes. But—"

"You said it yourself; we have to kill the dragon that took the Darkstone. Come with us; help us kill it. Isn't that your job?"

"It is, but I am a novice. I am not authorized to travel to the Dragon Lands. Only the Fang Hunters operate there," Spiro protested.

"I get it—you're not strong enough to handle a real dragon."

"That's—" Spiro balked. "It's against protocol."

"Say no more—you stay here in your little assigned territory chasing lesser dragons. We will kill the Elder Dragon without you." Caelan shrugged and turned around.

"Wait." Spiro bit his bottom lip as he thought. "Slaying an elder dragon is the greatest feat a dragon knight can achieve. My name would be etched into the stone at Slayers Hall, never to be forgotten." He closed his eyes and took a long deep breath. "I will accompany you and help you slay the creature. The Knight Masters will not be pleased I hunted outside of my assigned territory, but if I return with a tooth and talon of an Elder Dragon, they will have no choice but to honor me."

"Oh look, Azalea, your boyfriend wants to join us," Caelan replied.

Azalea put a small burst of energy into her fist and casually shoved it into Caelan's chest, knocking him back and onto the ground coughing. Vale paid no attention. He turned to Dante.

Dante nodded. "Dragons are outside of my expertise, but from what I have read, everything he is saying seems to fit. I am inclined to believe him.".

"Very well," Vale replied. "It seems our company is growing. I'd like us to be underway as soon as possible. Rivik, I would like to test your men, see what they are capable of. Can you arrange this?"

Rivik nodded. "Of course."

"Spiro, when will you be fit to travel?" Vale asked.

Shadows of the Dark Realm

Spiro stretched his body, starting with his arms and working his way down. "Probably tomorrow. If not, by the next day I should be near full strength."

"So soon?"

"I heal quickly."

Everyone parted ways either to rest, gather supplies, or prepare for the next stage in their journey. Rivik brought the warriors to Vale—a group of a dozen fighters consisting of eight men and four women. They all looked fit, fierce, and ready. The Rag'amorian people, it seemed, were as hardened as they were rumored to be aggressive. Each presented themselves and then gave their oath.

At that moment, something in Vale's pocket warmed and tingled with an abnormal pulsing energy. Perplexed, he pulled out the writ of passage, the one given to every team of Seekers that they were instructed to keep at all times.

"I've put together a little tournament to show you what they are capable of. We can have it ready by tonight," Rivik said, moving next to Vale.

Vale nodded. "Very good. Let's do it first thing in the morning instead. If you'll excuse me."

Vale grabbed Dante and pulled him away from the others. He handed the writ to the blue alchemist.

"What is going on with this?" he asked, his tone hushed.

Dante took the paper and inspected it. Words started glowing and lifting from the page.

Dante chuckled. "Well, that is very clever."

Vale scowled. "What is?"

Dante showed him a small marking on the page, very subtly stamped onto the paper. "This is a tracker enchantment. They must have put one on each writ. It would allow the palace wizards to see where each team is and perhaps listen in, should they wish."

"They are spying on us?" Vale growled.

Dante shrugged. "More like keeping tabs, I would say. This is a message. It seems the king would like an audience with you and I privately tonight, away from all the others."

"Why?" Vale asked.

Dante rubbed his hand over the parchment, and the symbols vanished. "It didn't say. The message was focused on emphasizing the importance of no one else overhearing."

Vale rubbed the side of his head. "Very well. When the others are asleep, we will meet in the tree line on the other side of the river, where we were when the dragon attacked."

Dante confirmed with a nod.

Night fell and the darkness grew until it covered the land completely. Vale waited. When he was sure the others were asleep, he snuck out and crossed the river to find Dante waiting. They moved out of sight, and Dante held out the writ, tapping it with his finger. A glowing blue mist streamed from the writ and formed in front of them into the appearance of a man. It wasn't a herald as Dante had expected. It was King Alistar himself. His non-corporeal likeness glowed like a spirit, his expression so detailed and clear he might as well have been standing in front of them.

"Vale, Dante, are you certain you were not followed?"

Vale nodded.

"Good," the king replied. "I have several things to discuss with you, and they must all remain secret. First, you must be careful. We sent over three thousand Seeker teams on this quest. The Court has informed me that many of the Seekers have already been killed."

"We saw the bodies at the gate. Many were already buried. There must have been hundreds of them," Dante replied.

"Thousands," the King corrected.

"Thousands?" Dante questioned. "How many of the Seeker teams remain?"

"Four."

Vale and Dante exchanged a long glance as the news settled into their minds.

"You very well may be the last hope of Parisia. You must be cautious. You must not fail."

Vale bowed his head. "We will not, my king."

"Good. Secondly, I spoke with Sir Brevioar. Imagine my surprise when the knight I assigned to your team came back before you even left the capital."

Shadows of the Dark Realm

"That's my fault, your majesty. I felt that his inexperience would make him a liability to our quest," Vale said.

The king's expression soured. "Impudent, disloyal, knave! Who are you to overrule my judgment? Who are you to defy my will? You, a disgraced knight, would question your king?"

Vale dropped to his knee and bowed his head. "My apologies, your majesty. I meant no offense. We had an altercation with a group of thugs. He was knocked out before even recognizing they were there. I felt that if he could not even handle himself in the capital, what chance did he have outside the wall?"

King Alistar took a long breath and cleared his throat. "I am displeased, but that is not what troubles me most. The man you took in his stead is called Caelan, correct?"

Vale nodded. "Yes. He is an archer and thief of some skill. We made him our fifth."

"Caelan is not a thief. He is a terrorist," King Alistar corrected.

"What?"

"He's a member of the Hands of Freedom, an anti-Parisian group of radicals. Vale, you are familiar with them?"

Vale nodded. "Insurrectionists who use extreme violence to create civil unrest and fear in the hopes of undermining the authority of the crown. They claim to fight for justice and the good of the people but have no qualms with killing women and children in their holy crusade."

"Our intelligence has linked them to several attacks on peaceful towns around the kingdom, as well as the magical bombing of Rivisia."

"Rivisia," Vale repeated. "I was there. I saw what remained after."

"We believe he is not just part of the Hands of Freedom, but that he is the one who planted the explosives and carried out the attack. I cannot express how important it is that he not be allowed to get his hands on the Darkstone. There is no telling what he would do with its power. You are to execute him as soon as possible."

Vale felt a deep rage burning in his heart, but he kept his expression calm. "Yes, my king, it will be done."

In the glowing projection, a face appeared next to the king's, whispering something into his ear. His expression softened.

"Another team has been lost. I must attend to this. Carry out your mission. Do not fail your king!" He waved his hand, and the glowing projection fizzled out.

Vale and Dante exchanged a glance.

"What are you going to do?" Dante asked.

"I've been ordered by my king to kill a man who murdered women and children. When the opportunity presents itself, Caelan will die." The two walked back to the burnt village in silence.

Perched on the thick branch of a tree near where they had been standing, sat Caelan. The foliage kept him out of view from the ground below, but from where he sat, he could see and hear everything. He rubbed his chin with one hand and the hilt of his dagger with the other. *This was going to be a problem.*

Chapter 15

The Perils of Friendship

Standing outside the town, watching through the gaps in the trees, cloaked in darkness, stood the man with the triangle scar on his hand. His eyes burned as he waited, frustration coursing through his veins.

"What happened?" a voice came from behind him.

The man with the scar scowled.

"The plan—she was supposed to be . . . "

"We did not expect him to be so formidable. It is of no concern. An inconvenience, nothing more," replied the man with scar.

"My master will not be pleased."

The man with the scar whirled around and faced the man in the black cloak, staring into the shadow cast by his hood. "Relax. Nothing has changed. Have you dealt with the other Seekers?"

"I have."

"All of them?"

"Two other teams live, but they will not interfere."

"Good. Her rise is at hand. It's time for the next phase of our plan. Are you ready?" the man with the scar asked.

"I am."

"Good. Do your master proud."

The man in the black cloak nodded and disappeared back into the shadows.

***

The next morning Caelan was up before the others. He said nothing but kept a close eye on Vale. He doubted Vale was the type to kill him when he wasn't expecting it. He also knew he was fast enough with that blade that he could if he wanted to.

Caelan noticed Azalea sitting by herself just outside the ruined town. He walked over to her and sat down.

"Silver for your thoughts?" He wrapped his arms around his knees, matching her posture.

"Wondering when you boys will learn that when you see a girl sitting alone, it's not an invitation to come rescue her. She might be alone because she wants to be alone," Azalea replied with a smirk.

"Ah, I wouldn't hold my breath. We menfolk don't tend to learn much of anything when it comes to women."

Azalea nodded in agreement.

"Since I've already ruined your alone time, might as well tell me what your thinking about."

"I'm thinking, next time that Royal snob snaps at me, I'm going to cook her like a roast boar."

"A bit reactive, isn't it? Here lies Celeste; she was snappy."

"For existing. Royals, living their lives of squalor, feasting on luxury, wasting more than others even have. They are all the same—a bunch of rich, entitled narcissists who think they are better than everyone because they were born into the right family. They didn't earn it or work for it. Everything they have was given to them as it was to their parents and their parents before them. Meanwhile, honest, hardworking folk are struggling. It's not right."

"Not a lot of starving people in Parisia," Caelan countered.

"There are more than you'd think. The Royals just do a really good job of keeping them hidden. They don't deserve what they have. I can't wait for the day when they don't have it anymore—when all the wealth is gone, and they get to see what life is really like when you can't throw gold at all your problems."

"That why you got caught in the royal treasury?" Caelan asked.

Azalea smirked. "Can't blame a girl for trying to take care of herself by reallocating the obscene wealth of the nobles."

"Blame? It's what I like most about you. How was the vault?"

"You wouldn't believe me if I told you. I thought I hated the Royals before, but once I saw how much they have just lying around in rooms collecting dust, now I really hate them."

"Hence the burning Celeste alive if she looks at you funny?"

"It's tempting enough to do it without provocation, but every time she speaks, she makes it that much harder to resist. Seven bells from seven hells, it would be one thing if she had some skill, knowledge, or anything that made us need her. She's not just a royal pain in the owa, she's useless. Why are we bringing her with us?" Azalea worked herself up as she spoke.

"You're failing to see the opportunity here," Caelan interjected.

"What do you mean?"

"The Darkstone."

"What about it?"

"A stone that could grant the deepest desire of your heart—wouldn't you want to use that?"

Azalea's brow furrowed. "Of course. Why do you think I agreed to go on this ridiculous quest?"

"No way that happens, though. Even as the heroes who save the kingdom, we'd never be allowed to use it."

"Why not?"

"You think the king of Parisia is going to let a Kinspira witch use the stone once we've returned it? He's not that emptos."

Azalea frowned. "No, you're right. I will find another way."

"We already have. That's what I'm telling you."

"How?"

"The stone is bound to the royal bloodline, right?"

"So?"

"Celeste is a member of the royal bloodline." He waved his arms for her to complete the thought process.

"Meaning as long as we have her, we can use the Darkstone without the King."

"Ding, ding."

"Meaning, I can't kill her."

"A small price to pay. You could always kill her after," Caelan winked.

Azalea smiled. "Bavaso . . . "

"What?"

"Now I have to put up with her the rest of the way."

"I'll leave you be. I want to see what these Rag'amorians are capable of." Caelan got up and made his way back to the burnt town. He saw Vale heading toward the square, and he followed him.

Vale made his way to the center of town where Rivik had gathered the warriors. He had the soldiers spar with each other in a make-shift tournament so Vale could observe both style and skill. They were all quite talented. They could have held their own against the Phoenix legion, which was no small feat.

The greatest of the fighters was a young blonde woman, Sera. She was attractive, strong, and fast. It was her skill and technique that Vale found so impressive. She fought with a pair of long, hooked daggers that allowed her to maximize the advantage of her speed. *Smart*. The last fight was between her and Rivik, who had sat out until this point. Rivik carried a spear made entirely of some strange green stone. It looked almost like an emerald shaped into a weapon, but no gem could be forged in such a way.

Rivik walked casually into the circle. Sera seemed oddly more aggressive in this fight. The others she'd dispatched with relative ease and minimal effort. Here she went all out. There was an intensity to her movement that contrasted its smoothness. Her body seemed to dance and nearly float as she moved around the circle like a leaf being tossed in the wind. Her face and the look in her eyes told a very different story. She was working very hard, her movements precise and controlled. She wasn't holding back anymore. Yet no strike found a mark. Rivik managed to dodge each of her attacks without even using the spear he carried to parry them. His agility and flexibility came so effortlessly it was like he saw the world in slow motion. The other fighters had impressed Vale. These two . . . were something else.

"That is enough." He interrupted the fight after Sera dove at Rivik and missed by a half dozen paces. "I am satisfied with this demonstration. I will take your oaths, and then you may go on your way. We will gather here tomorrow and depart at first light."

Celeste was surprised at how easily and naturally Vale gave orders to people he hardly knew. She was used to people doing as she said, but that was only due to her station. Vale didn't have a title, rank, or any position of authority over them, and yet when he spoke, they listened. It was unlike anything she'd ever seen before.

After the demonstration was complete, Rivik brought a map of the area and laid it out before the group. He explained the possible routes they could take, potential dangers, and the various things they might expect to encounter depending on the route they chose.

"Best bet is here. It takes us through Storvale, one of the largest cities in Rag'amor. Good place to rest, restock, and gather information before venturing into the Dragon Lands," Rivik explained.

"We keep talking about these Dragon Lands, but I've never seen them marked on a map. Where are they exactly?" Celeste questioned.

Rivik drew a circle on the map with his finger. "Northwestern Rag'amor, most of Baronia, the hills further north toward Vargr, and all the way across the Sapphire Sea."

"These lands belong to various kingdoms; why are they called the Dragon Lands?" Celeste asked.

Caelan rolled his eyes. "For a princess with a fancy education, you are as sharp as a ball of snow sometimes."

Celeste whirled around, facing the archer with her hands on her hips in defiant protest. "You should watch your mouth."

Caelan smirked and waved his hand dismissively. "Easy, princess, think it through."

Celeste glared at Caelan, her face red.

Rivik ignored the conflict and drew his finger across the map. "I suggest we follow this ravine to avoid any towns along the borders."

"Are you sure the ravine is the wisest path? It seems like a dangerous place if we got attacked," Spiro questioned.

"This path is not well known. It is out of view from the lands that surround it. It's the safest path forward. When we are in Storvale, it is big enough that a group of travelers won't draw much attention. Just don't go blabbing about where you're from. Parisians are not well-liked outside of the wall."

Celeste sighed. "It's only natural that people would be jealous."

"Your king has sent troops to attack and harass our people, interfere in our affairs, and cause enough trouble to be wildly disliked. There are many who would kill you simply for being Parisian."

"Those are lies. The king is a good and righteous man. Any action he takes is to create peace and harmony," Celeste objected.

"Believe what you will. But be careful. One other thing you should know," Rivik started. "You are not the only ones seeking the Darkstone. The armies of Rag'amor are being assembled. Spies are being sent out across the land. Rumor has it, it's the same in Vargr and Baronia. Any safety afforded to you by secrecy is over."

"What right do they have to try to steal what is ours? The Darkstone must be returned! It belongs to Parisia!" Celeste protested.

"Yours?" Rivik raised an eyebrow.

"The Darkstone was not given to Parisia, it was taken. Your people have no more right to it than anyone else. Many would kill to obtain its power. The Darkstone is one of the most powerful magics in the realm. Whoever possesses it can name themselves king, establish a land, and be fruitful, prosperous, and secure. Who wouldn't crave that power? You think because your people stole it first, that gives you claim to it? These are the thoughts of a child," Rivik stated.

Vale's hand shifted to the hilt of his blade. "You think your people have a right to it? Your king is working to claim it. You're not giving me confidence in our new arrangement."

Rivik smirked but seemed otherwise unphased. "You are mionogaol; we are bonded. We take oaths very seriously. To break an oath is to tarnish your word and your honor. We'd

Shadows of the Dark Realm

sooner die than bring that shame upon ourselves. You have our oath; thus, you have nothing to fear from us."

Vale grunted and nodded.

"You are right, though—if word has spread that the Darkstone is missing, we must be very careful who we trust with our purpose and mission. We must assume everyone we meet from here on out is a threat until they prove otherwise," Vale said.

Celeste looked intentionally at Caelan, who ignored her with a smirk.

"Let's go, we've got a lot of ground to cover."

Rivik rolled up the map and handed it to an older man who walked back toward the remains of their village. The group headed off toward the ravine that would lead them to Storvale.

Rivik, Sera, and three of the Rag'amorian warriors moved ahead of the group to serve as guides. The remaining Rag'amorians stayed back, guarding the flank as they moved. Caelan travelled in the front with the vanguard, trying to keep as much distance between himself and Vale as possible. No point in taking needless risks.

Rivik guided them along the river, following it through the forest for two days before the trees gave way to open fields of grass. While Rag'amor was far from desolate compared to Parisia, the fields and plains appeared barren and lifeless. The greens of the grass were marred with strips of yellow and brown. The songs of birds sounded drearier; the animals looked thinner. To Celeste's eyes, everything looked bleaker and impoverished. Had she seen this in Parisia, she would have thought a blight had come. For Azalea and Caelan, the lands looked rich and bountiful compared to much of what they were used to seeing.

They moved efficiently. The pace was quick but not so quick as to cause exhaustion. Periodically, Rivik led them to shade or shelter for short rests. He was a skilled guide and seemed to have an innate awareness of how hard he could push them and when they needed rest. They moved across Rag'amor, avoiding towns when possible and making stops to gather supplies and rest as needed.

Apart from Caelan, they tried to be discreet. Even after Rivik's warning, Caelan made it his habit to go to the tavern after the others had settled down in the inn. He would drink long into the night, laughing and joking—all but announcing their quest to anyone who would listen.

Rivik led them to a large town settled on the edge of a vast horizon of rolling hills, a final stop before the long trek of wilderness to reach the ravine. The town was lively, filled with shops and stables, surrounded by farms of open fields. While the others were settling in, Caelan made his way to the tavern. Vale stood outside, listening to the crowd as they laughed and cheered.

"He's quite the entertainer." Rivik turned and leaned on the wall next to Vale.

"Fools often are," Vale replied.

Rivik smirked. "I'll try not to take that personally. Any reason you're playing sentinel?"

"Someone has to make sure the fool doesn't get himself killed before we even reach the Dragon Lands."

"Nice of you to look out for him. You're a good friend," Rivik said.

Vale cringed. "No. I can't wait to be rid of him. But we need him, for now."

"Again?" Celeste asked, walking over to them.

Vale nodded.

Celeste huffed and pulled the door to the tavern open. "I'm putting an end to this!"

She marched over to Caelan, who was sitting on the bar itself with his feet propped up on the chairs around it. She grabbed his arm, causing him to spill his drink.

"Heeeey! Whaat's wrong with yooou?" Caelan asked, hiccupping.

"With me? What is your problem? Every town, you do the same thing. You continue to draw unwanted attention, putting us and our mission in even greater danger. I tolerated this nonsense when we were in Parisia, but it has to stop, right now!" Celeste demanded.

"Tolerated, did yoouuu? Weeell, I'm soooo soooorry princess. But I don't answer to you. Now get a drink or get out of my face." Caelan pulled his arm from her and downed the rest of his glass.

Celeste threw her hands in the air and grunted before storming out.

"You want me to stay with you?" Rivik asked.

Vale shook his head. "No. Only one of us need suffer."

The twilight faded into the full dark of night. The only remaining light came from the torches burning inside. Caelan stumbled out of the tavern, his feet shaky and his body wiggling like a long vine in a strong wind. He was so intoxicated he walked right past Vale without noticing. Vale sighed as he watched the intoxicated archer clumsily make his way down the street. Before he could move, two large thugs exited the tavern and turned to follow him. Could just be a coincidence, but they moved with purpose, closing the gap quickly.

Vale gave them a little lead and then followed, staying close enough to react if his suspicions were in fact accurate. Caelan turned a corner. The thugs rushed to catch up with him, disappearing around the corner as well. Vale's hand readied on his blade as he rushed to the alley. He could hear the sounds of a struggle, but by the time he reached the street, Caelan was nowhere to be found. It was as if he had vanished into the night. Vale turned his attention to the two thugs lying motionless on the ground.

Vale knelt over them, inspecting their coats. The pockets of the first had been emptied out. In the second he found a note:

BOUNTY: Parisian Seekers
REWARD: Large
REQUIREMENT: Alive only
INSTRUCTIONS: Bring to King Tomlin at the palace in Lunal

Vale moved out of the alley and scanned the area. Still no sign of Caelan. He left the unconscious thugs behind and made his way back to the inn. The king of Vargr had put out a bounty on Seekers. Things were about to get even more difficult.

Chapter 16

The Death Dragon

Even on horseback, it took six days to cross the rolling hills of Rag'amor. The occasional silhouettes of dragons flying far off on the horizon signified their growing proximity to the Dragon Lands.

After watching her fight with Rivik, Celeste became obsessed with Sera. She followed her around, requested tips and asked questions. Sera, though quite annoyed by the young royal's persistence, eventually gave in and spent whatever free time she had training her.

On the seventh day, they reached the ravine Rivik had spoken of. The ravine was a deep canyon carved into the earth. The path leading down into it was a steep, rocky slope, making the canyon appear like a mouth leading into the belly of the earth itself. They moved deeper and deeper into the gorge. The rock walls towering on either side serving as a marker for just how deep they had gone. It wasn't long before the surface itself was out of view.

"We rest here," Rivik said.

"It's barely past morning," Dante objected.

"Fire mages and goblin pillagers patrol the canyon by day. They tend to make for an unpleasant encounter," Rivik explained.

"No way to avoid them?" Vale asked.

"There are plenty of caves that spiderweb throughout. No telling where they will spit you out. At night, the canyon is vacant and passage much safer."

Reluctantly, they agreed to wait. Celeste trained with Sera. Caelan kept his distance, remaining alert, eyes never far from Vale. The sun started to descend over the great mountain peaks to the southwest, and darkness drew over the sky like a blanket. A quiet settled over the land with the fading of the celestial light.

"It's time."

Rivik led the group down the hill and into the canyon.

From atop her horse, Celeste felt her legs tremble as the group followed the path down. She was glad she didn't have to walk the path as she wasn't sure she'd have been able to. The stone cliffs towered higher and higher above them as each step took them deeper into the earth, as if being swallowed up by a great stone maw. It felt like marching into their own grave. After a moment, the initial intimidation began to pass, along with the fear that had gripped her heart.

The canyon was wide and spacious. A great river must have one time passed through here to forge such a deep tunnel into the earth. The rock walls climbed almost perfectly straight up into the sky and stretched as high as Celeste could see. Surprisingly, the bottom of the tunnel was lit by glowing pools of water and mystical floating lights that danced overhead, creating a dim, violet-blue light.

Caelan idly fingered one of his arrows. He kept himself behind Vale as he contemplated ending the Black Swordsman before he had a chance to attack. He knew it was coming; at some point, Vale would try to kill him. Caelan was confident in his own abilities, but having seen Vale fight, he wasn't sure if he would be able to best the Black Swordsman. It would be much safer to just put an arrow to the back of Vale's head. He could make it look like an accident, pretend he got jumpy and misfired. Though doing something so cowardly felt loathsome, it was certainly better than being executed himself. Was it really so wrong to kill someone before they killed you?

Finally, he sighed and pulled his hand from his quiver.

"What good is surviving if you can't live with yourself after?"

he muttered too quietly for anyone else to hear. "Then again, if I die, I won't be living at all. Tough choices."

A gust of wind crashed over him, causing him to freeze in place. His bow was free, and an arrow notched on reflexive instinct. Celeste crashed into him, not paying attention.

"Hey, why'd you stop?" she asked, grumbling as she stepped back.

Spiro and Rivik had also stopped.

Caelan held a finger to his lips in silent warning as his eyes turned up.

"Did you feel that?" he asked.

"It was just a gust of wind," Celeste protested at full volume. "What are you so worked up about?"

Caelan shook his head. "We are in a canyon. Wind should be coming from the west and hitting us head on. That gust came from above."

Celeste's face turned grim, and she glanced up. There was nothing to be seen. Just an endless void of black littered with tiny silver shimmers that pierced the veil in decorative patterns far above the earth. Celeste let out a sigh of relief. He was just being paranoid. Nothing was there.

A loud shriek echoed around them, and her heart skipped three beats. Caelan drew back his bow, aiming into the blackness. Celeste could see nothing. Caelan let loose his arrow, and it whooshed out of sight. A gust of wind slammed into them again, this time nearly knocking them back as the dragon flew into view, adjusting his course to avoid the arrow. Had it not done so, it would have slammed into the group with its extended claws. *How had Caelan even seen the dragon to know where to shoot?* Celeste thought. The group huddled together as the great black dragon swooped over their heads.

"The ralk is this?" Caelan asked. "Oi, dragon boy, you never said a thing about black dragons. Slip your memory? You daft goraum—useless piece of troll gwar!"

Spiro had his massive sword in his hands and stood at the ready. "It did not. I told you about regular dragons and elder dragons. This is neither."

"Are you having a laugh? You want to defend your position

on a linguistic technicality? I'm gonna shoot you in the foot, just know—it's gonna happen," Caelan challenged.

"Enough!" Vale interrupted. "We can argue later; it's coming back around. Spiro, what are we dealing with?"

Spiro shook his head. "A death dragon."

"Oh, ralk you, a what? You mean to say there is a dragon called a death dragon and you didn't even bother to tell us—" Caelan started.

"Caelan, not now!" Vale shouted, cutting him off. "How do we deal with it?"

Before Spiro could answer, the black dragon landed on the ground in front of them, making the stones under their feet tremble. The creature was massive and majestic. Its scales were a shiny, gorgeous black, so smooth they seemed almost wet. It had far more spikes than the silver dragon they'd seen before. Its eyes were lit like purple flame and a glowing violet mist emanated from inside the creature's mouth.

The group still huddled together, weapons at the ready as the dragon reared up on its hind legs, extending its head to look over them.

"You are an odd bunch. For what purpose have you traveled into my domain?"

The dragon's voice was a powerful basso that made the ground rumble as it spoke. Celeste gulped; the simple fact that the beast spoke struck her with fear. Dante uttered a spell, lighting up the arrowheads of every arrow in Caelan's quiver. Caelan had one ready but kept the glowing flame out of view of the dragon.

Rivik stepped toward the beast.

"What are you doing? Don't engage it!" Spiro grunted.

Rivik continued forward and whispered, "Be ready, just in case."

He returned his focus to the dragon, gripping his spear but deliberately not readying it as he locked eyes with the creature.

"We are just travelers passing through. We have no intention to linger or take anything from your domain," he answered.

Spiro gripped his massive sword, his body rocking back and forth with restrained energy.

"Never engage with a dragon; this is the most basic tenet of the dragon knights. Their words are enchantments that rob you of your mind," he muttered under his breath.

The dragon growled. "What do you seek?"

"Nothing beyond safe passage," Rivik replied.

"Lies. You are trespassers here. You will answer me, or I will consume you and learn what I want to know from your memories," the dragon replied, his voice like the rumbling of thunder.

Rivik stepped closer. "We travel under the protection of the Siochaol Agreement."

"What's that?" Celeste whispered.

Sera leaned over. "Siochaol means peace in Rag'amorian. After generations of endless bloodshed and death, Bag'Thorak, King of Dragons, formed a pact with the Kings of Men to minimize the conflict between our peoples."

The dragon's massive maw turned up into an amused sneer, revealing perfectly kept, razor-sharp teeth. "On what grounds would you call upon this right?"

"An elder dragon from your lands laid waste to our village without cause or provocation. Under terms of the agreement, we are to be allowed passage through all Dragon Lands to seek out and kill the dragon responsible. As long as we do not take what is not ours or commit any act of aggression against you, we have the right of safe passage," Rivik replied.

The dragon laughed. "It is decided—a game, then. If I am to be denied my snack, you will not deny my amusement."

"What sort of game?" Rivik asked cautiously.

The dragon grinned wide. "I shall give you a riddle. Answer correctly and not only will I allow you to pass, but I will guard you on your journey. Answer incorrectly, and you must offer me one of your men as a tribute."

Rivik looked back at the others.

"Agreed." Dante stepped forward.

Vale turned to him, "What? We can't!"

Dante pointed at the dragon. "If he doesn't let us pass, we have to find another route anyway. At least this way we have a chance."

Rivik nodded to the dragon. "Very well, let's hear it."

Shadows of the Dark Realm

The dragon chuckled, his eye fixed on Spiro for a moment before scanning the rest of the group. Caelan turned suspiciously. *Could the dragon tell that Spiro was a dragon hunter? Or was he reading too much into it?*

"Mighty and strong and covered in armor, I strike fear into all. In a flash with a dash, I'm suddenly quite small. In this way, I seem frail and tender, pale, all that might is to no avail. A clever trick—"

Before the dragon could finish, Spiro cried out, "You will not bewitch our minds with your draconic magic! Enough of this!" He lifted his sword and charged.

"Spiro, no!" Vale reached for the dragon knight, trying to stop him, but he was too late. The only one between the knight and the dragon was Rivik.

The dragon grinned as the knight charged toward him.

"Look at this fool." His mouth opened, and a ball of purple light grew between his jaws.

"Ralk!" Rivik cursed. He moved with such swiftness Celeste didn't even see it at first. In an instant, Rivik had stepped to the side and swung his spear, twirling it overhead. The dragon roared, and a purple beam of light burst from his mouth just as Rivik's spear slammed into the dragon's jaw, knocking its head to the side and the purple light off its course.

A Rag'amorian warrior screamed as the flame hit his arm. He was the only one touched by it, and the damage looked minimal. They got lucky.

The dragon stepped back and grinned. "Impressive. Now the Siochaol protection is void."

A creaking, crackling sound surrounded the group. The dragon smiled and cocked its head. Something broke out of the ground in front of them, but it was hard to make out what it was. Another did the same behind them. More rattling. More crackling. The Rag'amorian warrior who was hit by the flame shook and seized.

"Get away from him!" Spiro shouted, turning from the dragon.

"He was burned; he needs help!" one of the other warriors retorted.

"He was touched by the necroflame; get away!" Spiro shouted again.

The warrior ignored him, rushing over to tend to his friend's arm. The man with the burned arm continued to shake and then suddenly froze in place, his eyes turning a glowing purple.

"Rinar? Rinar? What are you?" the warrior asked, fear trembling in his voice. The warrior with the burnt arm, called Rinar, said nothing as he drove his sword through his friend's chest and twisted it.

The warrior fell to the ground dead as Rinar slowly walked toward the others.

"What was that?" Azalea shouted.

"It's part of the black dragon magic. If its flames touch you, then he can take over your mind and make you his thrall," Spiro replied.

"For the record, that would have been good to know BEFORE it happened. You know, just some friendly communication coaching," Caelan grumbled.

"Anything we can do for him?" Vale asked as the rumbling and crackling grew louder.

"He is mine now. I see his mind. I see . . . ohhh . . . so that is why you are here. Interesting," the dragon replied.

"He's gone. There is nothing to save him!" Spiro shouted before charging the dragon by himself.

Rivik rushed back, standing between Rinar and the group.

"Rinar, what is wrong with you? Get ahold of yourself."

Rinar was beyond hearing. He swung his sword aggressively but not skillfully. Rivik dodged easily and continued his plea as Rinar came closer and closer.

Vale's focus shifted between Rinar and the dragon who was battling with Spiro. At least the dragon knight was keeping it distracted, the rash fool. The group was so focused on Rinar, they didn't notice what was climbing up from the ground all around them.

Caelan aimed and fired, his arrow flying right through where Rinar had been. The thrall of a man moved at the last moment, dodging the arrow completely. It was an impossible dodge. Caelan cursed. Rinar's attacks grew more and more coordinated, more skillful, more dangerous as the dragon's control over his mind became more absolute. Rivik was fast and agile, but even his skill would not be able to keep up for long.

"Don't hurt him!" Rivik pleaded. "We can still—"

The lancer ducked just in time to avoid decapitation. He stood up to find Rinar's fist slamming into his temple, sending him flying through the air and crashing to the ground in a heap.

"Azalea, blast him!" Caelan shouted, pulling back an arrow as the thrall moved closer.

"He's too fast! It wouldn't hit him!" she replied.

"Fire at his left shoulder. Do it now!" Caelan cried.

Azalea threw her hand forward, and a ball of fire shot toward Rinar's left shoulder. As she predicted, he moved out of the way, dodging it just in time. As soon as he stepped, his head jerked back, Caelan's arrow piercing between his eyes. The purple glow faded, and he slumped to the ground. There was a collective sigh of relief before . . .

"Look out!" Rivik shouted, pushing himself up from the ground.

The others turned to look. The source of the rattling, crackling sound suddenly became very clear. While they had been focused on Rinar, a small army of skeletal warriors had risen from the earth below them. An army of skeletons blocked the way they had come, and the dragon and more skeletons cut off their path ahead. They were trapped. The skeletons killed several of their horses before the group could react. The Rag'amorians rushed at the skeletons at their flank, cutting them down and smashing them into bits. Azalea's flames provided support to the warriors, keeping the skeletons from swarming behind them. Vale dashed and cut a path to Rivik, who had been surrounded, only to discover that Rivik had already cut down several dozen skeletons and was surrounded by a circle of piled bones.

"Listen, Mr. Dragon expert, if we don't die here, you and I are gonna have a strong talk," Caelan shouted as he fired an arrow into one of the slow-approaching skeletons. Hundreds of piles of bones littered the rocky ground around them. Perhaps the undead warriors were not such a threat. They were slow, clumsy, and unintelligent.

As the last skeleton fell, its bones crumbled into a heap on the stony ground, a spectral sound surrounded them, like an eerie gust of wind. Every pile of bones began to shake and rattle, and they reformed, immediately resuming their slow charge toward the group.

"Ralk this!" Caelan muttered.

"You cannot win, foolish humans," the dragon rumbled.

Spiro had managed to keep the beast distracted but had achieved little more. The dragon's black tail swiped out, slamming into Spiro, sending the dragon knight flying back. He bounced across the rocks as he skidded toward Dante's feet.

"We need to get out of here!" Vale shouted.

"The caves!" Caelan started.

"Getting trapped in a cave would be our doom," Vale replied.

"They aren't caves; they are tunnels!" Rivik shouted. "They run deep into the earth. Some exit the canyon in different places. Even the ones that don't, the dragon won't be able to follow."

Celeste and Sera stood back-to-back, a circle of skeletons surrounding them. Each time a warrior cut down a skeleton, it reformed a minute later. Their push, though slow, was an unrelenting force.

"Get to the caves!" Vale shouted.

"The horses!" Celeste called out.

A wall of skeleton soldiers stood between the group and their mounts.

"Leave them," Vale commanded.

Sera, Celeste, and the Rag'amorians rushed to the closest cave on the right side of the canyon, rushing through its tunnels to where the canyon was almost completely out of view.

Rivik smashed a pair of skeletons advancing on Spiro's unconscious body.

"Get him out of here!" Vale shouted.

"Can't move him and guard him at the same time," Rivik cried back.

Fire arrows rained down on the pack of skeletons, shattering them. Azalea was casting as fast as she could, trying to burn the skeletons out of existence, but even her flames succeeded in little more than slowing down the relentless pounding of the undead advance.

"I got him!" Azalea closed her eyes, and her body began to glow. A moment later, she was a large wolf. She bounded across the canyon, clamped her jaw around Spiro's cape, and tossed the knight onto her back. With him draped over her, she rushed into the cave and out of sight.

"Run, little rodents. Hide. You will not survive." The dragon watched in amusement as the group tried to escape.

Vale was fending another group, cutting them down as he moved toward Rivik until the two fought back-to-back. Dante and Caelan were the only others still outside the cave.

"We need to buy the others some time!" Vale shouted.

"We need to get out of here. They are too slow to keep up," Caelan countered.

Knowing they were at his mercy, the black-scaled monster was content watching in amusement as they struggled to fend off his horde.

Dante threw several bottles into the air. They shattered on the rock walls and blue arms reached out to grab the skeletons, pulling many of them back and pinning them to the wall with a magical energy.

"It won't hold them for long!" he shouted.

They turned to run for the cave entrance. Just as they were reaching it, a funnel of purple flame crashed into the opening. The dragon swooped up into the air and sprayed his mind-controlling fire, cutting off their path.

"No, that is not your path," they all heard in their minds.

The blue arms fizzled out as Dante's spell diminished, and the skeletons returned to their creeping charge. The flames showed no sign of dissipating, and the dragon showed no indication of tiring. They were cut off and would not be able to rejoin the others.

"There's a tunnel on the other side," Rivik pointed.

"We can't just—" Vale started before realizing the futility of trying to get past those flames.

The dragon turned his head, and the flames moved toward them slowly enough that they could avoid it but not get around it. They rushed across the canyon as the flames grew closer and closer. Caelan dove inside just as the fire passed by where he was. The dragon landed on the ground and smiled a toothy grin.

"You are mine now." He pulled his head back, and purple flames shot toward them.

Just as the flame reached the entrance, a giant boulder crumbled and fell, sealing the entrance and blocking the flame. Caelan, Rivik, Dante, and Vale had avoided death by dragon flame only to find themselves cut off from the rest of their group and trapped.

Caelan sighed. "Well, that was fun. Wanna go again?"

Chapter 17

Revelation

Dante closed his eyes, uttered some unintelligible words, and the cavern walls began to glow a faint blue. It wasn't bright, but the light filled the dank passage well enough to navigate. As Rivik had indicated, the cave was in fact a tunnel, curving and twisting deep into the canyon walls.

Caelan pushed himself up and dusted off his clothes. "That goraum troll gwar of a dragon knight! What the ralk was he thinking?"

Dante rubbed his chin, staring up at the walls. "Perhaps he was saving us from having our minds taken over? We saw what happened to the man who was touched by the dragon's flame; perhaps its words could have a similar effect?"

"Riner. The man's name was Riner. I've known him my whole life. He was a good warrior and a good man. He deserved better than that." Rivik glared at the rubble blocking the entrance to the cave and separating them from the dragon.

Vale put his hand on Rivik's shoulder and stood wordlessly next to him.

"Now I have two dragons to kill," Rivik said, more to himself than anyone.

"Let's get moving. The sooner we get out of here, the sooner we can find the others," Vale said.

Rivik stared at the rubble for another minute before sliding his spear over his back and starting down the tunnel passage. Dante's magic seemed to have coated the walls through the entire tunnel in its glowing blue light.

Caelan kept his hand on his knife as they walked, trying to keep Dante between himself and Vale. In the open, Caelan was certain he had a chance against Vale. In tight quarters like these, the Black Swordsman had a distinct advantage. If Vale made his move here, in the tunnels, Caelan doubted he would be able to fend him off. But the further in they went, the less likely it seemed that Vale would attack him. If he was going to make a move, he would have done it by now.

It took a few hours for them to navigate the winding tunnels. Finally, after what seemed like forever, Caelan saw pale light glistening on the walls of the cave. They'd been underground so long, it was already morning.

Stepping out of the cave felt almost magical. The sun shining down providing its warm embrace. The smell of flowers and plants in bloom, the sound of animals and insects singing, the feel of a soft breeze on his skin. It was wonderful. He closed his eyes and soaked it all in, enjoying the fresh air. But then the cool touch of steel pressed against his neck, prematurely ending his reveling.

Caelan opened his eyes and glanced down to see the black metal blade of Vale's sword. He gulped. *This was it.*

"Dante, you and Rivik go on ahead. I'll catch up," Vale said.

Rivik planted his feet. "What is going on?"

"It is not your concern," Vale replied.

Rivik chuckled. "Not to be contrary, but I disagree. We are hunting a dragon. He is the only archer in our group, and from what little I've seen, he's a ralking good one. Losing him will make it much harder to kill the dragon. Being that I committed my life to this cause, I don't think it unreasonable to seek an explanation."

Vale sighed. "I have been ordered by my king to execute this man for the crimes of treason, terrorism, and murder."

Rivik raised an eyebrow. "Those are strong accusations. Is there proof of his guilt?"

Vale turned his blade so the sharp edge grazed Caelan's neck. Caelan carefully pulled his knife free and held it behind his back out of view.

"I am a knight. My sworn duty is to carry out the instructions of the king."

"Regardless of what your king tells you?" Rivik asked.

"The word of the king is law. I have no right to challenge it."

"What if the right thing to do is challenge it?" Rivik asked. "Not all kings are good. None of them are perfect."

"A knight who disobeys his king has no honor," Vale replied.

Rivik stood for a moment before nodding. "I see. This I understand. Without honor, we are nothing. Very well, I will not interfere further."

Caelan laughed. "Your honor is a joke, as is your king."

Vale turned, but Caelan was already in motion. His knife clanged into Vale's sword, knocking it back. Caelan leapt away, moving himself out of the blade's reach before Vale could ready a counterattack. He was standing with his back against the cave entrance as Vale squared off, standing between Caelan and any hope of escape.

"I wouldn't expect a man who murders women and children in hopes to bring disorder and chaos to an entire kingdom to understand honor," Vale snapped.

Caelan grinned. "Strange—what you call honor is nothing more than blind obedience." He started pacing back and forth, turning and shifting his position to try hide the purpose of his movement.

Vale chuckled. "I'm sure for an anarchist like you, the idea of serving something bigger than yourself seems absurd."

Vale thrust his sword forward quickly. Caelan slid his body to the side, dodging the path of the blade. Vale twisted, turning the blade and slicing through the air at Caelan. Caelan dropped down under the path of the sword. Then as he rose up, he thrust his knife at Vale's chest. Vale somehow managed to bring his blade around and parry the attack.

"You believe it is a knight's duty to obey his king without question?" Caelan asked.

Vale grunted in confirmation.

"What happens when your king commands you to do something wicked?"

"What?"

"Like killing innocent people who can't defend themselves. That's wrong, right?"

"Yes. Obviously. What is your point?"

"If the honorable thing is to do whatever your king says, but what he says to do is dishonorable, like killing villagers who have no weapons and have done nothing wrong, does that stop being dishonorable because your king commanded you to do it?"

Vale's stance weakened, the tip of his blade lowering a little as he considered the question. "My king would not do that. He is a good man. A man who, despite having incredible power and wealth, uses what he has to serve his people. He sacrifices for them; rescues them from horrible situations. He must make hard choices, yes, but they are always for the good of his people."

"Perhaps you have too much faith in your king," Caelan replied.

"I have faith in my king because I have seen his rule, his lands. He governs well. He is a worthy and benevolent king."

"Loyalty makes it easy to be blinded by a devil who disguises himself a saint. Your king is not the man you think he is."

"Lies!" Vale shouted through gritted teeth.

"I saw you in Elysia, looking at the posts. You were looking for the missing children."

Vale's eyes narrowed. "How do you know of that?"

Caelan smirked. "Every village has them. You were investigating, weren't you?"

"What's your point?"

"How did you get involved in all this again? Did you volunteer to lead a team of Seekers?"

"No. The king sent for me."

"The king sent for you, a man known most famously as the Disgraced Knight, to lead one of the most important quests in Parisia's history. Doesn't that seem strange to you?"

"He needed someone who he could trust to carry this task to completion."

"Open your eyes, rooki; he needed you out of Parisia. He didn't want you investigating."

"No, that's not it."

"Did you tell him? You must have, right? Captain of the honor brigade, you told him. What did he say?" Caelan pressed.

"That his royal guard would take care of it, but that he needed me here . . . " Vale's words began to slow as his mind raced. *Could he really have missed it? Was Caelan right? No. It couldn't be. The rogue was trying to confuse him.*

"King Alistar is not what you think. He may play the role of beloved king, but he is a monster."

"It's not possible. You don't know him like I do . . . " Vale felt his conviction waning.

"He what? What did he do to earn such blind devotion from you?"

Vale's sword nearly fell from his hand. "My father sold me to a band of mercenaries when I was a boy. I was forced to fight—trained and used as a weapon, passed around from group to group to kill on their behalf. King Alistar found me; he rescued me."

"Rescued you? He took you from one battlefield and placed you in another. He didn't rescue you; he just bought you, like everyone else," Caelan accused.

"No! He . . . gave me a home. He gave me land. He set me free. He didn't force me into his charge. He provided for me, said I . . . I . . . had been wronged by this world, and that, while he couldn't change the past, he could help make it right! That's the kind of man he is. He helps people, even when it comes at great personal expense."

Caelan laughed. "You are dim, aren't you?"

Vale roared and charged. The two danced, blades collided as Vale attacked and Caelan dodged, wildly moving in and out of Vale's reach. Caelan countered with a series of attacks of his own, which Vale deflected and dodged with crisp, skillful movements.

Their blades clashed and clanged together before the two pushed off each other, creating space between them as they stared each other down, looking for openings to exploit.

"You don't see it, do you?" Caelan asked with a smirk.

Vale growled. "Enough talking; you will not see another sunrise."

Caelan shrugged. "Maybe so, but it won't change the fact that he didn't rescue you. He just saw an opportunity to take advantage of your skills."

"You're wrong!" Vale shouted. "He never forced me into this. He gave me a choice—a choice I never would have had without him!"

Caelan shook his head. "What choice did you have?"

Vale's blade shook. "King Alistar came to me, said he could use someone with my skill to fight for him. He asked me to join a special unit, the Phoenix Legion, to help ensure what happened to me wouldn't happen to anyone else ever again. I chose to fight so that I could prevent others from being forced to fight the way I was."

Caelan laughed again. "He manipulated you. He offered you all this stuff to make it look like you had a choice, and then he used the one thing he knew you wouldn't be able to say no to."

There was another clash of blades as Vale attacked and Caelan defended. Despite all their fighting, it was Caelan's words that landed the only blows.

"How much shame will you allow him to cast on you? Hmm. You helped slaughter an entire village of innocent, defenseless people—good, kind people who just wanted to enjoy their little patch of the world. You helped cut them down like animals. Where was your honor then? Where was right and wrong?"

"That is not why . . . and that is not what—" Vale protested.

"It's no wonder you were forced out, branded unfit. Your legacy is shame, Disgraced Knight." Caelan jabbed again.

The sword in Vale's hand might as well have been an anvil. Still, he held it. He clutched it with all his might, holding on by sheer force of will.

"Is that why you took on this quest? To restore your honor? You think retrieving a stone can wash the blood of innocents off your hands?"

Vale's arm dropped to his side. "I did not kill those villagers . . ." His words were barely more than a whisper. His breathing was heavy, his eyes fighting back tears that threatened to track down his face at any moment.

"What?" For the first time in their fight, Caelan was stunned.

"I have killed more people than I can count. Most of them, deserving. None of them were defenseless."

Caelan scowled. "No, you can't rewrite history. You forget I was there. I've seen your memories. I know what you did. I told you I would kill you for what you did to my home."

"You saw my memories; tell me, did you actually see me kill a single villager?"

"I watched a helpless family rush inside their home just trying to survive. I watched you and another knight enter. I saw you exit with blood on your sword."

"Did you see the other knight leave?" Vale asked.

Caelan thought for a moment, picturing the scene in his mind. "No."

Vale nodded. "I didn't kill that family. When I went inside, the other knight already had. I killed him. That is my crime. That is my shame. I killed my own men."

Just saying the words seemed to break him. The sword fell from his hand, and his head hung to the ground. "I killed my own men," he repeated.

Caelan's eyes widened. "What are you talking about? I saw you chasing people."

Vale's body started to tremble. "That night haunts my dreams. I can see it all like it is happening around me right now. The king had ordered us to meet with your village leaders, negotiate terms for them to build an outpost. In exchange, they'd become a part of Parisia, and the magic that blessed our kingdom was to be given to their lands as well. As a symbol of our good will, the king had given my commander an ornate dagger made with a golden hilt and the largest ruby I'd ever seen embedded in the pommel. It was a beautiful, kingly blade." Vale covered his face with his hand.

"That doesn't make any sense," Caelan started.

"The elders were receptive and eager to enjoy the wealth and riches of our lands. The deal was struck without incident.

Our instructions were, before we left, to give the dagger to the elder as a parting gift. My commander drew the dagger and started to offer it to your elder. Before the elder could take it, something happened. Rather than give the blade to the elder, he used it to slit the elder's throat . . . and then he laughed. I saw it happen, but I couldn't believe it. My body froze in shock. I'd known the commander for years, fought side by side with him. He was not an aggressive man. He was not—" Vale's words caught in his throat.

"I stood there in horror, in stunned disbelief, as one by one they all lost their minds. Trained, disciplined soldiers lost all sense of themselves and began attacking the villagers. These were good soldiers with families and lives. Something happened—something I cannot explain. Each and every one of them turned. I tried to reason with them; I tried everything I could to stop them. The more they killed, the more they started to enjoy it. I pleaded with my commander to put a stop to it. He ordered me to burn the village to the ground. I refused. One by one, I tried to stop them. One by one, they attacked me. One by one, I killed them. My own men. My friends. I killed them until their blood stained my blade and ran down my arms to my elbows. I killed them. No matter how hard I tried, I could not save the village. And the carnage didn't stop there."

"Gods below." Caelan felt the strength leave his legs. He sank to the ground, unable to stand under the weight of this revelation.

"Once everyone was dead, the legion got on their mounts and started riding through the countryside, slaughtering anyone they came across. Towns, villages, hunters, farmers, monsters, a coven of witches. It didn't matter. They were consumed with a lust for blood that would not be sated. The Phoenix Legion had become mindless killers. It was my responsibility to stop them, so I did. I tracked them. They were in groups at first, but as days passed, they scattered. I hunted them and killed them until I alone remained."

"A man who killed his entire legion. That is why they call you the Disgraced Knight. The shameful traitor who turned on his own brothers, killing the very men who trusted him most," Dante said calmly.

Vale's eyes closed and he nodded.

"But you did not turn on them. You honored who they were by ending their madness," Dante offered. "You saved them from living as monsters."

Vale shrugged, "Some perhaps. It took months to hunt them all down. By the time I got to the last few, they had returned to Parisia. They had no memory of what they had done. They acted as if I were crazy, but I couldn't let it go. It was my responsibility to bring their victims justice, and now I am the Disgraced Knight. Caelan is right. Me . . . talking of honor? It is hypocrisy."

Caelan sat in stunned silence.

"Perhaps not. Tell me, when your commander turned, did his eyes go red?" Dante asked.

Vale thought for a moment and nodded.

"And the others?"

Vale nodded again.

"Did the hilt of the dagger seem to emit a red smoke?"

A third nod.

Dante sighed. "Caelan may be right, but not in the way you think. Can you picture the dagger in your mind?"

Vale closed his eyes. Dante pulled a vial from his coat, poured a small amount onto his fingers, and rubbed the liquid onto Vale's forehead. He swung his hand as if pulling something from Vale's mind. The space between Caelan and Vale lit up, and floating in the air was the magical projection of a knife, elegant and beautiful, finely crafted with a golden hilt and ruby gemstone. Caelan recognized the blade immediately, his jaw agape.

"That's it." Vale walked over to the projection. It looked so real, so lifelike, Vale thought he could touch it.

"That," Dante said, "is the Dagger of Arran Groaul."

Caelan slid his blade in its sheath. "That is not possible."

"Who is Arran Groaul?" Vale asked.

"An ancient kanji king, called the god of rage. That dagger causes anyone near it to go into a prolonged berserk state. Even the most peaceful person can be turned into a bloodthirsty monster if they are in the presence of that dagger when it is drawn."

"Why wasn't I affected?" Vale asked.

Dante exhaled. "There were stories of a few who were able to resist the magic of the blade, but their race died off long ago. That is not what should trouble you."

Vale slowly retrieved his blade and put it away. "What is it then?"

Dante waved his hand, and the image of the knife fizzled into vapor and vanished.

"King Alistar had this in the royal armory."

Vale's brow furrowed. "What are you saying?"

Dante stared into the distance as if talking to the sky itself. "I am saying the king knows full well what that dagger does."

Vale felt as if a wild boar had landed on his back. His legs buckled and nearly collapsed. His mind tried to push the thought away, but it kept smashing into his head like a battering ram. That night was one of the worst amongst a series of horrid memories that haunted him.

Vale's life was built on violence. He was forced to pick up a sword before he reached the age of eight. Blood and carnage, chaos and fear walked with him all of his days. Through it, he had learned of the special bond that is forged only by fighting side by side, of the uncanny kinship that develops between soldiers. It was a bond of brotherhood that could run deeper than blood. For most of his life, the men who fought beside him were the only family he had.

Vale had been forced to hunt and kill every member of his family because of that one fateful night. The guilt had crippled him. It was the source of his shame and ridicule for years. This revelation threatened to break everything he was.

The king had given him a purpose, forged his skills into something meaningful. Vale believed in the glory of Parisia, and he had devoted his life to the protection of its people. Never once had he doubted his purpose—never once questioned his calling. Not even after his family was murdered and he was cursed by witches. The same witches . . . His mind spiraled.

Dante rubbed his chin. "We cannot rule out the possibility

that the reason King Alistar ordered you to kill Caelan is to cover up what happened in Oakwood."

Vale's mind raced at the thought. "Wait. Let's be very clear here," he managed to get out.

Dante nodded. "What happened to Caelan's home, to those villagers, was not an accident. It was the king's purpose in sending you there."

Chapter 18
Visions

Purple flame battered against the entrance to the cave. Azalea looked back, realizing that the others had been cut off. She slid to a stop and stared at the wall of purple light bursting endlessly against the entrance. Azalea's heart sank; Vale, Dante, Caelan, and Rivik hadn't made it. Perhaps the flame had consumed them. *No. That couldn't be. They would find a way,* she assured herself. *Standing here wouldn't do them any good anyway.*

"We should get moving," Sera said, stepping further into the dark abyss of the cave.

Once they had rounded the first few corners, the dim light of the entrance was gone, leaving them in perfect darkness. Even in her wolf form, she could not see. The Rag'amorians took the lead. They held rocks in their hands and tapped them along the walls as they moved forward, allowing those following to navigate by sound. It was slow going. Hours passed, and Azalea wasn't even sure how far they had made it into the tunnels.

The prolonged darkness began taking a toll on her senses. With nothing to serve as a guide, she wasn't sure, but it felt like the tunnel was moving downward, deeper into the earth. Azalea couldn't help but wonder if that was going to make getting out even harder, but it wasn't as if they had an abundance of options. What else could they do? Go back and fight the death dragon?

"I can't believe we fought a death dragon," Celeste muttered to herself. "The Royal Library doesn't even have records of one. When I get home, I will add an entry to the Dragon Tomes and be the first person from Parisia to encounter a death dragon. My name will live on forever," her tone lifted to a gleeful pitch.

"I can see it now—children begging their parents for a bedtime story of the legendary Celeste. The hero who saw a death dragon, lost the fight, and then wrote about it in a book. Only a goraum royal would be excited about getting their owa kicked and running away."

Celeste groaned. "I wasn't talking to you."

"No. You were talking to yourself, you spoiled naiflo—"

"Alright, let's give it a rest—at least until we are out of these tunnels," Sera interrupted.

Azalea's legs began to burn as her muscles shook and threatened to give way. They had to be walking downward. Her calves hurt too much for any other explanation. The weight of the dragon knight laying limply on her back was starting to wear on her. Why was he so heavy? She would need to rest soon.

The clumsy warriors in the lead were getting all scraped up trying to navigate in the dark. She could smell their blood on the air. At least in her wolf form, her head was low enough to not have to worry about rocks hanging from the ceiling.

Then she noticed it—a scent on the air followed by a soft, almost rhythmic, echoing sound. They were close to something. They rounded a corner and the darkness fled.

Azalea blinked as the darkness gave way to a fantastic and beautiful light. The tunnel opened into a large cavern. They were still underground, but the large open chasm felt like stepping into an oasis. In the middle of the room was a large pool of water. The water seemed to glow, lighting the entire cavern with radiant blue light. The stone ceiling was covered in specks like glowing flakes of gold.

There were little fields of grass and trees adorned with enticing fruits. *How could such a place exist?* The air was cool but fresh, not like the stagnant air of the tunnels. *Were those birds singing?* Azalea's jaw hung open as she looked around the room. The Rag'amorians were far less stunned and began laughing and rushing around, exploring the arcane cavern. They gathered fruit from the trees and began eating it, tossing a variety of fruits back and forth as they jested and marveled.

Azalea, still in her dire wolf form, slid Spiro from her back onto a patch of grass before shaking her body and returning to her human self. She sighed and made her way to the lake in the center of the room. She pooled the water into her hands and drank it. It was cold. Not cool, but full-on cold, as if chilled with unseen ice. It was refreshing and almost sweet, like a honeyed wine, but . . . water.

As the others ate and drank, they were lost in the hypnosis of the mystical cave. Sera looked around. She'd been through this canyon before, explored some of the tunnels, but she had never seen this place. Everything here seemed to glow with its own bioluminescence. Flowers of every color grew up the walls and around the waters, lighting the room like decorative torches. Just being in the room made her whole body feel rejuvenated.

Around one of the rock outcroppings, Sera saw a set of flowers in the shape of bells striped with bright colors. She recognized them as Faiinder, a magical flower. It was beautiful and enchanting to see, but everyone in Rag'amor knew to stay away from them. Sera blinked as she watched Azalea walk over to the flowers. *What was she doing? Surely she wouldn't . . .* Sera's eyes widened as she remembered that Azalea was not from Rag'amor and didn't know what the Faiinder did. She reached her hand out and opened her mouth to shout a warning, but no sound came out. Her brain wouldn't project the words. She just watched silently as Azalea leaned down and sniffed the flower.

A glowing mist sprayed into Azalea's nose, and she shot back, her red hair flailing, and she sniffed again and again.

"Azalea, get away from that!" Sera finally managed to get out.

Azalea turned to hear the warning, but the room was already starting to spin. Colors swirled like ribbons dancing and streaking across the landscape before her. Suddenly the waters rose and formed into dancing images so lifelike and real. She could see what was happening as if the water was acting out a story before her. A woman was giving birth to a child.

Shadows of the Dark Realm

The crying baby was whisked away by a group of people in hooded cloaks. That was strange, yet those cloaks looked familiar.

The water shifted, following the group of cloaked figures carrying the baby up a hill to a rocky outcropping. On the ground was painted a symbol inside a circle. A collection of flames was placed evenly around the circle, and the design glowed a bright red-orange, as if it were made of fire.

"What is this?" Azalea asked, her mind feeling like a barrel of apples being rolled down a steep hill.

"It's a memory pool," Sera answered. "The waters are enchanted to show events from a person's life."

Azalea moved closer to the pool, staring at it. "Whose memory is this?"

Sera turned. "You were the first to drink from the pool; the magic is linked to you."

The water shifted, showing a circle of men and women in cloaks, their waists bound together, chanting as they held hands. The baby was placed in the middle of the group. A glow began to surround the circle, and an otherworldly beam of energy appeared to drift from each of the cloaked figures to the baby. One by one, the people in cloaks dropped to their knees and then evaporated into a mist that flowed with the beam and was absorbed by the baby. When the last figure was gone, someone outside the circle came over, scooped the baby up, and returned her to her mother.

"Well, that's some messed up gwar," Azalea said, more to herself than anyone else.

"I . . . I know that symbol," Celeste said. "I've seen it in the records of Parisia's history." She walked over to the water and reached out, touching the circular symbol glowing on the rocks in the background. The surface of the water went flat. She gasped and stepped back. The water rose again, forming a new image, this one unmistakable. It was the glowering face of her father. Celeste gulped and stepped further back.

"Wait, who's this ralker?" Azalea asked. "This isn't my memory. I'd remember a fancy noble, especially one with such a punchable face."

Sera looked at the image and then Celeste. "The water must have reacted to contact. I think this is one of her memories now."

Azalea cocked her head. "You're seeing this too? What a relief; I thought it was just me. Last time my head felt like this was when I got magically flung into Vale's memories. That was some weird gwar."

Sera shook her head. "No, it's what we are all seeing."

Azalea smiled. "So, what's this thing then?" she asked, pointing.

Sera looked and saw nothing. "Umm . . . Azalea, there's nothing there."

"No, the weird uni-goat thing," Azalea clarified. "Right here." Azalea turned and pointed to the creature she saw standing beside her—a creature that was not visible to anyone else.

It was an odd-looking beast with the head of goat but butterflies where its ears should be and a single horn swirling up in the center of its head. It had a fin like a shark on its back, eagle legs, and a long serpent-like tail with an alligator head at the end of it.

Sera shook her head.

"Seven bells from seven hells," Azalea muttered.

Celeste was still backing away from the pool of water, stumbling as she caught herself on the rocking ground.

"No, no. I won't go back!" she shouted at the water. "I'm never going back to that prison! You . . . can't . . . what . . . is happening?" Celeste's words slowed.

Sera forced herself to sit quickly. "It's the water. It puts you into a deep . . . sleep," she said before her eyes closed, and she slumped to the ground.

Azalea looked around to see all her companions sprawled out, most of them slumped in awkward positions.

"Great, everyone take a nice nap; get some rest in while I just stand here trippin' spirits again." Azalea sighed. "Well, at least I can talk to you," she said to the bizarre single-horned goat creature.

The creature turned and looked at her but said nothing, did nothing. Azalea groaned dramatically. "Well, aren't you just barrels of fun."

Shadows of the Dark Realm

Disregarding the wordless creature, Azalea walked down to the pool and watched the scene unfold. She ignored the floating caterpillars that burst into colorful confetti all around her. That was obviously the drug-flower talking. The others had seen what was in the water—that much at least had to be real. She tried to focus her mind and push aside all the wild, impossible things happening around her. In a magical cave it was difficult to distinguish what was real from what wasn't.

The water showed her a young girl sneaking out of the doors of some rich palace and running out to the pristine grass of a courtyard, only to be swept up over a man's shoulder and carried back inside, kicking and screaming. It showed her being tossed into a too-large, overly decorated room and then the doors were shut and locked. It was unclear from the water story how much time passed. The girl got older, people came and tended to her and brought her fancy meals, but she never left the room.

Tutors came and taught her classes. Whenever she did leave, she was escorted by several guards to a kitchen, library, or some other posh-looking room, and then escorted back. The girl was never outside or with other children, just sitting in her room, looking out her window with a lovely view of a world she never got to be a part of.

"Well, this is depressing; can we watch something else?" Azalea said, standing up and turning from the waters.

She ducked suddenly as a large bird appeared across from her, opened its mouth, and shot a squirrel at her head. She turned around to see another bird on the other side do the same. Squirrels flew all around her, and she rushed across the open cave, covering her head as she heard and felt the whooshing as they flew past. She dove to the ground, the cold stone on her skin making her mind feel suddenly clearer. The birds and the projectile squirrels disappeared.

"Ralking hallucinations. Why does this keep happening to me?"

"Yer a vessel, lassie. That makes ye highly sensitive to magic," said a mystical and familiar voice.

Azalea spun around to see on her other side a giant, three-headed boar with its combined twelve eyes and twenty-one husks.

"You again?" she growled.

"And ye did go snorting a hallucinogenic flower, didn't ye?" the right head added.

"How was I supposed to know? It's not like it was labeled, was it? You daft swine!" Azalea snapped.

The boar heads all laughed.

"Ye did notice that yer the only one who tried sniffin' a glowing flower inside a magical cave?" the left head answered.

Azalea extended her hand and flames engulfed it. "Keep talking; I've been craving roast pork all day."

The boar backed up and shook all three heads at once. "Beggin' yer pardon luv, we was only teasing a bit. Ye wouldn't begrudge us a wee laugh, would ye? Anyway, that's not the purpose of our being here."

"Why are you here?" Azalea let the flames go out.

"Because of dat thing, dearie." The center boar head nodded at the creature behind her.

"You can see uni-goat?" she asked.

The boar heads exchanged a glance. "That is called a Grimachopa. A veil beast—they look like a mix of different things because they exist between realms. Whenever one shows up, it means there is a coming danger that threatens to rip the veil between realms that would certainly end in a catastrophic loss of life."

Azalea felt her heart start to race. "If this creature is so doomy and gloomy, why am I the only one who can see it?"

"Because, dearie, ye would be the one to cause it," the center boar sighed.

"Cause it? I'm trying to prevent it."

"We aren't talking about the Dark Realm, dearie."

"What are you talking about, then?"

"The Spirit Realm. Just as the absence of the Darkstone threatens one veil, so your presence here threatens the veil to the other."

"I'm so glad you are telling me all this while I'm trippin' on magic flower pollen." Azalea closed her eyes and covered her face in her hands.

"We came here to warn ye. There is a rage that burns inside ye. It gives ye power. It also makes ye dangerous. If ye can't get a handle on it, that rage will result in the destruction of this world," the center boar-head answered.

"Ralk off! Who are you to tell me that? How would you know?"

"It would be strange if we didn't, dearie; we are Poarog, god of prophesies and dreams." The boar oinked loudly in amusement.

"A god pig? Gods below, why wouldn't that have been my first guess? And why should I trust you? This could just be part of my hallucination," she countered.

"Aye, we are not surprised ye'd think that. But be warned lassie; yer hate fer the Royals may bring about far more destruction then ye intend," the right boar head warned.

"Thanks. Got anything helpful for me? Or just random warnings and judgments?"

"When the threat is over, find the witches that cursed your friend. Help him lift it. This may change the turning of the wheel of fate," Poarog said, before vanishing into thin air.

Azalea's mind started to clear. She sat and stared at the flat pool of water for some time, trying to sort through what had happened. Eventually, the others started to stir. She was jealous. They got rest. She got a headache. How was that fair?

"You sure they came this way?" a voice echoed down the halls.

"Course, I'm sure. Look, should be just up ahead," a second voice answered.

"Looks like they split up—what a pain. Now it'll take us twice as long to finish 'em off," the first voice said.

"Yeah, we better charge extra for the inconvenience."

Several voices laughed.

"Alright, shut it, we are getting close. Don't want them hearing us coming." Both voices were male and had a sort of sinister tone to them.

"Don't worry, they haven't moved in hours. Bet we find 'em

down there sleeping. Easy pickings." Quiet snickering echoed around as footsteps approached.

Azalea stood. The others were still not functional enough to defend themselves. She could wake them, but all that would do is let their pursuers know and give them time to prepare. Her mind rushed as golden sparks danced in her vision. *Stupid flower.* That was it—she'd never sniff flowers again. *Ralk that.* She rushed over and shook Sera, holding a finger to her mouth as the warrior woman grumbled. Azalea pointed to the entrance. Sera regained her senses surprisingly fast. After a groggy moment, she nodded and got up, quietly waking the others.

Azalea shook Celeste next, repeating the warning for silence as the footsteps grew close. Even working together, they wouldn't be able to wake everyone in time or clear the room. Azalea felt her heartbeat quicken in her chest. Without the gloomy Black Swordsman or the Blue Alchemist to step in, it was up to her. She had no experience playing defender. She knew how to cause trouble; she'd mastered that craft years ago, but diverting trouble was a skill she had never tested.

Azalea rushed toward the entrance of the cave to cut off their pursuers. The tight walls of the tunnel would force them to pack in close and reduce their ability to dodge. She peered around the corner into the dark tunnel. They were already around the final turn. She could see their torches approaching as well as the shadowed silhouettes cast by the half dozen flames. An idea formed in her mind. This was going to be fun.

Azalea channeled her magic, waiting to give them as little time to react as possible. She lifted both hands and uttered the magic word, sending two crashing waves of flame through the tunnel toward the group of mysterious pursuers. Here's hoping she didn't take something out of context.

Screams erupted from the tunnel as several of the men were engulfed in her flame. Azalea looked over. At least the screams woke everyone up. The Rag'amorians rose and readied themselves. Sera moved toward the entrance with Celeste and Spiro. Azalea returned her attention to the tunnel. A glowing red sphere engulfed the group as the lines parted, and a man with pure black hair and orange eyes stepped forward.

"That's adorable. You thought those little flames would stop us?" His voice was different, not one of the two who had spoken before. "You are not the first team to have a mage, you know." He laughed and a wave of red energy flew towards her. It caught Azalea in the chest and knocked her back against the wall of the tunnel. Her ears rang as pain surged through her.

Sera rushed into the tunnel. She pulled a knife from her boot and hurled it at the approaching group. The blade thumped into the red sphere that surrounded the men and bounced away, clanging against the stone walls of the cave. Sera drew the twin blades from behind her back.

"No!" Azalea groaned. "You can't get through that barrier."

"Well, I'm not about to stand around and do nothing," Sera replied.

"Is there another way out of the cave?" Azalea asked.

Sera nodded.

"I'll slow them down; get everyone going."

Sera shook her head. "Rag'amorians don't run from a fight," she replied through gritted teeth.

"Both of you need to get out of here now. I will deal with these interlopers," Spiro said, moving in front of the two women.

"Oh good, captain got us into this mess in the first place and wants to play hero now?"

"That's not a real rank," Spiro retorted.

Azalea rolled her eyes. "Rooki, you almost got us killed. What would make you want to attack a dragon?"

"This is hardly the time for that discussion," Sera interrupted.

Spiro smirked, "I am a dragon knight. My sworn duty is to slay dragons. Was I supposed to forsake that oath because it told us a riddle?"

He stepped toward the approaching wave of mystery attackers. "If you blame me for what happened, let this be my righting of that wrong. I will deal with them. You go. Find a way out. I will catch up when I'm done here."

Azalea and Sera exchanged a glance.

"I don't mind leaving him to die," Sera said.

"Ohh . . . I like you," Azalea laughed.

They rushed back into the cavern. Celeste and the other Rag'amorians followed as they exited the cavernous room through a passage on the far side. Azalea cast an illusion spell over the entrance to make it look like part of the rock. It wouldn't fool a mage for long, but it would certainly slow them down.

They ran through the tunnels as fast as they could. At least the passage was leading up this time. They ran until their legs trembled and their lungs burned. Azalea gashed her arms repeatedly on the sharp edges of rocks as they moved, emphasizing speed over caution. Blood dripped and the pain throbbed, but she pressed on. Behind them they could hear the sounds of battle—metal clanging followed by screams of pain. Whatever Spiro was doing, he was making them work for it.

Then hope fluttered to life as they turned to see the tunnel light up with a stream of natural light. They found an exit. Azalea closed her eyes as they rushed out of the tunnels into the bright valley, then covered her face with her arm to give her eyes time to adjust.

"Well, well, well, so nice of you to come running right into our little trap," a man's voice rang out.

Azalea blinked and forced herself to look around.

They were surrounded by a half circle of warriors with bows drawn at the ready. Behind them, swordsmen with tall shields moved in front of the tunnel entrance. On the ledges above, mages. Azalea could feel it in the air. Their magic was ready.

"Now, unless you enjoy having your insides brought outside, I would suggest you put your weapons down," the man warned.

Chapter 19

Pursued

"That does not make any sense. Why would the witches curse you?" Dante peered at the Black Swordsman from across the fire.

After the fight between Caelan and Vale, the group had traveled through the woods, making their way to the other side of the canyon in the hopes that the others would think to do the same. When it grew dark, they made camp in a clearing in the woods. Caelan's role in the bombings went unaddressed as the revelation of the king's behaviors moved to the forefront of their focus. Vale shared parts of his story, mostly providing context for the pieces that Dante and Caelan had seen when they were in his mind.

"Revenge. They blamed me for what happened," Vale answered.

"You had nothing to do with that."

"It matters not. The Phoenix Legion massacred their entire coven. I was the last survivor of the devils who slaughtered their sisters."

"Hold on, let me get this straight. Your unit was driven mad by the Dagger of Arran Groaul. They rampaged around the countryside, slaughtering towns and villages. You made it your mission to hunt down and kill your own brothers-in-arms, but before you could stop them, they went massacre-manic on a coven of witches without your knowledge or presence. Then, once you'd redeemed your legion, you hung up your sword and started a family only to have a few surviving witches show up, blame you for what the madmen did, kill your wife and daughter in front of you, and then curse you." Rivik sounded more and more confused as he verbally processed what Vale had explained.

"Yes."

"Gods below, why did you not track them down and kill them?" Rivik asked.

"At some point, the wheel of vengeance must be stopped. They were victims of my failure."

"Yeah, until they killed innocent people. That makes them villains," Rivik replied.

"This curse is what I deserve."

Caelan scoffed and stood up. He glared at Vale for a moment before turning and stomping off into the woods, out of sight.

Vale stared at the ground, idly prodding the fire that lit and warmed his face with a long stick.

"Tell me about this curse." Dante stared more intently.

Vale didn't respond for a moment. Caelan appeared behind Dante, leaning against a tree at the edge of the clearing, with his arms folded across his chest. Vale sighed.

"They wanted me to feel what they felt. To live after those they loved the most died. Anyone I get close to, care for, or demonstrate any affection toward, will die. It's not always immediate, but it will always come."

"Demonstrate?" Dante rubbed his chin. "I see. So, the curse cannot sense what is in your heart?"

Vale shook his head. "I don't think so. It seems to be activated by what I express. I learned that the hard way."

"What do you mean?" Dante pressed.

"I didn't take the curse seriously at first. I became close with my neighbors, only to come home one day to find them murdered by thieves. My wife's parents died next, followed by a couple of students I was training. That's when I realized it. If I ever demonstrate affection, friendship, compassion, or concern for someone else in any meaningful way, my curse activates and they die—terribly, and usually in front of me."

"That is awful. How do you keep going?" Rivik asked.

Vale shrugged. "I don't have a choice. If I give up, all those who died would have been for nothing."

The silence that followed was disturbed only by the soft hooting of an owl in a nearby tree.

"Is there a way to break the curse?" Rivik finally asked.

"It wouldn't be easy," Dante answered. "A perpetual curse that hangs over someone for an extended period of time drains a great deal of magical energy. The witches would not be able to maintain that for long. They would need a magical item. My guess would be a Stone of Rebia."

Vale and Rivik stared at Dante as if to encourage him to explain further.

"Rebia was the little sister to Zular, king of the gods. She led an uprising against her brother. Zular defeated her and as punishment, cursed her to be the torturer of wicked souls on Mount Desparia. It is said that the tears of those she torments fall to earth as magical stones called the Stones of Rebia. They are a powerful source of magic, and they are fueled by pain."

"Destroying this stone could end my curse?" Vale's eyes lifted from the burning wood for the first time. His voice rose with them; for the first time, a subtle gust of hope washed over him.

"If I am correct and that is what they are using, yes. If you could destroy the stone and kill the witches who cursed you, then the curse would be lifted," Dante answered.

Caelan shook his head and stormed out of view, disappearing again into the dark. Vale prodded the fire with a stick, causing embers of orange light to slowly wisp through the air like little stars in front of them.

"Do you know where they are?" Dante asked.

"After their coven was destroyed in Taggoron, they moved to Vargr. I am not certain if that is still where they reside; it's been some time since I tried to track them."

Vale stopped talking, his eyes scanning but his body

unmoving and rigid. Rivik looked down from his stargazing. He slowly, subtly moved his hand toward the shaft of his spear.

"What's going on?" Vale held a finger to his lips, and Dante stopped speaking.

Then he heard it—the soft snapping of a twig in the woods nearby. Dante was certain this was the first sound he'd heard, so why was Vale on edge? It was just Caelan, right?

As if by magic, the entire tree line around the clearing was suddenly filled with armed men. Judging by their matching uniforms and armor, they were either a well-organized, well-funded group of thugs or part of an army. Vale didn't move, holding his position like a statue as he glanced over at Rivik.

"Well, it's about time we found you. We've got you surrounded, so be good lads and surrender peacefully and we won't have to hurt you," one of the men said, stepping closer to Vale.

"Sir, weren't there supposed to be four of them?" another knight asked.

The man who'd stepped forward froze in place. His eyes went wide as a whistling sound pierced the air. The knight behind him cried out and fell to the ground, an arrow stuck in the nape of his neck. Another whistle was followed by another scream. Another knight fell. Two more before the man in front could draw his sword.

"The archer! Find him!" he yelled, pointing his sword at the tops of the trees.

The forest erupted into a flurry of noise and activity as soldiers chased and scrambled to find Caelan. Screams echoed out along with sounds of clanging and clashing.

"Over there!"

"He's above us."

"I see him."

The utter chaos of the shouting was almost amusing. The man who'd given them instructions, their apparent leader, turned his gaze toward the woods as if staring into the dark would somehow help. It was all the distraction Vale needed.

In one swift motion, he turned, drew his black blade, and sliced. The motion was so fast, he'd stood up and faced the

Shadows of the Dark Realm

soldier before the leader even realized what had happened. He coughed and blood ran from his neck, pouring out like a gentle crimson waterfall. He caught the dripping red fluid, holding his neck with his hands as if it could stop the flow. The damage was done. The leader of the knights dropped to his knees before toppling over in a heap.

Dante blinked and Rivik was gone. The spearman was twirling his green spear through the air, and one by one the men who had surrounded them fell. Vale held his ground, defending against attackers who rushed into the clearing. Rivik hooked his way around the tree line, cutting down anyone who stepped into view, rushing in a circle around them, slicing through soldiers like they were nothing more than straw targets for practice.

Dante stood up, drawing on his magical energy. He lifted his hand and a blue sphere appeared around Vale just as a burst of lightning shot from the woods. The lightning hit the sphere and dissipated. These weren't just soldiers; they had mages with them. *How irritating.* Dante sensed the energy build up and brought his hands together, making a blue wall of magic that spread to the tree line just as fire, lightning, stone, and bursts of plasma energy flew into it. *They had lots of mages.* That must have been how such a large group got so close without drawing attention. They were using sneak spells.

Dante held the wall in place as spell after spell crashed against it. He felt the power drain from his fingers as the attacking magic began to overpower his barrier. He grunted and formed another just in time to stop an array of arcane arrows. The mages were good, coordinated, and powerful, and from the speed of their casting, there were at least twenty of them.

Dante reached into his cloak and pulled out a vial. He waited until a stream of attacks hit his barrier magic, then let it dissolve. He hurled the vial into the woods in the direction the spells were coming from. Blue acid rained down from where the vial broke against tree limbs. A few scattered screams rang out. The next wave of magical attacks was slowed, but that was it. Slowed was exactly what he needed. His vial had given him just enough time to prepare his next barrier.

This time, the blue wall was sparkling with silver embers.

The spells collided into his barrier in perfect synchronization, just as he'd expected. When each spell collided with the wall, instead of being absorbed or deflected, they were reflected directly back at the caster. Only a mage of superior talent could counter his own spell before it came slamming into him. These mages were good, but they were not that good. Dozens of screams filled the air as the woods lit up with human torches. Men in cloaks rushed around screaming before falling to the ground, silent and still.

Dante turned to see at least a dozen bodies surrounding Vale. The clearing was littered with even more. Vale and Rivik stood back-to-back, facing another wave of knights who had to climb over the mound of their dead comrades.

"Enough of this!" a voice shouted from overhead.

Dante looked up to see a man in a dark hood floating above the clearing. He turned to lift his hands but found them bound together with a cord of orange light. He cursed and tried to walk, only to find his legs bound together by a similar cord. Before he could move again, a beam of light smashed into his body and sent him flying back into a tree.

Pain rushed up his body as his eyes flashed. He was stunned. His body wouldn't move. He could still see, though. Vale and Rivik fought hard, their weapons flying like blurs through the air, cutting down the men who approached them. Dante was impressed. Rivik was holding his own, perhaps even equal in skill to Vale. The two of them together had wiped out a whole squad of soldiers.

The flying man fired off a burst of orange energy. It was shaped almost like an arrow as it crashed toward Vale's back. Rivik pushed Vale away, putting himself between the swordsman and the energy arrow. The orange streak seemed to pierce right through him, and then a wave of orange webbing danced over his skin, making his body shake and then crumple to the ground.

Vale gritted his teeth and spun around just as another arrow flew toward him. He twisted his blade, using it like a shield and deflecting the blast. A soldier charged, trying to grab him from behind. Vale reversed his grip and, without looking, stabbed the blade back into the approaching man's chest, all with his eyes fixed on the flying man above them.

The flying man slowly descended to the ground just across from Vale. He clapped slowly.

"Impressive. I would expect nothing less from the century slayer," the man said.

Dante tugged against his magic restraints, trying to get enough movement to use one of his spells. The binding was tight, and the magic was strong. *Why did he call Vale 'century slayer'?* That was the second time Dante had heard Vale referred to as such.

Vale aimed his blade at the hooded man. "What do you want?"

The man chuckled. Even his laugh sounded superior. "You are a Seeker of the Darkstone. King Gladio of Taggoron wishes to speak with you."

"About what?"

The man shrugged. "I presume he wishes to make you an offer."

"And you thought attacking us in the middle of the night would put us in a receptive mood?" Vale countered.

The man laughed. "Our instructions were clear. If you were not interested in speaking, we were to stop you by any means necessary. I had hoped you would come along quietly. But, alas, I expected too much from the Parisia's loyal mutt."

Dante closed his eyes, channeling energy into his wrists. He pushed the energy out as he tried to pull his arms free. The cord around his wrists finally snapped. Dante grinned and fired a blast of cyclical elemental magic at the hooded man. The magic shifted in flight from lightning to fire to ice to rock and back, each element swirling together.

Without even turning his head the man in the hood extended one hand and caught Dante's spell. He held the elemental magic in his hand, examining it as if amused by it.

"Impressive. There are only a few alive who could combine this magic in a single cast." He turned just enough to see Dante.

"Shame that I will have to—"

A whistle cut through the darkness. The man in the hood

twisted, but it was too late. An arrow pierced his hood, and a line of blood shot from it. He winced, and his hold on Dante's spell drained. The ball of elemental magic the hooded man had been holding at bay plowed into his chest and sent him flying back. He landed on the ground with a thud.

Dante tried to remove the binding on his legs. The magic should have come undone when the man collapsed, but it was still strong. More soldiers shouted in the woods, and Dante could hear them rushing after someone, moving away from the camp. Vale rushed over to Dante to help with his binding. He set his sword down and inspected the orange cord.

Dante looked at him. "What is a century slayer?"

Before Vale could answer, a voice came from behind him.

"He is. Vale, the Black Swordsman. The Captain of Carnage. The Disgraced Knight. The century slayer. Your friend has earned many titles in his life. Though that one is my personal favorite. Do you want to tell him the story or shall I?"

Dante looked past Vale to see the hooded man standing up and dusting himself off, as if he'd merely tripped. He shouldn't even be alive, much less capable of standing after taking that blast.

Vale gritted his teeth and picked up his sword.

"Ah–ah–ah." Orange ropes swung around Vale's arms, legs, chest, and neck, pulling him back and binding him to a large tree at the edge of a clearing.

"I guess I will then. Your friend here was hunting down some of his soldiers—something about a madness of sorts. Along the way, he came to a village. The village had exclusive access to a mine with a very rare metal called Nightstone. I'm sure you've heard of it. It's known for its strength, durability, and black coloring."

"This story got a point?" Dante asked.

The hooded man chuckled. "Brief version, very well. A group of bandits wanted this precious stone, so they kidnapped the village elder's daughter and took her away to their hideout outside of town. They were going to ransom her when the village elder found Vale and pleaded with him for help. Without a word, your friend tracked down the bandits and slaughtered them all, returning the girl to her parents the next morning. The elder was so grateful, he had the blacksmith forge Vale a sword made of pure Nightstone. A sword fit for a king."

"What does that have to do with his name?" Dante had almost gotten his hand into his cloak to grab one of his vials, but he had to move slow, keep the man focused on something else so he wouldn't notice.

"There were one hundred bandits in all. One swordsman fought his way through all of them. It took six hours of endless fighting, but by the time he was done, all one hundred bandits were dead. All to save a little girl he'd never met and a town he'd never been to. I wonder, what strange sort of man risks his life like that?"

Dante grasped the vial and took a breath. He moved quickly, tossing the bottle at the hooded man's face. The man waved his hand, and a gust of wind sent it crashing into a tree on the other side of the clearing. The tree trunk fizzled, and a moment later the tree was gone.

"A worthy effort, Blue Alchemist. But you are out of your depth here," the man said.

Vale pulled and tugged against his binding but made no progress.

"I tire of this; take them."

Dante saw a man hit Vale in the back of the head with the pommel of his sword. The Black Swordsman stopped moving. Dante turned, grasping for one last chance, one last move to free themselves of this. And his head seared with pain. His vision flashed bright, and the world around him faded into nothing.

Chapter 20

The Rite of Amends

Caelan dropped from the tree branch he'd been perched on. They were at a disadvantage in the woods. His adoptive father in Oakwood was a woodsman who had taught him how to move, stalk prey, and disappear in any forest. After his adopted father's death at the hands of the Phoenix Legion, his childhood living as an orphan in a foreign kingdom had refined his skills of evasion even further. His pursuers had been frustratingly persistent but still had nothing to show for it. Eventually, the fools bumbling around in the dark like ogres at a dance party gave up and started back to the clearing where Vale and the others were.

"They went through all that only to give up now? Three out of four isn't bad, right? Is that a compliment? Or an insult? Feels like an insult," Caelan muttered to himself.

He notched an arrow in his bow. Out of the corner of his eye, he spotted a solitary soldier wandering away from the others. Caelan aimed his bow and released. The man fell to ground, dead before he landed.

"That makes me feel better."

The main force was already moving out. A few stragglers were still lazily searching the woods in hopes of uncovering his hiding spot. One by one, even they gave up. *Laziness was becoming a real epidemic*, he thought. Caelan heard a rustling behind him. He froze and pressed his back into a thick tree, hiding himself behind it just as two more soldiers came crashing by. He took a breath and readied his blades. If they got close, he'd cut them down before they had a chance to signal anyone.

"It was only a matter of time with Lord Drako with us," one of the men said.

"If he's so great, why did he let so many of us die before subduing them?" the other asked.

"I'll let you ask him," the first replied. That ended their discussion.

Caelan stepped out from behind the tree when the men were out of sight. *The others had been captured? That meant it would be up to him to save everyone. Typical.* He moved quietly behind the two talkative soldiers to see if they'd reveal anything else.

"We better hurry, or we will have to walk all the way back to Maylor," the man said. *Maylor?* Caelan cringed as a wave of discomfort rolled through his shoulders. He was walking so close he was practically in line with the two men, yet somehow they still hadn't noticed him. It was sad, really.

"Maylor? Seriously?" Caelan sighed dramatically. "Why couldn't you be from somewhere else?"

The two men, suddenly very aware of Caelan's presence, froze and exchanged a glance. It was the last thing either of them would ever do, as Caelan sliced their throats simultaneously.

"I ralkin' hate Maylor." He cut off a piece of yellow fabric from one of the dead men's uniforms.

Quickly, he stripped the other one. He felt dirty wearing the clothes of a common soldier. *Gross.* He didn't have much choice. His bow and armor were a bit too distinctive to pass as a common soldier. Still, he felt naked without them. His boot and belt knives would have to do. He attached his daggers to the side of his hip and put on the dead man's sword. He gathered his armor and bow and wrapped them tightly into a bundle to disguise its contents as best he could. He used the yellow fabric to make a crude strap so he could wear the bundle over his shoulders like a pack.

"Caelan, what the actual ralk are you doing?" he muttered, putting on the dead man's armor and adjusting it. "This is a really goraum idea. So, of course, here I am doing it. Ralking Maylor."

Shaking off his disgust, Caelan rushed back to the clearing where his companions had been taken. A man in an orange hooded cloak held an arm out, and an orange-hued gate glowed in the middle of the clearing. In the light of the magical gate, he could see the barracks in Maylor. A few other soldiers stepped in and disappeared from the clearing.

"Sure, let's just walk into the light. What could go wrong?" he muttered again to himself before entering the clearing.

The hooded man turned to look at him. *There's no way he could have heard that, right?* Caelan kept his head down and walked into the glowing gate.

As he passed through, he felt almost weightless, and tingly, as if little waves of electricity were passing over his skin. His body was being lifted and pushed forward by a strong gust of wind, and a moment later he was standing in a yard full of soldiers. He knew where he was; he could smell it in the air.

He tried to move like a soldier to avoid suspicion, but it didn't matter. The chaos in the courtyard was all the distraction he needed. He made quick mental notes of the area, marking in his mind places to hide if needed. In addition to the large number of dead, Vale, Rivik, and Dante had managed to wound many others. Though that seems to have been more Dante's work. Mages and knights scampered around frantically helping wounded comrades away from the teleportation zone.

He searched frantically, finally catching a glimpse of Vale's black cape as a group of soldiers dragged the bodies of three men into the recesses of their keep. The glowing gate suddenly fizzled closed, and the man in the orange hooded cloak appeared, following the soldiers into the keep. *Well Caelan, you're really in it now.*

With everyone moving around frantically, it was easy to slip back to one of the walls where he could duck into the shadows and move out of sight. In the corner of the courtyard, there were stacks of barrels set against the walls. They looked like they hadn't been moved or touched in some time. He slung the makeshift pack containing his armor and bow and stuffed it into the corner, out of view. There was no way he could get out of the barracks with them strapped over his shoulder. He'd have to come back for them.

With his pack stored, he moved as quickly and quietly as he could. Caelan darted down passageways, through corridors, and to the barracks' gate. Two guards stood watch at the small, highly fortified door that led out to the city itself.

"Hold on, soldier, just where do you think you are going? All returning troops were ordered to the keep for an after-action report," one of the guards said.

Caelan shook his head. "Right, thanks for telling me what I already know. I was just there, wasn't I? What then, would I be doing here? Oh that's right, Capt'n sent me to bring back some extra healers. We took a bigger beating than was expected. We gonna stand here and argue and bicker like merchants, or you gonna open that gate and let me through?" he shot back, trying to make himself sound as much like a goraum soldier as possible.

"The captain sent you alone?" The two guards exchanged a glance.

"No, genius, he sent me with a whole bloody squad. You don't see 'em? They must have gone invisible again. They keep doing that. Cheeky lads, they are."

The guards folded their arms across their chests in unison.

"Fine, I'll go tell me capt'n I need an escort. Before I head back, what was your names again?"

"Why?" the left guard asked suspiciously.

"Well, when I explain to the capt'n why I came back without the healers he just sent me to get, I'd like to tell him who is to blame."

"Wait . . . that won't be necessary. We were just doing our jobs. Supposed to ask, you see."

They unbarred the gate in a hurry, shouted to the man above, and before long the path was clear.

Caelan wasted no time getting away from the barracks and out of sight. With as much work as the Taggoronian army had done to acquire his companions, getting them back would be no small feat. He'd need help. Lots of help.

"This Darkstone better be bloody worth it," he muttered under his breath as he made his way down the familiar stone streets.

The alleys seemed smaller and less intimidating than he remembered. Maylor was a city built across three large hills. An external wall was built around all three hills, enclosing the entirety of the city. In addition to the large outer wall, there were smaller walls separating different zones. Each hill was walled off from the others, with three large gates that were typically left open.

Each hill also had three walls encircling it. The top was for the rich and powerful upper class; the middle was for distinguished or accomplished citizens; and the bottom level was a slum for commoners, orphans, and other degenerates. It was like an undercity, despised by those above as being a leach on the overcity.

The outer walls of the hill to the west ran along the mysterious and dangerous Mirklan Forest that was home to all sorts of mystical creatures and even more fantastical rumors. In the center of Mirklan was a small lake that many rumored to have magical properties. While the waters and their potential were alluring, few who wandered into the woods were ever seen again. The forest provided better protection for Maylor than her walls ever could.

The west side of Maylor was the poorest and darkest of the three hills. No one with means wanted to live near the mystery forest. Rather than having the rich at the top of the hill in West Hill, the top tier was home to the crime lords. West Hill was controlled by two rival thieving guilds, a league of assassins, and two gangs of thugs who policed and controlled the streets. It was a difficult place to live.

"Home trash home," Caelan muttered. As he approached the open gate, a set of thugs stepped out, cutting off his passage.

"You lost, soldier boy?" one of them said.

Caelan had almost forgotten he was in the dead man's armor. He stood and stared at the thug guard cutting off his passage into West Hill.

"Oh, Lonnie, looks like he's lost and deaf. Well, why don't ye turn yerself around and march back to yer barracks before you have an accident?" another thug said.

Caelan pulled the metal vision-confining bucket off his head and tossed it aside. The sweet relief of cranial freedom made him sigh. His moment of euphoria quickly faded as he assessed the five thugs in front of him. Killing them could prove problematic, or it could work in his favor. West Hill was always a difficult-to-predict place.

"Two ways this goes. You can move out of my way, and I'll keep walking. It's nice. It's clean. It's less screamy and keeps all your blood inside your body. Or, and I really hope you choose this one, you can stand there. Before you can blink, I'll be stepping over your corpses." Caelan smiled as patronizingly as he could manage.

The five thugs reached for their weapons in unison, gripping their hilts and handles at the ready. Watching them was like watching ice melt on a cold day. They were so slow. Caelan grinned, readying himself to make his move.

"Caelan? Gods below, is that you?" The voice came from a man standing behind the guards.

The man was tall with light hair and bright green eyes. His face was covered with a light stubble which complemented an easy smile. It was a rugged, but natural charm. He wore gray leather armor that covered his shoulders and chest but left his arms completely bare, which may have been done more by necessity than choice. His arms were massive and looked as if they'd been sculpted by a craftsman for the perfect aesthetic. Tattoos looking like mystic patterns ran from his shoulders down to his elbows. Caelan hadn't seen the man in years but immediately recognized him. This was his childhood friend, Ash.

"You lot might want to move away. Caelan will cut you down before you even get your weapons free." Ash walked up to the guards standing in front of them, his presence menacing.

"You insult us. We can handle a single soldier!" the guard called Lonnie replied.

"Could you handle me?" Ash chuckled.

The guards each took a step back, their resolve crumbling like a tower of sand under a stiff breeze.

"Caelan would make short work of me. Unless you think the five of you could handle me, I'd repeat my urging for you to step back."

"Sir, there's no way you'd lose to some punk soldier," one of the guard-thugs protested.

"Boys, you're not listening. He's not a soldier at all. Caelan grew up here in West Hill. He is one of the fastest, most skilled fighters I've ever seen. He and I are mates going way back. Say another word that isn't moving out of the way and I might start taking it personal." Ash's words had hardly finished leaving his mouth when the guards held their hands up and stepped away with a sense of urgency.

Ash put his arms out and hugged Caelan tight. Caelan felt like he was being crushed by a rock troll.

"What on the god's cursed earth would bring you back here? You must have lost your senses after what you did."

"I need to speak with Xander." Caelan pushed him away.

Ash laughed. "That so? What, my oldest friend, do you think Xander will say when he hears you came back?"

Caelan couldn't resist smirking. "I imagine he will try to throw me into that Murmuck pit he's always talking about."

"If you're lucky. He'd probably offer me a hundred silver just for bringing you to him."

"But you're not going to," Caelan replied confidently.

Ash laughed but offered no confirmation as he walked with Caelan deeper into West Hill. When they'd moved out of view from the gate, Ash turned and lead Caelan on the path up the hill toward the crime lords.

"You know I owe you. I'll help you how I can, but it would be a lot easier if I knew what you were after," Ash said.

Caelan sighed, debating how much to reveal.

"You really don't trust me? After surviving that orphanage together, you really think I'd betray you?" Ash's demeanor shifted from jovial to a firm glower.

Caelan shrugged. "Who says I'm after anything? Maybe I just wanted to have my back cracked by one of your obscenely hard hugs?"

"Fine. Keep your secrets. Good luck with that."

Caelan put his hand on Ash's overly developed shoulder. "It's not that I don't trust you. After Josh, it's hard to really . . . "

"He betrayed me, too, you know. Difference is, after what he did, you got out of this place. You left me here to pick up your mess." Ash ground his teeth and turned his gaze up the hill.

Caelan stopped and looked at his friend. "I told you to come with me. I begged. You chose to stay."

Ash looked back and smiled, stuffing his hands in his pockets. "Aye, I suppose I did. Anyway, it's in the past now. No sense dwelling on what we can't change, is there?"

Caelan nodded in agreement. "Are you still running with Xander?"

"Yeah, he's made me a captain now."

Caelan smiled. "You're a king among vermin then."

When they reached the top of the hill, their path was blocked by a closed gate and four armed soldiers. Unlike the thugs at the entrance to West Hill, these four were well-equipped and looked quite capable.

"Stand aside, lads. We need to see Xander," Ash said.

Two large pikes crossed in front of them, barring their path.

"Oh, you'll be seeing Xander all right. We have standing orders should the great Caelan ever show his face in West Hill again—to capture him and bring him to Xander for summary execution."

"Well, that's hospitable." Caelan shook his head.

His instinct was to draw his sword and fight, but if he had any hope of getting his friends out of the clutches of the Taggorian keep, he was going to need Xander's help.

"I am a captain of the Shadowed Hand. I will vouch for this man and take full responsibility. Stand aside and let us in," Ash replied.

"I wish I could, captain. Sadly, our instructions don't leave any room for interpretation. You will both need to come with us." The guard motioned, and a moment later a dozen drawn weapons were aimed right at them as enforcer-thugs surrounded them.

They bound Caelan's hands behind his back and put chains around his ankles to keep him from being able to move far or fast.

Then they tugged a coarse sack like something you'd put potatoes in over his head.

It would have been amusing if it wasn't so annoying. He was being shoved and pushed into a wannabe castle that served as the base of operations for the Shadowed Hand, one of the two thieve guilds that operated out of West Hill. But Caelan had been in the fort too many times to count. He used to be a part of their network, so the thought that covering his head with a sack would somehow prevent him from knowing where he was felt insulting.

The gate opened and closed. He was pushed and guided through a large open courtyard with a building on each side, ensuring there was never a good breeze. The building in the back served as a sort of command center and makeshift throne for Xander, the king of thieves and one of Caelan's childhood companions.

Caelan felt his body buckle as he was shoved to his knees. The black sack was ripped awkwardly from his face. Thieves and manners were rarely good bedfellows. He shook his head to reorient and looked around the room. There was quite the crowd.

"Nice to see I'm still popular," Caelan remarked.

Behind him, along the back wall, about fifty people sat as if observing a wedding. Caelan was kneeling, with guards on either side of him, in the middle of the floor before the throne.

The throne was a lone seat set on an elevated platform to give it a sense of prominence and power. The simple chair failed at both. The man sitting on the make-shift throne wore a red robe adorned with red gems, all accompanied by his very red hair. His right eye was covered by a patch that concealed most, but not all, of a long scar. A scar Caelan remembered giving him.

"Ah, Ash, well done. You brought me the best gift for my birthday," Xander smirked.

"Your birthday is in winter you troll-tingling owa hair," Caelan snapped.

The smile on Xander's face faded, and he glared at Caelan. Without moving from his seat, he lifted his finger, pointing at Caelan.

"For your crimes against the Shadowed Hand, your abandonment of your responsibilities, and for all your many, many wrongs, I sentence you to death by Murmuck. Throw him into the pits. Let everyone hear him scream," Xander said.

"I can't let you do that," Ash interrupted. "Caelan is here to make a request of us. I think we need to hear him out."

Xander chuckled. "Ahh, still loyal to the boy you looked up to all those years ago, I see. Well, I must say, I am surprised that you, of all people, would speak up for him. But since you are a captain and I am a king, you have no power with which to stop me. Guards . . . "

One of the guards moved to grab Caelan. Ash grabbed the guard, pulled him close, drove his fist in the man's chest, and pushed him back in a coughing heap before anyone else could blink. The other guards moved more timidly. Ash glared at them, and they stopped moving entirely.

"Have you forgotten what he did for us?" Ash challenged.

"Have you forgotten what he did to us? What it cost us?" Xander replied.

"Sure, we lost something we'd have never had in the first place were it not for him," Ash scowled.

Xander cursed. "You bring up the orphanage one more time, and I'm gonna—"

"Right, so you do remember the pains in our stomachs after going days without food, the lashes on our backs for making too much noise, the freezing cold of the winter nights without blankets. We'd have died in that infernal place. You'll have to forgive me for feeling a bit of loyalty to him, since he's the reason we are alive. You must honor our code." Ash folded his arms across his chest, his feet planted in demonstration of his resolve.

"Our code?" Xander raises an eyebrow.

"The Rite of Amends," Ash said with a nod.

Xander laughed. "Doesn't apply."

"I say it does."

"Well, you're wrong."

"Perhaps we should let the committee decide. Or perhaps you just need a reminder. The Rite of Amends clearly states that if one person commits an intentional act that genuinely and significantly benefits another, that person is honor bound to a debt of repayment. Repayment must be given in the form of a great favor at the express request of the person who committed the benefiting act in the first place."

Xander sighed and sat back in his chair. "I am familiar with the Rite, thank you. You give him too much credit. It was the charitable Lord Orthenil who donated the food and supplies. He just helped orchestrate the deal. The Rite of Amends also states that the action cannot equally benefit the person committing the act. What he did benefited him just as much as it did us. The Rite of Amends doesn't apply here. Your position is invalid. Now stand aside and let me carry out my—"

"You still don't know?" Ash laughed. "What an unexpected world. The king of thieves is apparently not the most informed. You think he just helped broker the deal by being friends with the Orthenil boy?"

Xander's eyes narrowed, but he didn't respond.

"Lord Orthenil wanted to look like a patron of the community. His son befriending an orphan boy made a great story for his fancy guest parties. The Orthenil boy was a useless gwar who liked throwing his title around."

Xander rolled his eyes. "And the point of this is?"

Ash pointed to Caelan. "Little Ted Orthenil liked to get a couple of his noble friends together and play knights and thieves. Caelan would pretend to be a thief, and they, the noble knights, would take their wooden swords and smite him. By smite, I mean they beat him to within an inch of his life every time he went to the estate. If Caelan refused, little Ted Orthenil would complain to his father, and the food and supplies would stop. If he resisted, the food would stop. If he told anyone else what was happening, the food would stop."

"He sent supplies every week for four years," Xander said.

Ash nodded. "Every week for four years Caelan went to the little house of horrors, suffering under some new sadistic torture dreamed up by that little ralk, Ted."

Xander looked to Caelan and then back to Ash. "How do you know this?"

Ash shook his head. "Honestly, how *don't* you? The workers

at the orphanage used to talk about it all the time. Laugh, even. Silly little Caelan never learned."

"Why didn't they stop it, if they knew?" Xander challenged.

"Lord Orthenil paid them well and provided enough medicine to treat Caelan's wounds. He knew what his son was. So long as word didn't spread, he didn't care. Why would he? He's a noble, so what if his son had a predilection for being a nasty ralking sadist?"

"You think I don't remember? Orthenil's son was off-putting, but he was never violent."

"Not to you. He had a different outlet. Every week for four years, Caelan let himself get beaten so that we could eat. Tell me, great king of thieves, did Caelan ever ask you for anything?"

Xander shook his head.

"No favors? Silver? Nothing?"

Xander shook his head again.

Ash smiled brightly. "With that in mind, under the Rite of Amends, I'd say that you, great king of thieves, owe Caelan a debt. Failure to pay on such a debt would be a violation of our ways and call your leadership into question. When he makes his request, I'd suggest, for the sake of your leadership, you say yes, no matter how crazy it may seem."

Xander glared at Ash, his chest rising and falling and his face red as blood. A small vein on the side of his temple throbbed. Finally, just as it seemed he might pop, he closed his eyes, let out a long slow breath, and turned to Caelan.

"Speak. What would you have of me?"

Caelan grinned. "I want to break into the barracks and free a couple of my friends, and I need you and your men to help me."

Chapter 21

Motives of the Heart

---Vale---

Vale woke to discover he was bound by thick iron shackles, his wrists pinned uncomfortably together. He followed the chain to a steel ring mounted in the ceiling. The links went in one end and ran through some gears along the back wall. Vale recognized the device. His captors could pull on one end of the chain and hoist or lower him as they saw fit.

Light poured in from a long rectangular window that stretched the length of the wall behind him. In front of him was an iron door. Everything else was cold, gray stone. *Well, this is a lovely room.* Vale could practically hear Caelan saying, "Great." Even when Caelan wasn't around, he could still be annoying. The last thing he wanted was the archers' words in his head. *At least it wasn't a dark, damp dungeon.*

Vale had no need to test the restraints that bound him. Any group that put that much effort into catching someone wasn't going to overlook a loose bolt in the bindings. His energy would be better served waiting for the right moment. Standing in front of him were two men. The first was a thin, frail, middle-aged man with wispy brown hair, wearing a brown cloak with an orange sash. The second was the man who had attacked them in the woods. He was taller than average, with wide shoulders. The rest of him was hidden by the orange hood that covered his face in shadow.

"Vale the black blade." The hooded man's voice rumbled low and heavy as he held up Vale's sword, admiring it. "This is an impressive weapon—a blade that can cut through even the scales of a dragon. Have you ever killed one? A dragon?" he asked.

Vale stared at the man in willful, silent defiance.

"You will answer, my lord Drako!" The thin man put his face in front of Vale's, glaring threateningly. Vale slammed his forehead into the man's nose. The thin man cried out in pain, blood gushing from his nose. He clutched his face with his hands as he tilted his head up to the ceiling to slow the blood flow.

"You insolent nave!" the thin man started.

The hooded man laughed, interrupting him.

"He is not the type to kill and tell. I warned you not to get too close." The man in the hood turned his attention back to Vale. "What is your wish?"

Vale answered once again with silence.

"This does not have to be painful. I seek only information," the hooded man warned.

"Is that why I am here? Why you sent all those men to their deaths? To ask me about my hopes and dreams like I am some fledgling searching for my place in the world?" Vale asked.

The hooded man nodded to his thin friend who responded for him. "King Gladio wants the Darkstone for Taggoron. He plans to use it to make his kingdom the new Parisia. In order to do so, he must prevent the Seekers from retrieving the stone and returning it. The men who attacked you in the woods were under the orders of their king to detain or eliminate all Parisian Seekers."

"Why capture us, then? Wouldn't it have been easier to kill us and be done with it?" Vale asked.

"Kill you? How long would that last?" The hooded man chuckled with a note of amusement in his voice. "King Gladio's preference would be to turn the Seekers so they retrieve the stone for him instead."

"You think I would betray my king for yours?" Vale smirked.

The man in the hood paced back and forth, stopping at the mention of the king. "He is not my king."

"Then what are you doing with his soldiers?"

Shadows of the Dark Realm

"Using them. We share an interest in the Darkstone but not in what to do with it. Now, if you ever want to see your friends alive, you will answer my question. What is your wish?"

"My wish for what?"

The thin man smacked Vale across the face. "Don't be daft. Why do you seek the Darkstone? What wish would you ask of it?"

Vale tensed his jaw. "Do you understand what happens if the Darkstone isn't returned? This world will fall to ruin at the hands of the Shadow King."

"That's your only motivation, then? You are a selfless hero set out to save the world?" the thin man sneered.

"No. I am knight of Parisia, tasked by my king to embark on this quest to retrieve the Darkstone. It is my duty. I am bound by honor to carry out the wishes of my king."

The man in the hood laughed. "Perhaps that is where your quest began. Much has happened since. You've seen the dead Seekers at the gate; you know something is hunting you. One of your companions was possessed by the Red Empress. Then there's the king. He is not the man you thought he was. You've felt something was wrong in Parisia for some time. Now, you've learned that the king you swore to serve—devoted your life to and lost everything for—betrayed you by sending you to massacre an innocent village. Yet here you are. Do not insult me by pretending this is nothing more than a knight's duty. Duty will only drive a man so far."

"The only limit on an oath of fealty is the honor of the one who swears it," Vale replied.

"No, there is something more. What is your wish? Tell me!"

Vale nodded, staring at the ground. "Fine. The real reason I want the Darkstone is so I can put an end to all wars and create a world of peace."

The hooded man sighed. "Lie. What is your wish?"

Even in the shadows of the hood, Vale could see the man's eyes light up like orange flames. He felt something pressing into his mind. A pressure grew in his head as he felt this unrelenting compulsion to answer.

Vale licked his lips. "My wish . . . is to save my kingdom from the ruin that will befall it . . . To seal away the Shadow King once and for all."

The hooded man shook his head. "Lie. What is your wish?"

Vale ground his teeth, fighting against the force pushing at his mind, the tension growing, begging for release. "I . . . wish . . . to bring back my wife and daughter . . . and put an end to my curse."

The thin man stopped tending to his nose. He pulled a small dagger from his cloak and lifted it toward Vale's head.

"My lord, if he will not answer honestly, let me cut the answers from him. I will make him sing for you, my lord."

"No," the man in the hood replied.

"But, my lord," the thin man protested.

"A man who has suffered as much as he has will not give in to torture. At least, not the torture of himself."

"What are you thinking, my lord?"

"We have his friends in the adjacent rooms. The mercenaries should be returning soon with the remainder of his party. Perhaps hearing their screams will loosen his lips."

Vale glared up at the man, growling between clenched teeth. He tugged on the chains that bound him. A foolish and fruitless effort, but his body moved on instinct as anger coursed through his veins.

The man in the hood chuckled. "Easy, killer, I do not revel in causing pain. I would much prefer to solve this with civility. But if you mean to test my resolve, know this. I have waited too long for half measures. I will acquire the information I seek at whatever the cost. How much suffering is required is entirely up to you."

Vale glared at the man. If it were not for the chain that bound him, he would strangle the life from him here and now. He let his head sink.

"Ok, you win." The words felt heavy coming from his lips.

"Open your mind to me. Let me see what I need to see."

"What are you looking for?"

"A very specific combination."

"A combination of what?"

"Of blood and desire. Open your mind; I will not ask again."

Vale closed his eyes and relaxed his mind. He felt a pulsing, probing sensation, as if invisible fingers were reaching into his head and moving his thoughts around. Suddenly, it stopped. Rather than moving thoughts, the invisible fingers were now clutching them.

"Your wish is to erase yourself?" The man sounded confused.

Vale stared, his lips pursed. A moment of silence passed.

"How is that a wish?"

"Why is that any concern of yours?"

The hooded man stepped closer. "Call it curiosity. The Darkstone has the power to grant the deepest desire of its wielder's heart. The reach of its power is beyond our comprehension. It can make a kingdom flourish, change the past, alter reality. With the Darkstone, you could reshape the world. A power of endless possibility, and you would use it to end your life before it began? Why?"

"I doubt someone like you would understand."

"Explain it to me. If you hate your life so much, why not just end it?"

"I don't hate it."

"Then why would you wish to never have it?"

"So that they could live . . . " The words hung in the air. Vale forced himself to swallow as if trying to keep the emotions at bay. "If I'd never been born, my curse would never hurt anyone. All the people I've killed, all the people I've loved who are dead because of me, they would all be alive."

The hooded man stood silent for a moment. "You are a strange fellow. You've killed more people than you can remember, and yet still you've not slain nearly as much as you've suffered. You believe ceasing to exist would save those you love pain?" he asked, his voice almost sympathetic.

Vale nodded, unable to pull his eyes from the ground.

"But if you were never born . . . " the man in the hood added.

"They'd still be alive."

"But you wouldn't be here to see it."

"A sacrifice I would gladly make."

"Have you ever considered how many are alive who wouldn't have been because of you?" he asked.

The question was like fireworks bursting inside Vale's mind. He'd never considered that. His life had been filled with so much blood, death, and carnage that all he saw was loss. His heart was weighed down by so much guilt that all he felt was despair. *Could it be that there was more than death and doom in his wake?*

"You have neither the blood nor the desire I seek." The screech of iron grinding against uneven hinges echoed around the room. The door slammed, and the lock clanked into place. Vale didn't bother looking up.

* * *

-DANTE-

Four orange half circles pinned his arms and legs tight to the wall, with a fifth ring around his neck, making it impossible for him to move in any significant way. It was a well-designed cage for a mage, as Dante would not be able to move enough to activate any magic.

He heard the door to his cell open and watched as two men entered. The first was thin and forgettable. The second was the unforgettable man in the orange cloak. Even without having ever seen his face, Dante recognized him. His build, his walk—he was utterly unique.

"What are you?" Dante asked the man in the hood.

"That's an aggressive opener," the man replied.

"It is a fact. Magic is a powerful force, but it has one great limit—its wielder. No matter how gifted a mage may be, every creature has a max capacity. I would know; I am one of the strongest human mages alive. Yet you are on a whole other level. There can be only one explanation. You are not human."

"Fascinating. You think because my magic is stronger than yours, it means I'm not human. Perhaps this is your way of escaping a more painful reality? Your magic is not as strong as you think. Or perhaps I just prepare better." The man in the

Shadows of the Dark Realm

hood pulled a glowing orange gem from his pocket and lifted it up.

"An Espira? Where did you get that?" Dante asked, staring at the gem as if in a trance.

"You are not here to question me. Answer my question, and perhaps I will answer yours," the hooded man said.

"What do you want to know?" Dante asked.

"What is your wish?" the hooded man asked.

"You think I am just going to reveal my desires to you?"

"How is it you know what I seek?"

"These rooms are not so far apart. Surely you accounted for this. You wanted us to hear what happened to the others. You may have been able to break Vale by threatening our companions. That will not work with me."

"Of course not. You are immune to such common emotions."

"That's right. You can kill them, torture them, make me watch every second of it, and I will not feel a thing. So, what are going to do?" Dante stared into the shadow cast by the hood where the man's face was hidden.

"You seek the Darkstone for all its power, but you have not even begun to realize all that it can do," the thin man replied.

Dante squinted as he processed that thought.

"What do you mean? The Darkstone protected the kingdom of Parisia and made it prosper beyond measure for generations. What am I missing?"

"Does that mean you are interested in sharing information? How about this? As you are a man of intellect who craves knowledge, Lord Drako has authorized me to share with you a piece of information about the Darkstone that not even the Archivists of Parisia are privy to. In exchange, all we ask is to know what you'd wish for with the stone."

Dante thought it over, his mind scrambling to find any risk or danger in revealing his desire. Nothing came to mind. "Very well, tell me what you know, and then I will answer your question. But first, I want your names."

Lord Drako nodded, and his thin friend turned back to face Dante.

"Agreed. You have the distinct honor and privilege to stand

in the presence of the greatest lord in Taggoron, Lord Kade Drako. I am his faithful servant, Ammonia Amir Ludvar."

"Very good; go on," Dante nodded, committing the names to memory. The name Drako sounded familiar but why, he could not recall.

"It is a seemingly small piece of information with rather shocking and significant implications," Ammonia started.

"Let me hear it then."

"The Darkstone is considered an Inherent magical object, as it was forged to maintain the veil between worlds and uses Inherent magic to do so. However, the additional power that it offers, to grant wishes and make prosperous a nation, comes not from Inherent Magic but Source Magic."

Dante felt as if all the air was robbed from his lungs by the sentence. He stared, unable to move, as the information struck him silent. *It could not be. There was no way.*

"Impossible," Dante managed after a long moment of silence. "That would mean—"

"The prosperity Parisia has enjoyed for hundreds of years has come at some great cost. Someone has been fueling the stone in order to maintain the effect of its power," Ammonia replied.

"What could fuel something like that for so long?"

Ammonia shook his head. "It is your turn to answer the question, I'm afraid."

"My answer will not help you. If what you told Vale is true—that the stone grants a wish from the heart—I am the one person alive who cannot wield it."

"You would back out of our arrangement?"

Dante shook his head. "I am not backing out. I am telling you I have no heart with which to make a wish."

The hooded man stepped forward, lifting Dante's necklace from under his shirt. "That's what this energy is. You've made yourself an emotional tether to try and keep you connected?" Kade put his hand over Dante's chest. "You are right; you can't help me. Would that be your wish? To have your heart restored?"

Dante nodded.

Kade chuckled, "It's almost tragic, isn't it? The thing you'd wish for is the very reason your wish would not work. We are done here. Let's go."

They made their way out of the cell and down the stone hall out of sight.

* * *

-RIVIK-

Rivik was sitting in the corner, his ankles and wrists bound to a chain that was attached to a metal ring set in the stone floor. His head was tilted back, his gaze focused on the ceiling. He was humming idly to himself to pass the time, not really paying attention to what was happening in the other cells—or at least, wanting to seem as if he wasn't.

> There was a journey, a distant journey
> That took him far away,
> Wandering night and day
> To distant lands, with blood-soaked hands
> He had to fight away,
> And at night lie awake.
> For on his journey, wrought full of worry,
> His hands were gory, he fought for glory.
> He told the story.
> Of lands far away and wonders man had made
> But all that glory, his epic story...
> Could not change the way,
> His heart would long to say
> For bluest seas, and wandering hills
> Fertile lands, and mystic thrills
> For fair as these green hills he'd roam
> They were not the hills of home

Rivik's voice echoed harmoniously around the stone walls as he sang. When he'd finished, he looked at the two men in his cell.

"First ones free, boys. If you want more, you have to buy me a drink," he smirked.

Kade cocked his head to the side, his features still completely hidden by the shadow of his orange hood.

"The Song of the Wanderer—where did you hear this?" he asked.

Rivik exhaled through his nostrils. "Heard it? I wrote it."

The two guests in his cell exchanged a glance. "You are the Bard of Rag'amor?" Ammonia asked.

Rivik smirked. "Is that what you came here to talk about? Didn't realize I had such zealous fans."

"Your song about the Breaking of the Black Mountains—it reminded me of things I'd long forgotten. You have quite the way with words." Kade's voice lifted a full octave.

Rivik smiled. "Wait, you didn't really go through all this to ask about my songs, did you? That'd be really sad."

"We kept eyes on the others, but you and your fellow warriors are not known to us. My lord desires to know why you are seeking the Darkstone," Ammonia asked.

Rivik looked up at the ceiling. "I couldn't care less about some stupid stone."

The two exchange another glance. "You are seeking the Darkstone at great personal peril. You don't expect us to believe that you don't want use of its power," Ammonia replied.

"What you believe is none of my business. It changes nothing. Everyone thinks their lives would be better if they could just get this, have that, change this. They think a wish could solve their problems, that magic can fix their lives. It won't. Nothing achieved by magical means leaves any lasting impact. Not interested," Rivik replied.

"Why do you risk your life, then?" Ammonia asked.

"Revenge. A silver-scaled dragon attacked my village. Killed my friends. I mean to end it. Not with a wish, but with my own hands as the gods intended."

"You can't be serious," Ammonia started.

"Leave him be," Kade said.

"My lord, we should at least—" Ammonia protested.

"No. There is no deception in his words. A man with no

wish cannot help me. A man with his purpose, I will not hinder. He will be released as soon as we are finished with the others."

Boots came tromping down the hall, cutting off the conversation.

"Lord Drako! Your presence is required at the barracks gate. There are some strange creatures seeking an audience with you," one of the soldiers announced.

Kade grunted. "Strange? How?"

The two guards looked nervously at each other. "Well, they look like small humans but have these little wings for starters."

Kade growled so loud Rivik thought he saw fire shoot from the man's nose. The man in the orange hood stormed off without a glance back, his servant on his heels.

"Watch them," Kade's voice echoed down the hall as he disappeared from sight.

Guards swarmed the halls, positioning themselves at either end, with groups of four moving to stand at the entry to each cell. Something had them very worked up. They weren't just standing guard; they were on edge.

Rivik stood as he heard a commotion at the far end of the corridor. There was smashing, confusion, yelling, and then a loud whistling sound. Rivik blinked as the whistle turned into a *thunk* as an arrow pierced the head of one of the guards facing him. The guard slumped lifelessly to the ground. *This was getting exciting.*

Chapter 22

Vargr

Azalea grunted as her knees slammed against the marble floor of the palace. She pursed her lips as she peered up at the court before her. She was at the bottom of several wide marble steps that led to a platform boasting an ornate throne with a seat on either side. In the central seat sat an overweight man with a large belly. He wore a fancy colorful robe and large, unnecessarily gawdy jewelry. Azalea immediately hated him. He sat lazily on his chair, looking down at her as if bored with her existence. In his right hand, he held a tall gold scepter with intricate golden carvings and embedded gems.

Sitting in the seats on either side of him were two exquisite-looking women, who even Azalea had to admit were utterly breathtaking. They wore thin, revealing dresses—one purple, the other green. Both girls were leaning into the central seat, giggling and whispering into the ear of the man in the middle. They fawned over him as if their only means of self-worth came from the scraps of attention he offered. *Pathetic*.

Hanging from the ceiling was a grand, black banner trimmed with silver. In the middle was a howling wolf's head stitched in shining silver. Azalea recognized the flag immediately. She was in the palace of Vargr.

The walls on either side of the throne were lined with

knights in shining silver armor holding large pikes. The throne consisted of three central chairs around which a few mages in their bulky robes stood like statues. Two more men stood on the top of the stairs leading up to the platform. They wore an unfamiliar red and black armor with thin, red, flowing robes and fur that covered their shoulders. Something about the style and coloring of their armor suggested they were not part of the king's normal retinue.

A young man, maybe in his late teens, was dressed in fancy, black clothes with silver on the shoulders, giving him the appearance of some esteemed military leader. He glared at the king on his throne.

"This is madness. Father, you must hear me."

"No, boy, you forget your place. You may be my son, but you have not seen enough sunrises to lecture me. I am the king. I decide how this kingdom will be run. I know what is best for it. Were you anyone else, I would have you in stocks. But since you are my son, I will give you the opportunity to prove yourself."

"I won't fail, father."

"We will see. You will lead the 2nd Brigade in their mission to obtain the Darkstone. Succeed, and you will earn your place by my side. Fail, and . . . I have other sons."

The young man stared for a moment before finally bowing. "Yes, my king," he said, his tone biting in spite of his bow. He turned and stormed out of the room in a huff making sure to stomp his feet down hard with every step.

"Sorry to interrupt family business, but we brought you what you wanted. Where's our money?" a man's voice came from behind her.

Azalea glanced back to see one of the mages that had been waiting for them when they got out of the cave.

"What he wanted? Oh, you better not be talking about me. I will burn the flesh from your body." A loud crack filled the room.

Azalea felt her jaw burn as the man backhanded her in the face so hard it knocked her off balance.

She lifted her hands, fire raging through her. "You goraum—"

"Don't interrupt," the man warned her.

The flames went out, and her wrists suddenly felt heavy and cold, like stone. She turned, and a mage behind her wagged his finger at her. She cursed and finally submitted. When her resistance faded, the spell petrifying her hands faded with it. She'd need a different method.

"Now, our money," the mage demanded of the king.

The king nodded lazily. "Yes, yes, of course. My administrator, Clancey, will take care of all of that on your way out."

"There's just this one little thing, yer majesty. You asked us to find ye this girl and bring her to ye. Well, we already had a contract to bring her to some fool in Maylor. That got me thinking. If that many people want this girl, mayhaps we settled on too low a price, being that she's so in demand." The man grabbed Azalea's hair and pulled, forcing her head back hard.

"You can't be serious." The disinterested expression drifted from the king's face as he leaned forward, pushing away the girls on either side of him in the process.

"'Fraid I am, majesty. See, we gots hired to by our last employer to hunt down all these groups seeking that fancy stone thing that the dragon stole. He was gonna pay us for each group we brought in. Then, wouldn't ye know it, some monster or other crazy thing starts killin' 'em all before we can snatch 'em." the mercenary answered.

"How is that my problem?" the king asked, his glare growing as he leaned forward in his elaborate chair.

"Seems we got a bit of a bidding war going on. Ye don't want to pay, that's fine; we can just sell her to the other guy," the mercenary answered.

"I could have you killed with the snap of my fingers," the king warned.

"Aye, but not before I kill her. I guess it all depends on how badly you want her alive," the man said with a cocky grin.

The king's expression soured even further. Azalea noticed that the two men in the foreign red armor seemed even more agitated by this suggestion.

"You are gambling with your life and the lives of all of your men for a few extra silver?" the king asked.

The man chuckled. "Beggin' your pardon, mi'lord, but we is

mercenaries. Gamblin' our lives for silver is what we do. And we are not talkin' 'bout no few extra. I thinks this girl is some kind of prize. Yer gonna have to pay a premium for her."

"Guards!" the king shouted. A line of pikes moved in unison as the king's guard stepped forward toward the band of mercenaries behind Azalea.

"Ah, ah, ah! Nother step and I make a mess of yer fancy floors." The mercenary leader slid the edge of his dagger against Azalea's throat. *Great, I'm going to die because a couple of addle-brained men want to compare egos*, she thought.

"Enough!" one of the men in the red armor shouted. The king's guard stopped, and all eyes in the room moved to him. He put his hand over his chin, and Azalea noticed a distinct triangle-shaped scar.

"What's this, then?" the mage-for-hire asked.

"King Tomlin, with your permission, I believe I have a way to make sure everyone gets exactly what they deserve." He looked to the king, who nodded in approval and lazily waved his hand.

The man stepped forward and removed his helmet. He was tall with black hair and tanned skin. He looked strong and confident with a constantly serious expression on his face that even a full smile couldn't dispel.

"Who's this, then? He don't look like no advisor," the mercenary leader asked.

Azalea felt the blade tighten against her neck.

"You are quite right. My name is Valron. I represent a party interested in ensuring that this deal goes through without issue," the man in the red armor said.

"And why does we care what you think?" the mercenary leader challenged.

"The king has failed to appreciate your work. After all, finding the girl was no small or easy task. I'm not sure many could have succeeded as you have. I think it's fair to say that you and your men have earned a proper reward," Valron started. The mercenaries murmured loudly in agreement.

"Yer right about that. Alright, since ye seem to be the brains here, I'm listening," the mercenary leader smiled.

"Where I come from, quality results are met with quality rewards. I would like to offer you twice the agreed-on price and a promise of future contracts in exchange for your delivering the girl unharmed. Of course, your majesty, I will personally be covering the difference, so your coffers remain unchanged. Is this agreeable?"

"Now we're talking. Alright, we got a deal. You show us the money, I'll hand over the girl," the leader said.

"Before we do, I want to give you something greater than all the silver in Vargr's vaults. What I offer you goes far beyond anything you've ever imagined." Valron smiled and lifted his hand. Two men in similar armor walked past, carrying two large chests.

"What's this, then?"

"Where I come from, it is customary to share a drink together after coming to terms. It is a gesture of friendship and good faith. I would like to share a drink with you and your men in honor of the successful completion of our transaction," Valron explained.

The two men opened the lids to their chests to reveal rows of short, stout glasses, each filled with a red fluid. It looked almost like a whiskey but with the hues of a light red wine. They carried the chests in their hands and walked around the room. Each mercenary pulled a glass free from the chest. The leader took one, and Valron grabbed the last one. The mercenary raised an eyebrow, inspecting the liquid.

"My new friends, this is not just any common drink. This is called Demoa. It is the finest of spirits from my country." Valron lifted his glass. The others all stared at him, holding theirs but not making any motion to drink it. Valron smirked and gulped down his glass in a single swig. The mercenaries watched him, and then, when after a moment nothing noteworthy happened, they cheered and empty their own glasses.

"See, that's how you do a deal right there," the mercenary leader said, nodding to Valron.

"Not all your men are drinking?" Valron noted, pointing to two men who didn't take a glass.

Shadows of the Dark Realm

"Those two? Nah, don't mind them; they are followers of the goddess, Virtua."

"The goddess of self-control? Really?" Valron raised an eyebrow.

"Don't take it personal; their devotion to the goddess demands they don't consume alcohol of any kind. Makes them dreadfully boring. But their blades are sharp, and they do what they's told. Makes up for their company being so dull."

Valron shrugged. "It makes no difference in the end."

The mercenary leader squinted and looked at him. "How about you go get that silver you promised us now? I got big plans —" His voice cut off suddenly. Groaning echoed around the room.

"W-w-w . . . what is . . . what is going . . . ahhhh . . . gaaww!" The mercenary leader suddenly grabbed his stomach and cried out in pain. He reached out and grabbed Valron by the arms for support. Valron smiled, his eyes glistening with delight.

The groans turned into cries, which turned into screams. The king stood up from his throne, eyes wide as he pointed at the scene below.

"G-g-guards, kill them!"

Pikes leveled once again, the knights that surrounded the throne moved slowly, cautiously toward the stairs.

Azalea glanced back to see the mercenaries dropping to the ground, their bodies contorting and changing. Their skin, limbs, and faces all blurring and shifting into something unrecognizable and then reforming. Azalea slid away from the group, pushing herself along the ground as all around her men turned into monsters. The scene felt familiar. Something about it shook her to her core. Her body trembled, and her strength left her. She felt this surging tug of crippling fear engulf her. All of a sudden, she wasn't herself. She was a little girl, trembling and afraid as giant, monstrous creatures surrounded her.

The two mercenaries that hadn't taken the drink drew their blades and stood back-to-back, facing their former friends as the monsters encircled them. What was strange is that none of the monsters looked the same. Some had multiple limbs like an octopus. Some had scales. Some had claws. Others had large mouths.

Each creature was horrifying to behold and bore little to no resemblance to the person they had been only moments before.

Red fog like a mist began to fill the room.

"What have you done?" the mercenary leader asked as he dropped to his knees.

Valron laughed. "You humans are all the same—shallow, petty, vile creatures. I have revealed your true form. Under that visage of flesh, you are all monsters."

Azalea closed her eyes and buried her face in her hands, curling her body into a ball as tightly as she could. The room was filled with screams, blades slicing, metal crashing, teeth biting, claws ripping, and bones breaking. She could hear blood spilling and spraying around the room as the scent of copper stung her nose.

"Valron! What have you done? You should have told me what you were planning! Your monsters have made a mess of my palace, and I will expect you to clean it up!" King Tomlin shouted.

With the sounds of carnage fading, Azalea slowly dared to peek out from her curled-up ball. The floors were coated in blood. Bodies of men and monster alike lay mangled on the ground.

At first, the king's guards had seemed like an excessive show of force. Now, not a single one remained. The two beautiful women managed to shriek their way to the back corners of the room where they were curled up, each making themselves as small as possible. Both were stained in the blood of the fallen knights as they shook violently in place. The king stood, eyes wide, legs trembling, on the edge of his platform, looking down at the scene below. Valron and the other three men who wore similar armor were now standing together, along with three monsters.

One of the monsters stood like a human. It had smooth, yellow-brown skin with fur growing out from its neck and over its shoulders. Four massive, bulky arms with bone spikes protruding in a line up each arm. Its back looked like a giant beetle with bony spikes running down the middle. Azalea recognized it as a Krogal.

The second was a Malgor, a giant creature that had the wings and tail of a dragon, the body and legs of a bull, the torso and arms of a man, and a head like a dark, furred goat man with massive goat horns.

The third, a Bogon, looked like a skeleton man with four horns on his head and the face of a rabid beast. *What sort of devilry could turn men into creatures such as these?*

"Dear girl, why do you hide your face? Surely, you are not afraid?" Valron leaned down in front of Azalea and smiled softly, like a father comforting their child.

Azalea stared back at the man, dumbfounded at his sudden gentleness. Valron placed the palm of his hand against her cheek. Azalea's gaze narrowed as she looked into his bright blue eyes.

"You don't remember?" He laughed again. "My child, we have been your guardians since you came into this world. You need not fear us. We are your most humble servants," Valron said.

Azalea blinked and her jaw dropped. "Servants?" she barely managed to get out.

Valron nodded.

"You are the Vas Noomi—the vessel. Your mother made a pact with Vespera. When she became pregnant with you, the kinspira used all their magical power to strengthen and form you into the perfect vessel to host the Red Empress. For you, my dear, are the chosen one. We are the guardians charged with your care."

"Spare me your noble protector speech. Your job was to protect the fragile vessel that your psychotic spirit-lady wants to use as a play-toy so she can rule the realm of men once again, right? I'm nothing to you but a tool," Azalea started.

"What has happened to you? Your mind has been twisted from your purpose." Valron's eyes narrowed as he saw the pendant around Azalea's neck. "Oh, I see. This is the work of the Blue Alchemist." He grabbed the necklace and tugged it.

"Nooo!" Azalea cried out, trying to grasp at the stone that kept her mind safe.

She was too late. Snapping the chain from her neck, Valron

squeezed the magical stone in his hand and crushed it into powder.

"You are free now, my dear."

"Valron! Are you listening to me? I . . . I demand you clean up this mess at once! And . . . and . . . you will need to provide me with new soldiers to replace the guards you killed!" the king commanded in a wavering voice.

Valron turned and started walking up the stairs toward the king.

"What are you doing? We had an arrangement! The girl belongs to Vargr!" The king's voice weakened and trembled as Valron got closer.

"Did you really believe we would leave the vessel for the Red Empress in your incapable hands? Did you think the Red Empress would settle for being your little puppet? You are a fool. With the Darkstone in her hands, she will regain all her former power, and she will cover this world in the light of her glory!" Valron declared.

"You can't do this! I . . . I am the king—"

Valron laughed. "The king of what? You are powerless. You are weak. You will shed tears of scarlet."

Azalea watched as Valron grabbed the king by his head, his thumbs digging into the king's eye sockets. Blood began to run down the king's face as he screamed. Valron effortlessly lifted the king's body off the ground. He kicked and flailed and screamed as the sound of creaking bones echoed around the room. Azalea gasped and covered her mouth to keep from screaming when she heard the king's skull crack.

The two royal concubines screamed as they saw the king's body lying in a heap on the floor. Valron smirked and descended the stairs.

"Enjoy," he said as he walked past the three monsters.

They cackled with glee and rushed up the stairs toward the two women. Azalea pushed herself to her feet. She was not going to be like one of those stupid girls. She was not easy prey. She pushed the fear and the shock down deep.

Valron held out his hands pleadingly, his face wrought with confusion. "My child, what are you doing? We have rescued you.

Now we will take you to get the Darkstone, and you can become your destiny. You will be the most powerful and glorious being in this realm."

"I . . . am not . . . your . . . child!" Azalea shouted through gritted teeth. She extended her hands, and a river of flame burst from them, blasting into Valron. He walked through the flames as if completely unphased by them.

"You will have to do better than this," he said with a confident smirk.

Azalea gritted her teeth and pushed a wave of energy like a hammer through the funnel of fire. It hit Valron and sent him flying across the throne room. He crashed into the wall with a loud thud, and his body slid to the ground. Azalea felt herself levitating as a cloud of magical energy formed under her feet. She lifted three of the fallen knight's pikes and hurled them at the Malgor monster. Just before they hit, she enhanced their tips with fire. They pierced through the Malgor's torso, and the creature fell dead to the ground.

Azalea flew across the room, riding the cloud under her feet as it launched forward, following her will. She ducked down and scooped up one of the women just before the skeletal monster beset her. She hooked her path around the back wall, trying to reach the other woman, but it was too late for her. The Krogal had moved much more quickly and had already torn the woman to pieces. The four-armed creature turned to see her as she flew toward it. Azalea launched another wave of energy, this time hitting the Krogal and sending the creature flying out the palace window to splatter on the ground below.

She didn't have time to think. She had to rely on her instinct, which was telling her to get out as fast as she could. With the concubine draped over the back of her cloud, she soared toward the window. If she could clear the palace, she would be out of their reach. Then all she'd need to do was find her friends.

She could see the light, feel the heat of the sun. Her heart raced and lifted. She was going to make it. But then a shadow was cast in front of her. In a flash, Valron was standing at the edge of the window, blocking her path. He was too quick—she didn't have time to react.

"I'm sorry to have to do this to you my child, but you've left me with no choice," he said, his voice sounding oddly sincere.

He lifted his hand, and a ball of glowing black light shot out and hit her in the head. Azalea felt her feet lift off the cloud, and she flew backwards. Her vision blurred and drifted to black. So close . . .

Chapter 23

The Turning

Celeste jumped as something or . . . someone splattered on the street not a stone's throw from where she was bound to the wheel of a trader's cart. She jumped so hard she slammed her shoulder into the wheel as a black, oil-like fluid sprayed out from the body as it slammed into the ground. Some of the oil sprayed onto her face and shoulder. It was warm and thick. *Disgusting.*

A half dozen mercenaries had remained behind to watch her, Sera, and the other Rag'amorian warriors. The rest had taken Azalea into the palace. Spiro never returned. Celeste suspected he died in the cave. Still, some part of her was holding on to the hope that he'd reappear and rescue them from their current predicament.

The Rag'amorian fighters had their arms bound behind their backs with a thick rope. A second rope was used to tie them all together. That rope was attached to the half-wall that lined the upper terrace of the palace gardens. Sera and Celeste were separated from the others and tied to the slaver cart they'd been transported here in.

The mercenaries had been on edge since the screaming started a few minutes ago. The body splattering all over the ground marked a break in their otherwise surprisingly disciplined watch. The moment the body landed, they froze.

Celeste couldn't blame them; it was a shocking thing to witness. The mangled mess of bone, blood, and flesh was undoubtedly not human. Yet it had come from the palace tower.

Their captors stared in shock. Two stood near the cart, staring up at the window from which the creature had exited. The others moved closer to the broken mess of a body. Where Celeste couldn't even think enough to close her mouth, Sera was on her feet in an instant. Before Celeste realized she'd moved, Sera was using the rope that bound her hands together to choke one of the guards.

The guard tried to grab for his sword, but she'd positioned herself perfectly, using her body weight to pull the man's head back. He flailed and struggled for a minute before going still. The other captor guard turned and drew his blade. Sera managed to pull a dagger from the dead man's belt. As she lowered his body down, she cut the rope that bound her.

"Naiflo! I'm gonna cut you into little pieces and feed them to —" the man started.

His words were cut off mid-threat as Sera threw the dagger, and it pierced his throat. Instead of threatening, he was now gargling. Sera lunged forward, pulled the dagger free, and turned as the mercenary collapsed to the ground. She knelt down and cut Celeste's bindings while Celeste could do little more than blink. Sera's movements were so precise, each movement setting up the next one. It was incredible.

"Free the others; I'll deal with the rest," she said, slapping the blood-covered dagger into Celeste's hands.

By the time Celeste managed to get to her feet, Sera had grabbed the dead man's sword and taken out the other four guards. Celeste rushed over and cut the Rag'amorians free.

"We need to go!" Celeste shouted, making her way to the cart where their confiscated weapons were stored and retrieving her royal sword.

"No!" Sera grabbed her daggers and started toward the palace.

"We can't help her. She's under palace guard. We need to get out of here while we can," Celeste instructed.

"You would leave your friend?" Sera asked, her brow furrowing.

"She's not my friend. She's a Kinspira who hates my family and tried to kill me. Even if I wanted to save her, we can't risk it. We may be the last hope for Parisia. I'm not about to risk millions of lives and the destruction of our realm to save one witch with a bad attitude." Celeste grabbed Sera's arm and pulled.

The tug did nothing to budge Sera's position, but after a moment, she relented. They rushed down the stone steps, away from the palace and toward the main city below. A warning bell rang out from the palace as they rushed away. Vargrian soldiers hurried past them in the other direction, charging toward the palace, not paying them any attention. *What was going on in that palace?* Celeste wondered.

The elegant stone path led them down a shallow hill into the center of the city. The homes and buildings were nice, sturdy structures made with gray brick. They were clean and well-maintained. Even so, they appeared to be slums compared to the capital city of Parisia.

They slowed as a large group of people had gathered in the town center around a merchant table. The crowd clogging the street was oddly enthusiastic. Celeste looked around to see two men standing behind the merchant table wearing captivating black and red armor unlike anything she'd seen before. The table was lined with large barrels of alcohol.

"The king has ordered a new celebration in honor of this joyous day! For you, the good people of Vargr, he sends his kingly gift—a fine spirit unlike anything you've had before. Drink up my friends; this round is on the king!" one of the merchants shouted.

The Rag'amorians snickered among themselves and started toward the stand.

"Something is off. We should keep moving!" Sera warned.

"Come on, it's a crowd; the perfect place to get lost. We can blend right in," one of the men protested.

"Wait!" Sera repeated, extending her arm to cut them off.

"What's the harm. boss? Let's grab a drink before we hit the road," the man pressed.

Before he could take a step, there was an unnerving scream from off in the distance. Celeste looked around, trying to find the source of the scream. Two men in similar black and red armor walked into the market from one of the side streets. They headed toward the other two merchants, appearing unconcerned.

The sounds from where the two men had come grew louder. Screams filled the air. Other unnatural noises accompanied them. Chaos ensued. Monsters burst into the market from the side streets in full rampage, charging into the crowd and sending people flying. Many in the crowd cried out, clutching their stomachs and falling to their knees. Celeste watched as the people's bodies broke and snapped, then reformed in different ways. Spikes, claws, tentacles, teeth, even their skin looked different.

The market transformed from a crowd of jovial people to a congregation of carnage and calamity. Celeste covered her mouth to stifle a scream as she watched person after person turn into a gruesome monster and proceed to tear those who hadn't changed into pieces. Doors burst open, windows shattered, and walls were smashed, followed by a choir of screams belting out from every direction. It was happening everywhere, all around them.

"To the gates! Run! Now!" Sera ordered, leading the charge through the horrific chaos in front of them. They rushed ahead as monsters rampaged around them, tackling people, biting them, shredding them in a sea of slaughter.

They pushed through the town center, fighting and slashing their way past the crowds, sprinting where they could. The screams grew louder and closer as the onslaught tightened around them. Bodies dropped and blood sprayed around them like rain. Celeste ducked as a four-armed creature dove for her. She slid under the monster, and it plowed into the Rag'amorian next to her. The man grunted and tried to push the creature off him. Celeste gasped as she watched the creature rip off the man's arms and discard them before sinking its long fangs into the man's neck.

The market swarmed with monsters as more and more of the people around the merchant table transformed. Several Rag'amorians fell as monsters closed in around them. Unlike the townsfolk, the Rag'amorians went down slashing and thrusting their swords, but, in the end, it made no difference. Sera cut the head from a creature that looked like a purple-skinned human with an octopus for a head. They pushed, ran, and fought their way through until they cleared the market. Even still, there were monsters and screams all around them. They ran and ran until Celeste's legs and lungs burned.

Finally, the gate was in view. Hope was on the horizon. Hope mixed with terror as Celeste saw something on the rooftops, something big and dark moving out of the corner of her eyes. She dared not look for fear that doing so might slow her down. One of the Rag'amorians rushed out ahead.

"We are almost there! Let's go!" he cheered.

Before he could turn toward the gate, a large, black, spiked leg pierced through his chest. Blood spurted from his mouth as he slumped to the ground. Celeste screamed as she stared up at a massive black spider with a human torso where the head should be. The spider monstrosity moved in front of them, cutting off their path to the gate. On top of the human torso, growing out of the spider's abdomen, was an oversized spider head with large pincer fangs that dripped with an opaque fluid. Its large, red eyes moved as the head turned unnaturally far to the side. The fangs opened and closed, then, impossibly, the nightmare spoke.

"Wwwhheere are you going, seekers of the stoooone?" The voice was feminine and almost enticing with its soft, whimsical tones.

"Did that thing just talk?" one of the Rag'amorians asked. "Oh no, I'm not having a conversation with that monster." He lifted his spear up and pulled back, preparing to hurl it.

The spid-trocity lunged forward with terrifying speed. It thrust one of its eight creepy legs forward, piercing the man. Celeste froze, unable to process what just happened. The spid-trocity pulled its leg back, and the man fell dead. The Rag'amorian warriors that had started with a dozen fighters were down to four, including Sera.

"You are Seekers of the stoooone; I can smell it on you," the spid-trocity said, her voice like a sweet melody tuned slightly off key. Her eyes closed.

A glowing red portal appeared just to the side of the creature, and a man in that same red and black armor stepped through.

"I am busy; what do you want?" the man asked, his voice thick with annoyance.

"Don't give me your attitude, Valron. Yoooou told me yooou wanted to speak with any Seeeeekers. I have found yoooou some Seeeekers," she answered.

Valron raised an eyebrow and turned to face Celeste and the others.

"I see. So, you are Seekers from Parisia on a quest from the king to retrieve the Darkstone?" He nodded and a smile formed on his face. "This is good news. Today is a glorious day that will mark a glorious return! You have the opportunity to be a part of it." He waved his hand and a small case containing five glasses appeared, each filled with a reddish-blown liquid.

"You don't really expect us to drink that do you?" Sera challenged.

Valron chuckled. "That depends on you. I offer you a great gift."

"Pass. We've seen what that does—transforming people into those things."

"Your form is fragile and frail. The new world she will form is for the strong. I offer you a chance to be remade, to shed your weakness and become so much more. All you have to do is drink." Valron extended his hands, his voice inviting and filled with sincere passion.

"You are offering to kill us and turn us into monsters to join your little horde," Sera retorted.

Valron's smile increased. "If you must be crude about it, then yes. You, as you think of yourself, are already dead. I offer you new life. You can be reborn as one of her loyal subjects, bathed in power and glory to destroy her enemies, or you can return to the earth from whence you came."

He turned to the spid-trocity and said, "Let them choose. If they refuse to drink, kill them . . . slowly." He looked over his shoulder. "That is all the time I have for now. Tata. I look forward to seeing your glorious new forms."

Shadows of the Dark Realm

A red portal appeared, and Valron vanished just as quickly as he arrived. Celeste blinked as her mind raced. The spidtrocity was too fast and too large to outrun. Maybe if Azalea or Dante were here, or even Caelan, they might stand a chance, but they had no hope. Even skilled warriors hadn't been able to launch an attack against the creature. Who knows, maybe it wouldn't be so bad. Maybe she would still maintain a part of herself. It was better than nothing, right? Better than death?

There was something about the fluid that called out to her. Like an invisible pull tugging her in. It made her feel warm, safe, and strong. It was like a cozy blanket on a cold night wrapping around her. How could something that felt so good, that looked so enticing—so delicious—really be bad? Celeste shook her head. No, these were not her thoughts. *Were they?*

She closed her eyes and found herself in her room as a girl. The door was locked, and the large window that overlooked the balcony from high up in the tower was sealed, leaving her no opportunity for escape. She paced around the room. She knew every tile, every crack, every stain on the floors, the walls, the ceiling. This room had contained her for her entire life. Her father called it "protecting," but she knew what it was. A palace suite can be just as much a prison as any cell. The bars just look nicer.

She could see her younger self pacing, crying, calling out, and bashing her hands raw against the door. Years passed with little or no contact with the outside world save the occasional tutor. The few conversations she had, everyone was always jealous of her birth, her station, her luxury. She'd have traded it all for just a taste of freedom. She'd hardly been allowed out of her family's estate in her first ten years of life. Just looking at this unnatural liquid made all her fears and worries fade away. It was like her memories of that place, the pain, and the loneliness all vanished. This was the answer. This was what she had been looking for. This would make everything better. All she needed to do was drink.

"Celeste, what are you doing? Stop!" Sera called, reaching out to grab her wrist.

Celeste pulled her arm away. Nothing was going to stop her

now. She picked up the glass and smiled, lifting it to the spid-trocity.

"Celeste, you can't drink that. You know what it will do to you!" Sera challenged, desperation in her voice.

Celeste smiled. "Don't worry so much. This is not a danger. It's a gift. I will show you."

She lifted the glass to her lips and smiled, her other hand on her hip. She could feel the eyes of the spid-trocity watching her intently. She tossed her head back and with it, the glass over her shoulder. For a moment, it appeared she had gulped down the drink, giving her just enough time to draw her sword. She thrust forward, kicking her leg, sending the other glasses clanging to the ground as she drove her sword into the spid-trocity's defenseless underbelly.

"You can keep your poison. I grew up in a cage. Never again," Celeste shouted before turning to the others. "Go! Get out of here! Find the Darkstone! Take it back to Parisia!" Her words were cut off as she dove out of the way of a stabbing spider leg. Celeste rolled as she hit the ground, barely dodging another stab.

"Yooooou will paaaay for that, yooooo foooool!" the spid-trocity cursed.

The spear-like legs crashed down with alarming speed and precision. Celeste's strike had done very little damage. She stepped and twirled as best she could, trying to regain her footing, but the monster was too fast, too dexterous for her to avoid. She slipped and landed on her shoulder, then quickly turned to her back. If she was going to die, she was going to see it coming.

A black spiny leg drove toward her. Instinctively, she shut her eyes. A loud scream, not of pain but a scream full of energy—of passion, a battle cry—echoed around her. Celeste opened her eyes to see a glimmer of silver flash by. The pointed leg split, and the bottom segment flopped away from the rest. The spid-trocity screamed in pain and reared back, off-balance.

Two daggers flew past, driving into the creature's soft underbelly. It stepped back, stumbling and nearly toppling over now that it was missing half of one of its legs. Standing over Celeste was a man with silver hair in bright silver armor holding an obscenely large sword. He looked down at her.

"Well done, girl; you have spirit. On your feet, we must take leave of this place." Spiro reached down and lifted her as if she weighed no more than a flower petal.

"W-where have you been?" she asked.

Spiro smiled. "Well, after dealing with the lot in the cave, I found you all being taken prisoner. Rather than volunteering to join, I followed from a distance. I watched and waited for the right time. Before I could make a move, you'd freed yourselves. I've been trying to catch up ever since."

"But why didn't you—" she started.

Spiro shook his head. "You want me to talk or to fight? Get the others and get going; I'll catch up." He turned.

"Wait!" Celeste shouted.

Spiro looked back and raised an eyebrow.

"That's the way we need to go. You're sort of blocking the path," she said.

Spiro smiled. "Well, then, let me clear it for you." He charged the spid-trocity as Celeste rushed back to the others.

Before Spiro could reach it, a blast of red surrounded the spid-trocity, consuming the creature and turning it into dust as a screech echoed from above them.

"A dragon?" Celeste shouted.

Spiro waved them forward. "No. Worse—much worse," he said, a note of distress in his voice.

The shadowed creature flew into the clouds and out of view. Spiro's eyes scanned the sky frantically.

"What is it?" Celeste asked, trying to find a sign of the massive creature.

"A Valrox—a demon monster from the Spirit Realm. They must have brought it through the veil somehow. We need to move fast," Spiro declared.

"I can help with that," a man's voice came from behind them. He was young, thin, with short dark hair and unmemorable features. He wore yellow robes that were two or three sizes too large, and he was walking toward them.

Sera pointed her knife at him. "And just who are you?"

He held up his hands defensively. "I am a mage from Vargr. I escaped the palace where the monsters were killing everyone. I , , , I can get you out of here. I can open a portal. But you have to take me with you." His voice was weak and pleading.

Spiro exchanged a look with Sera and put his sword away. "Do it now, and you will have our protection."

Before Sera could protest, the mage extended his hand, and a glowing yellow portal appeared a few hundred paces down the hill.

Spiro raised a brow. "Really? You couldn't make it closer?"

The mage looked down at the ground. "I'm sorry. I'm a novice. Portal magic is . . . tricky."

Sera led the Rag'amorians toward the portal, and the others followed. Spiro caught up with them and then took the lead. He slid to a stop suddenly as the ground shook beneath them. Standing in front of the portal was a massive creature. Its bird-like wings were covered in red and gray feathers that looked tattered and mutilated. Its neck was skinless muscle tissue. Its skeletal rib cage was fully exposed and contained nothing but a glowing purple heart. Its head looked like the skull of a great eagle with a massive beak. Its jaw opened beyond the beak and was littered in sharp teeth. Its eyes glowed purple, the same light that filled its empty ribs filling its mouth. It looked like a twisted, skeletal griffon but with seven black, whipping tails, the rest of the creature made of bone and moving independently of the others.

This was a creature to haunt even the bravest of dreams. It had landed directly in front of the portal through which they needed to escape.

"Ralk," Sera cursed.

Chapter 24

Escape Plan

Xander walked over to the side wall of the private room they had gathered in. The wall was lined with a lattice of diamond-shaped boxes from floor to ceiling, each stuffed full of tightly rolled scrolls. Xander pulled a scroll from one of the boxes and walked over to the long, rectangular table in the middle of the room, then spread the parchment across the stone slab.

The scroll was a blueprint of the center hill barracks, complete with a detailed mapping of the streets that surrounded the building. The details were great enough that the blueprints could pass for the product of the architect himself.

"Just for clarity's sake, you are using a custom of our people to force my hand into helping you so you can try to sneak into the most secure building in the entire city— into a building that was designed to prevent unwanted people from getting in or out and is the literal home to hundreds of soldiers, guards, and mages who patrol the spaces. Not to mention the magical wards and alarms that are undetectable and unavoidable littered throughout the barracks that will make any effort to sneak in virtually impossible." Xander looked up from the table and stared at Caelan.

"Oh, come on, we both know you love a good challenge. This

is going to be fun. The original lords of West Hill back together again!" Ash said, smacking Xander on the shoulder.

The tap was meant to be soft but knocked Xander forward so hard that his hip slammed into the table. He winced and tried to hide the jolt of pain from his face.

"There are two places they could be holding your friends: in the dungeon, three floors below the surface of the barracks, or in the cells four floors up. We will have no way of knowing which—unless you know something I don't," Xander said.

"Xander, Xander, Xander, when are you going to learn? I know a lot that you don't," Caelan grinned.

Xander scowled, saying, "You're going to need two teams to search both places. I hope you have a plan, and it better be a good one. Rite of Amends or not, I will not risk my people for some goraum idea that will never work."

Caelan smiled with his lips while glaring with his eyes. "First thing we need is a good distraction."

"A good one? Like starting a big public brawl outside the barracks?" Xander asked.

Caelan covered his face with his hand and sighed. "That's terrible. How are you the king of thieves?"

Xander grunted as he folded his arms across his chest.

Caelan grinned. "Since you have apparently learned nothing in my absence, let me teach you. A good distraction requires three things. First, it needs to draw attention. Then, it needs to demand a response. Lastly, it needs to be natural enough that it doesn't look like an obvious distraction."

Xander lifted one hand and started stroking the thin goatee that decorated his jaw. "How are we supposed to get their attention without making it look like we are trying to get their attention?"

Caelan smiled. "We make it look like you were trying to do something else, and it went wrong. Do you have a mage that can do a swarm spell?"

Xander broke eye contact. "I'm not going to like this, am I?"

Caelan's smile grew. "The soldiers are responsible for the protection of the palace. First, Xander, you and a few of your best men will sneak into the palace treasury and snatch the most valuable things you can find. Second, we will spread the word in the market that at midday tomorrow we will be distributing all the treasure from the palace to anyone at the gate. That will draw a large, excitable crowd. Put a few thugs with weapons in there to get them worked up, and it'll look like a riot."

"That's exactly what I said to do!" Xander scowled.

Caelan grinned. "No, it's completely different. Next, we'd place notices around town from a made-up secret society: The Brotherhood of Equality. The Brotherhood's mission is to create equal opportunities for everyone by sharing the wealth of the rich with the poor. We make sure some get to the barracks, and word will spread. That will put them on alert so when chaos breaks out, they won't suspect anything else is going on."

"Why the swarm spell?" Xander asked.

"Use it inside the treasury. Start throwing everything you can into it so the wealth of the palace is scattered throughout the city. That will create city-wide chaos. Everyone will start rioting in the streets, trying to get their hands on royal wealth, which will require all the soldiers to exit the barracks to respond. The king will demand they take the time to go collect all the stolen wealth and retrieve it. It will also trigger every alarm and warning ward in the city that will force them to disregard them all until the situation is resolved," Caelan explained.

A slow grin formed on Xander's face. "Then the only thing you'd have to deal with would be guards left behind. Still, there are enough guards in the barracks that you wouldn't get far. Even if every thief and thug in West Hill worked together, we wouldn't be able to overwhelm the guard."

"It's about time for the merchant's showcase, right?" Caelan asked.

Xander wagged a finger at him, and his smile widened. "You're thinking we donate some barrels of ale to the good guards-folk to show our "appreciation" and spike it with some Somna root?"

Caelan nodded. "They will assume it's the annual bribe for leaving West Hill alone. It'll knock enough of them out that the impossible suddenly becomes doable."

"You didn't just come up with this, did you?" Ash shook his head.

Caelan smirked. "No, I didn't. Oh, one last thing. I'll need your man on the inside to get my stuff—my bow and my armor; I stashed them here." Caelan drew a circle on the blueprints with his finger.

"That's easy enough," Ash said.

Xander folded his arms again and reapplied his stern gaze. "One problem," he said cryptically.

"You aren't competent enough to break into the palace treasury to use the swarm spell? I thought of that. I even made a step-by-step guide for how to do it," Caelan started.

"The scope of this far exceeds any requirement for the Rite of Amends," Xander cut him off. "A debt I may owe, but the debt is not so great as to require this. I do like your plan, but I cannot commit such a great force to it. Not without something in return."

"Xander, come on, you can't be . . . We have to do this. It's Caelan," Ash protested.

Xander shook his head. "I do not feel the same loyalty to him that you do. Nor am I willing to risk so much for his benefit. Anything goes wrong, he leaves, and we are the ones left holding the bag."

"I thought you'd say that. Which is why I know there are two things in it for you. First, if my sources are correct, the Gem of Marion Wei is kept in the palace treasury. While you are throwing the rest of the wealth into the swarm spell, you could keep that one for yourself. Not only would that make you richer than anyone in West Hill—stealing a magical gem from the palace—that would make you a legend. Stories of Xander, the great thief king would be told for generations," Caelan replied.

"And second?" Xander pressed.

"The dungeons are where they hold captured thieves. No one has ever rescued his men once caught. You would not only be able to get your men back but also make a declaration of your supremacy. Do that, and all the thieves working with your rival will come flocking to you. How nice would it be to put an end to the competition once and for all?"

"Well, you seem to have thought of everything. My last question: many of the guards will be passed out and unresponsive even to the alarms, but that won't take care of all of them. You will still have a lot to deal with. How do you plan to overcome that?" Xander challenged.

"Best if you don't know my plan, and I don't know yours. That way, if either of us are captured, we can't burn the other."

"Trust through distrust. Very well." Xander nodded.

"Your men will certainly be in the dungeon below the barracks, so that'll be your task. Ash and I will take the cells on the 4th floor."

Xander stared for a moment. "This had better work. Rite or not, you screw me on this, and I will cut off your hands."

Caelan smirked. "I'd be nervous, but you'd have to figure out which was the dull end of your knife first."

Xander chuckled and slapped Caelan on the back. "Don't make me regret being glad to see you."

"You get those spiked barrels delivered and everything in place. I'll make you a folk hero that thieves and vagabonds will sing of for all time," Caelan said.

They shook hands before Caelan and Ash left the room and made their way back down West Hill.

"How are you planning to deal with remaining guards? I can fight a lot of them, but even in reduced capacity they will outnumber us considerably," Ash commented.

Caelan put his hand on his friend's oversized shoulder. "You still with that girl who has a witch sister?" he asked.

Ash laughed. "No. Turns out the witch sister was the normal one."

Caelan rolled his eyes. "I've had meals that last longer than your relationships."

Ash chuckled and shoved him. Caelan took three steps to one side before regaining his balance.

"You get a message to the witch sister?" Caelan asked.

"What are you thinking?" Ash asked.

"Run, boy, run," Caelan said.

Ash stopped and grunted as he looked up at the sky. "I hate run, boy, run."

"No, it was your favorite," Caelan protested.

"No, it really wasn't."

They chatted as they made their way back down to the slums where they had grown up. Then they parted ways, Ash heading off to find the witch girl while Caelan made his way to Center Hill. He found a tall residential building that overlooked the barracks and snuck his way up onto the roof where he stayed, watching the guards and learning their patterns as best he could. A few hours were not enough time to really feel prepared, but it was better than nothing.

He watched as a group of Xander's men brought a cart filled with barrels to the barracks gate. They wasted no time cracking open the barrels and distributing the ale. Even from the roof, he could hear the guards eagerly laughing and helping themselves. At least Xander was cooperating thus far. Whether he would remain true to the plan was yet to be seen.

The next morning, Caelan found Ash waiting at the gate to West Hill. Ash was not dressed in his normal sleeveless leather chest plate but wore the gear of a low-ranking barracks guard. He gestured with his head to a box containing a prisoner's uniform.

Caelan shook his head. "Oh no. I play the guard. You can be my prisoner."

"All I could get on short notice. The prisoner uniform is two sizes too small for me."

"Meaning you asked for these sizes specifically, and now it's too late to change them," Caelan retorted.

Ash smirked. "Get dressed, convict! Brad the Blood Butcher of Bornio is making an appearance." Ash folded his arms across his chest.

Caelan rubbed his temples with his fingers. "Oh, that's terrible."

"It's a perfect criminal name, and it's alliterative."

"It doesn't even make sense," Caelan protested.

Ash ignored him and said, "From the witch," holding up a small woven bracelet, which he then slipped onto Caelan's wrist.

"Enchanted?" Caelan asked.

"It's a familiarity spell. When people look at you, they will have this nagging thought in the back of their minds that they know you from somewhere. It'll make them more impressionable when I tell them you're a blood-thirsty criminal. Now get dressed."

Caelan scowled and grabbed the box of dirty clothes before making his way into an alley and changing into them. He attached his knives behind his back, tucked out of view by the grungy, too-loose shirt.

"It smells like griffon gwar," Caelan said, cringing.

They made their way to the barracks and waited out of view. Once the alarms started, they could make their move. It didn't take long. A minute later, alarms rang out around the city. The barracks gates clanged open. As the sea of soldiers rushed out, Ash fitted Caelan with chains around his arms and started pushing him through the gate against the tide of armed men rushing past them. The farther in they got, the fewer soldiers remained until they were practically alone.

Before they could clear the courtyard, the gates slammed closed. Half of the guard posts were empty, and the rest were filled with guards who were actively struggling to stay awake. The plan was working beautifully. They moved toward the stairs when a pair of guards cut them off.

"Oi, where you think you're going?" the guard asked.

"Taking this one up to the cells for questioning," Ash responded.

"I haven't got no word of a prisoner being brought up." the guard said.

Ash shrugged. "I don't know what to tell you. Maybe with whatever is going on, word didn't get to you yet."

The guard's eyes narrowed as he appraised Caelan. "Who is this anyway?"

Ash grabbed the back of Caelan's shirt and jerked him. "This here, boys, is Brad the legendary Butcher of Blood from Bornio. He's one of the most wanted men in all of Taggoron," Ash boasted.

"Butcher of Blood from Bornio? Why they call him that?" the guard asked, his face crinkled in frustration as he tried to understand the name.

Ash cleared his throat. "Well, he killed seventeen people . . . with his bare hands."

"Then why they call him the butcher? If he used his hands, wouldn't he be the—"

Caelan nudged Ash in the ribs. Ash pulled back on his shirt and shoved him forward. "He chopped 'em up after, didn't he?"

The guards seemed to find this answer more palatable.

"But how does one butcher blood, exactly?"

"What are you on about?" the other guard asked.

"Well, a butcher is someone who runs a meat shop. The act of butchering is to slaughter or chop up an animal. Blood is a liquid. You can't exactly chop up a liquid can you? So, they shouldn't really be calling him the Butcher of Blood, should they? Bloody Butcher—that makes sense. But that name is just confusing."

This was not going well. Caelan knew he needed to do something to move it along. He lunged forward and snapped his teeth at one of the guards, causing the man to jump back in surprise. Ash tugged on him in time to keep the guard from needing to respond.

"I'd keep my distance, boys. He's broken out of three prisons already and always kills any guard who makes eye contact with him when he does."

"I remember now; I've seen him before. On , , , a wanted poster, must have been," one of the guards muttered, his voice trembling.

The two guards stepped back and shuffled away carefully, avoiding Caelan's gaze. Ash pushed him inside, and they started up the stairs.

"My contact stashed your weapons on the fourth floor, in case we need to fight our way out," he said as they climbed.

The winding stone staircase leading up to the cells above was wide and sturdy, well cleaned but lacking in any decoration or detail.

"So many stairs . . . " Caelan complained.

"It's four floors." Ash made no effort to hide the mocking tone in his voice.

"Yeah, and then a long corridor to the protected wing,

another set of stairs, and another hallway. When we rescue them are they going to be like, 'Thank you, Caelan you are our hero and the most amazing man ever!' No! They are going to be like, 'what took you so long?'"

"You are walking pretty slow . . ."

"Shut up, it's a lot of stairs."

As they exited the stairway to begin down the long corridor, some guards were frantically running around and others looked nervously from their posts.

"Stay back! Don't get too close. It's Brad the Butcher of Blood!" Ash shouted down the halls.

"You really need to fix that," Caelan whispered through gritted teeth.

Ash was having entirely too much fun with this. When they reached the fourth floor, they had to pass a guard station. A young guard rushed past, and Caelan stepped to the side and slammed into him. The young guard shoved Caelan away and glared, his hand falling to the hilt of his blade. Ash jerked Caelan over and shoved him toward the far wall.

"Keep moving, convict!" he shouted and gave the guard a nod.

The guard collected himself and started off. Ash suddenly rushed forward toward the guard station and shouted, "Prisoner escaping! Brad the Butcher of blood is getting away! Sound the alarm! Get him!"

Guards charged into view, moving away from the guard station in the middle of the hallway. Ash turned and pointed to the young guard who had yet to notice the small bracelet Caelan slipped onto his wrist when they collided. The spell worked perfectly. As soon as Ash suggested the guard was a convict, the guard's appearance changed.

"W-w-what are you doing? G-g-get away from me!" The young guard looked confused as the others started creeping toward him.

The other guards continued to close in on him. He shook his head and sprinted down the hall in the other direction. The guards gave chase, leaving only two posted at the station.

They stood next to each other, blocking the path forward as

Ash approached with Caelan in tow. Ash smiled and stepped close to them. Without a word, he drove his fist into the stomach of the guard closest to him. The man keeled over, only for Ash to send him toppling the ground in a heap with a shot to the face. The tandem attack was so quick that the second guard barely had time to blink before Ash twisted his body and slammed his elbow into the man's temple. He was down in a single hit.

Caelan slipped out of the chains that bound him before making his way past the now-empty guard station. He turned into the small room where Ash's contact had placed their weapons. The schematics they'd used were perfect; everything was exactly where it should be. Caelan felt relief as he slipped out of the prisoner's garb and put on normal clothes again. He slung his quiver over his shoulder and held his bow. Uniforms and tricks weren't going to help them from here.

When they stepped out of the room, they nearly crashed into a man in an orange hood walking by. He stopped.

"You. I've seen you before," his voice rumbled like rolling thunder.

Caelan notched an arrow and held his breath. Ash shoved him down the hall.

"Go get your friends. I'll take care of this one."

Ash squared off against the man in the orange hood, putting himself between the stranger and Caelan. The hooded man turned slowly, as if unconcerned.

"You want to get to him; you will have to go through me," Ash warned, lifting his fists into his fighting stance.

The man in the hood chuckled. "Is that supposed to intimidate me?" he asked, a note of amusement in his voice.

"I'll give you one chance to walk away. One way or another, we are leaving with the prisoners," Ash stated.

The man in the hood sneered. "They are of no concern to me. Your friend, however—you've saved me time by bringing him to me. Thank you."

Ash charged. His fists caught the hooded man in the stomach, then the head. Ash froze for a moment. It had been years since he had to throw more than two punches, yet this man took two and seemed completely unphased. Ash shook it off and pressed his attack. He hit the man in the head three more times, and the stomach over and over as Ash turned each swing into a series of consecutive blows.

The hooded man made no attempt to block. He took each punch and was somehow still on his feet. This was unnatural. No one should be able to take blows like that without showing some sign of struggle. Normally, he'd jump at the challenge to face an opponent like this, but, under the circumstances, it was unnerving. He moved and danced, striking hard and fast. Despite the lack of resistance, he kept himself moving, always ready with a counter. Still the hooded man made no effort to block or fight back. Not a single blow seemed to have any effect.

"Fight me, rooki!" Ash shouted.

He jabbed his fist directly at the man's hooded face. The man dodged it at the last second. He jabbed again. Nothing. He punched faster and faster, his arms moving in a blur, his fists disappearing entirely as he thrusted and punched. The hooded man moved his head back and forth, leaning a little to avoid each strike with impossible, effortless precision.

Ash's arms began to burn as his body tired. How could anyone be this much better than him? The man wasn't even trying. This wasn't a fight; the man was toying with him. The more irritated Ash got, the more he had to hold himself back. Driving into a blind rage would only make things worse. He paused, holding up his guard while trying to catch his breath and consider a new approach.

"My turn," the man in the hood said.

In a blur the distance between them disappeared. Ash felt his body slam against the stone wall behind him. Something felt cool on his back as he slid down the wall, his mind drifting, vision fading to black. He'd never even seen the man move.

Chapter 25
The Guide

Celeste jumped back as one of the bone-tails slammed into the ground where she had been standing. Even working together, the group was barely able to fend off the seven striking tails.

"Don't let the tails touch you; they are poisonous!" Spiro warned.

Celeste could practically hear Caelan saying, "Why wouldn't they be?" The group huddled together as best they could, each focusing on one of the tails and trying to defend the group against it. The Valrox cocked its head back and forth, watching them with its glowing, smoky eyes.

"Hey, novice. You got anything in your bag of tricks?" Spiro called out.

The mage stood frozen, staring at the monstrous demon-bird creature with his fang bared.

Sera grabbed him and shook. "Listen, you keep standing here like a statue, and we are all going to die. I get it; you're afraid. But there's a time to be scared and a time to act. Snap out of it."

"Shrink! I . . . I can use a . . . shrink spell," he finally managed.

Spiro grinned. "That'll work. How small can you make it?" he asked.

The mage shook his head. "I . . . I can't shrink spirit creatures. I . . . only . . . smaller objects . . . like us."

Spiro swung his blade, deflecting a bone-tail strike. "Your great solution to our problem is to make us smaller? What the ralk?"

"Hold on!" Sera interrupted. "That could work. How small can you make us?"

"Field mice," he answered.

"All of us at once?" she asked.

He nodded.

"Do it!" Sera commanded.

Spiro shook his head. "This is a really bad idea. How is—" But before he could finish, he started to glow.

Celeste turned to see the monster facing them becoming larger and larger. Doubling in size. Tripling. No, the creature wasn't growing. Celeste looked at the stones at her feet. Where two had been hidden by her boot, now a single stone appeared massive.

"Run! To the portal!" Sera shouted.

The crew charged toward the massive skeletal creature. Crossing a few stones felt like sprinting across the entire city. For all their effort, they had covered so little ground. They still weren't even to the skeletal monster blocking their path. Celeste gripped her side as pain surged through it. Her legs, her lungs, and her core all burned. What was Sera thinking? Why did this seem like a good idea?

The shadow of the Valrox loomed far greater as they scurried toward it. They were, Celeste was certain, running to their doom. Before the Valrox had stared at them; now its head turned furiously as it stomped from side to side. Each stomp made her nearly loose her footing as the earth trembled beneath her, but she pressed on. Even from here Celeste could see its smoking eyes darting back and forth, scanning for any sign of them. Sera was a genius, coming up with this so quickly. The creature was so large that shrinking had made them basically invisible to the monster.

They reached the shadow cast by the Valrox. They kept running. Celeste's heart thumped so loud and hard in her chest, she wondered if it would break free of her body. Still the creature scanned the horizon looking, searching, not finding. It roared a terrible, deathly roar. With a great flap of its wings, the creature took off into the air, flying up and away, circling the area for any sign of its prey. A few minutes of running later, and they reached the portal. Jumping through it, Celeste felt her body tingle with an electric energy before she landed softly on a pile of grass. The blades were huge, considerably taller than she was. The trees towered into the sky around them. They were in the clearing of a wooded area.

Celeste ducked down when she heard voices, then realized how unnecessary it was. The grass hid them completely.

"Look at him trying to free himself. The beast is too dumb to know it's captured," a man's voice mocked.

At the edge of the clearing, gathered around a tree, was a group of six men, bandits by the look of them. Their skin looked dirty; their hair and clothes looked unkempt. Everything about them looked rough and uncivilized. *Had they never heard of a bath?* They certainly didn't seem to have ever taken one. It was like the dirt on their skin was covered in dirt. *Gross.*

The others laughed and jeered as they circled around a tree. One of the men stepped to the side, creating an opening that allowed Celeste to see what they were focused on. Tied to the tree with its arms behind his back was a large, mostly human-looking creature. It was a full head taller than the men that surrounded it. It had jet-black, braided hair cut into a mohawk that ran down behind its back. Its skin was a deep blue-gray and two tusks like those of a boar lined the sides of its mouth from its bottom jaw.

It looked muscular and strong with the body of a god. The only thing covering it was a hide loin cloth and leather belt. One of the men in front of it was brandishing a large knife. That's when Celeste noticed all the little cuts covering the creature's body. They were torturing it, playing with it like it was a toy. It grunted and pulled at the ropes that bound it. The rope was thick and wrapped around its body and the trunk of the tree several times. Still, Celeste was surprised its rippling muscles didn't tear through the restraints.

"What is that?" Celeste asked, unable to take her eyes off the creature. He somehow looked human and unlike anything she'd ever seen at the same time.

"That's a troll berserker," Sera said. Her hands gripped her blades as she watched.

"A troll?" Celeste had read about trolls, seen pictures sketched in bestiaries. Different types of trolls had very different looks, but none of them were depicted like this.

"They are noble creatures—proud, intelligent, loyal. He doesn't deserve this," she said through gritted teeth.

"Why are they doing this?" Celeste asked.

Sera shook her head. "Troll tusks are often taken as a prize and worn on necklaces like a badge of honor."

"Why?"

"Many believe wearing the tusk of a troll proves they are a great warrior. Though, I've never met a great warrior who needed a trophy to prove their worth."

Sera's attention shifted as Spiro and the few remaining Rag'amorian warriors circled around the Vargrian mage.

"What do you mean you can't reverse the spell, boy?" Spiro demanded, grabbing the young man by his cloak.

"M-m-my name is Y-y-yolan," the thin mage protested feebly.

"Tell me again that you shrank us, knowing full well that you didn't know how to put us back!"

Sweat was already dripping from young Yolan's face as he looked around desperately for help.

Sera sighed and walked over. "Put him down. He's the reason we are alive right now."

Spiro sneered before dropping the mage.

Yolan landed on his feet and stumbled back, flopping onto his rear.

"T-T-The spell . . . d-d-doesn't have to be reversed," he said weakly and almost too quiet to hear.

Spiro pointed his finger at the mage. "What do you mean?"

"It . . . it wears off . . . in a few minutes," Yolan sputtered.

"Haha, look at that, boys. He's got a tear. Little beast is

crying." The booming voice of one of the men surrounding the troll pulled her attention back.

Sera turned to the bandits torturing the troll. She started pacing back and forth, her hands gripping the handles of her blades so tight her knuckles turned pale. She stomped back and forth so hard even her small body was wearing down a few blades of grass.

Sera looked down at her hands as they suddenly felt tingly, like all the sensation was leaving them. Her skin felt numb; her vision blurred. Then every part of her body felt like it was being stretched and pulled at once. She winced at the awkward sensation. When her eyes opened, everything was normal again. The grass was no longer towering over her head but rather barely reaching her ankles. The others appeared equally disoriented.

"What's this ralk? Where'd you come from?" The bandit with the knife gasped in surprise.

"Step away from the troll," Sera warned, her voice rumbling as she restrained her rage.

"What did you say?"

"Step away from the troll or this forest will be your tomb," Sera warned again, her head turned down as she glared at the men.

"What's this?" the bandit laughed. "Are you confused, girl? This isn't a kitchen. Are you lost?"

"Last chance." Sera stood statuesque even as the bandits moved to surround her.

The thugs started to circle around Sera, grinning wickedly.

"Spiro, help her," Celeste pleaded.

Spiro shook his head. "This is not my fight. A troll is of no interest to me."

Celeste turned to the Rag'amorian soldiers, but they stood back, seemingly amused.

"What is wrong with you? We have to help her," Celeste shouted.

None of them moved. Celeste growled and drew her sword.

"Fine! I'll do it."

"Stay out of this," Sera said flatly, looking back at Celeste. "They are not yours to kill."

"Oh? Is that right? Listen to her. This . . . woman . . . thinks she can threaten us? Why don't you show her what we do to girls who forget their place?" the bandit with the knife sneered.

Three of the bandits rushed at her from different sides at once. Sera dove between them, throwing a dagger at one of the bandits. The throw seemed oddly slow. The bandit stepped aside, and the dagger slammed harmlessly into the tree behind him.

"Is that it? You're gonna have to do better than that, sweetheart," the bandit taunted.

Sera deflected an attack from one of the bandits and pushed him away, hurling her other dagger. It flew wide and missed the bandit, also sinking into the tree behind him with a loud *thwump*.

The bandits laughed. "You've got spirit, sweetheart, but don't feel bad. You weren't meant to be out in the big bad world. Let me show you how it's done."

The bandit sliced his blade at her. Sera leapt back, dodging the attack. Before he could react, she dove forward, rolling across the ground past the bandit and sprinted further away.

He laughed. "You see, boys? She talked fierce, but like the woman she is, she's running off scared."

The other bandits laughed. Celeste resisted the urge to draw her sword. *What was Sera doing? Had the shrinking spell impaired her vision?* Celeste had thought her a much more competent warrior than this showing was indicating. Sera planted her feet suddenly and spun around.

"What happened to all that killing us, sweetheart? Lose your nerve?" the bandit asked.

Sera shook her head. "You are not mine either. Your lives belong to him." Sera ground the toes of her foot into the ground. Celeste saw it—the wooden handle of a short axe. Sera had slipped her foot under the flat metal of the side. She kicked her foot up, and the axe launched into the air.

"What are you—" the bandit started.

A grunt from behind him cut him off. Celeste realized what was happening only a moment before the bandits. Sera's throws hadn't missed their mark. She wasn't trying to hit the bandits.

She was cutting the ropes. Dropping from the tree as his bindings fell to the ground, the troll reached out and snatched the axe from the air. He roared with delight.

The bandits started backing away.

"W-w-what have you—"

The troll moved in quick bursts, leaping from one bandit to the next, driving his axe down into their skulls. Each one pleaded for his life, begging and backing away.

"P-p-p-please don't hurt me; we was only playing. We didn't mean anything."

When their pleading didn't work, they tried to run. Not one blocked the troll's attack. Not one could dodge it. Six leaps. Six strikes. Six dead bandits. Once they all lay dead, he rested the blunt end of his axe over his shoulder.

The troll stood still, looking down over the bodies of the bandits who'd been cutting on him. His breathing was loud and heavy. He squeezed the axe tightly in his hand. Slowly, the large creature turned and walked toward Sera.

"Easy there, big fella." Spiro put his hand on his sword and stepped closer.

The troll glared at him but said nothing. He just kept walking. Sera stood perfectly still as the troll towered over her, bloodstained axe in hand. She stared up at him. He stared down at her. Their eyes were locked for what felt like an eternity.

The troll snorted. "You," he spoke, his voice deep and heavy.

Sera stared silently back. With her daggers still stuck in the trees, she was completely at his mercy.

The troll dropped to one knee and lowered his head, kneeling before Sera. "You . . . save . . . Grom." The troll kept his head down. "Grom . . . The Bone Breaker . . . pledge life to serve the lady."

He reached his axe behind his back and cut off the tip of his finely braided hair. Clutching it in his hand, he offered it to Sera. "This . . . my vow."

"Umm . . . Sera . . . what's happening?" Celeste asked, her hand still clutching her sword.

"T-trolls have been known to devote themselves to someone who does them a great kindness," Yolan explained. "The cutting of his hair is a token of his vow, a binding offering that he will not betray even to his death."

"How do you know that?" Celeste asked.

"My primary studies are in beasts and creatures of the wildlands. My hope is to be a druid," Yolan answered.

"I am honored by your offer. You do not owe me this debt. I did only what was right—what I would want someone to do for me. Nothing more. You are a free troll. Go, be free," Sera tried to push the troll's hand closed.

"Grom . . . free. Grom . . . choose to follow lady." The troll opened his hand and pushed it forward with more insistence.

"We are on a dangerous quest. I can't ask you to join us," Sera warned.

"What . . . is lady's purpose?" Grom asked.

"We are retrieving a magical stone called the Darkstone from a dragon's roost," Sera answered.

"Grom . . . understand."

"And I am hunting the dragon that attacked our village. I mean to kill it," she added.

Grom nodded. "Grom help lady—"

"No, you don't need to—" Sera started to protest.

"So long as Grom live . . . Grom's axes . . . are for lady . . . Grom will obey . . . Grom will protect . . . Lady's enemies . . . Grom's enemies. Lady's friends . . . Grom's friends. None . . . will harm lady. Grom . . . help slay dragon."

"Very well, I am honored to have you, Grom. I will accept your oath so long as it is freely given." Sera placed her hand on the troll's head.

Grom nodded.

"I am Sera. These are my friends." Sera took the lock of hair and tucked it away.

Grom greeted each of the others with a grunt and a nod.

While they took some time to rest, eat, and recover from their escape, Yolan sat down next to Sera.

"You are . . . heading into the Dragon Lands?" he asked tentatively.

Sera nodded.

"Then . . . I think this must be where I leave you."

"No. We could use another mage. You need to come with us," Celeste said.

"I . . . am not cut out for this. I like books. Theories. I like to study and understand. I'm not made to fight monsters and dragons," Yolan protested.

"You realize what will happen to all your books if we fail? If the Darkstone isn't retuned, the Shadow King will return," Celeste started.

"Where will you go?" Sera cut her off. Celeste glared in frustration, but Sera ignored her.

Yolan shrugged. "There is a mage school in Taggoron. I was thinking of going there. After what I just saw, I don't think I feel safe in Vargr anymore."

"What you just saw is the fate of this entire realm if we fail. You want to go hide in your libraries? Good for you, but there won't be any libraries when the veil breaks. That'll be on you." Celeste started up.

"Travel safe and thank you for your help. You probably saved all our lives," Sera said, interrupting Celeste again.

Yolan stood up. Sera shook his hand. Grom grunted. The others offered a nod or a wave at most. After bowing in respect, Yolan the wizard started off, disappearing into the woods.

"We should get moving. We have no idea where we are or even which direction he teleported us into. We will need to find a way back to the canyon so we can regroup with the others," Spiro said, rising to his feet.

"If they are even alive," Celeste remarked.

Sera scowled. "They are alive. Rivik knows better than to die on me."

"Either way, we need to go. If those monsters continue to spread, this area could get overrun very quickly," Spiro pressed.

"Grom know . . . Dragon Lands . . . through Valley of Dry Bones . . . to big water. Grom . . . take lady there."

"Is this Valley of Dry Bones a deep canyon that dips deep into the ground?" Sera asked.

Grom shrugged. "It . . . way to Dragon Lands."

Sera nodded. "Ok, take us there."

The troll walked ahead, guiding them through the woods as

Chapter 31

Potemania

"Help! Please help!" Caelan turned to see a woman, middle-aged and blonde. Her cut-up face was covered in mud as she sprinted toward them. She repeatedly tripped over her long tunic, scrambling as she fell over and over again. Even at a distance, the terror in her eyes and voice were unmistakable. Caelan grunted as she bumped into him at full speed. Despite her small frame, she practically knocked him over as she tried to keep running.

"Whoa, whoa, whoa, what's going on?" he asked, grabbing her shoulders to hold her still and stabilize her.

"Let me go! Please! I have to get help! Monsters! The village —" she panted.

Caelan looked up. The winding path the woman had run down led to a small town. She wasn't alone. Rushing toward them was a huge crowd of people fleeing and screaming for help, with a horde of monsters on their heels. Caelan moved the woman behind him and pulled his bow free.

"What are you doing?" Celeste asked.

"Thought I'd have a picnic right quick. What's it look like, princess?" Caelan replied.

"This is not our problem."

"Says the girl who wanted to be a hero. How far you have fallen."

"We can't save Parisia if we die fighting for some random village. This isn't worth the risk," Celeste replied.

"Spoken like a true Royal. Run away if you want, princess. I'm staying," Caelan snapped before turning. "Ash."

Ash nodded and cracked his knuckles. "Just like that time in the Wandering Woods."

Caelan raised an eyebrow as he notched an arrow. "With the Aligari? How is this like that?"

Ash shrugged. "It's a really bad idea." He turned to Owen. "Stay with the villagers. If they run, run with them."

Ash walked straight down the path, allowing the sea of villagers to part around him. Caelan rushed up the hill next to the path and started firing arrows into the march of monsters.

"Goraum fool!" Celeste stomped her boot into the ground and dug her heels into the dirt.

She cursed as the villagers rushed around them. The Rag'amorian warriors exchanged confused glances as Ash stood alone in the middle of the path, waiting for the monsters to reach him.

"What are you going to do?" Kade asked, waiting for her response.

Celeste looked at the path ahead and back to where Ash was standing. Her mind was as forked as the crossroads she stood at. It was an impossible choice. The wave of monsters came to a halt in front of Ash, stopping to assess him, as if suspicious of a trap. An arrow pierced the head of one monster, and it slumped to the ground. The monsters turned and started moving toward Caelan's position at the top of the hill. Ash moved to cut them off. His fist drove into the face of the first monster to move, knocking it back.

Celeste watched as Ash kicked, punched, and dodged a series of attacks from a swarm of monsters, single-handedly holding their line back as Caelan's arrows rained down on them. Despite Ash's size, he was small by comparison to the towering beasts that surrounded him. Each time a monster tried to move on him, one of Caelan's arrows struck them. Ash held the line in place while Caelan reduced their numbers. Somehow, the two were holding their own.

The villagers stood behind Celeste and the others, watching as Caelan and Ash held back the enemy lines. The townsfolk creeped farther and farther away but kept their eyes locked on the fight. Spiro drew his sword and started toward the fray.

"Spiro, what are you doing?" Celeste asked.

"Dragons are not the only monsters who need slaying," Spiro shrugged.

The Rag'amorian warriors followed as Spiro charged into the monster mob. Celeste sighed and drew her sword. Before she could take a step, Kade's hand grasped her.

"I need you alive. Stay here," Kade said before his body lifted into the air.

Orbs of fire and chains of lighting rained down as Kade flew over the crowd of monsters. Orange beams crashed into the ground, incinerating everything they touched. The swarm of monsters diminished within moments to a scattered few before Kade landed on his feet. One of the creatures, a large minotaur, lunged at him. Kade grabbed the bull-man, lifted him into the air, and pulled him in two.

Ash kicked one of the monsters around him away, sending the creature flying backwards through the air. He turned and looked at the sudden open space around him. Two arrows whooshed past him, one after the other, dropping two small creatures that were rushing toward him.

Spiro and the Rag'amorians were battling off a few of the remaining monsters. A small pack of goblins who had been in the rear of the herd were charging toward Kade. Kade turned to face them when the ground under his feet started to glow. A yellow aura filled with various shapes and symbols surrounded him. Kade started to move, but he was stuck. The yellow light surrounded him like a cage. Kade pressed against it. The light grew brighter and pushed him back. His calm, confident demeanor suddenly shifted to a wide-eyed panic as the pack of goblins charged toward him, their crude weapons ready.

"Ash!" Caelan shouted and nodded to the goblins.

Ash barreled toward them, closing the gap between himself and Kade. The goblins were closer and moving quickly as he set out to intercept them. Caelan scanned the horizon. On the hill across from him was a single goblin wearing a large skull headdress decorated with colorful feathers and beads. The goblin was dancing and waving a large wooden stick over his head. There was a glowing yellow circle under his feet, similar to the one under Kade.

Caelan lifted his bow and lined up his shot. The goblin was far away, farther than Caelan was confident he could hit. He pulled back hard on the bowstring and held his breath. He let all the noise around him fade, felt the breeze against his skin, and released. His arrow tore through the air, flying across the chasm toward the goblin.

The goblin moved its head to the side and Caelan's arrow stuck into the grassy hill behind him. The goblin snickered and bobbed its head back and forth tauntingly as it faced Caelan. It waved its arms in mockery so dramatically that it didn't notice the second arrow before it pierced its head. The goblin swarm was nearly upon Kade, who was trapped in the yellow light. Ash dove into them just before the first few reached Kade. The goblins scattered as Ash bowled them over. As the goblin on the hill fell, the circle containing Kade disappeared. It didn't take long for the rest of the monsters to fall and only a pile of corpses to remain.

"What was that?" Caelan asked as he retrieved a few of his arrows from the monster's bodies.

Kade growled, "A shaman."

"A goblin shaman managed to contain you? You mean to tell me, Dante couldn't take you, but that little dancing monster was too much?"

"Not all magic is equal," Kade answered, seeming even more annoyed.

"Little goblin magic is your weakness?" Caelan pressed.

"Watch it," Kade warned.

Celeste stood with her hands on her hips. "It's over now, let's get going."

"Patience, princess," Caelan jested.

"Every day the Darkstone is gone, Parisia is vulnerable. My home is in danger. So excuse me for not wanting to stop and smell the flowers," she snapped.

"We have to wait for Vale anyway. Does it really matter if we do it before or after we reach Stormdale?" Caelan replied.

"Thank you! You saved us!" The blonde woman from the village threw her arms over his shoulders and hugged Caelan.

They were whisked away by the mob of grateful townsfolk who celebrated and danced, throwing a feast in their honor. Games were played, dances were danced, and drinks were drunk. The sun released its hold on the sky and drifted out of sight. The jubilation of the townspeople, rescued from certain, horrific death was more intoxicating than the strong drinks they poured as the festivities went on long into the night. They lit a great fire, singing and dancing around it, celebrating their heroes, the saviors of Artiome.

The group sat around a smaller fire in what the villagers had called 'a place of honor'. Owen was fidgeting with a unique-looking set of gloves. Celeste stirred the stew in her bowl idly as she stared at her reflection in it.

"What's the matter with you?" Caelan asked, sitting down next to her.

"You proud of yourself?" she snapped, looking up at him. "You risked all our lives, our mission, the hope of Parisia, to save a group of people you've never even seen before, for what? For this? To feel good about yourself? Does your ego need inflating that much?"

Caelan leaned back. "My ego? You think this is what happened? Did I miss something, or were you like this the whole time and I just didn't notice?"

"No one ever notices. It's just foolish little Celeste. Whatever. Do you think I want to leave people behind? To do nothing while people die? You really think I'm so heartless? What you seem to have forgotten—what all of you seem to have forgotten—is why we are here. The king did not send us into these gods-forsaken lands to put down a monster population. Someone has to keep us focused. We've been lucky so far. Every time we engage in an avoidable conflict—every needless fight we get in—there's a chance that one of us dies. What if we needed them to be successful? What if that person was the difference between our retrieving the Darkstone and our failure? You are thinking about the moment. I'm looking at the bigger picture, the greater good. There is too much at stake for you to be so reckless with our lives," Celeste said.

"Ah, now I see what you mean about the noble thing," Ash started.

Caelan chuckled and nodded.

"What's that have to do with anything?" Celeste stood up, spilling her stew and putting her hands on her hips.

"Nobles have the luxury of choosing what to care about, of believing that your character is based on your intention. I'm a good person because I mean well," Caelan mocked.

"When you grow up on the streets with nothing, you learn that intention doesn't matter. Even the most wicked of people believe their actions are justified by some nobler purpose. Character isn't about intention. It's about action. It's about doing the right thing even when it's not the easy thing. Life is a series of choices: the right thing and the wrong thing. No matter how you slice it, the greater good is never a reason to do nothing," Ash finished.

"Oh, are we to take lessons in morality from a thug and an insurrectionist?" Celeste retorted.

"I can't change the past, princess. But mistakes of yesterday aren't fixed by doing wrong today," Caelan sighed.

"Valuing the lives of an entire kingdom, of my home, is wrong to you? Caring more about the hundreds of thousands of lives that would be lost in Parisia over the few simpletons in an insignificant town—that's wrong? Because what if we'd all died? Hmm? Did you even stop to think about that? What happens to Parisia?"

"Even without the Darkstone, Parisia has an unclimbable wall and an army to defend them. Maybe your kingdom will be in danger tomorrow. These people were in danger today. If we died trying to save them, we died doing the right thing. Doing the right thing can never be doing the wrong thing," Ash explained.

"I don't need this." Celeste stomped her foot and huffed off back to the inn where they were staying.

Shadows of the Dark Realm

Kade watched her go but remained seated on his log chair by the fire.

"What's gotten into her?" Caelan asked, more to himself than anyone else.

"You think she's got potemania?" Ash asked.

"What does that mean? Potemania?" Kade asked.

"Power madness. Magical objects are said to have a corruptive influence on the mind. The more we pursue them, the greater their hold becomes. Potemania is said to cause a person to become so blinded by their desire—their goal, greed, whatever it is—that it consumes every thought until their lust for power brings them to ruin," Caelan answered.

"This is something you believe in?" Kade smirked.

"Something clever to say, wizard . . . mage . . . magic ralk-face? What do I even call you?" Caelan asked.

"It never ceases to amaze how quickly people will use magic to justify themselves. It's like you are allergic to responsibility. It doesn't take magic to corrupt the heart. The human heart wants to be corrupted. Power, control, greed, desire, revenge, mission—you don't need a reason, just an excuse. Power doesn't corrupt. It merely magnifies."

They sat in silence, listening to the crackling of the fire before Owen stood up and walked over to Ash.

"Um, here . . ." he said, tossing the gloves into Ash's lap.

"What's this?" Ash asked as he examined the gloves.

"I thought these may help."

Ash pulled one of the gloves over his hand and made a fist. Across the knuckles was a thick metal plate. Ash looked at it and then up at Owen.

Owen smiled. "I've always been good at making things. You are a strong fighter but fists versus monsters . . . The gloves have padding inside to protect your knuckles while the plate on the outside will help you do damage even to things with thicker skin."

Ash stood up and wrapped his arms around the little man, hugging him tightly and lifting him off the ground. He set Owen down, and Owen stepped back, adjusting his shirt and blushing.

"Y-you like them?"

"I do. I'm going to find something to punch." Ash grinned and put on the other glove.

He walked away from the fire and toward the woods. Owen chuckled and headed back to his seat, giggling to himself. Caelan stared into the dying flames in front of him. After a few more minutes of silence, Ash, Owen, and Kade headed back to the inn, but Caelan remained. He sat in thought as the sounds of celebration faded, and the crowds returned to their homes. His mind sprinted back and forth as he tried to process the future.

Caelan groaned when he stood up. Everything around him rocked like he was on a small boat in a heavy storm. The drinks had been stronger than he'd thought. He clumsily stumbled his way back to the inn. Once inside, he managed to climb the stairs and headed down the hall where their rooms were located. The hall itself was dark, lit solely by the moon shining through a large window at its end.

The Rag'amorians—Spiro, Owen, and Ash—were already asleep in the room on the left. Celeste had her own room on the right. Caelan felt so off balance he ended up leaning against the wall, using it to keep himself upright as he walked. He reached the door to Celeste's room and noticed an unnatural blue light shining under her door. Curious, he rested his ear against it. He could hear voices. Someone was in there with her.

"Have I not always looked out for you? Tried to make sure you were well treated? I loved you like my own daughter. In all your life, have I ever asked you for anything?"

A silence hung in the air. The voice sounded vaguely familiar. It was male, older, refined, probably annoyingly educated. His voice had that tone that only comes from someone who has read a few too many books.

"No . . . " Celeste's voice sounded heavy.

"After all I have given to you and done for you, I ask this one thing, and you continue to fight me on it."

"I'm not fighting you; I'm just saying, I don't see why I can't—"

"You really need me to repeat myself? You know how I hate repeating myself."

"I'm not, I just think—"

"Celeste, you have a good heart. You care about people. It's an admirable quality. But thanks to your father, you're not experienced enough in these things. You don't understand how the world really works. That's ok. It's not your fault. Sometimes the greatest wisdom is knowing who to listen to."

"But—"

"Your family is counting on you. Your people, all of Parisia, is in your hands, Celeste. If you mess this up because you wanted to prove something—if you fail because you were trying to save some savages at the edge of civilization—then everyone in Parisia will die. An entire kingdom will die, and it will be your fault. Do you understand me? I know you didn't ask for this, but the weight of our kingdom is in your hands. Do not let me down."

Caelan could practically feel the expulsion of air through the heavy wooden door.

"I-I won't let you down."

"That is why you are my favorite niece. I know you will make me proud." The tone of the other voice softened and suddenly sounded warmer.

There was a sort of sizzling, bubbling sound, and the blue light emanating from under the door went dark. There wasn't someone in the room with her; she must have been using a Phorasee orb. Those weren't easy to come by. Caelan peeled his ear from the door and quietly stepped across the hall into his room.

He opened the door to his room and stepped inside. He swung around after closing the door and collided face first into a man in a cloaked hood. His mind was suddenly alert as instinct kicked in. Caelan pulled a knife from behind his back and dropped his weight, preparing to pounce on the intruder. The man turned and saw him. He held his hands up and open, revealing he carried no weapon. The action caused Caelan to pause for a moment as he assessed the man. Slowly, the man pulled down his hood. He didn't have the bearings of an assassin, but the best ones rarely did.

"I mean you no harm. I was sent to give a message to Caelan. Are you Caelan?"

Caelan tightened his grip on the knife. If this intruder didn't choose his next words carefully, they would be his last.

"Who are you? What do you want?" Caelan asked.

"The Blue Alchemist sent me. He told me to give this message to Caelan and no one else."

"Why should I trust you?" Caelan replied.

"Dante said you'd be suspicious. He said if you were, to tell you, 'Death to the Hands of Freedom.'"

Caelan sighed and stood up straight. "Ok, fine. What's this message?"

"Perhaps you should sit down."

"Just spit it out. I'm tired."

"Vale is dead."

Chapter 32

The Gate of Monsters

Dante sat, trying to decide which stone from his necklace to activate. He needed to feel something, even if it was artificial, but what? Vale was gone; that should have generated sadness, but it was more complicated than that. Vale had done the logical thing, what any hero would, and sacrificed himself so others could live. Perhaps he should choose pride, honor, or respect? Watching the others, he finally settled on sadness and let the magical crystal in his necklace pump simulated melancholy through his body, making his heart feel heavy.

Dante had used a spell to contact a wizard from Blackwater Marsh to get a message to Caelan. The others needed to know. They continued their journey for four days, moving quickly toward Lunal. Vale's sacrifice had given them a sense of driving purpose. He'd given his life so they could escape and rescue Azalea. They would not let him down. They had hardly spoken a word during their travel. At night, Rivik would sing songs to try to lift their spirits. Mostly they just added to the lament. With each passing day, Dante wondered if his message had been delivered.

As they traveled, Grom scouted ahead. His troll senses being superior than those of a human, he could give them more warning of any coming dangers they might encounter. They were still in the wilds, but they were getting closer to their goal.

That night, as they did every night, they gathered around a fire.

"You want to talk about it, wizard?" Rivik sat down next to Dante and offered him a piece of cooked meat.

Dante took it. "He did what needed to be done. I'm not sure what else there is to say."

"Losing someone is hard. Especially someone you've fought with and entrusted your life to. It's ok to be sad."

"No sense in too much lament; we will likely be joining him very soon," Dante said.

"That's hopeful."

"It's practical. Valron leaving Vargr to look for us can mean only one thing," Dante explained.

"Which is?" Sera asked.

"Azalea is no longer there. Likely, I fear, he's opened a door to the Spirit Realm and taken her into it. Time is running out," Dante said.

"Wait, if he can open a door to the Spirit Realm, why does the Red Empress need Azalea?" Sera asked.

"When she was banished, her body was destroyed. Without one, she is vulnerable. Any wizard with a soulstone could turn her into nothing more than an item of power. She could possess someone, but then her power would be limited. That's why she needs Azalea," Dante explained.

"What's so special about Azalea? Couldn't any powerful mage do the trick?" Sera leaned forward, fascinated.

"For a time, yes. But Azalea is not just a magic-user. Valron called her the Vas Noomi."

"I don't know what that is," Sera responded.

"A Vas Noomi is a type of spirit vessel. Children in the womb are especially susceptible to magical alteration. If she is a Vas Noomi, that means there would have been a group of mages weaving magic into her before she was even born. Then, once born, they would have continued enhancing her capacity for magic to increase her limits. The Red Empress ruled Parisia when she possessed an average kinspira witch. If she had a Vas Noomi..."

"Who would do that to a child?" Sera's voice dripped with disgust.

Dante shrugged. "Her followers are not known for being reasonable."

"What happens to Azalea if the Red Empress takes over?" Rivik asked.

"Two beings cannot occupy the same space. It goes against nature. In order to make the perfect vessel, it needs life. A golem would not do. Azalea isn't meant to be a temporary host. In order for the Red Empress to truly have control, Azalea would be obliterated."

"And the only way to save her—" Rivik started.

"Is for us to enter the Spirit Realm, find her, and bring her back before the Red Empress can complete the ritual," Dante nodded.

"Here I was, worried it was going to be dangerous." Rivik made his way to a flat patch of ground and lay on his back.

* * *

The next morning, they ate, gathered their supplies, and moved on before the sun had even climbed over the edge of the horizon. They traveled through the day. As the sun started its descent, they spotted a sizeable town. Stone walls, defense towers. If it had a palace, it would have been its own capital.

"Do we risk checking it out?" Sera asked. "We're close to the capital. Monsters could have easily taken it over by now."

"Monsters no . . . smell . . . human," Grom answered.

"Do we have anything that resembles a plan?" Rivik asked.

"From what Sera told us, Azalea was taken to the top of the palace. If Valron opened a portal to the Spirit Realm, he likely did it there. If the monsters haven't come here . . . " Dante started.

"They are likely still in Lunal. Ralk. Rescuing Azalea from the Spirit Realm is one thing. If the portal is at the top of the palace, how are we even going to get to it?" Rivik questioned.

Sera smiled and, standing up on her tip toes, kissed Rivik on the cheek. "Easy."

Rivik folded his arms across his chest. "I hate it when you say 'easy.'"

"You men are all the same." Sera's smile grew. She puffed out her chest and deepened her voice to make it sound like a mockery of a man's. "How am I going to overcome these challenges all by myself."

"I don't sound like that," Rivik protested.

"It's easy. We get help."

"We cannot just—" Dante started.

"Sure, we can," Sera cut him off. She gave Rivik another kiss on the cheek and started toward the town. "Meet me at the tavern. You know what to do," she called back.

"Wait. Hold on! You did not tell us your plan. How are we supposed to know what to do if you do not tell us what you are thinking? What is she doing?" Dante looked completely out of sorts.

"She's recruiting," Rivik chuckled.

"That makes no sense. We are headed to Lunal, a city overrun by terrifying monsters the likes of which this world has never seen. When we get there, we'll have to fight our way through those monsters to the palace in hopes that the portal to the Spirit Realm was left open. And if, by the blessing of the gods below, it is, enter into the Spirit Realm to rescue a witch from one of the most powerful and vindictive beings to ever enter this realm," Dante stated.

"And . . ."

"She is going to what? Walk into a tavern and invite a bunch of people we have never met to come join us on this suicide mission? Not for gold or for country—just because she asks them to?" Dante asked.

"Exactly." Rivik smiled and put his hand on the alchemist's shoulder.

Dante frowned. "That makes no sense. No reasonable person would answer that call, not for a stranger. She has no chance of success."

Shadows of the Dark Realm

"I know, isn't she great? Come on, let's go watch." Rivik smacked him on the back.

Reluctantly, Dante followed Rivik down the hill and toward the city in the distance. Grom had already left, following Sera without hesitation.

The town gate was manned by two guards on the ground and another two perched on the walls above. As they approached, one of the guards on the wall called down to them.

"Halt. What business do you have in Cannin?" the guard asked.

Rivik and Dante were still catching up and didn't hear what Sera said in response.

"The troll—he with you?"

Sera nodded.

"Just in time for the Guild Brawls. If you want to register him, take him to the town hall. While you are here, you will abide by our laws: no stealing. no scamming. Rules for any unsanctioned brawl: no killing, maiming, breaking bones, gouging eyes, or any other thing that has a permanent effect. All fights must be one-on-one unless prior agreements are made. Am I forgetting anything?"

"You break something, you pay for it. Pretty simple. Don't ralk about. Don't be an owa," another guard answered.

Once he had finished his well-rehearsed speech, he stepped aside. Sera nodded again, and they made their way in.

Cannin was even larger than it looked from a distance. All of the buildings were made of stone and decorated with wood. Each of the buildings was two or three stories tall. Yellow banners, each with a black, howling wolf's head, were mounted on poles all throughout the city. The people passing by in the streets, like the city itself, were hearty and stout but had no sense of style or form. Apart from the flags, there were almost no decorations or colors to be found.

Finding the tavern wasn't difficult. A wooden sign with a carved overflowing goblet hung from the second floor and was so large it was visible from blocks away. Sera turned to face the others.

"We can't all walk in together. Give me some time, then you

can come in. Rivik, don't ralk it up," she said with a playful smile.

She twirled around and marched herself into the tavern, leaving them outside to wait. Wait they did. Dante sat and watched the sky darken. Rivik leaned against the building across the street. He closed his eyes and let his other senses take over while Grom stomped back and forth, pacing and listening.

"She's all right, my friend," Rivik offered to the troll. "Sera knows what she's doing."

"Why we wait? What wait for?" Grom questioned.

"The right moment," Rivik answered.

"When . . . this moment?"

"I'll let you know," Rivik chuckled.

The tavern, which had been a gentle rumble of sounds and chatter, grew louder. With each passing minute, the rumble was growing to a roaring thunder of sound. Cheers. Clapping. Stomping of feet. Banging of tables. The sounds grew louder, but Rivik remained still. The longer it went on, the more the sounds began to bleed together, combining like a choir of chaos. Finally, Rivik stood up and walked to the door. Grom practically knocked him over as he rushed to follow him inside.

The tavern was a large, open room with a bar set along the far wall. To the right was a small, elevated stage with a stool and a few unattended instruments. The rest of the space was cramped with small wooden tables and little wooden chairs that seemed a bit too small for grown men. The room was poorly lit and smelled of sweat, blood, and a mixture of other unpleasant aromas.

All eyes were fixed on Sera, who was standing atop a table, holding an oversized metal cup of ale that she was pouring down her throat. The room was cheering and clapping in delight as they egged her on. Sera finished, extended her arms, and threw the mug down onto the floor, which resulted in even louder cheering.

"Good men of Vargr, I promised you entertainment and entertainment has arrived. I present to you the Bard of Rag'amor, here to regale you with his finest work." She waved her hands in the air, and the room filled with shouting and applause.

Shadows of the Dark Realm

Dante looked around, surprised. "She certainly has them worked up."

"You have no idea." Rivik pulled off his spear and pushed it into the alchemist's hands, forcing him to hold it. He walked up onto the stage and picked up the lute, slinging its strap over his head, and he danced his fingers across the strings, plucking them quickly as he got a feel for the instrument.

The cheering quieted, and the attention turned to him. Rivik smirked and began to strum an energic tune.

"There once was a knight
so ordinary.
No tales would be sung
of his glory.
No adventures did he share
Or enemies he'd lay bare.
Soon he would fade
Forgotten.

All those battles that he fought
Led to nothing.
All the trials that he wrought
Disappointing.
But when darkness rose at Vree
And all the others did flee,
This one knight
Stood his ground at Bardone

Standing alooone
At the cliffs of Bardoonne
He slashed, and he sliced, and he slew
And he ran every monstrous beast straight through.

So rise,
Rise, brave knight, riiiise
Let glasses, and glory, and your fabled story riiiiiise.
Rise to the skiiiies,
May every song that we sing

Stir within us that same feeling
To riiiiiise
Rise, brave knight, riiiiiise
When all around you are through.
The greatest glory that can ever be is to riiiiise
Rise, brave knight, rise.
And at the end of days be it true
That you found the courage to . . . rise."

Rivik set down the lute and bowed as the crowd cheered. The sound was deafening. He bowed again, but this time when he stood up, he reached his arms out toward Sera. The room quieted as the focus shifted back to her.

"Men of Vargr, I call on you. Lend me your blades, your axes, your shields. I am not your people. I have no gold to offer you. But for those of you who are brave enough, for the true warriors of Vargr, I offer you something far greater. Glory. Fame. Legend. Come with me, bleed with me, die with me, and you won't be listening to the songs of other heroes. You will be the heroes for which others sing. Come with me, and the tale of the wolves of Caninn will be sung in every hall and tavern across the land!" Sera's voice was impassioned and captivating. Her words were saturated with conviction and challenge.

A stunned silence fell across the room.

"Or hide here in your safe little tavern and be outdone by a Rag'amorian woman." Sera shrugged. Many laughed. Others objected. Once again, the room filled with so much sound it was impossible to hear.

Rivik gave her an approving nod and walked to the door. She had them. They may not know it yet, but she had them.

* * *

The next morning, the four stood at the edge of town, waiting. With the gate behind them, there was a large street that ran along the inside of the wall and the main street that ran perpendicular to it. The two streets formed a large T shape that extended from one side of the town to the other. All the zeal and energy from the night before had worn off with the sobering light of the morning sun. They waited, alone.

"It was a valiant effort but an impossible request. We will have to think of another—" Dante was interrupted by the loud blaring of a war horn.

As if coordinated, the entrance to the city flooded with people pouring in from every street and alley around. Men and women dressed in a variety of different armors and brandishing a dizzying array of weapons marched toward them.

Rivik put his hand on Dante's shoulder and leaned in, speaking softly. "Told you she'd do it."

Dante blinked, trying to make sense of what he was seeing. There were far more people here than there had been at the tavern the night before. The crowd came to a stop at the edge of the main street before the gate.

"Sorry we are late. Took a minute to get everyone ready," one of the men shouted.

"We are glad to see you." Sera smiled and walked over. She clasped hands with the man.

"Wolves of Cannin, are we ready?" The man turned around and lifted his sickle in the air.

The crowd cheered and stomped and slammed their swords into their shields in response.

"Halt!" came aloud, authoritative woman's voice.

Metal boots thudded against the stone, creating a thunderous rumble that resonated all on either side. Sera turned to see a sea of soldiers swarming toward them, boxing them in. The soldiers moved as one, in neat rows filling the streets. Each carried a large shield, a sword at their hip, and a long spear in their hands. The soldiers wore thick plates armor in yellow and black, each one branded with the head of a howling wolf.

In the front of one of the units, a woman stepped forward and removed her helmet. Her face was attractive but fierce, her eyes like a bird of prey as she scanned them.

"You do not have permission to be here. This is an unauthorized gathering and could be viewed as sedition." She let her words hang in the air as she slowly pulled her blade from its scabbard. The motley militia began to murmur. "You came here to fight, to free Lunal, our capital city, from the clutches of an invading horde? That is not your job. The glory of Vargr is not your responsibility. It is ours. So, if you think you're leaving this city without us, you've got another thing coming."

She marched over and looked at Sera. "Are you the leader of this little uprising?"

Sera shrugged, "I guess so."

"I'm Aurora, commander of Black Wolves battalion." She extended her hand. Sera shook it.

"Sera."

"You're not from here. What's your purpose in Lunal?"

"We need to get to the palace to rescue a friend of ours before, well, she gets turned into a weapon that is used to destroy the world."

"I see. Well, you need to get to the palace. And we need our city back," Aurora said.

"Sounds like we should work together."

"You rallied this lot; I'd rather have you with us. Let's discuss on the way." Aurora turned. "Soldiers, prepare to march. Unit one, you will lead. Unit two, let the militia pass and take up the flank."

As they marched, they worked out a plan. Sera would take a large group of skilled fighters. Once they entered the city, they would stay on the outskirts and try to reach the palace undetected. Aurora would lead the main force through the gates and into the town center, engaging any monsters they found and making as much noise as possible to draw attention away from Sera's group. Once they reached the palace, most of the fighters with Sera would split away and move toward the main group, flanking any monsters they were fighting. Sera would select a few fighters to join them in storming the palace.

Cannin was only half a day's march from Lunal, and they arrived just after the sun reached its zenith. As they approached the city, it was quiet. Strangely quiet. Sera had expected to see some monsters roaming around. Instead, littering either side of the path were rows of dead monsters. *What had happened here?*

Had they turned on each other? Had some other force already attacked? What was going on?

The gates were left open and unguarded. Sera and Aurora exchanged a nod.

"May the gods below bless you and bring you luck," Aurora said.

Sera repeated the evocation, and the two parted.

Dante, Rivik, Sera, Grom, and a squad of a little over two hundred soldiers moved along the walls, trying to stay as far from the main streets as they could. Even as they moved, they could see some of the monsters roaming around aimlessly through the streets at the town's center.

Aurora's unit charged in, moving ahead of Sera's team. There was a great commotion. Screams pierced the air, followed by roars and the stomping of feet. The battle was commencing. The plan was working. Monsters from all over the city started moving to the center of town to fight the Vargrian army.

Rivik and Grom moved to the front, guiding the others between buildings and through the city. Thanks to the battle, no monsters were in their path. Things were going well—too well. Something bit at Sera's stomach—an odd feeling of unease. It shouldn't be this easy. Aurora's troops were fighting to draw the attention of the monsters, but she never expected to avoid all of them. Where were the stragglers? The wanderers? They didn't see a single living monster. Then she noticed it.

As they ran, they passed multiple slain monsters. Never in a group. Never on a main street. Just single monsters cut down and left on this path. As if someone had taken this route before them and, intentionally or not, cleared the way. It was as if they had taken a leisurely stroll. There it was, the palace, right in front of them. Not a single encounter along the way.

"Go!" Sera instructed with a firm whisper.

Sera had selected five men to stay with them. The rest of the soldiers who had come with them readied their weapons and charged toward the unsuspecting monsters in the center of town.

"Well, this is it," Rivik said. "Let's go!"

"It's about time. I've been waiting."

They froze as they heard the voice behind them.

Chapter 33

The Man in the Orange Cloak

The next morning, Caelan woke in his room with a throbbing pain in his head. The light from the morning sun burned into his mind. He tried to push his eyes closed enough to blot out the unrelenting light, but it only made the throbbing worse. He hadn't taken much stock of the room after his encounter with the mysterious messenger the night before. To cope with the news, he'd gone downstairs and consumed another bottle of the town's potent liquor.

Could it really be that Vale was dead? Had the news come from anyone but Dante, he would have doubted it. *What was this strange feeling that even drink could not wash away?* Vale was his enemy, champion of the kingdom he hated. Vale was a part of the Phoenix Legion who had massacred his hometown. There was no world in which he should do anything but rejoice in his death. He didn't feel like rejoicing.

Caelan rolled out of bed and fell farther than expected. He hit the floor with a loud thud. *What sort of inn uses bunk beds? When had he gotten on the top one? How did he not remember?* He let out a loud groan as he got to his feet.

He took a breath and closed his eyes, standing up straight. He muttered a quiet vow.

"As Ekidar is my witness, I swear vengeance. On my life, I will put an arrow between the eyes of Valron."

Shadows of the Dark Realm

Caelan drew his knife and dragged the blade across his hand, letting exactly three drops of blood drip to the floor before wrapping his hand. Spiro was snoring in his bed loud enough to shake the earth. The few remaining Rag'amorian warriors were sprawled around the room, still sleeping. Only Kade was missing. He stepped out into the hall. The door to Celeste's room was closed. Caelan tried to recall the voice he'd heard the night before. He knew the voice from somewhere but couldn't place it.

As he tried to clear his head, something outside the hallway window caught his eye. There was a small group of villagers standing at the edge of town with a sizable unit of soldiers across from them.

"Great, someone is having a party without me. That's rude," Caelan said to himself as he retrieved his bow and went to the other side of the inn, where he climbed out the window and up onto the roof. He kept low, using the pitch of the roof to keep himself out of the sight of the troops below.

He leapt from the inn to the roof of the building next to it. The building was a little shorter but ran close to where the soldiers were gathered. He laid out, peeking his head over the top to see what he could. The soldiers were wearing Baronian armor, which emphasized the use of dragon scales as accents to the otherwise heavy plate. The army was lined up in even rows. Four sections, five wide and ten soldiers deep, all standing at perfect attention. In front of each section was a single horseman. The horsemen must have been their captains. Each had a long, decorative, orange cape and a plumed helmet to make them easily identifiable.

There were a group of five others who seemed different from the rest. Four men in orange and white cloaks and a larger man in full knight's armor who stood at least a head taller than the rest. In front of the four horsemen was another horse, devoid of its rider. Four guards stood on either side of a single man wearing the fanciest armor and the most ornate cape. It was clear this was not a happy gathering. The man in the fancy armor stood forward from the others as he spoke to the villagers and . . . Kade?

* * *

"And you haven't seen anyone suspicious? No new arrivals to town?"

The town elder, an old man who could barely stand upright, looked into the general's face and shook his head.

"No, sir, our quaint little village is very much out of the way for most travelers. Other than Lord Drako from Taggoron, we haven't seen anyone for weeks, save you and your men of course. If you'd like to stay, we can offer our best accommodations, though we do not have space for such a large troop."

"You'll understand that I can't just take your word for it. We have reports of Parisia spies in this area. On our way in, I couldn't help but notice the monster corpses outside of town. I'd love to know how your quaint little village managed to defeat them. Perhaps I should be sending my men here for training. What's your secret?" The general grinned a smug, self-righteous grin.

The elder started sweating and his voice broke. He began mumbling. "W-w . . . Th-those—"

"Save it. We will come back to this Lord Drako in a moment." The general held up his hand.

He snapped his fingers, and two of his soldiers walked over, dragging a small boy with them. The general gripped the boy's shoulder and squeezed, holding him firmly in place with one hand. With the other, he drew a long dagger from his belt.

"This is your grandson, is it not? Fine looking young man. I'm sure he has a bright future ahead of him if he lives to see it. Now, let's try this one more time. Where are the spies from Parisia?"

"Please, m'lord, I've told you everything I know. Please don't hurt him." Tears welled up in the elder's eyes as he fell to his knees.

Kade stepped forward, putting his hand on the elder's shoulder.

"This is not your business, Lord Drako. We have no quarrel with Taggoron. But should you insert yourself, my men will not hesitate to kill you," the general warned.

"You would threaten the life of a child?" Kade asked, his eyes narrowing. Memory flooded Kade's mind, taking him back to a time he wished he could forget. The scene in front of him froze in place as his mind played the scene of his past...

* * *

He pictured his mother. She was beautiful. Dark black hair that shined like the midnight sky. Crystal blue eyes and a smile that rivaled the warmth of the sun. Her voice was sweet and loving. She carried herself with an unbreakable kindness, despite all she had to overcome. He remembered being on the run, always going from one place to another, his mother always looking over her shoulder. She warned him of a bad man, a man that was searching for them. The only way to be safe was to stay on the move. She may not have been physically strong, but she had a force of will that, even as a child, he could see.

Then the dreaded moment that haunted him. It was dark. Rain pattered against the roof of the house as the dark sky lit up with flashes of light. There was a sense of gloom in the air. Earlier, when they had gone to the market to get some food, his mother seemed more on edge than usual. When they reached the house, she urged him inside quickly and latched the door.

It was as if he was watching it happen right in front of him, not from his own eyes but from outside himself. There he was, a young boy, huddled in the corner of the packed closet, pulling a thin blanket to his chest as he hugged his knees and rocked back and forth. There was something about the look in his mother's eyes—a rushed panic that told him not to question her when she pushed him into the closet and slammed the door. She'd warned him not to make a sound. A moment later, he heard yelling. One voice, his mother; the other, a man.

"Did you really think you could hide this from me, Liara?" the man accused.

"W-w-what are you talking about? I-I am not hiding anything from you."

Something shattered against the wall, and the man's voice

got angrier and deeper—too deep. Kade felt himself shiver at the effect of this bellowing voice.

"Do . . . not . . . lie . . . to me!"

He tried to peek under the closet door, but all he could see were feet. His mother's voice was muffled as she cried.

"Y-you're scaring me," she sobbed.

"You should be afraid. Did you think I wouldn't find out what you did?" His voice was so deep, it felt like the floor was rumbling.

"How did you know?" she started, her voice stabilizing.

"How could you do this? After all I have given to you, you betray me like this?"

"How? How could I not? I knew what you would do. I won't let you!"

"Let me?" The man's bellowing voice filled with amusement as he started to laugh. "You think you can stop me? Tell me where the boy is."

"You'll just kill him," his mother protested.

"He's an abomination, a threat to everything I have built. The other elders, they tolerated our little fling, but this . . . this is too far. The boy cannot be allowed to exist."

"Then I'm glad I sent him away," she said defiantly.

"You what?" he practically screamed.

"I took the coins you gave me when you abandoned me, and I invested them in his future. I had friends take him far away and made sure I didn't even know what direction they went. You can do what you want to me, but your son is far from your reach, and you'll never find him."

"Lies. You would never send away your own son! You'd be ensuring you never saw him again! You wouldn't!"

"Wouldn't I? I'm a mother. There is nothing I wouldn't do to keep my son safe. It broke me to send him away. I've never done anything so painful in all my life. But I did it. I did it to keep him from you! My son will have a chance to grow up to be a better man than his sad excuse for a father. I ripped out my own heart to keep him from you!"

"No, you didn't." Kade heard a sound unlike anything he'd heard before and saw blood pour out onto the floor. He heard his mother gasping for air, coughing desperately before her body collapsed to the ground. He could just barely see her through the crack under the door. Eyes wide, body still, blood pooling under her. A moment later, something dropped down on top of her.

"That . . . is what having your heart ripped out feels like."

The man stomped out of the house. Kade remembered that room, that moment, that waiting. Everything in him driving him to run to his mother. He had to wait. He knew he needed to be sure that his father, the man he'd never known, the man who had left his mother when he tired of her company and now killed her, was gone.

When he finally dared rush out, he scooped his mother's body into his arms and rocked it as he cried. He cried as if his tears could bring her back. As if his mourning could fill the hole his father had punched into her chest. That was the last day he ever cried. That was the day he learned who his father really was. That was the day he began plotting his vengeance.

In all of his years, any time someone threatened to harm a child or took action against them, he felt himself transported back to that room, to that horrible closet he'd have given anything to escape. No matter how powerful he was, that room never stopped haunting him. It was where his rage was born. A rage he would unleash on any who caused him to feel that way again.

* * *

"You're a long way from anyone who would be scared of you, Lord Drako. Maybe if you'd brought your house guard with you," the general sneered.

"I don't need a house guard." Kade walked forward, locking eyes on the general.

"Warren!" the general called out.

A large man stepped from the ranks of soldiers and marched toward Kade. Kade paused, which added to the general's sense of confidence.

"Now you get it? Warren is my champion. He's won six last-man-standing tournaments, each one to the death. He has bested over forty fighters in duels and slain over two hundred men. His strength is unrivaled. Facing him is facing certain death. Take another step, Mr. Nobleman, and it will be your last."

Kade smirked and stepped defiantly forward. Warren lifted his large, two-handed sword and swung it in a wide arc toward Kade's head. Kade stood perfectly still as the blade moved closer. It struck him in the head, and still he did not move. As metal hit skin, the blade shattered on contact, the forged steel turning to a sparkling powder as it misted past Kade, not even breaking the skin.

"W-w-what are you?" The general's eyes grew wide. He stepped back, releasing his grip on the elder's grandson.

"You would hurt a child?" Kade glared and stomped forward.

Warren stared in shock at his shattered blade and then at his stomach. Kade left the dagger behind after plunging it into the large knight's chest. Warren dropped to his knees, clutching the hilt, blood pouring to the ground below.

"I will not forgive you. Nor any who stand with you," Kade warned.

"Y-y-you'll regret this! Mages! Blast him!" the general ordered.

Four men in orange and white cloaks rushed forward from behind the ranks of soldiers and aimed their outstretched arms at Kade. Funnels of flame burst from their hands and covered his body, engulfing him completely. The general exhaled in relief.

"Fire?" Kade took another step forward. "I was born of this."

He moved through the flames as if completely unaffected by their destructive power. The flames were so hot, they seared the grass beneath his feet but left not a mark on him. Kade darted forward. He seemed to disappear completely from the funnel of flames, engulfed in the light so not even a shadowed silhouette could be seen. It was if he'd evaporated.

It happened fast. The mage's cried out one after the other as their hands flew into the air, cut from their arm one at a time until all four of them were screaming, both hands severed from their bodies. There he was, walking calm and casual as if the mage's spells had been nothing more than a cool breeze.

Kade continued his slow walk toward the general, leaving

the mages to writhe on the ground in pain. The general stumbled and fell before trying to crab crawl away and reach his men. As Kade approached, they stepped back as well.

"You. I shall give you one chance. Flee this field right now and never return, or I will consume you one by one. You have this moment and not a moment more. Turn and flee. If you hesitate, I will kill you. If you look back before you reach the trees on the horizon, I will kill you. If you stop to catch your breath, I will kill you. Run and do not stop running, or you will not see the dawn of another day." His eyes flashed, and flames burst from the sides of them.

One man put his hand on his sword. Kade darted so fast it looked as if he teleported. He grabbed the man by his throat, lifted him with one arm off the ground, and with the flick of his wrist, snapped the man's neck.

"Decide," he bellowed. The disciplined, ordered army cried out, turned, and fled. Not one hesitated. Not one looked back. Not one stopped running. The general tried to follow but tripped over himself. He crawled back as quickly as he could, but he was too slow.

"P-p-please let me go . . . I swear I will never come back. I'll . . . do anything. You want money? I . . . I am a very powerful man. I can get you whatever you want." The general continued to plead and beg as he pushed and slid himself away.

"You will shed crimson tears," Kade said. He swung his hand across the general's face.

The general cried out as blood poured from his eyes. He covered them with the palms of his hands and managed to get to his feet, stammering and crying out in pain as blood dripped through his fingers. He ran as fast as his legs could carry him. He ran until he felt the sharp sting of a blade pierce his armor and into his heart. He coughed and fell to the ground. Standing on the other side of the blade was the village elder. His hands shook as he let go of the hilt.

Chapter 34

The Realm of Spirits

"It can't be." Rivik practically dropped the spear in his hands.

Standing across from him, leaning casually against the wall across from the palace courtyard, was a man in black armor with a black cape, holding a black blade.

"Miss me?" Vale smiled.

Sera walked over and hugged him tight before pushing him away. "How are you here? We watched you die."

"Yeah, about that," Vale grinned.

"The curse that kills anyone you care for won't let you die?" Dante asked.

"Oh, it lets me die. I just don't get to stay that way," Vale shrugged.

"That sounds unpleasant," Rivik cringed.

"It is," Vale nodded.

"Where did you go?"

"I figured you'd end up here eventually, so I cleared a path and waited. I didn't expect you to bring an army with you."

"My girl likes to accessorize. What can you do?" Rivik shrugged.

Dante grasped Vale's hand. "As good as it is to see you, we should get moving. We do not know how long we have or what obstacles await us."

Shadows of the Dark Realm

They made their way into the palace. The occasional monster roaming the halls was dispatched quickly. The once-great walls were stained with gore. The stone floors were covered in remains. Bodies were littered around the room, torn to various degrees of shreds. They climbed the stairs that led to the throne room, circling up and up until their legs burned, fighting monsters along the way. Finally, the stairs opened to a hall that led to the throne room.

The doors were guarded by a pair of bulky orcs. Vale moved toward them, but Sera rushed past him.

"Take it easy, dead man walking. We don't want you getting hurt." She looked over her shoulder and winked.

The two orcs seemed amused as Sera walked toward them. They sneered, nudging each other as they moved to either side of the hallway to catch her in a pincer attack. Sera fake-lunged toward one, shifting her weight and driving her dagger into the heart of the other. She'd pulled her knife free and was already midair before the second orc could react. He was too late. Her knives drove into his head from opposite directions before he could even lift his crude axe. Sera walked casually over to the palace doors and waited for them to catch up.

"That's my girl." Rivik nudged Dante proudly before blowing her a kiss.

Dante shoved the doors open with a magical burst of energy while the others stood ready for whatever was behind them. Nothing. They looked and then stepped inside. The large throne room was empty—no monsters, no people. Just a mess of bodies, a few blown out windows, and a large portal door of waving black smoke in the back of the room behind the king's throne. The soldiers with them exchanged a nervous glance as they appraised the black, smoky void.

"Why don't you lads stay here and guard the portal so we don't have any surprises when we get back," Rivik said, putting his hand on one of their shoulders and grinning.

The man nodded in appreciation as the others looked visibly relieved.

"There is something foreboding about this," Dante muttered.

"Very insightful, thank you," Rivik remarked.

"I would advise caution; the Spirit Realm is dangerous in ways you cannot even imagine," Dante warned.

"What should we expect?" Sera asked.

"The realm of spirits is an unnatural place: skies red like blood, clouds black as night, and the ground a dark sea of sand and death. Endless lightning storms, impossibly tall mountains and the air itself a toxic fume. Plants do not grow. Birds do not sing. Mortal life does not last. As soon as we enter the world, the spirits that reside there will be alerted to our presence—some to feed, others to possess, others . . . far worse. We would do well to move quickly and spend as little time there as possible."

"Well, it sounds lovely. I, for one, am really excited to go there," Rivik grinned.

"Staring at it won't make what we are about to do any easier," Vale replied. He gave them a reassuring nod and then stepped into the black hole. Just like that, he was gone.

On the other side of the portal, Vale squinted, holding his arm to his forehead to shade his eyes from the sudden intense light. It felt like stepping out of a dark cave into the bright midday sun. He blinked, letting his eyes adjust.

The throne room was gone. He found himself standing on a path surrounded by green grass littered with brightly colored flowers that almost appeared to glow. The path wound along up to the top of a series of rolling hills. To one side was a beautiful meadow that made even the finest gardens in Parisia look like a volcanic desert by comparison. In front of him, the path disappeared into a tranquil-looking forest. To his left, a cliff dropped down to a sparkling sapphire river below.

On the other side of the canyon were more luscious green fields, tiered with several terraces and rolling waterfalls pooling into little lakes, creating white, foaming steps that made their way down gradually to the river below. The mist coming off the water was a perfect white sprinkled with soft purple and blue. Behind the waterfalls and the snaking river leading into them were lush green mountains.

At the other side of the canyon was a great white city, like a pearl on the horizon. An arching bridge reached across the canyon to some place out of view on the other side of the forest.

This was not what Vale had expected. This was something from a dream.

Sera appeared next, followed by Grom, then Rivik and Dante. It took them a moment to process what they were seeing.

"You had me all worked up." Rivik smacked Dante on the arm.

Dante squinted as he took in his surroundings. "This is not the world that was described in the tomes."

"This is paradise," Sera laughed. "Why would anyone want to leave this place?"

"Be on your guard. This place is all wrong," Vale warned.

"Smell . . . good . . . feel . . . good." Grom's eyes narrowed. "Something . . . coming."

Glowing lights like little floating orbs danced from the woods, moving playfully through the air. Behind them, a half dozen tall, thin, almost human-looking people walked towards them. They were dressed in thin, flowing fabric. Their bodies were lean and smooth, their skin a sort of pale brown, like sanded wood. Their hair was flowing long and white.

"Druids? Here?" Dante asked in disbelief.

A faint, melodic song seemed to whisper on the breeze as the group approached. Vale's hand fell to his blade.

"Hello there!" Rivik walked ahead and held his arms out.

Several of the female druids giggled. The one male walked right up to Rivik with a warm smile and hugged him.

"Welcome, travelers. Welcome! You have found the palace of our Lady Iluthi. Here you will find peace and rest for your weary heads. It would be our pleasure to take you in, provide you with food and drink, and attend to your needs for as long as you wish to stay," he said, his voice like a poem being sung.

"Very kind of you. We are here searching for a friend of ours. Perhaps you could help us?" Rivik asked.

"Oh, we are always pleased to help new friends. Tell us, who is it you seek?" the male druid asked.

"A woman with bright red hair," Vale answered.

The druid's eyes lit up. "Oh, yes. We have seen a redhaired maiden. She was quite fair. She is at our Lady's palace as an honored guest as we speak. We can take you to her. Come, come."

Dante glared. "Were you not just heading in the opposite direction? You would go out of your way to help total strangers? Why?"

"Well, it is not out of our way. It is always a delight to visit our Lady's palace. Helping people is our custom. Why would we not help you?"

The glowing orbs pulsed with warm light. A soft, shimmering dust rained down from them onto the group. Vale felt the tension release in his shoulders and arms as his body relaxed. He released his grip on his sword. He felt deep inside himself that he should trust these people. They were clearly friends who wanted to help. He should listen to them.

"Please, show us the way," Rivik gestured. The male druid smiled brightly and turned, guiding them back toward the forest.

"We do not see many who look like you in these parts. Where have you travelled from?" the druid man asked.

"I doubt you would have heard of it," Dante answered.

The female druids parted, allowing the group to pass, and then followed with the glowing orb lights floating overhead.

Between the serene sounds and the sweet smells, Vale felt a great burden lifted from his shoulders. The weight of responsibility and guilt he'd carried for as long as he could remember seemed to evaporate.

Everything around them felt magical. The closer they came, the more exquisite the trees looked. They were majestic, as if the trees were made of glimmering gold and the leaves were precious gems.

"Our Lady will be thrilled to meet you. She loves guests from foreign lands. Says they are so interesting," the druid said.

Vale's eyes felt heavier than usual. He was so relaxed, so comfortable, he could practically fall asleep while on his feet. He let out a long sigh of relief as all thought began to fade from his mind. He wasn't sure why they were here or what they were doing, but it didn't matter. He knew he never wanted to leave.

His trance was broken when a spray of something warm splattered against his face. He wiped his hand across his face and looked at it. *Red? Was this blood?* He glanced up to see Grom's axe in the male druid's head.

"What have you done? Why did you do that?" Sera asked in shock.

"Smell . . . too good. Nothing good . . . smell that good," the troll replied.

Vale burned with rage. *How could this filthy troll commit an act of horrid violence against such a lovely creature? It was monstrous. I should kill the beast.* His hand tightened on his sword. The urge to put the troll down boiled over inside him. He resisted, fought against it. Clenched his jaw. The harder he fought, the more he wanted to destroy Grom.

The female druids cried out, tears streaming from their eyes. They cowered together, hugging one another for support and protection. Seeing them only ignited Vale's rage.

"No trust . . . Grom kill them," the troll said, raising his axe back up.

"Don't do it. I won't let you hurt them." Rivik moved between the troll and the druid women.

Vale felt relief. Rivik would stop any more senseless violence. It would be ok. Everything in him yearned to return to the euphoria he'd felt as they were walking. It was different now. Vale watched Rivik. There was something different about him; his eyes lacked their normal piercing gaze. Instead, they looked almost dull, glossed over.

"Rivik," Sera warned.

He turned to her. "I won't let your troll slaughter such innocent creatures. They were helping us. They have done nothing and deserve to be protected."

"Help? No . . . Smell venom . . . They not right . . . Grom sense trouble."

"Step back, troll; I won't tell you again." Rivik rested his hand on his spear.

"Wait." Dante closed his eyes. "*Apocalpyti orama*"

The forest turned from luscious, life-bearing trees to gnarled, curling, nightmarish branches and leafless vines growing all around. The sky turned red, and the world suddenly looked exactly as Dante had warned.

The druids hissed as everything around them started to change. Their fair, smooth, sensual skin peeled away, revealing rough, pale skin that looked like a light knotted wood. Their hair was like serpents swimming and slithering through the air. Their pupilless eyes glowed yellow. Their bodies were covered in long leaves that covered their torsos like long togas with a train that dragged on the ground behind them. Moss grew in patches over their skin, and their shoulders and arms were covered in thorny, wooden spikes.

Vale felt his body jerk as if some controlling force had released him. His senses snapped back, and his mind cleared. It was like stepping out of a thick fog.

The will-o-wisps descended on them. Dante reacted, tossing a vial in the air and using magic to shatter it. A flash of lightning descended from above and hit the jar, sending energy forking out. A separate strand hit each ball of light and connected them with an electric energy. Dante lifted his hands and uttered some incomprehensible words. Shards of ice broke from the glowing orbs, and they froze in place, dropping to the ground with a series of thuds.

"Foolisssh humanssss. You have noooo bussssinesss in thiss placcce. We will take you to the Red Empress, and you will be her sssacrificesss," one of them said.

Before the creature had even finished speaking, Vale lopped off the head of one of the snake creatures. Rivik similarly had run his spear through the heart of a second. Grom leapt onto the one who had spoken and crumpled the creature to the ground under his enormous troll weight. His axes stopped the snake creature from uttering another word.

Sera drew her knives and drove both into one of the creatures. The remaining two hissed loudly and ran into the dark woods.

"Well, that's confusing," Rivik said, looking at the sky.

Sera punched his arm.

"Ow, what was that for?" he asked, rubbing the spot.

"You know what you did," she accused.

"Come on, that's not fair. You know I can't resist old haggish ladies with moss arms and snakes for hair. Their natural allure is so enchanting, who could resist such paragons of beauty?" He shrugged playfully.

"You're hopeless." She rolled her eyes, a soft smile crossing her lips.

"What was that?" Vale asked. "I felt it in my head, like something was compelling me."

"That was glamour magic," Dante answered.

"What is glamour magic?" Sera asked.

"It is an old magic, perfected by fairies but used by a variety of fae creatures. It alters how others perceive you. Like, we could use it on Grom to make it so when others saw him, they wouldn't see a troll, they would see a human. It is like a magical disguise."

"Grom . . . troll . . . No hide." He beat his chest with his fist proudly.

"It was an example, not a suggestion," Dante explained. "Glamour magic is very draining as it has to be maintained. The more eyes on you, the more magic is required. I have never heard of a glamour being used on anything larger than a house. The amount of power it would take to create a glamour over an entire realm is unfathomable."

"You think this is the work of The Red Empress?" Vale started.

"No. No, this is not Vespera's magic. This is something else. Something stronger," Dante interrupted.

"Stronger?" Rivik asked nervously.

"It had occurred to me before that while the Red Empress may have been the most powerful being to enter our world, that does not mean she is the most powerful being from her own," Dante said.

"This place is absolutely lovely. Where to next?" Rivik asked.

They were standing in the midst of a valley between two great mountain passes. The mountains were black slate stretched like shadows into the sky, blocking out any view of what was on the other side. The valley snaked with twists and turns heading down into a dark, corrupted forest.

From his vantage point, Vale could see on the other side of the woods was a winding stone bridge surrounded on either side by a river of liquid magma, bubbling and boiling. The small path led to a black keep, walled and twisted. Its towers were turned and broken. Stone blocks floated in the air as if they were nothing more than weightless leaves caught in a strong draft of wind.

Vale smirked. "You're not going to like my answer."

"Let me guess. We start with the creepy forest of doom. Then, if we survive that, we make our way across the winding path of death until we reach the castle that screams 'do not enter.'" Rivik sighed.

"Scared?" Vale smirked.

"What's there to be scared about? It's not like we are marching into a living nightmare surrounded by lava," Rivik chuckled.

They made their way into the dark woods, weapons drawn and ready. They moved quietly and carefully, not wanting to disturb anything that may be nearby. Overhead they saw imps floating lazily past. Ghouls and specters hovered among the trees, typically around pools of water. Their glowing essence made them easy to avoid in the dark woods. They heard sounds unlike anything they'd ever heard, and all the while felt the presence of someone or something watching them.

"I have a question," Rivik whispered to Dante.

"What?" Dante replied.

"Are all the creatures here . . . evil?"

"How do you mean?"

"In our world, some people are good and others are bad. Some creatures are docile and others hostile. I was just wondering if it's the same here."

"I do not know for certain. I would suggest we treat everything we encounter as hostile," Dante replied.

They managed to make their way through the forest without incident and were almost to the other side. Vale could see the winding path to the creepy castle. A ledge to their right led alongside the cliffs, creating a walking path with a sudden drop off on one side and the steep, rocky slope of a mountain on the other. The path hooked out of sight not far from where they stood. In front of them was a great chasm that split the earth, cutting them off from their goal.

The only way across appeared to be a winding stone bridge that led over the chasm. It was wide enough to cross but narrow enough to require careful steps along the way. On the other side, there was thick shelf of rock like a beach before the bubbling sea of lava that served like a giant moat around the palace. A single, narrow stone path provided the only visible passage to the palace on the other side of the lava lake.

Floating over the lava on tails of fire were guardian creatures. Their bodies were made of pure flame, and their chests, heads, and arms were covered in armor made of volcanic rock. They towered at twice the height of a normal man and were carrying rock blades as they patrolled all along the lava near the bridge.

"Fire elementals," Dante answered before anyone asked.

"What do we do?" Rivik asked.

"The bridge is too narrow to maneuver. If we try to cross it, we will be defenseless and exposed. We need another means to cross," Vale replied.

"Well, I left my wings back at the village, so any other ideas for how we can do that?" Rivik asked.

"I can try to fend them off, but there are many of them, the path is long, and pure elementals are very difficult to stop. Crossing that bridge will likely be our death," Dante said.

"We didn't come all this way just to turn back," Sera protested.

"No, but we can't help Azalea if we are dead, and we don't even know that's where she is," Rivik said.

"I've got this. Wait here, and I'll come back with Azalea," Vale said.

"Whoa, hold on." Dante grabbed the Black Swordsman's arm.

"I can't die, remember? I'll fight and die my way through until I reach the other side. It might take a minute, but I'll get there."

"Being burned alive over and over again—you realize how painful that will be?" Rivik asked.

Vale smirked. "I've felt pain before."

"It's not simple as that," Dante cautioned. "You forget, we are in a different realm. There is no way to know if your curse has power here."

"You mean . . ."

"I mean, there is a very good chance that if you die in this realm, you will not come back," Dante warned.

Vale nodded. "I see. What other choice is there?"

A screech filled the air like the cry of a great bird. Sera turned, following the sound. The path to their right was lit like a large flame.

"That sounds like a—" Sera's eyes grew big and she started toward it.

"No, no, no, you have no idea what that is." Dante stepped in front of her, trying to block her path.

Rivik put his hand on the alchemist's shoulder. "You aren't gonna win this one."

"Nothing good can come from this," Dante warned. "Every moment we spend here puts us at a greater risk. We need to stay focused, find a way across that bridge."

Sera pushed past him and started down the path, with Grom unquestioningly following.

"No point in fighting what you can't win. Who knows, maybe there's a secret path to the castle around this bend?" Rivik smiled his annoyingly charming smile and turned to chase after Sera.

"A secret path . . . in the wrong direction? This is utter foolishness," Dante protested.

"Perhaps. But sometimes the best solution to a problem is to find a way around it. Besides, we came to rescue a friend, not lose another. Let's go," Vale said.

Vale chased after them, with Dante reluctantly following. The stone path grew more and more narrow as the mountain wall grew closer and closer to the edge of the cliff. Just as the path threatened to give way, it turned. Around the corner was a valley leading into an enclave surrounded by rocky cliffs. Vale could see numerous caves, some on the bottom level and a few others on ledges at multiple points up the rock wall.

One of the cliffs, just above the surface, held a massive nest that was easily visible, even from the ground. Vale slid to a stop, in shock at the scene before him. On one side of the enclave was a large basilisk with its snake body coiled around an egg. On the other, a massive eagle made of fire, glowing with orange and red flames, its feathers curled as it screeched in rage.

"Is that a—" Vale started.

"That is a phoenix," Rivik confirmed.

Chapter 35

The Father's Shadow

Caelan made his way down from the roof. By the time he got back inside, the excitement at the edge of town had woken the others who were all scrambling out of the door of the inn to see what was going on. Spiro was in full armor, hand over his head, gripping the hilt of his stupidly large sword as he ran. He stomped with purpose, moving ahead of the others. Ash, Owen, and Celeste were close behind but failed to keep up with his rapid pace.

By the time Caelan caught up to them, Spiro had stormed past the villagers on an arrow's flight toward Kade. As he walked, he pulled his sword free and whirled it in front of him, his quick walk moving to a rushing charge.

"Deceiver!" he shouted, letting the tip of his blade drag against the dirt before swinging in an upward arc at Kade, threatening to cut him in half.

Kade smirked and stepped back casually. The blade missed him by a wide margin. Spiro used the momentum of his failed attack to bring his blade around faster. Again, Kade dodged. Spiro would not let up. He swung and thrust his blade over and over again, Kade dodging each one as if Spiro's attacks were in slow motion.

"Spiro! What are you doing? Stop this at once!" Celeste commanded.

The dragon knight ignored her, his string of attacks continuing. The effortlessness with which Kade dodged them should have discouraged him, but Spiro wouldn't stop. He attacked until the blade in his hand shook and he could hardly hold his sword up any longer.

"Are you quite finished?" Kade asked, sounding annoyed.

"I won't be done until I have your head!" Spiro's chest was heaving up and down as he took deep breaths.

Spiro lifted his sword. He took a step forward to lunge but was stopped as an arrow pierced the ground in front of him.

"As much as I love watching you make a complete goraum fool of yourself—and I do love that—you need to stop," Caelan interrupted.

"I will not!"

"How about you try using your words for a minute?"

"He is an imposter! He must be slain," Spiro responded.

"You mean he's not Lord Drako of Taggoron?" Ash asked.

"I mean, he's a monster," Spiro explained.

"He doesn't look like a monster," Owen said.

"Right? Just an annoyingly perfect face," Caelan added.

"I will not let you live to spill your lies, you undead elven lich!" Spiro screamed and swung his blade again. Kade dodged even more easily than before.

"You think I'm a Baelnorn?" Kade laughed.

"What else could wield such magic? I knew when you sensed the Skellar there was something unnatural about you. No normal human could have done that. But now, seeing you walk through mage fire unscathed . . . " Spiro shouted.

"What's a Baelnorn?" Owen asked.

"A Baelnorn is made when an elf surrenders his life to be forged into a lich. They become undead sorcerers of terrifying power," Spiro explained.

"Why?" Caelan asked. "Elves are already immortal."

"I read about these in the Royal Archives. According to the legends, they do so to be made a guardian of their people. Unlike most liches, Baelnorn are not by nature malevolent, but they cannot be trusted. You don't surrender your immortal life without reason. Baelnorn are fanatical in their purpose and will do anything to achieve their mission," Celeste explained.

"It would explain his flight, his awareness of other undead creatures, his magical power, and his ability to wield multiple types of elemental magic," Spiro said.

"I am not a Baelnorn," Kade replied.

"Lies. You are not human. No human could do those things," Spiro started.

"I am human, in a sense. I can explain. But not here." Kade turned and whispered something to the elder. The elder nodded and lead all the villagers back to town.

Beyond the town, in the distance, was a forest filled with tall trees stretching high into the sky. Kade led them to the other side of it, using the thick wall of trees to shield them from the sight of the village.

"What is going on?" Celeste put her hands on her hips.

Spiro pulled a silver medallion out of his cloak. The medallion bore the image of a tree but with long flowing hair instead of branches. He held it up to Kade.

"Touch this," he commanded.

"The mark of Lady Anima. Really?" Kade glared.

"Are you afraid? If you are not a Baelnorn, this shouldn't bother you at all."

Kade groaned and took the medallion in his hand. He pressed it to his forehead and then his neck and handed it back.

"What was the point of that?" Owen asked.

"If Kade were undead, as Spiro suggests, when he touched the symbol of the goddess of life, it would have burned him," Ash explained.

"That is not possible," Spiro muttered. "This is some sort of trick."

"Hey, quick question," Caelan interrupted. "Can a Baelnorn thing or whatever shatter a steel blade with their face?"

Spiro's brow furrowed. "No, they are not impervious to steel."

"Well, before he walked through fire, I watched a soldier's blade shatter like a piece of glass when it struck his face. So, if he's not a Baelnorn, why don't you take a breath and let him explain?"

"If I sense a single lie leaving your lips, I will end you." Spiro turned and glared.

Kade ignored him, focusing on the others. "You know me as Kade Drako. That has not always been my name. I have had many. I was born one thousand years ago when the worlds of Sidhe and of men were still connected."

"So, not human then?" Caelan commented.

"My mother was human. A lovely woman—sweet, kind, protective. She also had an innate magical aptitude that she didn't live long enough to develop. My father is Bag'Thorak." He stopped and waited.

"Bag . . . Thorak," Spiro repeated in disbelief. "How is that?"

"I can do you one better. Who is that?" Caelan asked.

"Bag'Thorak?" Kade smirked. "The king, eldest, and most powerful of all dragons."

"You dare utter that name?" Spiro interrupted. "I have lost countless brothers who gave their lives trying to bring him down. You dishonor them by using his name to support this ridiculous story. I should cut you down where you stand!"

"Tell me, dragon knight, what is the rarest type of dragon?" Kade asked.

"An orange dragon. We know nothing of them. The only reason we even suspect they exist is due to a few extremely rare sightings."

"Wait, so you're saying your mother was a human, and your father was a dragon? How would that even be possible?" Ash asked.

"I suppose I'll show you." Kade shrugged.

"Oh, no, please don't. I think we all know how that would end," Caelan started.

An orange mist surrounded Kade as he closed his eyes. His body grew, his skin changed. The smoke around him grew thick so that only a shadowy silhouette could be seen expanding larger and larger. Finally, as the smoke cleared, the creature in front of them looked unlike anything they'd ever seen.

He had long, plate-covered legs, bending knees, and a torso

shaped like a man but covered in layered orange and black scales. His shoulders were like a horned pauldron. His neck grew long like that of a lizard. His face was a hybrid of man and dragon, and he was adorned with a crown made of horns and a set of spikes running down the back of his neck. He had four great wings: two large wings on the top and a smaller pair underneath. The dragon-man stood towering over them, his long, orange and black tail swaying behind him.

"This is what an orange dragon looks like." Kade's voice was suddenly deeper. His words came out slow but felt heavy. "We are a cross between dragon and man. Satisfied?"

Kade turned his head to the side as the orange mist appeared around him again. His form shrank as scales gave way to flesh, and a moment later he appeared as he was—a man.

"Monster!" Spiro started to charge forward. Ash grabbed him by his armor and tugged him back.

"Release me! I will slay this devil!" Spiro demanded.

"Calm down, dragon boy, I'm gonna need you to shut your mouth for a minute. I'm trying to sort this out," Ash said.

"Sort it out? I am a dragon knight. I live to slay dragons. He is a dragon. The son of the dragon king! What part of this has you confused?" Spiro snapped.

"It's a bit more than that, isn't it?" Ash challenged. "You swinging your sword and slinging your rage like a rabid werewolf is really distracting. So, Imma need you to just stand there and keep your mouth shut," Ash stated.

"Or what? Surely you do not think yourself capable of standing in the way of a dragon knight."

"Or I'm going to hit you so hard you won't wake up till tomorrow."

"I have a sacred quest! You will not stop me!" Spiro tried to pull free and charge Kade.

Ash shook his head, pulled the dragon knight's shoulder to turn him, and drove his fist into Spiro's face. Spiro's head turned violently to the side. His body froze for a moment and then collapsed to the ground in a heap.

"Sorry, he was bothering me. Getting back to it, can you

explain to me what I just saw? How is it you look human?" Ash gestured to Kade.

"Dragons possess a unique magic called Polymorph. Lesser dragons cannot use it, but any mature dragon can, for a time, take on human form. The stronger the dragon, the longer they can hold the form without changing."

"Then . . . they—"Ash started.

"Yes, sometimes, in human form, a dragon will mate with a human. And in very rare cases, sometimes a human woman will become pregnant. Typically, the spawn of a dragon and human does not survive its birth," Kade explained.

"Because they are um . . . " Owen started.

Because their fathers eat them," Kade said.

"That's terrible," Owen replied.

"Dragons are a proud race obsessed with pedigree. The lord of each type of dragon is worshiped like a god amongst his kin. Pure lines are so sacred, even breeding between types of dragons is considered a violation of the way of the dragon. While most dragons find mating with a human amusing, offspring are considered an abomination, an offense to all dragonkind."

"Because you're part human?" Caelan asked.

"Dragons believe their power and their worth comes from the prestige of their bloodline. An impure bloodline, like one mixed with weak, frail humans, should be far lesser. But, despite our tainted blood, orange dragons are often more powerful. Our existence threatens the core of what dragons believe about themselves. So, they call us an abomination and try to end us before we ever begin."

"How did you survive, then?" Caelan asked.

"My mother deceived my father, then hid me from him. For years, she kept me safe by moving us from place to place, so it would be harder for him to find us. Eventually, her luck ran out. When he found out about me, he hunted her down and killed her. I heard it happen, watched it from my hiding place as he ripped her heart from her chest. I swore a blood oath that when I was I able, I would kill him. Last we met, I almost did," Kade replied.

"What happened?" Caelan asked.

"Another dragon interfered, and my father managed to escape."

"If you almost killed him before, why not track him down and finish the job?"

"The Sidhe."

"Yeah, Sidhe, of course. Why didn't I think of that? Imaginary magical people with little shiny wings. What else could it be?" Caelan replied.

Kade grunted. "They are not imaginary, I can assure you. Dragons have two weaknesses: other dragons and spirit magic. The Sidhe were the greatest wielders of spirit magic in this realm. So, after he escaped, my father flew to the Kingdom of the Sidhe and forced them to use their magic to make him invulnerable. With their protection, my father is unkillable."

"Oh, perfect, an unkillable dragon. Sounds lovely," Caelan replied.

"What happened to the Sidhe? Did your father kill them?" Ash asked.

"When I discovered what they had taken from me, I killed many of their kind, until a young prince called Legari pleaded for mercy. He swore he would take all the Sidhe from this realm, and they would never return. I vowed to him that if ever he broke his oath—if ever a Sidhe crossed back into this realm—I would devour his kingdom and leave the world of the Sidhe in ash. Once they left, I bound the portals between our realms and removed all knowledge of their kind from this world. They became nothing but bedtime stories and faded into myth."

"That's why you want the Darkstone? You want to remove the protection around your father so you can finally kill him?" Caelan said.

Kade nodded.

"Why did you need someone else's wish? Couldn't you just do it yourself?" Caelan asked.

"You ask many questions."

"Well, it's not every day you learn you're traveling with a half-dragon on a quest to save the world from the Shadow King while also supporting his secret vendetta against his father, the king of all dragons," Caelan replied.

"Very well. The Darkstone is more complex than you know. A simple wish is not enough to undo the magic that protects my father. I need the right wish to help me unlock a greater power in the stone."

"Unlock the stone—what do you mean?" Celeste asked.

"Think of the Darkstone like a treasure chest that has been locked inside another treasure chest. Your uncle used the treasure in the first chest, but there is even greater treasure inside the second."

"Ok, so how do we unlock it?" Celeste asked.

"A shared wish."

"Are you serious? That's all it takes? Two people wanting the same thing?" Caelan challenged.

"Not just wanting, desiring in their hearts. There is a power, a sort of magic created by the sharing of dreams and desires. When two people hold the stone and their heart's desire is similar, the wish becomes enhanced by that power. Alone, my wish is not enough, but with a Royal whose wish is similar, I could finally avenge my mother," Kade explained.

"You know a lot about this stone," Caelan said.

"Yes. It's amazing what you can learn when you have one thousand years to learn it."

"Fair. Since you're an expert, how exactly does it work? The Darkstone, I mean. Say we succeed? We just pass it around like a pitcher of ale? Wish, grant, pass it on sort of thing? Do we make all our wishes at the same time?" Caelan asked.

"The Stone can be used either individually or as a group. Though there are some who suggest that the power of the wish is reduced when multiple people use it at the same time. It is not known, as very few outside of the King of Parisia have ever used it. But what I can tell you is that before you use the stone, you must be prepared to pay its price."

"What price?" Caelan asked.

Kade smirked. "You were told the Darkstone has the power to fulfill the greatest desire of your heart, to make your deepest wish a reality. You were all deceived. The stone has incredible power. Using it comes at a terrible cost."

"Sooo, it is true then," a booming voice echoed from overhead, interrupting their conversation.

The voice was followed by massive gusts of wind that nearly toppled the whole group. With a thud, a great green dragon landed next to them. "You have aligned yourself with these creatures? I suppose it should be expected, with your mixed blood."

"Ermgal," Kade glared.

"It was unwise to transform. Now we who hunt you know where you are," the green dragon replied.

"I'm sure you lesser dragons are eager to prove your worth to my father. You will regret it," Kade said.

"This is your tomb, mixed-blood," Ermgal laughed.

The green dragon raised his head and roared; green flames erupted from his mouth into the sky.

"Ralk it." Caelan drew back an arrow and fired it at the dragon's exposed neck.

Just before the arrow struck, the dragon disappeared, leaving behind a green, vaporous cloud. Caelan scanned the area, trying to figure out what happened. A green cloud suddenly appeared behind him, and in it, the green dragon.

"What cute little pets you have. I'm going to enjoy eating this one," Ermgal cackled.

"Don't worry, little man. There's just one." Ash squared off to face the dragon. Owen moved sheepishly behind him.

"Look again," Ermgal laughed.

The ground shook and thundered as a yellow dragon landed behind them, shouting its fearsome roar into the sky as it stood tall on its four legs. The tremors continued as a red dragon, then a blue, a purple, and two browns landed, encircling the group. Owen gasped and took off running, holding his head between his hands as he dashed quickly between a gap in the yellow and red dragons. He made his way to the forest, rushing past the tree line and disappearing into the woods. The dragons paid him no heed.

"Your father promised an extra reward if we brought you back alive. Seems he wants to devour you himself. Surrender to us and we will eat your friends quickly with minimal pain." Ermgal's booming voice made every word rumble like thunder.

"I got something you can eat." Caelan fired another arrow at the green dragon.

The arrow once again pierced nothing but green mist as Ermgal vanished and reappeared.

"It's over, tainted one. Surrender, and we take you to your father; resist and we rip you apart and deliver him the pieces."

Kade laughed, a bright smile on his face.

"What are you laughing at?" Ermgal demanded, anger surging in his voice.

"You still don't get it, do you?" Kade asked.

"Get what?"

"All my life you have hunted me, hated me for what I am—an impure half-breed. I have evaded you for a thousand years. You think after all that time, in a place like this, in the Dragon Lands themselves, I would let down my guard? How foolish your arrogance has made you. You think you have trapped me? You have plunged headlong into your own doom."

"What are you talking about?" Ermgal grumbled.

Kade pointed to the ground.

Ermgal looked down to see a glowing circle of yellow light under his feet. Not just his feet—the same yellow circle glowed under each of the dragons. He tried to step off it, to move his massive body, but the light glowed brighter, and his body refused to budge.

"What is this? What have you done?"

"Ermgal the Hunter and his famous squad of dragons. Seven dragons to hunt an abomination. Always seven. Lilithima, it's time," Kade said.

A smaller pattering of wings filled the air as seven flying Sidhe floated up above the tree line. They looked human in every way, save the large glimmering wings beating rapidly in the air behind them. Their features were soft and ethereal. They were beautiful to behold, as if magic radiated from their very skin.

"Sidhe?" Ermgal roared. "There have not been Sidhe in this realm for—"

"A thousand years, yes. I'm quite aware. Yet to my surprise, these appeared in Taggoron not long ago. I'll admit my initial instinct was to do what I told them I would do should any of their kind ever set wing in this realm again, but it occurred to me this annoyance could be an opportunity." Kade smiled and started chanting. Colorful crystals appeared all around him, floating in front of his hands.

"Enough!" Ermgal roared.

Green mist covered him. He disappeared for a moment and then reappeared in the exact same spot. His eyes, once filled with the flames of anger now stretched wide with terror. He was trapped. Fear seized the mighty dragon, and he lashed and clawed frantically at his luminescent cage. The walls glowed and sparked with little glistening flakes. The magical field hissed on contact but did not budge. The other dragons raged in similar fashion, like caged beasts tugging against their restraints. The red breathing fire, the blue breathing ice—nothing broke the barriers of light that contained them so completely.

The Sidhe hovered in a line above the dragons, holding their hands together with their eyes closed as they reinforced the barriers. The crystals in front of Kade started to glow and pulse. A line of light like a glowing rope linked each crystal to one of the dragons of corresponding color.

The dragons cried out and struggled, clawing against their spirit cages to no avail. With each passing moment, the color began to drain from the dragons' scales and the crystal started to glow all the brighter.

"What is this feeling? What are you doing?" Ermgal asked.

"This is a Soul Trap. It's an ancient spell, all but forgotten since it requires both Sidhe and dragon magic to use. It can drain the lifeforce of just about anything. It turns your power into a crystal that can be used, forged, or even absorbed. You see, I knew any road to my father would have to go through you. Alone, none of you are a threat. But even I couldn't take on seven dragons at once. So rather than wiping the fairies out of existence, I offered them a chance at redemption."

"You . . . will not . . . get away with this—" Ermgal started.

"Your souls are mine. This is your end," Kade cut him off.

He extended his hands, and the strings of light grew thicker. One by one, the dragons turned to dust as their very essence was being pulled into the crystals. Only Ermgal remained, glaring angrily as he watched his companions vaporize. Kade walked over to him, looking at the towering green dragon.

"That's enough, Lilithima; you and your friends may go. But if I see you again, even at a distance, I will go to Aethirum Astra and extinguish the race of Sidhe like the dying ember of a burned log," Kade warned.

"You want us to release him?" Lilithima asked. Kade nodded and waved his hand. The Sidhe released their hands and turned away, flying off into the distance. The further they went, the dimmer the yellow light under Ermgal became.

"You should have drained me like you did the others. Your death will be slow," Ermgal sneered.

A green mist surrounded the dragon, and he vanished. Kade moved, ducking his head and thrusting his arm out at the open air. Suddenly the mist appeared behind him. Ermgal's teeth crashed together where Kade's head had just been. The green dragon roared, its deep voice caught in its throat as Ermgal began to choke. Kade pulled his arm back. Blood coated his forearm as he clutched in his hand a large beating heart. The green dragon fell limp to the ground. Kade cast the heart away, letting it bounce against the rough earth and roll into a small bush.

"Your soul is not even worth having."

Chapter 36

The Palace of the Red Empress

"What are they doing to it?" Sera asked.

Glowing blue arcane ropes wrapped around the wings and legs of the phoenix, keeping it restrained. Holding the ropes were a half dozen water sprites.

"It looks like the water sprites are helping the basilisk. I assume that is a phoenix egg they are after," Dante said, rushing up next to them.

"Why?" Rivik asked.

"Snakes and water sprites hate fire birds. Phoenix are immortal creatures born out of the ashes of their predecessors, so their numbers never diminish. However, it is extremely rare for a phoenix to reproduce. Once that egg hatches, there will be another immortal bird in the world. My guess is they want to stop that from happening," Dante explained.

"We have to help her!" Sera shouted, drawing her blades.

She moved toward the water sprites.

"Wait!" Dante shouted.

"Don't try to stop me, wizard." She turned and glared.

"You can't hurt sprites, not with your weapons." Dante shook his head. "Your blades will pass right through."

"We have to do something!" Sera said.

"Leave them to me. The basilisk is all yours." Dante grinned and walked toward the phoenix.

Shadows of the Dark Realm

"You're going to fight the water sprites—with the power to get you wet—and leave us to deal with the giant serpent with poisonous breath, regenerative properties, and a glare that can turn you to stone?" Rivik asked.

"Is that a problem?" Vale asked.

"No, just making sure I knew the plan. Let's go kill the king of serpents." Rivik held the shaft of his spear along his arm. He charged the giant snake, leaning forward as he ran.

The basilisk turned its head, fixing its gaze on Rivik. Rivik closed his eyes, feeling his way toward the creature as he ran at full speed. Grom moved toward the back, staying out of the serpent's view. The snake opened its mouth, and a purple smoke wafted out, hovering just in front of its body.

"Rivik, freeze!" Vale shouted as he moved in toward the snake.

Rivik's boots slid along the ground. He looked ahead as much as he dared and saw the purple smoke. He crouched down and stepped back.

"I need an opening," he shouted.

"Grom . . . make way." The troll lifted his axes above his head and leapt into the air, covering the distance between himself and the basilisk in a single massive bound.

He landed, slamming his axes down using the full force of his momentum. The axes cut through the basilisk's tail in two places. The basilisk's head shot up as it hissed in pain. The purple smoke cleared. Rivik pushed forward, charging the creature while its gaze was turned. He readied his spear, lifting his head to line up his target. To his horror, he could see the basilisk moving its head back down, its gaze falling closer and closer.

"Gwar!" he muttered to himself.

If he caught the creature's eye, he'd become the newest statue in the Spirit Realm. If he looked away, he would miss his mark and the serpent could catch him in its deadly jaws. The serpent's eyes grew closer and closer, nearly upon him. He had to decide, and fast. One eye was aiming right at him. One eye was all it would take. If only he'd been a little faster.

A gust of wind burst past his face as a glimmer of light nearly struck him. He turned a little but followed the sound to see a large dagger pierce the basilisk's eye. Once again, the serpent's head lifted up, moving his gaze safely away. Rivik put both hands on his spear and drove it into the serpent's exposed neck. The spear sank in deep, and Rivik hung from it for a second. His spear cut through the serpent's scales, slowly causing him to slide down its body until, at last, his feet reached the ground. Rivik looked back to see Sera blow him a kiss as she drew another dagger.

"Rivik, twist your spear!" Vale shouted as he rushed forward.

Rivik wrenched the sharp tip of his spear to the side, widening the gash in the basilisk's neck. Vale drove his blade into the gap, getting his black sword far deeper than Rivik's spear. He lifted, slicing through a portion of the serpent's neck. His blade pulled free, and he whirled it around. The basilisk turned, opening its jaws and lunging its head to gobble up Vale and Rivik in a single bite.

Two axes buried into the snake's head near its eye sockets as Grom used his axes like hooks to climb the massive serpent. The strike stunned the snake-monster just long enough for Vale to slice his blade in the other direction, completely severing the snake's head from its body. Black blood sprayed and splashed over them.

The basilisk's head thumped to the ground with a squishing sound as its body went limp. Rivik put his hand on Vale's shoulder before putting his hands on his knees and leaning down to catch his breath. When his heart stopped thumping like a drum, he turned to see Dante standing with his arms folded, six puddles of water around him.

"What took you so long?" he asked.

Rivik started to reply but then the companions heard a new voice.

"Mortals do not belong in the Realm of Spirits."

Vale and Rivik exchanged a glance before looking at the towering bird of fire that now glared down at them. They heard her voice clearly, but her mouth did not move. It was like she spoke directly into their minds. They stared in stunned silence for a moment.

Shadows of the Dark Realm

"Voice in head . . . how she speak?" Grom asked, looking around. "You . . . hear?"

"Be careful what you think. Phoenixes are telepathic. They can hear your thoughts and speak into your mind. They also have insight and foresight," Sera said excitedly.

"That's a surprising thing for you to know," Dante said.

"She saw one when she was a girl, climbing through the mountains in Vargr. She's been obsessed with them ever since," Rivik explained.

"Why have you come to the land of spirits, mortals?"

"Don't lie," Sera warned.

"One of our companions was taken from us, brought here to be used by the Red Empress. We came to rescue her and stop that from happening," Dante answered.

"I see. I am Missanja. I have lived two thousand lives. Never in all of my days did I think I would be indebted to mortal men. Yet, you have risked your lives to aid me and save my whelpling. What would you ask of me?"

"Could you fly us across to the castle, and bring us back once we rescue our friend?" Sera asked.

Missanja stared. "You have saved the rarest and most precious thing to me, and that is all you ask for in return? Very well. I can take you two at a time. Pair as you wish, and we shall begin. But first . . . " The phoenix flapped its wings, and a circle of fire surrounded her egg, not touching it but swirling like a vortex all around it.

Vale and Rivik went first. The phoenix flapped its mighty wings, lifting them off the ground and carrying them in her massive claws to the castle on the other side. She gently dropped them onto the roof before flying back to get Sera and Grom. Finally, she returned with Dante.

"I will be waiting with my egg. Signal me, and I shall return to bring you across," she spoke into their minds and flew back out of view.

From the roof there was a door which opened to a winding staircase that led down into the palace. Vale opened the door and stopped.

"Where do you think the Red Empress would be keeping Azalea?" Vale asked.

"Vespera's greatest weakness is her arrogance. She wouldn't bother with a secure location or a dungeon that could be guarded and secured. If she has Azalea here, odds are she has her in the throne room or at the top of the tallest tower."

"No reason to hide. I can't imagine she gets lots of company in a place like this," Rivik said.

Vale went first, cautiously moving down the stairs. At the bottom was a long hallway with four doors. They tried the first, a waiting room with nothing but chairs and decorations.

"Room . . . empty," Grom stated.

"I don't like it," Vale said.

"Not a fan of terror chic? Wouldn't have been my first design choice either. Her decorator really needs some tips," Rivik said.

"This place is abandoned," Vale said.

"I hate to say Rivik might have been right, but we don't know for sure that the Red Empress would have brought Azalea here." Sera shook her head.

"You don't have to act like it hurts to say it," Rivik protested. "Anyway, we've come this far, better check it out,"

They moved to the next door and pushed it open. Inside the walls were tall and made of pure black stone. The room was massive and felt luxurious. Red banners and flags were hanging from the four walls and ceiling. They'd found the throne room. The throne itself was a red velvet chair with black arm rests and a giant black skull hanging over the seat like a canopy. A plush, red runner stretched from the base of the throne all the way to the entry on the other side of the room.

Black, carved gargoyles lined the walls, each one eight feet tall at least. The rest of the room was completely open. No other furniture, save a tall fireplace opposite the throne. Rivik walked into the room, looking around before making his way over to one of the gargoyles.

"This is some really detailed craftsmanship." He bounced his spear across his shoulder idly as he leaned in close.

. . .

"Get back . . . not . . . stone . . . " Grom warned, pulling his axes from behind his back.

Suddenly, the eyes of the gargoyle Rivik was looking into flashed red. In a blink, the stone turned to leathered flesh, and the winged creature attacked, swinging its claws at Rivik. *Rivik is too close. He won't have time to react,* Vale thought as he raced toward them.

Rivik seemed to disappear, dropping down so quickly as his body spun in a crouched circle. The gargoyle's massive claw swung high, missing Rivik completely. The creature extended its arms and stepped off its pedestal right into Rivik's spear. Vale stared for a minute, not even sure how it had happened. Rivik had not only reacted with incredible speed, but he'd also managed to predict the creature's move and counter it all, while seeming completely effortless.

"Ok, when the decorations start trying to kill you, that's where I draw the line," Rivik said.

The gargoyle shattered, and piles of rubble bounced along the ground. As if in response, one by one, the eyes of every other gargoyle in the room lit up.

"Come to Grom." Grom smiled excitedly as he extended his arms and readied himself.

"Let's get out of here!" Dante urged.

"You go . . . Grom play."

A loud scream filled the air. A woman's scream coming from some unseen place above them.

"Azalea!" Vale shouted.

"The tower!" Dante added.

"You go; we'll be right behind you," Rivik said.

"We can't just leave you," Sera started.

"Don't waste time arguing. Get Azalea; we will take care of the decorations."

Sera, Dante, and Vale made their way out of the throne room and rushed through hallways. They ran from one corridor to the next until they found a set of stairs leading up.

"This way," Vale guessed as much as said.

"How do you know?" Sera asked.

Vale shrugged. "I don't. The sound came from above us. At least this is moving in the right direction."

The stairs seemed endless, winding in so many tight circles they started to feel dizzy. When they reached the top, they found a small walkway leading to a sturdy wooden door. Vale didn't bother to slow down; he used his momentum and slammed his shoulder into the door, knocking it open.

Laying sprawled out on a stone table floating several inches above the floor, was Azalea. Her arms and legs were stretched out and bound by arcane rope. A series of gemstones were positioned in a circle around her, and a larger center crystal floated above her. Four mages in red robes stood chanting, one at each corner of the table she was sprawled out on. Azalea was groaning and writhing from whatever they were doing to her.

"Who are you?" One of the mages turned, glaring angrily. "How dare you interrupt our work!" His words turned to gargles as Vale's sword pierced his throat. His eyes went wide as he clutched his neck, blood pouring from between his fingers.

"What were you saying?" Vale glared at the other mages.

One lifted his hand, a ball of fire forming in his palm as he aimed it at Vale. Sera's dagger pierced his hand, and he cried out. Clutching his wound, he fell to his knees, his face curled in pain.

Vale crossed the room to the mage on the far side. He stepped back, pleading.

"No . . . wait . . . you can't . . . you have no right!" He protested until the moment Vale separated his head from his neck.

The final mage barely had time to move before Dante hit him with a burst of magical energy. His body froze and then shriveled until it turned into a mound of dust on the floor. As the mages died, the arcane ropes binding Azalea vanished.

Sera rushed to Azalea's side. "She's still breathing."

Vale moved to the other side, taking her hand in his and looking down at her. He let out a sigh of relief when he felt her gently squeeze his hand in reply.

"Well, well, well, look who we have here," a woman's voice came from behind them.

In a flash of red light, a woman appeared in a long, slender, red dress that clung to her curves. Her skin was fair, her hair black as night. She wore a red crown shaped like a circlet of feathers as she walked slowly toward them. She looked beautiful and terrifying at the same time. Her movement was refined and enchanting. Her hips swayed as she stepped closer, her body seeming to flow as she walked.

"If it isn't my old friend; good to see you again, Dante." Her words were sweet and pure honey pouring from her lips.

A burst of light flashed next to her, leaving in its place a man with short blonde hair wearing a pair of thin square glasses. He bowed slightly to the Red Empress.

"My lady, King Aeon would like to see you." His voice was high and formal.

"He can wait. I have special guests to attend to," she replied without turning to acknowledge the man.

The blonde man sighed. "Gods don't like waiting, my lady."

"He . . . can . . . wait," she repeated, a slight edge to her voice.

"Very well, I will tell him." He shrugged before disappearing again with a flash of light.

The Red Empress rolled her eyes and turned her attention back to Dante.

"After all these years, imagine my surprise. Dante, how are you?"

"What is she talking about?" Vale turned to Dante.

"Not now," Dante replied, reaching into his cloak.

"Tsk tsk tsk." The Red Empress wagged her finger. A red glow surrounded Dante and lifted him into the air, immobilizing him. "I may still be recovering from your binding and banishing me from my own vessel, but do you really think you can come here, into my realm, and take what is mine? Even at a fraction of my power, you're no match for me."

Azalea groaned on the table, drawing the Red Empress's gaze. One of Sera's daggers flew through the air, stopping inches in front of the Red Empress's face. The blade, suddenly surrounded in a red glow, floated harmlessly out of the way. She turned her gaze to Sera.

"Foolish child." She motioned with her head, and Sera's

knife turned and flew straight into her shoulder. Sera cried out in pain, dropping to her knee.

Vale lunged, only to be caught in a red light himself.

"Your friends are quite slow, Blue Alchemist," she laughed.

Vale gritted his teeth and pushed with all his might. His legs felt heavy, his body resisting his own instructions. He pushed anyway. It burned in every fiber of his being, but he pushed and took a step closer.

The Red Empress stopped and looked at him, her eyes narrowing. "That . . . is not possible."

Vale managed another step.

"How are you doing that? You shouldn't even be able to blink." She glared angrily.

He pushed through the pain, taking one slow step and then another.

She laughed. "What do you expect to do? Hmmm? It's pointless. You will never reach me like that."

Vale smiled. "I'm not trying to reach you. I'm trying to distract you."

The Red Empress's eyes grew wide as she turned too late. Azalea had managed to sit up, and her hands were already extending. A wave of purple energy slammed into the Red Empress, launching her into the wall. She hit it with a thud and dropped to the ground. Her magic holding Vale and Dante flickered out.

Dante hit the ground and pulled a vial from his coat. He fired several bursts of blue energy at the Red Empress with one hand and tossed the vial with the other. A blue smoke surrounded her.

"A spirit drain potion? Really?" the Red Empress scoffed.

"It will give me plenty of time to do this!" Dante rushed forward.

He pulled a small blue gem from his cloak and grabbed her by the throat. Wrenching her mouth open, he shoved the gem inside it and forced her to swallow it down. The smoke was making her weak and tired; the Red Empress tried to protest but was unable to do so.

"A soul trap gem is more powerful in the Spirit Realm. This

will keep you contained here for a long time—plenty of time for me to get Azalea well beyond your reach." Dante grinned victoriously.

Dante lifted his hands and muttered a spell. A great ball of ice formed around the Red Empress, freezing her in place. He looked down at her, barely visible through the thick ice, and smiled, dusting his hands together.

"Well, that will hold her for—" he started.

The ice began to melt away, and the Red Empress thrust her arm forward, shattering the frozen shell around her. She stood up and glared.

"Did you think your parlor tricks would hold me?" She lifted her hand.

Dante's eyes grew wide. If he could feel fear, this would have been a moment for it. He'd used three layers of magic that should have held her for a month or more, and she had broken free in less than a minute. This was not good.

Chapter 37

The Fang Collectors

"All of this was a set up?" Caelan asked.

"Yes," Kade answered.

"Why?"

"We are in the Dragon Lands now. If you are going to survive long enough to obtain the Darkstone, you are going to need better weapons."

"You want us to use these little crystals in a fight? Just toss them like a rock?" Caelan jested.

Kade walked over to one of the crystals that were hovering in the air where the dragons had been pulsing with a soft hum. He put his hand on it and closed his eyes, uttering unrecognizable words. The crystal began to pulse louder and glow brighter. There was a brilliant, almost blinding flash, then hanging in the air where the crystal had been was a thin, curved shield. Kade turned and tossed it to Celeste.

"For you, Celeste, I give the Shield of Argon."

She jumped out of the way, and the shield hit the ground with a thud.

"I don't know how to use a shield," she protested.

"Learn. I need your wish, so I need you alive. That is an enchanted dragonscale shield. It will repel any weapon and resist any magic," Kade answered.

Kade walked to another crystal and repeated the process.

This time the crystal was transformed not into a shield but into a pair of glossy, dark gray daggers. He tossed them to Ash.

"You are strong, but fists will avail you not against what we face. The twin daggers of Roa Cal Gar will be your weapons. One will drain the magic of any person or creature you cut, the other will drain their energy, weakening them for a time."

The next crystal formed into a quiver with a dozen arrows.

"For you, archer, the Quiver of Blagarok. The quiver will never empty. The arrows will pierce nearly anything, and they will return to your quiver after they find their mark."

Caelan notched one of the arrows and fired it into a tree in the distance. He reached back and the arrow vanished from the tree and reappeared in his quiver.

"Well, I'll be an ogre's foot wart," he grinned gleefully.

Kade turned the remaining crystals into a spear, a sword, and a gemstone.

"Now, we can get started," Kade said.

"Hold on. You must think us daft as murmuck gwar if you expect us to believe you did all this just to make us weapons."

"No. That was one of several reasons," Kade replied.

"Oh, I do love a good list. Let's hear it."

"First, they were an obstacle in our path. As agents of my father, they would have interfered when we moved for the Darkstone. Rather than waiting for them to strike, I preemptively removed them from the equation. On a personal level, Ermgal was the dragon who interfered when I fought my father. He is the reason my father escaped," Kade replied.

"Well, gwar, you really thought this through," Caelan smirked.

"Now, if we can continue? Before we move forward with our quest, there are several things we will need to obtain."

"No," Celeste said. "We can't afford all these delays. We need to stay focused."

"And how, child, would you like to focus? Do you know where the Darkstone is? What is your plan to find it? Wander around from roost to roost until you find the right treasure horde?" Kade paused to make the weight of the absurd thought sink in.

"No; surely someone saw—" Celeste protested.

"A dragon . . . in the Dragon Lands. You think someone in a nearby village just happened to see a dragon flying by with a small stone clutched in its claw and, from that briefest of moments, knew they were looking at the Darkstone?" Kade pressed. "What happens when you do find it?"

"Caelan sneaks in and steals it; that's why he's here."

"A thief so talented he can avoid the enhanced senses of an elder dragon? A shade isn't that good."

Celeste put her hands on her hips and glared. "Well, what do you suggest then?"

"You see what we've been working with?" Caelan rubbed his eye.

"There are several items we need to find to safely transport the stone. I'd rather not explain it multiple times. Gather your party. I will meet you back in the village; we can go over the plan from there," Kade answered.

"Who put you in charge?" Celeste stomped.

Kade turned to look at her, little orange flames dancing from the corners of his eyes. Celeste scoffed and stormed off back toward the village.

"Ralk, I better go find little Owen before he wanders into trouble." Ash rushed off in the direction Owen had run.

Kade and the Rag'amorian warriors were already walking away, leaving Caelan standing alone near the unconscious Spiro.

"No, it's fine. I'll take care of Spiro. Don't worry about it, guys. I insist . . . Go have a nice leisurely walk back. I'll just tote his heavy owa all on my own," Caelan shouted.

No one replied. No one turned back to help.

"I know you can hear me. Nothing? Awesome. You guys are the best." His voice trailed off as he started talking more to himself than the others. "His armor looks like it weighs as much as a goraum horse and buggy."

Caelan tried to use his body weight to lift Spiro up. He grunted and practically collapsed. "Yup, that's too heavy."

* * *

Shadows of the Dark Realm

Owen was clutching his knees to his chest, rocking back and forth with his back to the wall of a small house. Tears streamed from his eyes, and even from a distance Ash could see the man was sobbing. He took a deep breath and walked over. Without saying a word, he sat down next to Owen. He held his head back and looked at the sky. Owen sniffled, and his sobs softened.

"I ran away again. Just like with my son. Just like always. No matter how hard I try to be brave, I just . . ."

"I've seen a lot of gwar in my time—street fights, monster attacks, mobs, uprisings, but I'll tell you, getting surrounded by a group of ralkin' dragons? Believe me, most people would run same as you," Ash answered.

"You didn't," Owen said.

"No. But I have before. I just had a lot more practice standing my ground," Ash shrugged.

"How . . . how am I supposed to save my son when all I do is run? I'm hopeless. I'll never be anything more than a coward."

"Who says you ran because you were a coward? Maybe you ran because you have something to live for. You can't help your son if you get eaten by a dragon," Ash offered.

"You think I ran so that I could stay alive to help my son?" Owen blinked.

"I think that when the moment comes for your son, you will be the bravest of us all."

"What if you're wrong? What if my son suffers because I am too weak, too scared, too . . . me?"

"I'm not wrong. But tell you what, when we find your son, I'll help you get him back." Ash smiled.

"Y-y-you would do that?" Owen stared, a note of disbelief in his voice.

Ash nodded.

"Why?"

"Some people are dealt a bad hand in this life. They don't deserve it, didn't ask for it, it's just the way the cards fall. You got a bad hand. I know what that's like; I had someone help me with my hand. Now, I'll help you with yours." Ash reached behind his back and pulled out the daggers Kade had given him.

"What's this?" Owen asked.

"Special daggers. The dragon-man gave 'em to me. I'm not much good with blades. Like to fight with my fists. Maybe we teach you to use them?"

Owen's eyes lit up. "I've got a better idea! Quick, take off your gloves."

Ash furrowed his brow but started removing the gloves. He handed them to Owen who gripped them and the two blades with a dopey grin.

"I know just the thing. I need to go find the blacksmith. Give me some time," he said, standing and rushing off.

"Time to what?" Ash called after him, but the little man was already around the corner and gone from sight.

* * *

Spiro woke to find himself tied to a chair. He stretched and strained, but the ropes wrapped around his chest and legs were so tight he couldn't even budge.

"What is the meaning of this? Release me now!" he demanded.

He was sitting in the middle of a large two-story room. The floors were a bright wood. Round tables of a matching color were spread across the room, each surrounded by chairs painted a deep green. He could see the Rag'amorians leaning over the rails of the balcony above, staring down at him. Celeste was sitting in a chair at a nearby table. Ash and Kade stood directly in front of him while Caelan was leaning against a post off to the side, picking at his finger with a small blade.

Celeste pushed back from the table and walked toward him. She stood tall, kept her chin up, and held her hands behind her back as she paced back and forth, looking like a proper entitled noble.

"When I saw you fighting that dragon when we first met, I thought, this brave knight could be a real boon if he joined us. Your expertise as a hunter of dragons could be invaluable in completing our quest. But you continue to make rash, unreasonable choices that put our mission and our lives in danger. Spiro, you've become quite the liability. I'm very disappointed."

"I am a dragon knight. It is my sworn duty to slay dragons."

"Well, this will be the end of your journey with us. I won't let you jeopardize us."

"Good. I wouldn't defile myself by keeping company with dragon lovers. To think you'd throw your lot in with his kind? I misjudged you," Spiro started.

"Half dragon, actually," Caelan smirked. "Turns out he's better at killing dragons than you are, dragon knight."

Spiro scowled. "What do you mean, better? I've killed four dragons on my own."

"He killed six at once. Funny you don't get along. You both hate the same thing," Caelan replied.

Spiro looked down at the floor and then up at Kade. "You hate your own kind?"

"My kind?" Kade chuckled. "Dragons view me as an abomination. They wish to kill me simply for what I am. What love do I owe them?"

"Your father is the king."

"Yes."

"You'd go against him?"

"I will kill him."

Spiro's eyes lit up. "You could do this?"

Kade nodded.

"To kill the king of dragons would be . . . " his voice trailed off. "Please, give me another chance. I will do better. I promise, I won't jeopardize your quest. I'll listen. I'll do whatever you need me to do. If there's a chance to bring down the dragon king, please, don't send me away," Spiro pleaded.

"I'm touched. Really. Deep-down feeling in all these feely places, but as moved as I am by your empty promises and hollow words, we have no reason to trust them," Caelan answered.

"You can trust me. I swear."

"No lie ever began that way. The thing is, Spiro, you are a mystery to us. We don't know you. We can't trust you."

"What does that matter? I have sworn on my honor as a dragon knight. Our interests align. It would be foolish for you to turn down my help," Spiro countered.

"Tsk. An oath sworn on the honor of a stranger means

nothing if that stranger has no honor. Knowing someone—their history and what drives them—helps one to understand their behavior. You ask for trust but offer us no reason to give it. An alliance of convenience doesn't make me trust you any more than I already don't," Caelan pressed.

Spiro closed his eyes and sighed. "I grew up in a little village in the mountains of Baronia. It was a cozy place, the essence of serene. We had cool mountain water, a mine, a hot spring, and just enough farmland to not have to worry about food. It was safe, comfortable, peaceful. You'd swear it was the friendliest, happiest place in all the land. A paradise that almost no one knew about.

"My family lived near the mine. I am the youngest of seven: six brothers and a sister. There was this girl, Leana. I'd loved her since we were kids. She had one of those smiles, you know, the ones that can take the breath from your lungs. My sister and I had gone down to a nearby waterfall for a swim as we often did. It was a favorite for all the kids we grew up with.

"I remember hearing screams. The scent of burnt wood and flesh stinging my nose. I was afraid. My sister, she wasn't scared of anything. She rushed back up the hill to see our home, our perfect village, ablaze. By the time she got there, almost everyone was dead. The fire raged everywhere. I chased after her, but she was older than me and faster. She ran into our home to try to save our brothers. She came out alone, covered in black soot.

"That's when I saw it, perched on the rocks of the mountain above the entrance to the mine, just watching us in amusement. Its glowing eyes were fixed on my sister. I grabbed a hammer, but it was too late. The dragon's tail smashed into me, knocking me into the wall of our neighbor's house. I felt the flames kiss my skin as I watched the dragon swallow my sister whole. Everyone I had ever known was dead, murdered by a dragon for its own amusement. I thought I was next and knew there was nothing I could do about it. The dragon had finished my sister and was creeping closer to me.

"I closed my eyes, expecting death. When I opened them, four knights stood in front of a headless dragon's body. They took me into their order. Taught me how to fight, how to slay the monsters that destroyed my home. Every time I see a dragon, I feel those flames, and I see my sister disappearing inside the mouth of one of those beasts. My rage boils over, and I lose myself to it," Spiro explained.

Caelan stared for a moment before walking around behind Spiro.

"Caelan, what are you doing? I said he's not coming with us. I don't care about his little story," Celeste started.

"Alright, we can give you another chance. But if you screw it up again. I'll kill you myself." Caelan cut the rope binding Spiro to the chair.

"Caelan, stop it. This is not your decision." Celeste stomped her foot.

"You do what you want, princess." Caelan ignored her.

"Kade, stop him!" Celeste commanded.

Kade didn't move. "You seem confused. I need your wish. That doesn't mean I serve you."

Celeste folded her arms across her chest and huffed.

"You going to enlighten us on these obstacles we have to overcome before stealing the Darkstone?" Caelan asked.

"I can. Where is your friend, the little one?" Kade asked.

"He's working on something, been at it all day. Go ahead; I can catch him up to speed later," Ash replied.

Kade nodded. "In order to obtain the Darkstone, there are three things we will need to acquire: a Glyphstone, some Slumbaspice, and a Volkili Prismward."

Caelan pursed his lips. "Naturally, we need all of that. I agree. For the others' sake, why don't you tell us what those are."

"A Glypstone detects magical energy. Acquiring one will help us figure out where the Darkstone is being kept. Slumbaspice is a strong incense that is known to put dragons into a very deep sleep."

"Right, exactly. And the Vokaloki Primewiz thing?"

"Volkili Prismward—it's a special container that allows the Darkstone to be transported safely. Without it, carrying the stone would be disastrous," Kade explained.

"How long will it take to find them?" Celeste wailed like an angry cat.

"Slumbaspice is easy. Most towns in Baronia have it. I will handle obtaining a Glyphstone. It's the Volkili Prismward that will be the greatest challenge. I know where one is, but it will require us to charter a ship and sail to a remote island in the heart of the Dragon Lands," Kade explained. "I know a crew that can get us there, but we need to leave quickly."

"How quickly?" Caelan asked.

"As quickly as we can. If we miss this voyage, we will likely have to wait weeks," Kade answered.

"Weeks? We don't have time for that!" Celeste started.

"Then we should hurry. We can make way for Blackwater Marsh, restock there, and press on to Stormdale."

"That's where we are supposed to meet Vale, right?" Caelan asked.

"Yes. It's a port city. The ship we need sails from there," Kade answered.

Just then, the door to tavern burst open. Owen rushed inside with frantic, excited energy. He practically sprinted to Ash.

"I finished them!" he said, handing the gloves to Ash.

They looked different. They were thicker and heavier, with a hard plating over the top. Ash turned them over, inspecting them.

"I don't understand. You redesigned them?"

"Put them on; I'll show you," Owen practically squeaked as his body bounced excitedly.

Ash slid the gloves over his hands, examining them again.

"How do they feel?" Owen asked.

"Good." He banged his knuckles together.

"Now push your wrists back, then drop them down quickly," Owen smiled.

Ash looked confused but did as he was instructed. There was a soft click when he brought his wrists back. When he dropped them down, there was a soft ringing sound, like a blade being drawn quickly from its sheath. Daggers sprang out of the plate on the top of the glove, protruding past his knuckles like extensions of his arms. Ash lifted them up and looked at them, his mouth dropping.

"You said you fight with your fists because you're not good

with blades. Well, now you can use them like fists," Owen smiled.

"You made these, little man? And so quickly?" Kade walked over and grabbed Ash's hand, inspecting the weapons as he twisted his wrist back and forth.

Owen gulped and nodded, his eyes drifting down.

"This is impressive work. Converting daggers to gauntlet blades—I've never seen such a thing. You have quite the talent." Kade nodded approvingly, releasing Ash's hand.

"I may not be brave, but I am good at making things. You've all kept me safe so I could search for my son. I had to do something. When he offered to help me rescue my son, I just—I wanted to do something to repay what that means to me," Owen replied.

"I do not understand what you hope to accomplish. Your son was sold. Whoever bought him will not surrender him easily. Having the means and the lack of morality required to own someone is a dangerous combination. What do you plan to do? You can't fight. You can't even stand your ground." Kade's eyes narrowed.

Owen swallowed back tears as he looked up into Kade's face. Even in his human form, Kade towered above the little man.

"I know I'm not strong or brave. I know I can't fight. I have to try. When I find my son, I won't run away. I will stand. I will fight. I will do whatever I have to do to get him back. He's my son. I let him down before. I won't do it again." Owen's words were firm and confident.

"You are everything my father was not. You may not have the strength to take back your son, but you have the heart. You are what a father should be. If we find your son, I will help you." Kade's lips twisted into a subtle smile.

"Are you kidding? You just said we need to hurry to catch the ship. Now you want to waste time searching for a slave boy who may or may not be anywhere near here?" Celeste glared.

"We don't have to detour. We can just check as we go. If we find something out, we can figure out what to do from there," Ash suggested.

"I will not tolerate a delay," Celeste started.

"You can do what you want, princess, but you may be doing it alone," Caelan replied.

Their conversation was broken up by a commotion. They made their way outside to see what was happening. Three men in bright silver armor with long, flowing white capes were sitting atop horses at the edge of town.

"More soldiers?" Ash asked.

"We need to go—now," Spiro said, a sense of urgency in his voice.

"Why, who are they?" Celeste asked.

"You don't want to know," Spiro answered.

"Seems weird that she would ask if she didn't want to know," Caelan replied.

Spiro sighed. "They are the Fang Collectors. An elite unit of dragon knights."

"You don't want to see your friends?" Caelan challenged.

"Not my friends. They are savage and merciless hunters. They must have been drawn here by the other dragons. If we don't get out, they will shut the village down until their inquisition is up."

"A few dragon knights don't concern me." Kade folded his arms across his chest.

"These ones should. They have killed over two dozen elder dragons. Each time they kill one, they grow stronger. If they realize what you are, they will never stop hunting you."

Chapter 38

The God of Spirits

Dante stared in shock. There was no way she could be this powerful. Not in her present state. His mind refused to believe what his eyes were telling him. He stood staring at the Red Empress's hand as a glowing red orb formed. His mind rushed, trying to think of some trick or spell he could use. There had to be something. He sighed. After all this time...

A flash of light appeared next to her, and the blonde man from earlier reappeared, standing beside her with a smile.

"I am so sorry, my lady, the king insists." He blinked and the two vanished in a ball of light.

Dante stared at the space where the Red Empress had just been. *How was she so powerful? It should not be possible.* His mind raced in pursuit of answers.

Vale exhaled. "That was... close."

"Let us not press our luck," Dante replied.

Vale walked over to Sera to help her up. She held up her hand to keep him back.

"Help Azalea; I'm fine." Sera clenched her teeth together, and in a single quick jerk, pulled the blade from her shoulder. She grunted in pain as she let the dagger drop to the ground. Tearing a piece of fabric from the bottom of her shirt, she tied it around her wound.

Azalea lay still on the slab she had been placed on, passed out from the sudden expulsion of energy. Vale scooped her up and carried her from the room. With her weight on his shoulders, he moved much more slowly than the others. Dante led them down the stairs of the tower, through the halls, and back to the palace roof. Vale laid Azalea down on the flat surface, leaving her with Dante and Sera as he went back into the palace to retrieve Rivik and Grom.

When he entered the throne room, Rivik and Grom were still fighting. The floor was covered in piles of broken rock stacked in little mounds all around. More gargoyles were pouring in through the doors on the other side of the throne room.

"We've got her; let's go!" Vale shouted.

"Mean knight . . . spoil fun," Grom grunted.

"It's ok, we can save some for our next visit," Rivik offered.

"Next time . . . friend right," Grom grinned.

They made their way out of the throne room and back the staircase leading up to the roof. Vale started up when the gargoyle's pursued, pouring into the hallway after them. Vale stopped.

Rivik pointed, "We got this; go make sure the others get across."

Vale shook his head.

"Listen, this is a great spot to hold them. We'll keep them here. Signal us before your leave, and we'll be right up," Rivik insisted.

Vale grunted, leaping up the stairs two or three at a time. By the time Vale reached the roof, Dante had already signaled for Missanja. The great phoenix had just deposited Azalea and Sera on the other side and was already flying back. He waited until the phoenix was close and called down the stairs for them to follow. He heard no response. He moved over to where Dante was standing as the phoenix landed in front of them, ready to take them across. Vale looked back. Still no sign of them.

"What are you doing? We must go," Dante urged.

"We can't leave them." Vale moved toward the stairs.

"Bad idea. She can only take two of us at a time. Waiting does not help them, it puts them in more danger," Dante challenged. "They handled themselves for this long. They can make it another minute."

"They were supposed to come up when I signaled. Something is wrong."

Dante stepped in front of Vale to impede his path to the stairs.

"Move, alchemist. I am not about to leave them." Vale's words faded as he smelled something odd. His legs suddenly felt shaky and his eyelids heavy. He glanced down to see Dante holding a smoking vial of blue liquid, the vapor wafting to his nose.

"Deep breaths," Dante coached.

Vale leaned his weight on Dante, trying to hold himself up as he felt his strength leave him. His body was like an overcooked noodle, soggy and formless, but his mind remained sharp.

Dante dragged him back and nodded to the fire bird. As Missanja scooped them up in her mighty claws and flew them back across the lake of lava, Vale saw Rivik and Grom rush out onto the roof. A steady stream of gargoyles was chasing out after them. The two worked well together. Moving in tactful tandem, one attacked while the other defended. Each time, a new pile of rubble formed on the ground. Missanja set Dante and Vale down softly and flew back up for one final trip.

Vale felt an anxiety growing in his heart. He took a deep breath and tried to push the worry away, concern he knew he could never show. She returned shortly with Rivik and Grom, both seemingly unharmed.

Grom clanged his axes together. "This place . . . fun . . . we stay?"

After a few minutes, Vale felt his strength returning. He pushed himself to one knee, glaring at Dante.

"Why?" His single word a great accusation.

"You were not thinking clearly. Missanja could only carry two at a time. If you had stayed to go rescue them, you would have been sacrificing yourself for nothing," Dante replied.

"You don't know that. I don't leave people behind."

"That is precisely why I did it. I trusted they had it handled. You were about to take a stupid and unnecessary risk."

"It's not your decision to make," Vale challenged.

"I made it anyway. I will not let you throw your life away on some fool's sacrifice."

"Sometimes sacrifice is required."

"Perhaps. I will not make it."

Vale's eyes grew wide, and his jaw dropped. "You would let this quest fail just to save your own life?"

"Yes. I was clear with the king when this started. I told him he should send someone else."

Vale's face grew red. "For the sake of humanity, you would—"

"For the sake of humanity, I must live."

"I never took you for a coward, Dante."

"It is not cowardice but conviction. When the Red Empress burned the Royal Library, she destroyed thousands of years of knowledge: medicine, magic, technology, tools that can advance the human race far beyond anything you can imagine. The hope of our world is not some stone; it is knowledge. I have found a way to restore that knowledge. Until my work is complete, I cannot die."

"What good is that knowledge if no one is around to use it?" Vale challenged.

"I am not saying no sacrifices will be needed. Just that I will not be the one to make them," Dante said.

"Maybe we can finish this discussion somewhere else. Someplace not in the Spirit Realm?" Sera asked.

"Azalea hasn't even woken yet," Rivik pointed out.

"She is right. If Vespera gets back and we are still here, it will not go well for us," Dante explained.

"Listen to the Blue Alchemist. His words are wise," Missanja's voice echoed in all of their minds as she flapped her wings and settled over her egg.

"Missanja, you saved us and allowed us to rescue our friend. We are—" Sera started.

"You do not need to express gratitude, child. You have given me much and asked from me little. Perhaps there is hope for the race of men after all. Before you depart, allow me to share a gift with each of you." She lifted her head and spread her wings.

Shadows of the Dark Realm

A wave of yellow-orange energy burst from her chest and engulfed the group. The world faded away. The mountains, the red sky, everything drifted to a peaceful and serene blackness. Each of them could see only themselves and the great bird of fire standing before them.

"Blue Alchemist," Dante heard her voice in his head, "I know what you have lost. You do not need the Darkstone to restore it. There is a potion ... "

"You mean the Teli-orchum potion of perfect restoration?" he asked in his mind.

"Yes."

"I thought it was just a legend."

"All legends come from somewhere. There are two ingredients required to complete the potion that are nearly impossible to obtain."

"They are?" Dante pressed.

"The first I can tell you. The second I can give to you. The first ingredient you will need is an Ambrosia leaf. The second ... is this." Missanja pulled a feather from her side and winced, a tear dripping from her eye. Dante grabbed an empty vial, and she blinked her tear into it.

"The tear of a phoenix," he thought in utter amazement.

"Take also this, though it is not for you." She reached out and offered him the feather.

He took it and looked at her, confused. "Is this what I think it is?"

She nodded her great head. "The time is coming when you will hold the fate of many in your hands. It is a terrible choice you must make, to choose who lives and who dies. Choose wisely. The consequences extend far beyond what lies in front of you."

She disappeared from Dante's mind, leaving him standing in a black void to consider what she had said.

"Rivik." She turned her attention to the spearman. "I see now desire in your heart and find none in your mind. Tell me, what gift may I offer you?"

"I don't need anything," Rivik replied.

"I could offer you many things."

"I need none of them. Thank you for the offer, truly, but it's not needed. Life is what it is. Sometimes it's good. Sometimes it's bad. Trying to change it only prevents you from seeing what you have."

"Strange. I will admit I did not think your kind capable of such noble virtue. What to give a man who desires nothing? I have just the thing. Hold out your hand."

Rivik did as instructed. Missanja extended her wing over it and Rivik felt a warm, soft metal in it. He held it up. It was a simple gold ring that seemed to dance with liquid flame. Mounted on the top was a small stone of orange, yellow, and red carved to look like fire. It was exquisite in its design. He looked at the ring and raised an eyebrow.

"You know who it is for," he heard in his head.

Rivik bowed, and his view turned to black.

"Sera." The phoenix shifted her gaze. "You seek power so you can protect those who do not have it. This is a worthy goal but be cautious. Power, even when sought for the noblest of reasons, has a way of bringing out the most horrible things. For you, I give the Amulet of Arthona. May it protect you as it once did her."

"Vale, you have devoted your life to atoning for the wrongs of others in your past. You carry with you a weight of responsibility that is not yours. You think the world would be a better place if you would have never existed. My gift to you is perspective."

Vale's mind flooded with images. A woman laughing and playing with her children. A peaceful village filled with people going about their day. Families. Friends. Laughter. Cheer. Faces flashed one after the other in rapid succession, like the strobing of a light. Hundreds, thousands of people all smiling and doing ordinary things.

"What is this?" Vale asked.

"You see only loss, so you believe that is all there is. You have never looked at the lives that continued because of you. These are all the people who would be dead or have never been born if it hadn't been for something you did. Every one of these people owes their life to you."

The images flashed faster and faster, almost too much to process. It was overwhelming.

"Why show me this?" Vale asked.

"In death, there is life. In life, there is death. Focus only on one and you will be lost in despair. You think the scales of your life are weighed toward death because death is all around you. In truth, the scales lean heavily toward life. For the lives you have taken have been to spare others. My gift to you is peace. Be free of your burden, brave knight."

Vale felt strangely warm at her words. His body felt somehow lighter, like the relief that comes from taking off heavy armor after a long battle. He felt himself relax.

"Lastly, brave and loyal Grom. There are few with so pure and noble a heart as you. My gifts to you are the golden axes of Nilandul. Forged by the god of war himself, the blades will never break, never grow dull, and will always return to their owner. With them, I see many glorious victories in your future." She extended her wing and placed two large, golden axes in his hands. They were remarkably light and beautifully crafted, and when he moved them, he could hear them sing.

"Shiny . . . Grom . . . like . . . thank you . . . bird lady."

"May your blades remain as true as your heart, troll-friend. Your time grows short; you must depart. Go with the blessings of the fire god."

When their senses returned, they each bowed to Missanja as they made their way back to the forest they'd just come through. The path back was uneventful. Avoiding the monsters in the woods proved easy enough as the group made their way to the portal connecting the Spirit Realm and the Realm of Mortals.

The black smoking void hummed right where they left it, providing a sense of relief to the whole group, save Grom, who seemed a little disappointed to be leaving. Vale exhaled when they finally reached the smoking portal.

"Alright, let's go," he started.

"Leaving so soon?" a man's voice came from behind them.

Vale felt every muscle in his body tense at once.

"Who's asking?" Dante called out.

There was a tension in the air like an electric current. Vale knelt and cautiously slid the still unconscious Azalea to the black, sandy earth beneath them before turning around. Sitting lazily on a massive black throne that had not been there a moment before, with his head resting on his fist, was a pale man. He looked young and had long, straight, white hair that flowed gently in the breeze. His eyes glowed a ghostly green. Around his neck hung a black amulet that contrasted his smooth white skin that looked as polished as marble. He was wearing black pants and a black trench coat with long pauldrons over the shoulders. The sleeves were long, and he wore it open with nothing underneath. A glowing green crown hovered near his temples rather than resting on his head. He looked thin but athletic. Resting on his throne was a glowing green sword that was taller than a normal man. Behind him were four ethereal knights and the blonde man with glasses they'd seen earlier.

"Mind your tongue, mortal! You address a god! You are in the presence of King Aeon!" the blonde man with glasses shouted. The man in the chair waved his hand dismissively, looking bored, his gesture silencing the blonde man.

"You have entered my realm without invitation or permission. This is a great offense and a violation of the law. The only punishment for such a transgression is endless death." His voice was low, and his words lingered on his lips.

"Man threaten . . . Grom . . . kill him?" The troll readied his axes.

"No, Grom, that would not be a good idea," Dante advised.

King Aeon smirked and leaned forward. He held out his hand, and Grom's soul ripped out of his body. The troll was a frozen statue as a translucent green copy of his physical form hovered in the air. Aeon tightened his hand, and the glowing soul cried out and compressed. He opened his hand, and Grom's soul returned to its normal shape and snapped back inside his body. The troll shook, his legs wobbling as a tear rushed down his cheek.

"What did you do to him?" Sera glared.

Aeon sighed and lifted two fingers, and glowing green chains wrapped around each member of the group, binding them and tugging them to the ground. Each one dropped to their knees, barely able to sustain the weight suddenly thrust upon them by the spirit chains. A current surged through their bodies, making it feel like their life was slowly being sucked out. He uttered no words. This raw power wasn't even an effort for him. Spears pierced the earth all around them, forming green glowing cages. King Aeon smiled a joyless smile.

"Explain to me what a group of mortals are doing venturing into my realm before I lose my temper."

"Your Majesty, if you would permit—" Dante's words were labored under the magical weight pressing down on him. Aeon shrugged, and the chains binding Dante disappeared into green dust.

Dante held up his hands. "We did not intend to or knowingly violate your laws. Our friend was brought here against her will by—"

"Vespera . . . " King Aeon sat back in his chair and rubbed his smooth chin. He laughed without smiling. "Go on."

Dante looked at the others before continuing. "Vespera's plan was to turn our friend into a mortal shell, a Vas Noomi that she could claim to remain in our realm forever. We only came here to rescue her before Vespera could complete the process."

King Aeon raised an eyebrow. "That is quite the accusation. Restless spirits may linger in the mortal realm for a time, some even temporarily take possession of your kind, but it is forbidden for any spirit to claim a mortal shell. I am sure you have evidence to support this claim?" he stated more than asked.

"Your Majesty, if you were to use Arcane Sight on her, I think you would find that she has been enhanced and groomed by magic from birth for such a purpose. Every limitation that a mortal host would have has been removed, as if she was designed to be host to a powerful spirit."

"Very well. If I find otherwise, you will suffer an anguish you nay knew possible," Aeon warned.

He stood up and walked over to where Azalea was still lying unconscious. His eyes flashed even brighter green, and a glowing mist surrounded them as he moved his gaze up and down her body.

"This pains me to say, it seems your information is correct." King Aeon turned to the blonde man. "Wayla, bring her to me."

The blonde man, Wayla, nodded as he bowed and blinked out of sight.

"You are the Blue Alchemist?" King Aeon asked, looking to Dante.

"Yes, Your Majesty," Dante nodded.

"Then you are the one who returned Vespera here after her last escape."

"I did not do it alone, but yes, I was there."

"How is it a mortal defeated Vespera? And how is it you stand before me here? You're not elf-blood, and two-hundred years is an exceptionally long life for a mortal."

"It is a long story, Your Majesty," Dante replied.

"Long is a relative concept. I am infinite. Your entire life is, to me, no more than a breath. Explain to me how one such as yourself manages to avoid Mora's call."

"Perhaps you could release the others while I do? No reason to—"

"This is not a negotiation. You will tell me what I desire, or I shall turn your friends to wraiths and send them back to haunt your world," Aeon threatened.

"You," Vale interrupted. "You create wraiths?" His breathing was labored as he pulled against the glowing chains that bound him. With every movement, the grip and weight of the chains grew stronger, tugging him down lower.

King Aeon turned to Vale, who was being pulled onto his stomach. "I am the god of spirits. Wraiths, like all spirits, come from me and serve my purpose."

"And what . . . purpose . . . does the great god king have for sending monsters into the world to torture and kill innocent people?" Vale grunted, barely able to hold his head up.

"I do not send wraiths to your world. I make them from you. They are born from your hatred and cruelty, and they feed on it. Wraiths are a warning, a mirror that you may face your darkness and overcome it."

"That's—" Vale started. Another chain wrapped around his neck, pulling his head down and muffling his words completely.

"I do not wish to hear another word from you," Aeon said.

Wayla appeared in a flash of light with Vespera in front of him. Her hands were bound behind her back, and a glowing green muzzle was over her mouth. She was on her knees with her head down.

"Speak, Blue Alchemist. If I do not like what you have to say, I will allow Vespera here to do what she wishes to you. I will have my answers, or you will know a new suffering." King Aeon smiled.

"Both of your answers come from the same story."

"Then tell it before I lose my patience."

"My father was a royal librarian. He loved knowledge. He imparted that love to me. He used to say, 'The only question with no answer is the unasked one. The only problem with no solution, is the one that hasn't been found.' I grew up surrounded by books written by the most learned men in history. I absorbed them. I consumed their knowledge like water. So great was my appetite that soon there was nothing left for me to learn. I had reached the end of all the trails that had been blazed before me. So, I started doing experiments, testing the effects of combining magic and other ingredients into potions. Before long, my creations earned the attention of nobles, Royals, and even gods. One day, the Red Empress arrived, pretending to be a traveling noble. She ingratiated herself with the nobles, giving them gifts and buying influence, all while sinking her claws in deeper. Then, when she'd earned their trust, she betrayed them. She took over the kingdom and slaughtered any who opposed her."

Vespera pulled on her restraints and mumbled loudly into her muzzle. The sound was muffled and muted. The amulet around Aeon's neck glowed green, and Vespera shivered visibly and stopped.

"There, that's better. Continue."

"She became obsessed with securing her position by hunting down anyone who might have enough power to oppose her, which included my family. She killed my father and banished me from my home. It wasn't just people. She feared that knowledge might provide the means for others to resist her, so she committed the worst crime of all—she burned the Royal library."

"That's the worst part? You cared more for the books than your father?" Rivik asked.

"Of course not. I loved him. But he was a man, and men die. To destroy knowledge and the means to obtain it—that is an offense I could not forgive.

"I was living in the wilds, searching for a means to obtain my revenge. It was there I met a wandering stranger. He appeared to me first as a frail old man who walked with a hunch. His hair and eyes were wild, like a nomad at the end of his days and far beyond the reach of sanity. Most striking of all were his golden eyes. He claimed to have a brother who he was visiting and wanted to surprise. He said he could change his appearance with magic, but his brother would detect it, so he asked if I knew of anything that might help. I gave him an elixir, and we went our separate ways. A week later, another man approached me. He was young, strong, and attractive, but he had those same golden eyes. He smiled brightly and told me that he was the old man I'd met before. My elixir had allowed him to pull a wonderful prank on his brother, and he wanted to repay me."

"You met Vannic?" Aeon raised an eyebrow.

"The god of magic. Yes. I did not know who he was. I told him all I wanted was the power to stop the Red Empress and restore that which was lost. He gave me the ability to wield great magic, and he showed me how Vespera had tethered herself to the mortal realm and that I may break her link to it. I started training, learning to master the magic I was given. Then I met Marshall Delaluche, who had devised a plan. We worked together to systematically break down Vespera's defenses without her knowing and then ambush her. With her tethers severed, I opened the portal to return her here."

"Tethers, you say? Crystals arranged around her palace to sustain her power in the mortal realm?" Aeon asked.

"As you say, Your Majesty," Dante nodded.

"This was two centuries ago; how is it you are standing before me now?" Aeon asked.

"Using some of the knowledge Vespera tried to destroy, I was able to create an elixir of longevity that slowed the effects of time to one-tenth of normal."

"I am sure that made you quite popular. You mortals are obsessed with extending your lives."

"The potion requires the rarest of ingredients and has to be tailored to each person who uses it," Dante said.

"You kept it for yourself," Aeon chuckled.

"Not for myself. I kept it safe. I tried changing the nature of the human existence once, and it cost me everything. I used the potion only to buy myself time to set things right. I would not inflict this on anyone. Men live as long as we are meant to live. Nothing good comes from extending it."

Aeon nodded in approval. "Immortality is not nearly what it's cracked up to be."

"As you say," Dante bowed his head respectfully.

"The long-living mortal mage who defeated a spiritwalker. Now, what to do with you?" King Aeon paced back and forth, looking off in the distance as he rubbed his chin. "You returned Vespera, so I'm in your debt. But you trespass in my realm so you're at my mercy."

"My king, you must give them the endless death, make them examples so no other mortals will dare test your sovereignty again," Wayla urged.

"I've got it!" Aeon said, lifting his hand. He snapped his fingers, and everything went black.

Chapter 39

The Information Broker

Kade led the group away from the Fang Collectors and out of town. After circling around using the forest for cover to slip past the dragon knights, they moved quickly and carefully, staying out of sight until they were sure they were beyond detection. They traveled to the north and west as Kade guided them toward Blackwater Marsh.

Along the way, they saw several militia groups wandering in search of the Parisian Seekers but avoided them with ease. When they stopped for food, Ash worked with Owen, giving him some basic tips on fighting. At night, Caelan regaled them with tales of his adventures, forcing Ash to continually chime in to correct the details. With each tale, Owen stared in complete amazement. He laughed loudly at every joke, reacted to every moment. It was like he was living the stories as Caelan told them. His reactions made every story that much more entertaining.

When Caelan had told all his stories, Owen offered to share. To Celeste's dismay, Caelan and Ash encouraged him. Unlike Caelan's wild tales of conflict and battles, Owen's stories were a series of comedic misadventures. It was like his whole life was a string of bad luck that resulted in the weirdest experiences. He told them of his nomadic life with his wife and son as they traveled from place to place seeing the world. While Owen had been the only one laughing at Caelan's stories, everyone laughed at his; even Kade couldn't help but chuckle at some of the bizarre experiences of Owen's life.

Celeste was the only one not amused. She kept quiet as she listened but didn't speak, her mind never really focusing on what was being shared. Her resentment began to build after each story. *How could he be so casual? So playful?* It was like he didn't care at all.

"Come on, there's no way," Caelan objected to a particularly unbelievable story Owen told.

"I swear by the gods below, every word," Owen chuckled.

"Why would she . . . " Ash asked.

"Apparently, in dwarven culture, 'top of the morning' is a really offensive thing to say," Owen shrugged.

"But why would she even carry a flask of Minotaur urine?"

"Dwarves believe it's good luck. The Necra hate minotaur, so they use it as a sort of repellant."

"That's not right." Ash covered his face with his hands.

"Well, after that, he made it worse by telling her she was short-tempered, so she may have knocked out a few of his teeth." Owen shrugged.

"She sounds like quite the woman," Kade added.

Owen nodded. "She was."

Silence fell over the group before, one by one, they tucked in for the night.

"I'll take first watch." Celeste broke her long streak of silence.

When the others fell asleep, she snuck away, out of view and out of earshot, to a place she could use her Phorsee stone without being overseen or heard.

* * *

Owen opened his eyes, and it was still dark. He looked around. Kade and Ash were sleeping soundly. Celeste was nowhere to be seen. He sat up, suddenly feeling a rush of concern.

"She's fine, just wandered off to be alone." Caelan was sitting on a stump not far from the dying embers the group had fallen asleep around.

Owen drowsily walked over. A bright crescent moon peeked out behind the clouds as they dashed across the sky. The thick patchy clouds were lit as they passed in front of the celestial light. The cool air was refreshing, even calming. Caelan was staring up at the sky, clearing his mind as the clouds rolled silently by.

"If only life could be so peaceful," he said, more to himself than to Owen.

"I'm surprised to hear you say that," Owen yawned.

"Why?"

"Sorry, I didn't mean that to sound—"

"It didn't."

"It's just, your stories, they are so filled with action and adventure. You're so courageous and so calm in a fight, it seems like you love it." Owen sighed in relief.

"I don't know many who would choose this life. It just happens. Over time, you see enough conflict, you get used to it," Caelan smirked.

"I guess I just assumed. You seem like you're having fun." Owen's eyes narrowed as he processed.

"Honestly, I often dream of a simple life. I'd rather be in a cabin in the woods somewhere. Hunting, fishing, maybe try to grow some crops. Start a family."

"Why don't you?"

"I've asked myself that. If things had been different, maybe I could have. I don't know, I guess I've just seen so much wrong with the world, I feel like I have to do something to try and make it right."

"That makes sense. My people found a safe place removed from the world around us where we can live in peace. It would have been easier to stay there. But there was something inside me that drove me to leave. I felt that our people were so misunderstood, and hiding away in some secret village wasn't going to change that. I thought maybe I could." He looked down at his feet. "Turns out I was wrong."

"Were you?"

Shadows of the Dark Realm

"My foolish belief that I could somehow change people's minds just by living among them got my wife killed and my son turned into a slave," Owen exhaled.

"It's also the reason you met your wife in the first place, right? Without it, your son wouldn't exist."

"Maybe. Despite my hopes, all I've seen from people is ignorance, distrust, and hatred."

"That does seem to be our default state. We fear and hate what we don't know. Maybe that's why what you're doing is so important."

"How do you mean?" Owen asked.

"Forging a path is hard work. The one who goes first suffers and struggles for every step. For everyone who follows, the trek is easier. Maybe you're not going to single-handedly change how your people are viewed. But perhaps you could clear the path so that those who come after you can."

"I've never thought of it like that." Owen smiled as he leaned back and watched as the light of the moon brightened the sky through a gap in the rolling clouds, only to hide again as more rolled by.

* * *

Two days later, the group reached Blackwater Marsh, a large, walled city that stretched as far as their eyes could see. The location of the city made the walls seem like an unnecessary redundancy. The entire city was built on an enormous swamp. The buildings and walkways set on elevated platforms, allowing boats to sail underneath and dock at various points around the city.

The only way to the city on foot was to take one of two long, wooden bridges which were certainly designed with some clever defenses to ward off attacking foes. The expanse of the swamp was so vast, even a skilled archer couldn't fire an arrow across it. Any army that tried to take this city would suffer massive losses just to reach the city gates.

The wooden bridge swayed a little with the moving of the current underneath them as they made their way across it. As they got closer the traditional orange and white banners with the head of a dragon could be seen flapping in the winds above the gates and towers.

"This place is huge," Ash commented.

"Blackwater Marsh is one of the largest cities in all Baronia. It was once its own independent nation before the Conquest of the Karon'dar. Even conquered, Blackwater Marsh operates with its own set of laws and serves as the heart of information-gathering for the entire kingdom. It's also home to the spymaster's guild. Mind your tongues here. The walls have ears," Kade cautioned.

When they finally made their way across the seemingly endless bridge, their passage into the city was blocked by a group of guards in dark cloaks. Standing near them was a man in thin spectacles with a shiny, smooth head and face. He wore elaborate patterned robes that flowed over him almost like a woman's dress, and he adorned himself with opulent gold jewelry to accompany it. He posed with a sense of self-importance as he stood behind a large wooden pedestal that held a massive ledger.

"Welcome to Blackwater Marsh. State your name, purpose for your visit, and where you are headed." His words rang out surprisingly loud as he stared blankly down at them from his elevated platform off to the side of the gate.

"Who says this isn't our destination?" Caelan remarked.

"All who reside here are known to us. You do not have the bearing of a Marshan nor do you look like the type who would seek to make this their home. Hence, you are travelers. Conclusion—we are a stop on your journey, not the end of it. Now, if you would stop acting like a horse's owa and answer my question, you can be on your merry way, and I can be rid of the sight of you." The man looked down at them.

"He's charming," Caelan muttered to Ash.

"And you are as refined as naiflo's gwar." The man rolled his eyes.

"Did I say that out loud?" Caelan winced.

"You practically yelled it, my friend." Ash nudged Caelan hard enough to nearly knock him over.

"I tire of you. State your business, or be on your way," the man on the platform warned.

"I am Lord Kade Drako of Taggoron. These are my traveling companions. We are here to rest and gather supplies on our way to Dorth for the festival of boats. Provided there are no unanticipated delays, we will remain for no more than two days before continuing our journey."

"Welcome back, Lord Drako. It is always an honor to receive you, even if your company is questionable. Will you be lodging at your usual—" The man on the platform began writing on his ledger.

"We have not settled on arrangements, nor is that information required by the guild. I have answered your questions; now grant us entrance."

The man waved his hand lazily in the air and the cloaked guards separated, opening a path between them to allow entrance to the city. Once inside, Celeste hurried next to Kade.

"Why did you lie to that man about our destination?" she asked.

"Why would I tell them where we are going?"

"Isn't it required? What happens if they find otherwise?" Celeste asked.

"How exactly would they do that?"

"Well, if . . ."

"The law requires him to ask and us to answer. It does not require us to answer honestly. Keep your mouth shut, and we will be fine," he replied as he marched them through the narrow wooden walkways toward the center of the city.

Kade led them through the market past a beautifully decorated inn surrounded by all sorts of colorful shops and taverns. He turned down a side street and walked them to the edge of town, stopping at a tall, shabby inn.

"Here we are." He gestured to the building in front of them.

"No, we are not staying here. This place is filthy. What was wrong with that inn in the market?" Celeste challenged.

"Everything," Caelan answered. "It's crowded. Noisy. And indefensible. It's also the first place anyone would look."

"And this gwar hole is better?" Celeste asked in disgust.

"It's perfect. Two ways to enter, both of which are easily visible from the top floor. It's off the beaten path, so anyone approaching will be easy to spot. It's quiet. But once outside, it has access to five different escape routes. If someone comes for us, it would be easy to escape."

"Five?" Owen said, looking at the building. "I see the three roads."

"Rooftop exit. This is the tallest building on a thin alley. If the streets are covered, we can easily make our way to any number of other buildings—makes it really hard for someone to box us in." Caelan pointed up.

"Ok, so four," Owen nodded.

Caelan gestured to the edge of the street where a wooden half-wall was all that separated pedestrians from the drop to the swamp below.

Celeste looked over the edge and cringed.

"Ew. Jumping into a swamp is not a viable escape route."

"Look again," Caelan said confidently.

She sighed and looked over the edge, turning her head. Winding out of view was a set of stairs that led up to a nearly invisible gate in the wall. The stairs led to a dock below that had several small swamp boats currently docked at it.

"You are very perceptive, archer," Kade acknowledged.

Caelan folded his arms across his chest proudly.

"Which makes me wonder, why do you feign the fool?" Kade asked.

"What now?" Caelan questioned.

They got set up on the top floor, renting out several rooms. Once they had settled in, Kade walked over to Owen.

"Come with me," he commanded more than asked.

"Umm . . . ok. Where are we going?" Owen looked at him nervously as his voice trembled in response.

"What are you up to, dragon boy?" Ash asked, moving between Kade and the doorway.

"Move, and I will show you."

"Tell me, and I'll move." Ash folded his arms across his chest.

"Move, or I throw you into the swamp and we go without you."

Ash chuckled and stepped to the side.

Kade led them out the back of the inn and deep into the

center of the city, past the market and the town hall, to the tallest, most secluded building in the entire city. It had its own walls, guards, and towers. It appeared to be a city within the city. Just to the left was a large tavern.

"What's this?" Ash asked.

"This is the spymaster's guild. And this," Kade pointed to the tavern, "is home to the greatest intelligence network in all of Baronia."

"Why did you bring us here?" Celeste asked.

"This is where the Information Broker resides. It's said there is no secret she can't find, information she can't gather, truth she can't uncover. She sees all, knows all. Yet all that is known about her is that she, apparently, has a fondness for riddles," Kade answered.

"Ralk," Caelan said.

"What information do we seek?" Celeste interrupted.

"The whereabouts of a half-dwarf slave boy," Kade answered.

Owen covered his mouth with his hands to muffle a gasp. He turned to Kade, tears pooling in his eyes.

"Truly? You think there's a chance?" Owen started, his voice shaking even more than his body.

"A chance? No. A half-dwarf is a rare thing. I am certain the Broker will know something about him. I would be surprised if she didn't know exactly where he was."

Owen shrieked and jumped, wrapping his arms around Kade's neck and hugging him tight.

"Thank you! Thank you!" he sobbed. "I . . . don't even know what to say."

"Say nothing," Kade smiled.

"But . . . how could I ever repay this kindness?"

"Be the father your son deserves. That's all that is required."

Owen finally let go of Kade's neck, his body bobbing with nervous energy.

"No, we are not doing this. This is a distraction we don't have time for. Owen, we wish you luck and the favor of the gods. Hope you find your son. Let's go." Celeste turned to walk away. No one turned with her.

"Seriously?" she huffed.

"We are already here; might as well check it out," Caelan answered.

"We agreed he could come with us so long as he didn't slow us down. This is slowing us down. We got him this far. He can take it from here," Celeste started.

"No," Kade interrupted.

"No use fighting it; this is happening," Ash added.

Two men stood at the outside of the tavern like columns holding up either side of the door. They stared blankly ahead. As Kade approached, the two men turned and stared at him.

"What business brings you to the Den of Knowledge?
You are not students of her college."

Caelan raised his eyebrows at the oddly poetic tone.

"We seek an audience with the Information Broker," Kade answered.

"You seek what many desire but few are worthy of.
Let us see if your wits can fly as freely as a dove.
To enter the den of knowledge you must demonstrate your understanding.
A question asked, an answer given, a prompt one I'm demanding."

Kade nodded his acceptance of the terms.

"If you have me, you can't share me. If you share me, you don't have me," the man on the right said.

"Gods below, what the actual ralk is this?" Caelan started.

"It's a riddle," Owen interrupted. "I love riddles."

"Really?" Ash asked.

"Yes! Riddles I understand. It's people that tend to confuse me," Owen nodded.

"I . . . hate . . . riddles. What kind of shady tavern requires riddles to get inside?" Caelan sighed.

"Answer not. Enter not," both men said in unison.

"My arrows are about to enter your skulls." Caelan pulled an arrow from his quiver as he started to tug his bow over his shoulder.

"A secret," Kade replied, stopping Caelan's motion.

"How is that helpful?" Caelan asked.

The two men turned and stepped back, making a space for the group to enter.

"Oh, that's the answer. Ralk, I hate riddles." Caelan rubbed his head.

The double wooden doors opened to a large room. A long bar ran down one wall and was accompanied by layers of shelves that were stacked from floor to ceiling, holding bottles of ales and other spirits. Square metal tables were organized into neat rows, creating clear walking lanes. Each table hosted four chairs covered in a fuzzy royal blue fabric. Despite the impressive size of the room, there were only a half dozen people in it. A tall bartender stood behind the bar, and two guards were standing in front of two doors at the back of the room.

All eyes were on them as they headed toward the doors. The guards blocking them were twins, identical in every discernable way. Even their armor was identical. The only difference between them was the guard on the left wore a yellow cape and stood in front of a yellow door, while the guard on the right wore a red cape and stood in front of a red door.

"We are looking for the Information Broker. Can you tell us which way?" Caelan asked as they approached the guards.

"That is the question." The bartender walked out from behind the bar and stepped in front of them. "Access to such knowledge does not come easy. Before you are two doors: one door will lead you to the next test on your way to the Information Broker; the other leads to death."

"How do we know which door is which?" Spiro asked.

"There are two guards before you. One always tells the truth. One always lies. You may ask one guard one question. From there, you must pick a door. May the gods below bless your guess," the bartender said before walking off.

"Oh great, it's my favorite game: information or death. Let's flip a coin. Might as well, right?" Caelan grumbled.

"Not if we ask the right question," Owen countered.

"Right . . . " Caelan nodded.

"We pick a guard and ask him if he's the truth guard," Spiro suggested.

"No," Owen countered. "That wouldn't tell us anything."

"We could ask the guard on the left if his cape is yellow. Then we will know which one tells the truth and we can ask—" Celeste started.

"No," Kade said.

"Think about it. The first thing we have to do is figure out which guard tells the truth," Celeste protested.

"But we only have one question," Owen replied.

"How are we supposed to figure out which guard is which, and which door is which, with only one question?" Celeste grumbled.

"You're missing the point," Kade said. "It doesn't matter which guard tells the truth. Only which door is which."

"This is not worth the risk. I'm sorry. It's bad enough wasting time on this, but risking our lives? No. We can't. Our mission is too important. Need I remind you . . . " Celeste sighed.

"You don't need to do anything, princess. You don't want to come, then don't," Caelan replied.

"I agree with Celeste. I will not risk my life on this gamble," Spiro said.

"Then why don't you two go gather supplies from the market? We will meet you back at the inn after we are done," Kade shrugged.

"Kade, you can't seriously be willing to—" Celeste started.

Kade's eyes sparked with orange flame, and she stopped before finishing her sentence. Celeste sighed. She and Spiro made their way out of the Den of Knowledge and back to the streets of Blackwater Marsh.

"Any ideas for how to, you know, not die?" Caelan asked.

"It's a bit of a paradox. Without knowing which guard is which, we can't trust the answer we are given." Kade rubbed his chin.

"I've got it!" Owen declared.

"Got it?" Caelan asked.

Shadows of the Dark Realm

"I know what to ask and what to do. Do you trust me?" Owen said.

"You're sure?" Ash asked.

"I'd bet my life and the life of my son on it," Owen nodded.

"Proceed," Kade agreed.

Owen walked to the yellow guard on the left.

"Is the liar in front of the death door?"

"No," the guard shook his head.

Owen smiled and walked over to the red door on the right. He twisted the nob and pushed it open.

"Wait." Caelan grabbed his wrist. "How do you know?"

"It's not a paradox, it's an equation. Kade's point was the key. It's not about the guard. Your instinct is to try to figure out who is telling the truth. That's the trap. You waste your one question and still don't know which door is right."

"Riiiighhht," Caelan said.

"It's not about the guard. It's about the answer. If we were talking to the truth guard, yes would mean the liar was in front of death's door, and that was the other door. No would mean the liar was not in front of death's door and that death's door was behind the guard we were talking to. If we were speaking to the lying guard, then yes means the guard we are talking to IS NOT in front of death's door. No means the guard we are talking to IS in front of death's door. You see?"

"That's a steaming pile of nope from me. How do you know which one is telling the truth?" Caelan shook his head.

"It doesn't matter which guard tells the truth. Either way, YES means the guard we are talking to is NOT in front of death's door and NO means the guard we are talking to IS in front of death's door. The guard said no, so we know we want the other door. Simple." Owen took a breath.

"Ralk me, I need to shoot something," Caelan complained.

They stepped into a dark room with no furniture or decorations of any kind. Once they were all inside, the door behind them closed and locked. Caelan felt his heart racing as he scanned the room nervously. If they had chosen wrong, he'd need to react quickly to avoid the promised death. If avoiding it was even possible.

There was a grinding, rumbling sound. Caelan grabbed for his bow. Before he could ready it, the wall in front of them slid to the side, revealing a well-lit stairway. The carpets were elegant and the walls ornate. The stairway led down to a platform that turned to another set of stairs going down in the opposite direction. When they reached the bottom, they passed through a doorway into a long hall. At the end of the hall was another heavy ornate door. As they approached, the door they had come through slammed closed behind them.

The door in front of them opened to a small room just large enough for a single person to stand in. On the far wall was another door, this one closed, barring exit from the small room.

"So many ralking doors. You guys get them on sale or something?" Caelan asked, mostly to himself.

"You passed the first test. But now each of you must pass another. One riddle per visitor. Answer right, and you will be granted access to the Information Broker. Answer wrong, and you will be teleported into the swamp. This is not a group test. Each must solve the riddle on his own," a voice echoed around them.

"Ralk," Caelan cursed.

Kade stepped into the room first.

"Time goes before me. History is created by me. What am I?" the disembodied voice rang out.

"Here lies Caelan. He was riddled to death. He was unhappy about it," Caelan buried his face in his hands.

"Writing," Kade answered. The door swung open, and he stepped inside.

"I guess, better get it over with," Ash shrugged and stepped into the room.

"I have forests without trees, rivers without waters, towns without people. What am I?"

Ash scratched his head and repeated the question. He looked over his shoulder at the others.

"If anyone offers a hint or attempts to aid you in any way, you'll be dropped in the swamp," the voice warned.

"How can there be a forest without trees—or a river without

water?" He stood still, his mind racing as his wrestled with the riddle.

"Do you have an answer, or are you going swimming?" questioned the voice.

"Give me a minute," Ash protested. He rubbed his head with a groan. "An empty village? A ravine? Without trees you can't have a forest. I mean, picture it." He snapped his fingers. "That's it! There are forests, rivers, and towns . . . on a map. It's a map!"

The door opened, and Ash disappeared behind it.

Owen stepped in next.

"I breathe but have no lungs. I consume but have no mouth. I grow but have no life."

"Fire," Owen smiled.

Caelan stood alone in the room. "Great, that was fast. Ok. Let's get this over with."

"I fall but never break; I break but never fall."

"Ralk, I'm going swimming." Caelan shook his head. "You realize that doesn't make any sense, right? Is it two things? One that doesn't break and one that doesn't fall? Why do people do this? Honestly, does this make you feel big and important? Oh, I can make up nonsense that confuses everyone, and they will all pretend to like it. Well, we don't. I hate riddles. Here's how it's going to happen. I'm going make something up. It'll be wrong, then you tell me the answer. All of a sudden, it will be clear and obvious. I'm going to be standing here like a goraum fool."

"Perhaps you should concede."

Caelan started pacing back and forth, his fingers brushing idly over one of his arrows. "What if, instead of answering this stupid question, I just shot you in the face with an arrow? Wouldn't that be so much better?"

"This is a place of intellect, not violence. If you lack the mental fortitude to engage your mind in a higher level process, we have no use of you and no reason to speak."

"Ralk off, riddles are twists of words and logic built around deception of intent. They have nothing to do with intelligence. If you were as smart as you seem to think you are, you would know there are many different intelligences. But if you judge a fish by his ability to climb a tree, he'll spend his whole life thinking he's stupid. Oh, I'm an information broker. I am insecure with my own intelligence, so I make up stupid riddles to make myself feel smarter. You're ridiculous," Caelan mocked.

There was no response.

"What happens if I don't answer? I just sit here forever? Night and day, just stuck in this stupid little room?"

The door clicked and swung open. Caelan looked around, confused. "What's going on?"

"You have answered correctly. You may enter."

Chapter 40

Battle for Vargr

Everything was black. From the black sprang a cave, trees, dark clay ground, and a starless sky. Vale looked around. The others were gone. He was standing alone at the edge of the woods. In the clearing before him, there was a long, shabby hut on one side and a pen filled with chickens and pigs on the other. In the middle, a large fire heated a bubbling cauldron. Lines were hung between the roof of the hut and tree branches or posts stuck randomly in the earth. From the lines hung chicken feet, herbs, and other strange items—items that all had one thing in common: witches used them in their spells.

King Aeon appeared beside Vale with a smile. He gestured to the cave. Green vines tugged three figures from the dark chasm and deposited them a few paces from where Vale stood. Three witches dressed in red robes were forced to their knees before him. Their hoods were pulled back, revealing their wiry, gray, unkempt hair that looked more like nests for birds. Their faces were twisted and marred with age.

Fear and defiance raged in their eyes as they looked up. Vale recognized them immediately. Three faces he would never forget. These were the three witches who had murdered his wife and daughter. The witches who had cursed him so that anyone he ever cared for died. He had dreamed of this many times. Here they were.

"I trust you remember them?" Aeon asked.

Vale's blood boiled as if the flames of a fire had been heating it for hours. He clenched his fists as his rage gripped at his heart. He couldn't speak. He could hardly think. He simply nodded in reply.

"They have caused you much pain." Aeon extended his hand. In it was a long, black, twisted knife. "Rid yourself of them and be free of your curse."

"What trickery is this?" Vale turned to face the god of spirits.

"I loathe witches. Their kind like to use their magic to call my subjects from my realm without my consent. These three are particularly foul. They have wronged you. I am giving you a chance to make it right. Take my knife and do us both a favor."

"Earlier you didn't want me to speak. Now you want to help me put an end to the curse that haunts me? What's the catch?"

"No catch. No tricks. You kill them here, with this blade. They die in your realm, and your curse is lifted. It's that simple. I'm offering you the power to set yourself free." Aeon pressed the knife toward Vale.

Vale looked at it. The dagger seemed to glow. It was like it called to him, pleading to be used. He looked at the witches as he imagined it over and over again. It would be so easy. Vale reached out his hand, moving to the blade. Just as his fingers were about to grasp the blade, he grabbed Aeon's hand and closed it over the knife.

"No."

"No?" Aeon looked confused. "Do you not understand what I'm offering you? You mortals can be a bit slow."

"I understand. My answer is still no."

"Why?"

"You don't care about lifting my curse. You want to see what kind of person I am because you are trying to determine whether or not to let us leave your realm. If we wandered here innocently to save our friend, that's one thing. You want to see if that's really why we are here. How would you know? Instead, you are testing us. I assume that's why you separated us all. You're offering each of us something we desire, a temptation. Maybe that blade does what you say. Maybe it doesn't. If I take it, you question the sincerity of our reason for being here and you'll destroy us. So yes, I will pass."

"If it's not a test? If this is nothing more than an opportunity for you to get vengeance, what then?"

"Vengeance is of no use to me. The blood of my wife and daughter demands justice. Justice cannot be delivered on the hands of some cheap trick. It has to be earned."

"Here I was thinking the Blue Alchemist was the smart one," Aeon laughed. "Well, that turned out boring." He snapped his fingers, and once again everything was black.

* * *

Vale found himself standing with the others in the middle of the upper room of the palace in Lunal. The small group of Vargrian soldier's they'd left to guard the portal were standing tense, weapons at the ready.

"What the—how did you get here?" one of them stammered in confusion.

"It's ok," Sera spoke calmly as she turned to face the soldiers. "It's just us."

"What did you see?" Vale asked.

"The dragon who burned our village," Rivik answered.

"My best friend from when I was a child," Sera said.

"The day my daughter . . . " Dante commented.

"Glorious battle . . . puny elves . . . rivers of blood . . . " Grom added.

"What happened? How did you get back so quickly?" one of the soldiers asked.

"Quickly? We were gone for hours," Rivik replied.

"Hours? We've only been standing here a few moments. Soon as you stepped through, it was like the portal hissed closed, and then all of a sudden, here you were. I've taken longer to open a window."

Azalea groaned as her eyes blinked open. Vale laid her down on a table that had managed to survive the chaos of the palace. He leaned over her, looking for any signs of injury.

"Uhh . . . " She rubbed her face with her hands, brushing her long red hair to the side. "What . . . "

"Are you ok?" Vale asked.

"I'm . . . confused. What happened?" she asked.

A glowing blue circle emanated under Dante's hands as he moved them from her head to her feet.

"No signs of any tethers. What's the last thing you remember?" Dante asked.

"I was in a strange castle, and these weird mages were using some sort of magic on me. It felt strange, like my insides were starting to melt," Azalea groaned.

"Was it painful?" Dante asked.

"No, my insides were melting, but in a pleasant way." Azalea rolled her eyes. "Honestly, aren't you supposed to be the smart one?"

"How painful was it?" Dante sighed.

"Pretty painful."

"How long would you estimate it lasted?"

Azalea pondered for a moment. "I-I'm really not sure. I couldn't ever tell if it was night or day, so time just kind of passed. It felt like forever."

"Why does this matter, Dante?" Vale interjected.

"Vespera craves power. Like the Shadow King, she wants to rule our world. During her previous reign, she'd neglected to prepare a proper host. That was the weakness we exploited to send her back to the Spirit Realm. She will not make that mistake again."

"That's why she wants to possess Azalea?" Sera asked.

"No, possessing is different."

"How?" Sera pressed.

"Possession is when a spirit being takes control of a person's body by force. The problem with possession is, the person is still alive, still inside their body fighting for control. It is hard to sustain for a long period of time because, eventually, the host breaks free. Vespera's not looking to possess. She wants control. She's looking for a Vas Noomi."

"Vas . . . Noomi?" Grom grinned at the sound the words

made. He wandered around, repeating the phrase and chuckling to himself.

"A Vas Noomi is like a body without the baggage. It is an empty house just waiting for her to move in. To make a Vas Noomi, you have to destroy the person without damaging their body. From what I have read, the process feels like having your insides melted," Dante sighed.

"This has happened before?" Vale asked.

Dante nodded. "Not often; most malevolent spirits settle for possession because it is easier and requires less power. But yes, throughout history there have been several accounts of Vas Noomi."

"Why me? Does this have to do with that vision I saw in the water of my mother and those people in robes . . . ?" Azalea's voice trailed off, her words soft as she struggled to even keep herself upright. Vale offered her water and some food from his pack. She accepted both eagerly.

"You are quite special," Dante started.

"Don't coddle me, just tell me," Azalea groaned.

"I was not coddling. I was answering. Two wizards casting the same spell can have a wide variety of outcomes. Why? People have a certain propensity, or lack thereof, toward magic. The more sensitive a person is to the flow of magic, the more power they can wield. Vespera is immensely powerful, probably capable of rivaling the god of spirits without his items of power. If she were to take the body of a normal person, or even a gifted magic wielder, their limitations would become her limitations. Thus, she can only be as powerful as the vessel that contains her."

"So, she's looking for someone who can handle a lot of power?" Sera asked.

"Not a lot. Vespera will not be restrained. She wants to wield all her power, uninhibited by her vessel. That's where you come in." Dante gestured to Azalea. "From your mother's womb, Vespera was working to create the perfect Vas Noomi. A host body that would not only enable her to use all her power, but that would also enhance her power."

"You mean, she made me?"

"In a matter of speaking, yes. You were forged more than born. Forged to be the perfect host. If she obtains you, there is no telling what she will become. With the limited power of her previous host, Vespera ruled an entire kingdom and threatened to take more. If she were to acquire you, she could conquer this world. She would make herself a god."

"If she's so powerful, why does she want this world so bad?" Sera asked.

"Power has a way of warping the mind. Those who have it cannot see what they have, only what they do not. The thought of what they do not have consumes them like a plague," Dante answered.

"Why doesn't she start with her own world? Wouldn't that be easier?" Rivik asked.

"No, it would not. You met King Aeon, the god of spirits. What you experienced is not even a fraction of his power. He rivals the Shadow King himself," Dante chuckled.

The group exchanged a glance, taking a moment to process everything Dante had just told them.

"Why does it matter how much it hurt?" Azalea challenged, finally breaking the silence.

"Before she can destroy you, Vespera needs to form a nomasyncha—a link. The intensity of the pain tells me how close she was."

"To do what?" Azalea questioned.

"Transfer her power. Creating a Vas Noomi is tricky. A body is not meant to live without its soul. If she destroys you, all the power you have begins to fade, and you become a poor vessel. By forming a nomasyncha, she can transfer her power to your body. Then when she destroys you, she takes over and wields your combined power without having to fight to control it."

"How far do you think she got?" Vale asked.

"I think she formed the link," Dante exhaled.

"What does that mean? She can tap into my power?" Azalea asked.

Dante chuckled and then started to laugh.

"This is funny to you?" Azalea snapped.

"Yes. The timing is perfect." Dante covered his face, wiping tears from his eyes as he laughed. "She went through all of this to gain control of you."

"Right..."

"But because we interrupted her, now you could control her."

"What do you mean control her?"

"Think of the nomasyncha like a bridge. She made it so that she could bring her power into your body and control you, but because she was unable to finish the process, you could take her power and use it for yourself," Dante explained.

"How?"

"It is tricky, but somewhere inside you, you should be able to feel it—a connection to her like a source of energy that you have never tapped into before."

A loud crash against the wall made the room shake, cutting off their conversation. The guards were standing at the windows, watching the battle outside.

"How is it going?" Sera asked.

"Hard to say from here. It looks like Lady Aurora is holding her own."

"We can talk more later; let's go." Sera drew her daggers.

"Grom . . . kill monsters . . . Grom . . . love that! Lead the way, lady!" Grom grabbed his axes and cheered.

The others looked to Azalea, who was still barely able to sit up. Vale was leaning behind her helping her stay upright.

"Go help them. I'll stay with her," Vale said.

Rivik and Dante nodded, following Grom out. The troll was zigzagging gleefully down the hall singing to himself:

"Grom . . .
kill the monsters . . . yay
Grom . . .
kill the monsters . . . yay
smash them with axes
and kill them to the maxes . . .
Grom . . .
kill the monsters . . .
Yay, yay, yay

what a great day!"

By the time they reached the battle, Lady Aurora's forces were pushing the monsters back. Many of the smaller monsters had already fallen, leaving only a dozen or so of the larger ones. Dante was surprised and impressed at how few men Aurora had lost. She was in the front, moving between lines and shouting commands. Her men, and even the militia Sera had raised, responded quickly and decisively. She used her troops with their large shields to guard the front while having militia fighters attack from the sides and back, allowing them to dispatch monsters while taking minimal damage.

Her shield guards had managed to keep the larger monsters at bay, but her troops had managed to do very little to bring them down. It was only a matter of time before the lines broke, and their good fortune wore out. Sera, Rivik, and Dante made their way through the soldiers to where Aurora was shouting her instructions.

"How can we help?" Sera asked.

"Back so soon? Did you find your friend?" Aurora smiled as she gave instructions to a young foot soldier, and he rushed off.

Sera nodded. "Where do you want us?"

Aurora lifted her sword, pointing to one of the monsters. It towered above the others, looking similar to the ogre they had seen in Parisia, except this one had four arms and two heads.

"We've been using their size to keep them in check. We need to take them one at a time. I want to start there. If you can move around the side and get ready, I'll give you a signal to attack. We need to overwhelm the creature, so timing will be essential."

Before she even finished, Sera saw Grom charging toward the creature, arms extended.

"Kill the big one!" he roared in delight.

"Or . . . we can just go now," Rivik laughed, rushing after Grom.

"We will take care of the big one. Just keep the others off us," Sera said before charging forward.

Dante sighed and started casting a spell. Blue ropes burst from the ground, wrapped around the arms and legs of several of the monsters, binding them and pulling them down as they struggled against the restraints.

Grom moved quickly, darting out of the way of one of the ogre-creature's massive arms as it swung toward him. The troll looked like a dwarf in comparison to the massive creature. He leapt into the air, slamming his axes into the ogre's knee. The monster roared in pain. Grom rolled out of the way, narrowly escaping one of monster's hands as the creature grabbed for its injured knee.

The ogre swung a long pole-arm at Grom in retaliation. The metal shaft whistled through the air faster and faster as it descended on a path for the troll. Grom, who'd not yet recovered his balance from avoiding the other arm, was just rising to his feet. There was no time for him to move away.

Rivik's spear slammed into the monster's hand, piercing through it. The monster winced and opened his hand instinctively, dropping his weapon, which bounced harmlessly to the ground, missing Grom completely. With his spear stuck in the monster's hand, Rivik slid out of the way of the creature as it tried to grab him. The multiple attackers had done only enough to keep the creature off balance and disoriented. It was going to take a lot more to bring it down.

A volley of arrows struck the monster in rapid succession, turning its chest into a living pin cushion. It stumbled back, growling in rage, then pulled the spear from its injured hand and hurled it at Rivik. He dodged, and it stuck into the ground with a loud thump. Grom continued his attack on the creature's knee, his axes cutting around the joint. The ogre creature stumbled and dropped down to one leg.

Chaos erupted all around as Aurora's plan came together. Monsters charged. The frontal assault force held the line while the smaller group attacked from the rear, striking at the monster's undefended flanks. Aurora's troops worked together to bring the large monsters down. Dante's magic was able to immobilize several more, allowing the soldiers to execute them quickly. One by one, the monsters fell and the Vargrian army cheered as victory grew closer and closer.

Sera, Grom, Rivik worked together, slowly chipping away at the strength of the monstrous ogre-monster. Having given the soldiers the edge they needed, Dante came over to assist them.

"Honestly, what is the hold up? You are taking your sweet time with this one," he jested.

"Tall, dark, and ugly is tougher than he looks," Rivik panted as he moved out of the creature's reach.

"Grom . . . love monster . . . so much fun . . . " The troll was smiling from ear to ear, his eyes sparkling with joy.

"Rivik, when I give you the signal, I want you to charge. Before you get to his legs, stick the base of your spear in the ground, leaving the sharp end up," Dante said.

"You don't want me to dance, too?" Rivik asked.

"No one wants to see that," Sera remarked.

"Once your spear is in place, you will want to clear the area. I am going to pull the creature forward. When it hits the ground, Grom, kill it."

A wave of blue energy hit the creature in the back. It grunted and stumbled forward but didn't fall.

"Gwar. I need him leaning forward," Dante said.

"I got it." Sera darted forward, racing toward the creature before anyone could even process what was happening. The creature reared back to attack her, but she was too quick. She slid along the ground and drove her knife between the creature's large, exposed toes. It cried out and leaned down, lifting its foot.

"Go!" Dante shouted.

Rivik charged and stuck his spear into the ground just as Dante had instructed. He rushed forward, grabbing Sera and pulling her away as another blast of energy hit the creature in the back, this time knocking it forward. Rivik's spear pierced through the ogre's chest, skewering it. Grom wasted no time descending on the creature. His axes rose and fell in a flurry of strikes, each hitting the creature's neck. Blood sprayed and splashed into the air as the troll kept hacking. Grom was covered in blood before he stopped. When he was finished, he had chopped straight through the monster's neck, severing its large head from its massive body.

"Soldiers of Vargr, the city is ours!" Lady Aurora shouted, lifting her sword in the air. The sound of jubilee was so loud, the ground itself shook. The army and militia roared with excitement. The victory celebration was louder than the battle had been as they jumped, cheered, hugged, and shouted into the air with reckless abandon.

"Thank you," Lady Aurora said, grasping Sera's hand.

Sera smiled. "We should be thanking you. Your men allowed us to complete our mission."

"No. You raised the militia. You inspired the people to take back their home. Lunal is free of monsters, thanks to you," Aurora interrupted.

"What now?" Rivik laid his arm out across Sera's shoulder, leaning on her.

"We rebuild. I'm not sure how exactly. With the noble family all wiped out, we don't have anyone to govern us," Aurora said.

"Sure, you do," Sera nodded.

Aurora shook her head. "No, I'm a soldier. Wouldn't know the first thing about leading a kingdom."

"Don't sell yourself short. From what I saw, you are a great leader. Vargr will need that," Rivik commented.

"You've helped us free our kingdom; how can we repay you?" Aurora asked.

"We could use a place to rest, at least until she recovers." Vale walked up, dragging a very weary looking Azalea with him.

Aurora nodded. "Lunal isn't quite ready for guests. Let's get you back to Cannin. We will set you up at the inn, and get you food, drink, and supplies for your journey. I'll take care of whatever you need until you're ready to depart."

* * *

Aurora set each of them up with their own room. The inn keeper waited on them at Aurora's behest, ensuring they always had plenty to eat and drink. By night, Azalea stirred in her bed as sleep eluded her. Every time she started to drift, flashes of her time in the Spirit Realm barraged her mind. She sat up in a cold sweat, annoyed at her inability to sleep. She pulled on her robe and walked outside to get some fresh air. With her first step outside of the inn, she felt the blunt edge of a sword against her chest. She glanced down at the black blade and held her hands up.

"I stroll in peace."

"Sorry. Bad habit. Can't sleep?" Vale pulled the sword away and sheathed it.

"I keep seeing those ralking monks. Every time I close my eyes, I hear that chanting in my head. If I didn't get up, I was about to burn the whole inn down just to shut them up," Azalea replied.

"I'm not sure that's how it works."

"Only one way to find out." Azalea's hands were suddenly covered in purple flame. She shrugged and smiled, looking back at the inn.

"How are you feeling?"

"You mean after finding out I was magically designed to be a host for a spirit-being who wants to rule the mortal realm as a goddess, using my body to do it? Or do you mean realizing all those weird priests I grew up with weren't trying to impart life lessons; they were trying to mold me into a weapon for someone else to use? Or do you mean—"

"Let's just start with how you are feeling physically," Vale interrupted.

"Oh, fine as spring roses."

Vale nodded and turned his gaze back to the sky.

"Can I ask you something?" Azalea leaned back against the wall next to him.

"If I say no, are you going to ask anyway?"

"Yeah."

"Then by all means, ask away."

"Why did you come back for me?" She turned to look at him.

Vale didn't return her gaze. He stared up at the night sky and sighed. "If I didn't, the Red Empress would have taken over your body and thrown the whole realm into darkness. What kind of knight would I be if I let that happen?"

"Is that all? Just trying to save the world?"

"No."

"No?"

"I didn't catch many breaks in this life. I was a child when I had a sword thrust into my hands. I know what it is to be taken and used as a weapon for someone else's ambition. I came back for you because I could do for you what I wish someone had done for me," Vale answered.

"Well, is that a shocking revelation. Underneath all that armor, you're just a big softie, huh?" She pushed against his shoulder, but instead of moving him, she lost her balance and stumbled back.

"You should get some rest. Your body needs time to heal."

Reluctantly, she agreed and went back inside.

Azalea claimed she was ready to go after three days of rest and recovery. Vale made them wait another two just be sure.

"We're going to have to move quickly if we are going to catch up with the others at Stormdale," Rivik commented as they stepped outside of the inn.

"I will escort you until we reach Lunal. I need to check on how the cleanup is going anyway," Aurora commented.

As they traveled, they made light conversation, sharing ideas about the world and the future of what Vargr could be. Aurora had resigned herself to leading, at least until someone more suited for the task came along.

"Your reluctance to lead is what will make you great at it. Those who desire power are almost always corrupted by it. Those who resist power often find ways of using it for the good of others," Vale told her.

When they reached the gates of Lunal, they exchanged their goodbyes. Though they hadn't known each other long, battling an army of monsters bonded them together.

"Take care of yourself," Sera said, hugging Aurora tightly.

Aurora nodded. "You too. May the gods below bless you on your quest. On your return journey, you must come see us. You are heroes of Vargr. We will celebrate seeing you again."

With their goodbyes said, they turned to part ways. They hadn't gotten very far when they heard a voice call out from behind them.

"After all the work I did to purify this city, you go and kill all my creations? So rude. So ungrateful."

Sera recognized the voice. Her heart pounded in her chest as she slowly turned, hoping she was wrong. She wasn't.

Squatting on top of the wall just above the gate sat Valron with his hands crossed over each other and a playful grin on his face. He looked at them and cocked his head to the side. When he saw Vale, he looked confused.

"Wait—didn't I kill you?"

Chapter 41
The Crossroad

Caelan stepped inside. The space looked more like a wide hallway than a room as it stretched surprisingly far. There was a series of doors running along each side of the hall, each one labeled—some with kingdoms, others with races, and others with miscellaneous things Caelan had never heard of. Standing between each set of doors was an attendant in a light gray robe. The hall room was dimly lit and undecorated. At the end of the hall room, Caelan saw the others standing in front of a large desk with a massive chair on the other side. The wall behind the desk glowed with a peculiar pink light. The light displayed moving pictures. Caelan recognized several of the places: West Hill in Maylor, the Parisian Capital, and several others. It looked like some form of magic in which the light revealed things happening all around the kingdoms.

"Are those Seer Stones?" Caelan pointed to the projections as he walked up to the desk.

"They are," came a woman's voice in response.

Sitting behind the desk was a tall, thin woman with a long face and long blonde hair. She looked like little more than a skeleton with skin wrapped around it. She wore pink and white robes that glimmered even in the dull light. She wore a thin, silver necklace with an intricate charm bearing what appeared to be some type of rune and a thin bracelet made of silver beads. Her elbows rested on the desk as she tapped her fingers together.

"Welcome, welcome. It is always good to meet such worthy travelers. Tell me, what is it you seek?"

"You're not much of an information broker if you don't know that," Caelan commented.

Ash smacked him in his chest hard enough to knock the wind out of him.

"We are looking for information," Ash started.

"Naturally. That is implicit in your coming to see me, isn't it? Let's assume that I'm not a child that needs you to hold my hand and walk me to the point. Let's just get to it, shall we?" The broker smiled with her lips and glared with her eyes.

"We are looking for a boy—" Owen started.

"Quite a lot of those in the world. You may have to be more specific."

"Half dwarf, half human," Owen added.

"Well, that is more specific. I know of only three half-dwarves currently in the world. One is a girl. One is middle-aged. That leaves only one who fits your description. What business do you have with this boy?" The broker raised an eyebrow,

"He's my son," Owen almost shouted.

"I see. Well, I can tell you where he is. Or at least, where he was most recently. But, as I'm sure you know, I don't work for free. What do you offer as payment?" The broker leaned forward, her eyes scanning the group.

"Anything!" Owen shouted. "Ask whatever you want of me. If you can help me find my son, I'll give you anything you'd like. I don't have much coin, but I'll give you what I have!"

"I'm not interested in your coin. Information on a half-dwarf isn't worth much on the market, though it is worth everything to you. Perhaps you have something to trade. I have spies all over the kingdoms, Seer stones that allow me to view events as they happen, but even those are limited. If you can provide me with adequate knowledge that I do not already possess, I will give you the whereabouts of your son. Fair?"

They all looked at each other as they tried to think of an answer.

"The Darkstone was stolen from Parisia by an elder—" Caelan offered.

"Old news. What else?"

"The capital of Vargr was destroyed by a mysterious group serving the Red Empress who turned the city into monsters," Ash said.

"Saw it. Moving on." The broker waved her hand dismissively.

They went quiet again. Ash opened his mouth, but the broker lifted her hand to stop him. "My time is valuable, and you don't seem to have anything worth sharing. Time to leave. Guards"

Four men in light armor with curved swords at their hips and bizarre hats on their heads stepped toward them. Kade's eyes flashed, and an orange flame burst from them.

"You don't want to do that," he warned.

"I had heard rumors about the great Lord Drako of Taggoron. I'm sure my men would be no match for a half-dragon. But killing them and me will not help you acquire the information you seek." The broker smiled and waved the guards back.

"I don't have to kill you. I can make you feel a pain unlike anything you have ever known. I will make you talk," Kade threatened.

"Brute over brains. Disappointing. I was hoping to keep this civil." She reached under her desk and pulled out a glowing pink stone. She lifted it toward him, and Kade winced and stepped back. "This is a Faestone. Very rare. They are mined from deep caves rich with spirit magic. Dragons are vulnerable to spirit magic, right?" the broker smirked.

"You got a special rock to stop my arrow from piercing your skull?" Caelan notched an arrow and aimed at the broker's head.

"Not a rock no. But if you think I let you in here without a contingency to get you out, you are goraum rooki," the broker smiled.

"Ken-Dahi . . ." Owen said.

"That's interesting. The lost city of the Katuchi. What about it?" The broker turned and smiled, sliding the Faestone back out of view.

"I know where it is."

"Do you? Well, isn't that something? Many believe the city to be a myth." The broker smiled.

"We want them to believe that. How do you think a bunch of superstitious people would react if they knew there was a city filled with a cursed tribe? They'd blame every bad thing that happened on us and wipe us out." Owen crossed his arms.

"Ignorance often leads to fear and cruelty." She bobbed her head back and forth for a few moments, as if rattling ideas around in her brain. "That would be a worthy price. Very well. You tell me where the lost city is, and I will tell you where you can find your son."

"What will you do with the information?"

"Whatever I see fit," the broker shrugged.

"If you share the location, sooner or later, people will seek it out and destroy it. You'd be responsible for the death of an entire tribe of people," Owen warned.

"I have no interest in the genocide of your people. The secrets they have could be of great use to me." She waved her hand.

"Where's your map?" Owen asked.

An attendant walked over and rolled out a large scroll across the desk. The scroll was an intricate and detailed drawing of the entire area—forests, rivers, mountains, cities, each drawn out and labeled. Owen stared at the map for a moment, tracing his finger over a small river that ran through a thick forest, up into the Weeping Mountains on the far western border of Vargr.

Owen tapped a small point on the map. "Here."

"How would they build a city all the way up there?" The broker examined the area.

"If they put it somewhere easy to access, don't you think you'd have found it by now?" Owen asked.

"I suppose you're right." She sat back in her chair and tapped her fingers together.

"Well?" Owen encouraged.

"Normally I prefer to vet the information I receive, but, as your quest is urgent, I shall make an exception. Your son is currently being held in Misting Falls, a port city not far from

Shadows of the Dark Realm

Stormdale. However, you should hurry. My sources tell me the family that owns him is preparing to relocate—to where I am not certain."

Owen felt his heart lift. For the first time in years, he had a direction, a location for where he could find his son. His face glowed with excitement even as his body shook with nervous energy, his joy turning to worry. *What if they didn't make it in time? What if he got so close but still couldn't find his son?* His breathing grew heavy.

"Don't worry. We will find him. I'm sure we will make it in time." Ash patted Owen on the back. The gesture, intended to bring comfort, nearly toppled the smaller man.

"Touching. Now, if you will step back onto those blue circles on the floor, I will return you to town and you can be on your way."

* * *

Back in town, they tracked a very irritable Celeste who was pacing back and forth, ranting like a lunatic in the central square. Once they calmed her down, they returned to the inn and rested. Owen was unable to fall asleep, his mind too busy racing with possible scenarios of how the next few days could play out.

Before sunrise, Owen had all his things packed and ready. He made no attempt to hide his eagerness, packing up everyone else's bags while they slept. When the others finally woke, he gulped down his breakfast and stood at the door to the inn as the others took their time. He managed to pace himself as they traveled, at least, until Stormdale came into view. When he saw the docks, the ships, and the great sea of the dragon coast, he gasped.

"There it is!" he exclaimed, nearly giggling.

The road forked with a sturdy, wooden sign where the paths diverted. An arrow pointing to the coastal city read: STORMDALE. Another below it, pointing to the right, read: MISTING FALLS.

Owen let out a long, slow breath before turning to the others. "Thank you for all you've done for me. Maybe one day, I'll be able to repay you."

"You're leaving?" Ash asked.

"Of course. You've done more for me than I had any right to ask. I know I'm no good in a fight, but you all kept me safe. You helped me find my son. I know you have your quest. I can't slow you down anymore." Owen nodded.

"Your son is not just hanging around waiting for you. He's a slave. Whoever owns him is not going to give him up just because you show up. You're going to have to fight," Ash said.

"I know, but I can't ask you to come. You've got to catch your ship."

"We are coming." Kade folded his arms across his chest.

"What? No. You have to be kidding. We can't be doing this again. You said it yourself—the ship won't wait for us. We cannot afford delay," Celeste objected.

"Calm down. We have to wait for Vale and the others anyway," Caelan challenged.

"Fine. Let's be quick about it. I don't need to remind you—" Celeste closed her eyes and sighed.

"Then don't," Caelan chimed in.

It took them the rest of the day to reach Misting Falls. It was a large fishing village with a single dock for big ships and a series of smaller ones for fishing boats. The town itself smelled of salt and sand. Its wooden buildings were durable but looked weathered. Nets hung everywhere. Gulls of the sea sang and squawked as they flew overhead. The town had no gate or walls, just a few open paths leading to the primary streets that ran between the shops and market. Most of the homes were scattered around the town surrounded by patches of farmland. At the far end of the town, there was a large barracks attached to a private dock, and a series of large warehouses.

A rotund merchant in baggy, striped pants and a stained, white shirt stomped merrily toward them.

"Greetings, travelers! 'Tis wonderful to see you. My name is Arthur Reddington, fish merchant extraordinaire. If fish is your vice, I've got the best price. What brings you fine folks to our humble town?" His voice was so chipper and loud it made Caelan uneasy.

"We are looking for someone," Kade replied flatly.

Shadows of the Dark Realm

"That a fact? Well, someone you have found." Arthur Reddington smacked his oversized belly, causing it to jiggle, and then laughed at his own joke. "Only kidding. I suspect you meant someone specific. Perhaps I can point you in the right direction?"

Ash cut in front of Kade before he could reply. He walked over and pulled him into a side hug.

"Very kind of you. We are looking for an old friend. But it's very important he doesn't find out we are looking for him. You know what I mean?"

"Like a surprise?" Arthur almost shouted.

"Exactly like a surprise."

"If there's one thing, besides fish, of course, that Arthur Reddington loves, it's a good surprise. How can I help you?"

"Here's the tricky part. We haven't seen him in so long, we aren't even sure how to describe him anymore. We've been mostly communicating through letters. All I know is, he has this boy with him, tells us about him all the time—a half-dwarf. You seen anyone like that?" Ash smiled.

"You mean Lord Urik's little slave boy?" Arthur leaned back and looked at Ash suspiciously.

Ash snapped his fingers and pointed. "Exactly, that's the one."

"Of course, the private dock and warehouse belong to Lord Urik. He brings in the trade that keeps this town afloat. He's a very important man around these parts. Everyone knows him. But last I heard he sold the half-dwarf boy as part of some new trade with a lord to the north."

"Already? Oh no, we came all this way. Never seen a half-dwarf before. Do you know where he might be?"

Arthur shook his head. "I'm sorry to tell you I haven't the foggiest. Lord Urik—"

"That's enough, Arthur, you've bothered our guests plenty," a cold, gruff voice interrupted them.

"My apologies, Lord Urik, I meant no offense," Arthur stammered and stepped away from Ash as he shrank down as small as his large form could get.

The man before them wore a long, black coat covering a gray

tunic. He was average height and build, clean shaven with jet-black, greasy-looking hair that he'd pulled back into a ponytail. He had a long, thin sword with an ornate handle attached to his hip. He walked toward them slowly.

"I don't take kindly to strangers asking questions about my business," he said as he glared.

"That's funny, I don't take kindly to people who think they can own other people," Caelan replied, pulling his bow free.

"How I conduct my trade is none of your business. But since you are so curious, tell me, what slave are you looking for?" Urik asked.

"Varric," Owen said.

"I do not bother to learn the names of my property. Who is that?" Urik sneered.

"The half-dwarf boy," Ash said.

"Ah, yes, that one. What do you want with the boy?"

"Where is he?" Ash asked, an edge to his voice.

"Were you looking to buy? I have plenty of stock, if you're in the market."

"What have you done with him? Where is my son?!?!" Owen pressed.

"Ahhh, I see. You're the boy's father. He told me about you. Quite the story, really. The brave father, fleeing to save his own skin, leaving his son behind to fend for himself. Truly inspiring."

"Tell us where the boy is, and we will be on our way," Ash demanded.

"Oh, so sorry, you only just missed him. I sold him two days ago to a business partner from Kalkan."

"The northern kingdom?" Caelan asked.

"Indeed. They are flush with spice, and I'm looking to expand my horizons. Their ambassador is a bit of a collector. Having a rare half-dwarf made securing a profitable deal quite easy. Fortuitous, wouldn't you say? Seems you've come all this way for nothing. Though, I suppose if you were motivated you might be able to catch him."

"What do you mean?" Owen asked.

"My partner is stopping at the village north of here before making the long trek back to Kalkan. The village is two days' travel by boat, four by land. He should be there for a week gathering supplies and finishing up his business in Baronia. You could catch him. But—"

"But?" Ash asked.

"Well, that could jeopardize the deal I just made, which would cost me a lot of money. It's not good business. I'm afraid you wouldn't be leaving Misting Falls." He snapped his finger. Thugs came pouring out of the side streets, forming a wall between them and Lord Urik.

"This is gonna get messy." Ash raised his fists.

Caelan glanced over his shoulder. More thugs had gathered behind them.

"Celeste, when I go, get Owen out. Down the alley. We will keep them off you and come get you when we're done," Caelan said calmly.

"Wait, no. It's my son; I should stay," Owen protested.

"He's right. They won't be hard to kill, but in close quarters like this, it'll be hard to protect you," Kade agreed.

The thugs were impressive in number, especially to have mustered so quickly. They formed two lines, trapping the group between them in a pincer attack. The thugs jeered at them but held their lines, waiting for instructions.

Caelan didn't wait. He notched an arrow, lifted his bow, and fired in one swift motion. His arrow cut through the air. An archer he had spied on the rooftop grunted and fell to the ground with a splat. Caelan turned and fired again, each shot quickly following the last. He'd fired four times before anyone else moved, and each time an archer on a nearby roof fell. Like the calm before a storm, everyone froze. A single cry broke the lines, and the two waves of thugs charged in.

"Celeste, why are you still here? Go!" Caelan shouted.

Celeste nodded and grabbed Owen by the wrist, tugging him with her. She darted to the alley as the waves of thugs descended upon the group. She glanced over her shoulder as they ran. No one seemed to be following. She kept going, crossing two streets before nearing the edge of town where she stopped.

"This is wrong. I can't keep running away. I have to go back. I have to fight. He's my son," Owen shook his head.

He rushed back to the alley before Celeste could stop him.

"Wait!" she cried out, chasing after him.

He didn't listen, instead rushing back toward the fight. Celeste ran as fast as she could. He was surprisingly fast, and she was struggling to catch up. The alley was coming to a turn that would open up to where the others were fighting. Three thugs were standing in the street, away from the fray.

"Look, I ain't dying for this. I ain't never seen nobody fight like that," one of the men said.

Owen slid to a stop when he saw them. He closed his eyes, gritted his teeth, and roared, charging toward the three thugs, who each brandished a different weapon. Owen had nothing, not even a dagger. Yet he charged ahead.

"Wait!" Celeste called out again. Again, he ignored her.

"Well, look at what we have here, boys," one of the men sneered.

The three turned to face them. Owen charged right at them. He lunged forward, throwing his fist. The thug leaned back and dodged it easily.

"Uh oh, lads, this one's scrappy," he mocked as the other two laughed.

"And it seems he brought a lady friend with him."

Owen swung again and again. Each time, the thug moved out of the way. After a few more swings, he grew bored and caught Owen's arm, pulling the small man into his grip and turning him to face the others.

"Quit toying with him and put him out of his misery. I got the girl," one of the thugs said, walking toward Celeste, dragging his blade lazily along the stone ground.

Celeste lowered her head and charged. The thug squared off as she grew closer, readying himself. As he started to move, Celeste planted her foot and sidestepped suddenly, moving herself out of his path. She thrust her sword forward, driving it through the man's neck and pulling it free, barely breaking her stride.

The man slumped to his knees, clutching his throat as she rushed past. The second thug turned, surprised to see she had gotten past the other man. He didn't have time to react. His momentary hesitation was all the time Celeste needed to slice her blade at his neck and run him through the chest. She whirled on the third man who was holding a thick sword forged with a very unique curve. He lifted the blade, pointing it at Celeste.

"Stay back. Not another step, or I gut your friend, here," he threatened.

Owen drove his elbow into the man's chest and dropped his body down, slipping out of the thug's grip. He coughed and stumbled back just as Celeste lunged forward, running him through. Owen took her hand as she helped him up. He smiled and hugged her tightly. She broke the hug and pushed him away a moment later.

"Thank you," Owen said, breathing heavily. "You saved me."

Celeste could hear the fighting around the corner of the alley, just out of view.

"What were you thinking? Running off like that?" she scolded.

"I wasn't . . . It's just, it's my son. I can't let everyone else keep fighting for me. I can't keep running away." Owen hung his head.

"You're not going to stop, are you?"

Owen shook his head. "No. I-I can't. I have to rescue my son. Come on, let's go help the others." He started toward the corner.

"Two days by sea," Celeste covered her face with her hand.

"What?" Owen stopped, looking confused.

"The noble, Urik, he said the man who has your son is at a village that is two days travel by ship. It'll cost us at least four days to go there."

"If you need to get back to Stormdale, I understand. This is not your fight," Owen nodded.

"But it is. Those small-minded idiots are bonded to you. Even Kade is determined to help you. We can't afford to waste more time. I'm sorry." Celeste took a deep breath.

"You don't have to be sorry. I didn't mean to cause so much trouble. Let's go back and help them, and then I'll insist they leave. This is not your problem."

"I'm sorry," Celeste repeated.

Owen smiled softly. "It's ok. I am grateful for the help you all gave me. Grateful to have known you." His voice caught in his throat as he coughed. His hands moved to his chest as blood poured over them. A thin piece of metal stuck through his chest as he looked down at it and then up at Celeste. Tears flooded his eyes, and a sob escaped his lips.

Celeste pulled her sword free and watched as the thin man slumped to the ground, rolling onto his back.

"Va—" he started and trailed off, coughing and sobbing softly. "Varric . . . I'm sorry . . . " he said, gazing up into the sky.

"I'm not the bad guy here. I didn't want this. You left me no choice. The others aren't going to stop until you have your son. I can't let my kingdom fall for one man's reunion with his son. If you lived, how many fathers and sons would be lost? Someone has to think about the big picture." Celeste sheathed her sword and kneeled over him.

"I-I didn't . . . I didn't run . . . away . . . right?" Owen coughed and blood drained from the side of his mouth.

"You didn't run." Celeste bit her lip.

"P-please . . . tell my . . . son . . . I didn't . . . run . . . I-I tried . . . " Another tear rolled down the side of his face as Owen's eyes slowly drifted closed.

Chapter 42

The Elven Way

"You're the one who did this?" Lady Aurora drew her blade and readied herself.

Valron dropped from the top of the wall and landed on the ground in front of them as if it was nothing more than a small step. He walked slowly toward Lady Aurora, sizing her up. Vale rushed toward Aurora, drawing his blade as he ran.

"No! Aurora, run!" Sera called out.

"We cannot stop him. He is too powerful. We need to get out of here!" Dante urged.

"He's the one who sent me to that place," Azalea growled. "I'm going to burn the flesh from his bones."

"Azalea, no. You are not ready for him. We need to get you out of here," Dante pleaded.

Vale rushed past Aurora, his blade swinging at Valron's face. Valron dodged, moving his head out of the path. Vale brought his sword around fast, but this time Valron didn't bother dodging. He caught the blade between two fingers and held it in place. Vale pushed against his grip, trying to drive the blade into Valron's shoulder. Valron smiled and drove his fist into Vale's chest, sending the Black Swordsman flying back. He landed with a thud and slid to Rivik's feet. Azalea's hands became engulfed in purple flame. Dante grabbed her and pleaded again.

"This is a battle we cannot win. If you try to fight him, we all die, and he takes you back to the Spirit Realm."

"We can't beat him. We can't outrun him. Ralker always seems to know right where we are. If he's sending me to the gods, I'm going to make him work for it." Rivik readied his spear.

"He's mine." Azalea extended her hands and balls of flame burst from them, flying past Aurora. Valron swung his arm and deflected the fireballs with a sizzle, directing them harmlessly behind him. He disappeared and a moment later reappeared behind Azalea. He smiled a wicked, sinister smile. Before the others could move, he raised his hands as if lifting a crate.

Vale felt his feet break contact with the ground as his body levitated. He looked around to see the others floating next to him. A wave of invisible energy slammed into him and sent him flying back, this time farther than before. The others slammed into the ground and slid next to him. He tried to move but couldn't. His arms and legs felt tied as if by invisible rope. Even Dante was unable to escape the restraints.

"Resistance is pointless." Valron turned to face Azalea. Glowing red ropes burst from the ground, similar to the ones Dante had used to contain the monsters. They wrapped around Azalea's wrists and tugged them to her side, restraining her movement.

Before he could take her away, Aurora's blade cut through the red cord on one side, freeing Azalea's arms. Azalea moved quickly, blasting Valron with a magical flare.

Valron vanished just before the flare would have struck him. The attack may have missed but it forced Valron to release the magic holding the others in place.

Aurora whirled around, searching for the man, her blade at the ready. Vale saw it as if in slow motion. Valron appeared right behind Aurora. Before she even knew he was there, he grabbed her. Vale heard her neck snap as the crack echoed around them. Aurora's body crumpled to the ground, her head facing the wrong way.

"Interloping insect." Valron kicked her body aside like a piece of garbage.

"Nooooo!" Sera screamed and started to charge. Rivik

Shadows of the Dark Realm

grabbed her and held her back. She kicked and flailed, striking him several times in her blind rage, but he did not let go.

"I've had just about enough of you. Time to die." Valron raised his hand, and a glowing aura surrounded it.

A flash of light and a strange cracking sound filled the air. Valron was thrown back as three men dropped out of the sky: one in a red tunic, one in blue, and one in green.

"We will not allow you to bring back the Red Empress," one of them roared, his voice unnaturally deep.

The one in green turned to face them. "Be gone from here. Keep her from his reach."

Vale felt his body tingle. He fought against the sensation as he tried to focus on what was happening. Two of the men who had dropped out of the sky began to glow and transform. They no longer looked like men but three large dragons standing between them and Valron. The third, still in his human form, had his arm stretched toward them. Vale felt his body sliding back on the ground and then everything disappeared to black.

He hit the ground and groaned. He sat up on his elbows and looked around. The others were still with him, laying on the grass, all teleported here by the same spell.

"What was that?" Rivik groaned. "Were those ... dragons?"

"Where ... Grom be?"

They were standing in an open field at the edge of a massive swamp. A long, wooden bridge just past where they landed led to an impressively large city that appeared to float on the dark water.

"I know this place. This is Blackwater Marsh. We are near Stormdale." Rivik stood and dusted himself off.

"Strange ... " Dante rubbed his chin.

"What are you thinking?" Vale asked.

"This is the second time we have seen dragons attack Valron. This time they did not just attack him, they helped us," Dante said flatly.

"What do you think it means?" Rivik asked.

"It is difficult to say for certain. I suspect our quest has led us into something far greater than we realize."

"Well, they did us a favor teleporting us here. If we move

through the night, we can reach Stormdale by morning," Rivik suggested.

Sera was quiet as they traveled. She'd seen people die before, more times than she wanted to count, but something about Aurora's death struck a chord with her. Perhaps it was just the bond of battle, but she'd felt a strange attachment to the young commander. Watching her die, especially like that—it left a mark. Rivik said nothing, just made sure to stay close enough that she could sense his presence as they traveled.

"Butterfly . . . " Grom's voice was gleeful and almost childish. "Purple . . . butterfly!" he repeated.

The large troll, who had been swinging his axes and practicing battle cries as they journeyed, suddenly put his axes away and started frolicking through the field chasing a small, fluttering, purple butterfly.

"So, when did you find him?" Azalea dropped back to Sera.

"After you got taken to the palace, we managed to get free. I wanted to come find you, but Celeste insisted there was nothing we could do. We met Grom during our escape, rescued him from some hunters in the woods. He's been with us ever since," Sera explained.

"He's . . . enthusiastic," she commented.

"Yeah, I guess he is." Sera forced herself to smile.

"Only time I've seen him like that is when he was smashing his axes into those gargoyles," Rivik commented. "He must really love butterflies."

Vale, who had been scouting ahead, hung back to let Dante catch up.

"Something is bothering you," he said more than asked.

"How can you tell?" Dante sighed.

"It's written all over your face," Vale smirked.

"A question we should have asked from the beginning. Why?"

"Why what?"

"The Darkstone was housed in Parisia for centuries. While there were several attempts to steal, no dragon ever showed interest before."

"You're wondering why now?"

"More than that—why did Draka Mors steal it at all? He is an elder dragon; what is it he desires that he cannot obtain on his own? It would have to be something monumental."

"And why hasn't he used it yet?" Vale finished the thought.

"Yes! That is what is bothering me the most. He goes through all the trouble to steal a stone that can grant him the desire of his heart. Yet nothing has changed, no release of massive magical energy. He has had the stone for months and ... has not used it. Why? I know dragons like to horde treasure, but the stone is not that pretty to look at. Why steal it if he is not going to use it? If he is going to use it, what is he waiting for?" Dante asked.

"You think the king was telling the truth? That the stone requires Royal blood?"

"It does seem that way. Even that troubles me. I suppose it is possible that Draka Mors stole the stone not knowing that he would not be able to use it. That just seems so unlikely. I cannot help but think there is something at work here that we are not seeing."

"Like what?"

"There is a lot at play here, Vale. Much more than I would have guessed when we started," Dante shrugged.

"We will figure it out together."

"For king and country?" Dante grinned.

"No. If we survive this, I have some questions for our king."

"I do not blame you," Dante replied. "It is strange to think I worked so closely alongside him for so long, and I saw nothing. Now, thinking back, I cannot believe how blind I was. The king has much to answer for."

They traveled through the night, stopping only to eat and rest for a bit before pressing on. As day broke, they could hear the crashing of the sea in the distance. The scent of the ocean air grew stronger with each passing step. As they followed the path over the hill, they came to a crossroad. The larger path to the left lead down into the valley below and to a large port city. The sign read: STORMDALE. The path to the right curved and turned to a much smaller town, hardly visible on the horizon: MISTING FALLS.

They took the path to the left and made their way to the port city. Stormdale was massive. Stone walls built all the way to the water surrounded much of the city with large gates left open during the day to allow travelers in. The docks themselves were larger than most cities. Shops lined the streets and walls, providing a wealth of trade and opportunity.

There were a dozen stone docking stations built out onto the water, with floating wooden bridges allowing better access for incoming ships. Each station could dock up to six massive ships. Once docked, the crew would enter a guarded registration building before exiting out the back. Each station had a single arching stone bridge, with two guard towers on either side that led to a central floating station with a series of buildings. From the central floating station was one long, wide bridge lined with a dozen guard towers that led to the city itself.

Large spikes jetted out from the water along with deliberately placed rocks, preventing any ship from trying to sail past the docking stations. It was an impressive display of architecture and design that allowed Stormdale to be a massive seaport while keeping the city protected from pirates or even invading fleets.

The city itself was enchanting. Smooth white stone streets, beige brick houses and shops lined with brown wood trim, and roofs topped with orange-gray shingles. Colorful banners and flags were draped between buildings. Arches and columns created openings between bridges and raised walkways. Birds sang their songs. The soft rumble of waves dashing against the shore created a soothing audible ambiance. The fresh sea air made everything smell clean. The soft bell of a distant buoy bobbing in the water accented the hustle and bustle of a city alive with energy.

There was a great summer palace with hanging gardens to the east, a merchant's guild to the south, and every kind of shop and store imaginable. This was the jewel of Baronia.

"So how are we supposed to find the others in a place like this?" Rivik chuckled.

"Let's start with inns and taverns. We can work our way toward the docks," Vale instructed.

They made their way from place to place through Stormdale,

asking barkeepers, merchants, and anyone else who may have noticed a group of travelers, but to no avail. Travelers came and went like the tide, and their faces were even sooner forgotten. If their friends had arrived, no one seemed to remember seeing them. As the sun began to descend, they made it to the long street that ran parallel to the docks.

A man with lustrous blonde hair walked past them. He was tall and slender, with soft, refined features. His skin was a creamy pewter color. His eyes were a vibrant azure. No hair grew on his face. As he walked the tips of his fingers brushed just below his knees, making his limbs appear lanky and stretched beyond normal human proportions. Most notably, his ears extended up to a fine point, rather than a rounded edge. He seemed to glide more than walk as he moved with an unnatural eloquence and grace. It was like water running downstream. He wore a flowing, teal tunic stitched with ivory thread.

"Your beast is blocking the road. Keep him on a leash, or keep him out of the way," the man said as he passed, knocking his shoulder into Grom's.

Before Grom could move or anyone could stop her, Sera grabbed the elf by his robes. She drove her knee into his chest, causing the wind to burst from his lungs, dropping him coughing to his knees.

"I'm not sure I heard you correctly. Want to try that again?" She put her foot on him, pushing him down so he couldn't stand back up.

Vale's hand dropped to the hilt of his blade as two dozen harpoons were suddenly aimed at them. A group of elves had surrounded them without them even noticing. *How could they have been so quiet?*

The elf gasped and laughed, "Do you?" The elf groaned out an uncomfortable laugh.

The sharp points of two harpoons pressed against her. She held her hands up and stepped back. The elf stood and dusted himself off.

"Grom . . . no like elves . . . elves mean . . . " Grom gripped his axes.

"That feeling is mutual, beast," the elf replied.

"Call him a beast again," Sera warned.

"You are as uncivilized as your little pet. Striking your betters? You will rue this day."

"Endril? Endril, is that you?" Another elf walked over.

He looked similar in many ways—tall, lean, gray-blue skin, bright blue eyes, and pointy ears. That was where the similarities ended. Where the first elf looked elegant with refined, noble features, this one looked rough and unkempt. His onyx hair was pulled back into a sloppy ponytail that was mostly hidden behind a dirty, red bandana. His ears were pierced at the top and bottom, the holes connected by a single earring designed to look like a chain. He wore studded, brown leather armor with a red sash over his shoulder and a red cloth belt tied around his waist. He looked like a thug.

The elf Sera had struck, Endril, rolled his eyes and scoffed. "Get out of here, Shivanariandu; this is none of your concern."

"Aw, Endy, you know I hate it when you call me that." The thuggish elf wrapped his arm around Endril and pulled the blonde elf down, ruffling his hair.

"Fine, Shiv, get off me." Endril pushed the dark-haired elf away.

"Alright, Endy, you can go." Shiv laughed and turned to face the group, smiling.

"This is unacceptable. You have no right to intervene here!" Endril protested.

The other elves, who had encircled the group, pulled back their harpoons, and started walking away.

"Wait! Where are you going? You don't work for him!" Endril cried out.

"Bye, Endy." Shiv turned around and waved.

Endril, who had carried himself with such refinement and grace, stormed off like a scolded, pouting child, leaving the dark-haired elf standing in front of them.

"What's his problem?" Rivik asked.

"Endril? Oh, he's harmless as raindrops on a lake. Takes himself a bit too seriously is all. But enough of all that, let's get down to business."

"What business is that?" Vale asked.

"You the ones Ammonia told me about, right? Looking for passage on me ship?" he asked, resting his hand on his hip.

"Are we supposed to know who that is?" Azalea snapped.

"Oh, come on, you know the butler-looking chap, works for some fancy lord of something. Said he was making arrangements for some mission of great import."

"Kade Drako?" Vale asked.

Shiv snapped and wagged his finger at Vale. "That's the one. Told me to keep me eyes wide for a knight in black armor and a man in blue robes. Didn't say nothin' bout no troll though. Yer quite the bunch aren'tcha?"

"Because you're exactly what people picture when they think of an elf. You look like a sewer person, and you smell like rotted fish," Azalea snapped back.

Everyone grew silent as Shiv glared for what seemed like an eternity.

"Don't like it, sweetheart? You want to dance?" Azalea added.

"Oh, I like you. Want to come see my ship?" Shiv winked, clapping his hands together.

Azalea rolled her eyes.

"Fine. Play hard to get. I got plans tonight, anyway."

"Can you take us to him?" Vale asked.

"To him? You mean he's not with you?"

"Genius, don't you think you'd see him if he were with us?" Azalea snapped.

"Ah, all you humans look the same to me," Shiv shrugged.

"They should have been here days ago," Dante said.

"So, what's keeping them?" Vale asked.

Chapter 43

Reunions

A butcher's knife swung toward his neck as the thug brought his weapon down. Kade caught the thick knife in his hand. The thug wielding it grunted, trying to drive it down. Kade smirked, and, lifting the man off the ground with one hand, he threw him into a nearby stone wall. The man smacked against it hard and went limp, adding to the pile of bodies that surrounded them.

Ash stepped over a pile of dead thugs, making his way toward Lord Urik, who had one guard left next to him. Spiro was finishing off one of the last remaining thugs, leaving Urik and his guard alone.

"W-w-wait . . . we . . . we can work something out . . . no need to . . . " Urik backed up. His guard turned and fled, leaving him alone.

"What's the name of this collector?" Kade asked, as he approached Urik.

"I'll tell you, just . . . promise to let me go."

"You'll tell me, or I'll pull every bone from your body one at a time," Kade warned.

Urik shrieked, "O-ok, ok . . . I sold him to a Lord Braydon Narxi. He lives in Rilio City. But he'll be staying in Coppers Mill for the next week. You . . . you can take my ship to get there. W-w-whatever you need. Just don't hurt me—"

Kade grabbed Urik by his throat. The noble squirmed and kicked, flailing about as he gasped.

"Y-you . . . p-promised," he groaned out between gasps.

"No. I didn't." Kade snapped Urik's neck and dropped him to the ground.

There was a collective sigh of relief as the fight was finally over. Ash smiled.

"Owen, you hear that? We got it." Ash turned, and his smile faded.

Down the alley he saw Celeste hunched over Owen as he lay on the ground. She was clutching his head and calling out to them. Ash rushed down the alley, sliding to a stop just before reaching them.

"Nooo . . . " he pleaded against what he was seeing.

"Ralk!" Caelan cursed. He fired an arrow into Urik's body, and then another and another as he cried out in anger.

"What happened?" Kade asked.

"We . . . we got away. But he insisted on coming back. He wanted to fight. I tried to stop him, but he's fast. He ran ahead, and before I could catch up to him, these thugs had him. He tried to fight them, but . . . but they killed him before I could reach them," Celeste sniffed and looked up from Owen's lifeless body.

"You got all of them?" Caelan looked at the thugs.

Celeste nodded. "I only wish I had been quicker. Then maybe he'd still be here."

Caelan knelt down over the first thug. His dagger was still in its sheath. His thick sword was on the ground next to him. He checked the other two and then Owen.

"There was nothing I could do. I told him to stop. He just—he wouldn't listen," Celeste explained.

"What do we do now?" Ash asked.

"Not to sound unsympathetic, but with Owen gone, there's no reason for us to continue. Even if we rescued the boy, we'd be putting him in greater danger with what comes next. I say we finish the quest, then we can figure out what to do about his son," Spiro sighed.

"We can't just . . . " Ash paced back and forth.

Caelan sighed. "He's not wrong, though. Before, it made sense. We could reunite them and go our separate ways. Now, we'd be rescuing the boy only to leave him alone or place him in even greater danger. I hate to say it, but for now, he might be better off where he is. We get the Darkstone, then we set things right."

"We're wasting time here." Kade pushed past them and started toward Stormdale.

No one spoke. They walked the entire way in silence. When they reached the gates of Stormdale, they saw a thin man in a brown cloak waving at them. He rushed toward them, only to stop a few paces away to correct his posture, adjust his tunic, and walk in an overly formal and dignified manner.

"My Lord Drako, it is excellent to see you." He bowed low as he spoke.

"Ammonia, have you acquired what I asked?" Kade questioned.

"Of course, my lord, I wouldn't dream of disappointing you. I have secured a room near the docks where there is enough Slumbaspice to put every dragon in the Dragon Lands to sleep." His voice rang with pride.

"Good. We will go get settled in while we wait for the others," Kade replied.

"Begging your pardon, my lord, but the others are already here."

Kade's brow furrowed in confusion. "Already? Are you sure?"

"How is that possible?" Caelan asked.

"I am unsure as to the logistics of their arrival, but I am quite sure it is them. They got in a scuffle with a group of elves by the docks. I had to send our captain friend to rescue them—a feat he was more than happy to charge us a premium for," Ammonia answered.

"Take us to them," Kade commanded.

Ammonia bowed and then guided them through the massive city. For such a large place, it was remarkably well-kept. In Caelan's experience, cities with high traffic often showed extra signs of wear and were considerably dirtier. Stormdale was picturesque and clean, as if out of a dream.

"I've never seen a city like this," Caelan remarked, marveling at the architecture.

"No, you wouldn't have. Stormdale was built by the elves," Kade answered.

"This is an elven city?" Ash chuckled. "Gods below, look at us now, Caelan, two slum rats from Maylor in an elven city. It's beautiful; why don't they help design other cities?"

"Elves never travel inland," Kade said.

"Why?"

"Elves are drawn to the sea. They can't stand being far from it."

Ammonia led them around a bend and down the wide stone streets until they cleared the final set of buildings. The horizon was covered in a massive expanse of sapphire water stretching in all directions as far as they could see. With the exception of a few distant islands, the great mass of glimmering water was all that could be seen. Caelan froze, his jaw dropping at the sight.

"You'll catch flies like that," a familiar voice called out.

Caelan turned to see Vale, hand resting on the pommel of his sword as he stared at them. Caelan's jaw dropped even further. He was certain his chin hit the ground.

"Vale?" he managed.

"Were you expecting someone else?" Vale looked around.

"You're dead—they told us you were dead," Caelan managed.

"Not anymore," Vale shrugged.

Caelan looked confused but rushed over and hugged Vale, pulling him close. Vale held his hands out, not sure how to respond. Finally, he settled on patting Caelan on the back.

"What's gotten into you?" he asked.

"Shut up, no one likes you. You're the worst." Caelan shoved him away.

The group sat around the docks and spent most of the evening catching up: the journey to the Spirit Realm, the encounters with the Red Empress, the Information Broker, and

Owen's death. Celeste remained quiet—uncomfortably quiet—while Spiro attempted to bond by interjecting too frequently.

When everything else was shared, Caelan started the story of Kade's great revelation. He led up to the reveal itself and let Kade take over. It took a minute for the others to come to terms with the fact that their companion was in fact a half-dragon. Dante, in particular, had a copious number of questions. Azalea was more focused on the logistics of a dragon mating with a human.

"So, you turned dragons into magical crystals, and then turned those crystals into weapons?" Dante tried to wrap his mind around it.

Kade reached into his pocket and pulled out a necklace. He tossed it to Dante. Dante examined it carefully.

"What is this?" he asked.

"The Crystal of Amon Lia. Wearing that will enhance your magical power and significantly increase your resistance to any magic used against you," Kade said.

"You are giving me a gift forged from a dragon soul?" Dante looked at it and then at Kade.

Kade nodded. "Our mission is dangerous. Proper tools and weapons increase our probability of success."

Kade pulled a sword from his pack and tossed it to Sera. "This is the Sword of Skylar, a fierce warrior dragon. It will increase your strength and your durability considerably."

Sera examined the sword while Kade pulled free the last item. He tossed a long green spear to Rivik.

"I've got a spear," Rivik chuckled.

"Not like this one. That is the Spear of Athlia. It is imbued with the power of lightning. When you wield it, it will allow you to move faster and strike with a magical energy," Kade answered.

"Well, why didn't you just say that?" Rivik removed his old spear, handing it to an eager Ammonia.

When Kade had finished giving out his gifts, Vale stood and waited for everyone's attention.

"When our quest began, we were five strangers. We didn't know, or particularly like, each other. We shared nothing but a goal. Now, we share scars and stories, we've shared laughter and tears. We've come a long way together. We've made new friends and new enemies. We've been hungry, tired, and afraid. We've fought dragons and monsters. We've seen things we didn't know existed. Our adventure has forged us together. Everything we have seen and endured has led us to this. We are close to the end. The danger is far from over. If we are going to survive what comes next, we need to work as one, think as one. We can't rely on luck to save us any longer. If we intend to secure the Darkstone and escape with our lives, we need to be a team. We need to do this together."

The group nodded in agreement.

"Well, this is awkward," Caelan said.

"What?" Vale glared.

"We're not quite ready to sail for the Darkstone."

"What do you mean?"

Caelan looked to Kade, who brought the others up to speed on the items they would need if they were to succeed in stealing the Darkstone.

"Ammonia has acquired the Slumbaspice. Before we can sail for the Darkstone, we still need the Gylphstone to find it and the Volkili Prismward to transport it," Kade explained.

"You know where these are?" Vale asked.

"I do. The elf captain you met, Shiv, will take you to an island temple where the Volkili Prismward is located. You'll need to retrieve it and return here."

"What do you mean 'retrieve it?'" Rivik asked.

"The Prismward is a valuable elven artifact. The elven elders could be reasoned with, but they don't surrender their treasures lightly," Kade answered.

"So . . . steal it," Caelan interjected.

"That would be easier, yes."

"And why are you not coming with us?" Celeste asked.

"We have another task," Kade answered.

"We?" Azalea asked. "And just what are you doing while we are sailing around, mister half-dragon?"

"While you retrieve the Prismward, I will take Dante to obtain the Glyphstone. We meet back here, and then we will be ready to sail for the Darkstone," Kade answered.

"Why Dante?" Vale asked. "He's the strongest, most stable magic user here. I will need him."

"Excuse me? I think—" Azalea started.

"No," Kade interrupted.

"Oh, I know you didn't just—" Azalea put her hands on her hips and glared.

"You are not a stable magic user. The precision required to obtain the Glyphstone, you do not possess."

"Oh, I'll show you what I possess," Azalea snapped.

"You are being hunted by a man called Valron. Every moment you waste being difficult, he draws closer. If he finds you, he will take you back to the Spirit Realm, and the Red Empress will destroy your soul and take control of your body. But by all means, let's continue to argue," Kade replied.

"If you're so big and tough, why don't you fight him? Not much of a dragon man if you can't handle one little wizard, are you?"

"Valron wields spirit magic. I can't help you against that. Our best plan of action is to be quick. Get the items we need, get the Darkstone, and then with any luck, we can use it before Draka Mors realizes it's gone," Kade answered.

"You should all get some rest. Tomorrow, we set sail," Vale said.

One by one the group dwindled as each person made their way back to the inn. After the others had gone, Caelan wandered down to the edge of the docks, closer to the water. Ash was sitting alone, holding his head in his hands as he stared at the ground. Caelan sat down next to him.

"Hey."

"Hey," Ash answered without looking up.

"You remember that kid we used to run with? The blonde one who got excited about everything?"

"Worsley? The one who couldn't tell his colors apart and thought he was invincible?"

Ash nodded. "That's the one. He thought he was the greatest thief the world would ever know. But in reality, he was—"

"Complete and utter rubbish. He couldn't steal a flower from the dead," Ash completed the thought.

"Yeah, he was near useless, wasn't he?"

"Near? That's generous."

"Useless, but it was hard not to like him. He just had that way, that indescribable quality."

"He was like a puppy. So loyal. So dependable, but he needed you for everything. He'd do stupid gwar and make you crazy, but then he'd hit you with those sad little eyes and there was nothing you could do," Ash recalled.

"You took his death hard."

"I did."

"This one, too?" Caelan asked.

"This one, too," Ash confirmed.

"I'm sorry," Caelan sighed.

"We were so close. So close to reuniting him with his son. It's just, it's not fair."

"Life rarely is. We don't pick the cards life deals us. It's how we play those cards that makes us who we are. You may not have gotten him to his son, but you gave him hope. You helped him find his courage. He got dealt a gwar hand. You helped him make something of it. In the end, that's all any of us can do."

A silent appreciation hovered between them.

"Thanks, Caelan. I think I just need to sleep it off." Ash rubbed his face and sighed.

They left the dock without noticing Kade, perched in the shadows on the wall above where they were sitting, listening. He sat for a moment, thinking. It had been a long time since he allowed himself to connect to or care about others. He spent the better part of a millennia convincing himself that friendships and attachments were distractions and weaknesses. He needed to forego them, at least until he got his revenge. Yet somehow, despite all his defenses, Owen had managed to worm his way in.

"It's rude to listen in on other people's conversations."

Kade turned around to see Azalea walking toward him with a smirk on her face.

"You should be sleeping," he replied.

Azalea sat down next to him, dangling her feet over the edge of the stone wall and looking out over the sea, its melodic rhythm soothing her restless mind.

"It's hard to sleep knowing you're being hunted by some godlike beings."

"I'm familiar," Kade nodded.

"Don't patronize me, owa; you're a dragon. How would you know?"

"I'm a half-dragon."

"Oh, only half-near godlike power. That must be so terrible for you. Would you like a handkerchief?"

"You have great power, yet here you are. I know what it's like to feel alone. Humans consider me a monster because I'm part dragon. Dragons call me maladictia; it means cursed one. They consider me an abomination. My mere existence is an offense to them. They have hunted me for a thousand years and will not stop until I am destroyed and their order restored. So yes, little human, I am aware of how you feel."

Azalea blinked. "Well, gwar, that's intense. Any advice, since you're kind of an expert?"

Kade couldn't tell if her question was sincere. When he looked into her eyes, he saw, at least, her fear was.

"There are many ways to cope with fear. Sooner or later, you will have to face it. What you do will determine whether you rule over your fear, or it rules over you."

Azalea sighed. "So, this feeling doesn't go away?"

Kade shook his head. "It's been a thousand years for me and . . . no, not really."

"How do you live with it? I know it's stupid, but I just feel like they could show up at any moment and—"

"It's not stupid. Not for people like us."

"Like us?" she asked.

"We live under the shadow of threat. It hangs over us as an ever-present danger. Most never know what it's like. That fear, though unpleasant, gives you an edge. It keeps you alert. Use it. Train. Prepare. Grow stronger. Push yourself beyond what you think you can handle, so that when they show up, you are ready. Turn your fear into a weapon that fuels and strengthens you. Wear it like armor. When they show up, because they will, take all that fear and inflict it upon them. Burn their world down around them until they have nothing left. Then, when those who hunt you lay in ruin, you will learn the fear they gave you is what gave you the strength to destroy them."

Azalea stared at him for a moment. "I . . . Thank you."

Kade nodded to her. She sat next to him, watching the soft white form of the waves dashing against the shore and listening to the calming, rushing sound it created. Thunder roared in the distance as storm clouds rolled over the horizon.

"So, your mom, you know, with a dragon? That's gotta be weird."

Kade rubbed his temple.

"You know, like . . . you know? When you turn into a human does—"

"This is not a conversation we are having."

"I'm just asking," Azalea protested.

"Don't."

Chapter 44

The Sapphire Sea

Shiv's ship was a massive three-deck galleon with red-gray sails and a dark wood hull. The ship looked masterfully crafted and was immaculately maintained. Rope ratlines like ladders allowed sailors to reach the masts and crow's nest. The figurehead at the front of the ship was an intricately carved dragon's head with its mouth open wide. The wood creaked as the ship bobbed in the water under the lift of the incoming tide.

A bulky elf with a long, black mohawk and tattoos covering his exposed arms stood on the railing of the deck, shouting out instructions. Elves were rushing in every direction—some loading crates, others adjusting lines, cleaning, or unloading supplies. The crew must have been at least two hundred strong. Even in the chaos, their movements looked coordinated and graceful. It was as if their bodies had no weight, and they were just gliding over the docks.

"Isn't she a beaut?" Shiv said, walking up behind them as they stood marveling at the massive sea vessel.

"That's not a ship, it's a floating fortress," Caelan said.

"Aye, you'll be glad for that when the storms come," Shiv grinned.

A line of elves pushed past them, carrying stacks of long, thick harpoons under their arms. They walked together, an elf at each end of the stack marching them up the plank and onto the ship. Small, square windows lined each side of the ship just under the main deck, and through the openings they could just see what appeared to be massive crossbows.

"What in the name of the gods are those?" Azalea asked, pointing to the square windows.

Shiv put his arm around her and smiled. "Those, my lovely dear, are elven ballistae. They fire those large bolts you see my men loading."

"And just what do you have to fire those at on water?" Celeste asked.

"Apart from the obvious—dragons, we use them for hunting and fighting off sea monsters and pirates."

"Sea . . . monsters?" Grom shifted his weight, looked visibly concerned.

Rivik laughed. "You love monsters."

Grom shook his head. "Not . . . water monsters."

Rivik seemed surprised. "What kinds do you see?"

"The most common are kraken, leviathan, sea serpents, deep fiends, merfolk, and drow," Shiv answered.

"Drow are real? I thought they were just legends," Dante said.

"What . . . drow?" Grom asked.

"Dark elves—nasty lot. They live at the bottom of the sea in their submerged kingdoms. Breathe underwater. Love massacring entire ships that sail into their territory . . . or just grabbing sailors off the edge and pulling them into the depths to drown," Shiv answered.

"Grom . . . no like . . . drow."

"Fear not, my trollish friend. You see those barrels there?" The elf pointed to a line of barrels hanging over the side of the ship, mounted horizontally and bound together by a line of rope.

Grom nodded.

"Those barrels are rigged to slowly drip Mangi powder into the water as we sail," Shiv laughed.

"Mangi powder?" Spiro asked.

"It's like a drow repellant. The buggers hate the stuff. A sprinkle of that in the water, any drow within a league of us will swim away screaming. See, mates, you got nothing to worry about. So long as your gold is good, ol' Shiv here will get ye where yer goin'."

The bulky elf with arm tattoos waved his arms back and forth until he caught Shiv's attention.

"All aboard. Next stop, Salamandri." Shiv glided effortlessly up the plank and onto the ship.

Kade and Dante stepped to the side, getting themselves out of the way.

"When you return, meet us at the Bounty of the Sea Inn," Kade instructed. "We will be waiting with the Glyphstone."

The group said their farewells to Dante and Kade before making their way onto the ship. Grom walked up to the plank and grunted before shaking his head and freezing in place.

"What's his problem?" Celeste asked, trying to push around him, but the large troll blocked the plank access completely.

"Trolls . . . not made for water . . . No float . . . No swim."

"Then don't fall in it," Celeste scolded.

"It's ok, Grom, we've got you." Sera put her hand reassuringly on the troll's shoulder.

"Sorry, lady . . . sea scary . . . Grom—"

"It's ok to be scared," Sera interrupted. "We all have things we are afraid of. Look at the size of this ship. You've got nothing to worry about, big guy. Besides, if somehow you end up in the water, I'll make Rivik dive in and fish you out." Sera smacked the troll playfully.

Grom grunted. "Grom . . . no like boat."

"Firstly, it's a ship. Secondly, if you can't handle it or you're too scared, stay here. We don't need to be holding your hand the whole time because you're worried about getting wet." Celeste rammed into the troll to move him out of her way and pushed past him, muttering under her breath something about a stupid troll.

"Grom . . . no stupid." Grom frowned.

"Don't listen to her." Rivik stepped to the other side of Grom. "You are a strong and brave warrior and a loyal friend. You've helped us so much. I'm not sure we'd have gotten this far without you and your mighty axes. Sera and I, we are in on this. We have to sail. You don't. We can part ways, or you can wait here for us to return. Keep the fire burning for us in the inn. It's up to you. We are not going to force you on a ship against your will. We won't think less of you if you choose to stay."

"He's right. If you want to stay here, no one will think badly of you," Sera nodded.

"No!" Grom folded his arms in front of his chest. "Grom . . . go with lady."

The troll stomped his way up the plank, his heavy body making the wooden beam creak from the strain.

The elf who had been shouting instructions to the crew moved in front of Ash before he could step off the plank onto the deck. He stared deep into Ash's eyes and planted his feet. Despite being taller, he wasn't as big as Ash, but compared to the other elves who were thin and long-limbed, he looked massive. Ash looked around until he saw Shiv walking over.

"*Thas nan ta polemiseis ochino?*" Shiv whispered to the muscular elf. The elf grinned and nodded.

"What is your name?" Shiv asked.

"Ash Hargrave."

"This is Mathias. He's my first mate and a practitioner of Valium Habatha Ashlowhe."

"I don't know what that is."

"It's an Elven fighting style," Shiv smiled.

"A fighter?" Ash raised an eyebrow, appraising the bulky elf more thoroughly.

"He would like to challenge you to a fight."

"That right? Why doesn't he just say so?" Ash smirked and cracked his knuckles.

"Mathias only speaks to the crew and people who he has fought in the circle."

"Is this really the best use of our time?" Celeste questioned.

"When, where, and what are the rules?" Ash looked Mathias up and down.

"After we leave the harbor. We do it here on the main deck. The crew loves watching Mathias fight."

Ash nodded in agreement, and Mathias smiled before moving out of the way.

A bell rang from the docks as Shiv's ship pulled away. The

ship bobbed as the waves lifted and lowered it while it departed. Elves were climbing up and down the shrouds, making adjustments and ensuring the sails deployed properly as they moved farther and farther from land. A whisking of wind propelled the galleon forward, and the mainland drifted farther and farther from sight.

Once the sails were set, the crew hurriedly gathered around the main deck. Shiv led Vale and the others to the wall of the quarterdeck so they could have an unhindered view. Elves were everywhere—leaning over the railing of the quarterdeck, hanging from the ratlines, lining both sides of the main deck, even sitting on the foreyard, cheering with wild excitement. Shiv drew a large, white circle in the middle of the ship with a piece of chalk before standing and lifting his hands to his crew.

"Naus Menalius, it is time; for your entertainment pleasure, one of our guests has graciously agreed to become Mathias's next victim." The elves roared with laughter and cheered so loud Shiv had to wait for them to stop before he could continue. "Allow me to introduce, Ash."

The elves booed and jeered.

"What did you get yourself into, chief?" Caelan asked.

Ash shrugged as he pulled off his gloves and tossed them to Caelan before stepping out into the middle of the deck. "No idea. He said it was a fight."

"You ready?" Shiv turned his attention to Ash.

"You haven't told me what I need to be ready for."

"Right. This is Elven Circle Boxing. Rules are simple: no weapons, no biting, and everything else is fair game. If your opponent taps, you stop—though you won't have to worry about that."

"Is that a fact?"

"Mathias has fought in over two hundred matches. He's never tapped once. Never lost for that matter."

Ash nodded approvingly. "Well, I've lost plenty. How do we know when the fight is over?"

"Every time your opponent steps out of the circle you get a point. The fight is over when one fighter gets to twelve points, one fighter taps out, or one fighter loses consciousness. Simple enough?"

"Stay in the circle. Don't get knocked out. Got it."

Mathias stepped inside the circle, and the elven onlookers roared with excitement. He squared off and raised his fists, gesturing for Ash to join him. Ash stepped into the ring but took no stance. He stared into Mathias's eyes while keeping his hands at his side.

"What's he doing?" Azalea whispered to Caelan.

"He's studying."

"Fight!" Shiv shouted.

Mathias's feet sprang to life as the large elf began bouncing. He moved quickly on his toes, bobbing gracefully from side to side, letting his arms sway a little as he moved. Ash stood perfectly still. Mathias stopped bobbing for a moment as his right foot planted. He twisted at his hips, and his fist drove straight for Ash's chest. Ash turned, and his hand came up in one quick motion, knocking Mathias's fist away. Mathias launched into a series of attacks, punching furiously at Ash who turned and blocked, deflecting one strike after another.

"Wouldn't it be easier if he stopped holding his hands down like that?" Azalea insisted.

"It would," Caelan answered.

"So why doesn't he?"

"He will. Just . . . watch."

Mathias jabbed. Ash blocked it. Before Ash could react, Mathias's foot slammed into his chest, knocking him back enough for him to step out of the circle.

"One point, Mathias," Shiv called out.

Mathias's movements were quick, yet powerful. Each motion led into another with minimal energy being wasted.

"You see what he's doing?" Caelan asked as the fight continued.

Azalea shook her head.

"He's timing his strikes. The elf bobs and bounces so he's ready to counter. He stays on his toes to sense the motion of the ship. Every time the ship moves enough that Ash has to shift his weight, he strikes."

"Mathias, nine. Ash, zero," Shiv called out.

"Why is he just letting himself get knocked around? He's barely thrown a punch. He's about to lose," Azalea questioned.

"Mathias has a form Ash has never encountered before. He's also used to fighting on a moving ship. Ash is not. He's learning how Mathias fights before engaging."

"Mathias, ten."

"Seven bells from seven hells, the fight's going to be over before he starts fighting back." Azalea folded her arms across her chest.

Ash stepped back into the circle, wiping a bit of blood from his lip. He grinned and finally lifted his hands. Mathias jabbed. Ash blocked and countered, striking the elf squarely in the face. Mathias attacked again, and again Ash blocked and struck him. This time Ash pressed it, driving his fists into the elf's chest in a fury of blows that sent the elf stumbling back.

The bulky elf planted his back foot, stopping himself just before he reached the edge of the circle, resulting in deafening cheers from the crew. Mathias swung a quick hook at Ash's jaw. Ash ducked and drove his fist in a rising uppercut that caught the elf under his chin and sent him off his feet. Mathias landed on his back, outside the circle. The crew went silent. Even the waves seemed hesitant to make a sound. Mathias groaned and rolled over. He tried to push himself up but stumbled back to the deck. Ash walked over and helped the elf up, supporting his weight. The elf, whose face was already showing signs of bruising, looked at Ash in disbelief.

"You . . . hit hard," he managed to get out.

Ash laughed and helped Mathias to a bench along the wall. The elves applauded in delight at the unexpected turn of events. With the fight over, they dispersed, getting back to their duties.

"Quite the show." Shiv walked over to Ash and shook his hand. "Welcome aboard The Moonslit Maiden."

Rather than using the stairs, Shiv leapt impressively high, grabbing the railing of the quarterdeck and pulling himself up and out of sight.

While the others got settled in, Ash and Mathias were leaning against the railing of the forecastle deck, Ash watching the sea and Mathias turned facing the ship. The two spent most of the day talking about fighting. Mathias's eyes glowed with excitement as they discussed different techniques and strategies. Spiro stood not far off, staring out at the waters, appearing lost in his thoughts.

"You are not like other fighters," Mathias remarked. "Don't say it's because you're human. I've fought humans. Lots of them. There's something different about you. The denseness of your bones, the thickness of your skin, even your heartbeat is different."

"I've heard rumors of the heightened elven senses. First time I've ever fought one, though," Ash chuckled.

"So, it is true? You're not like other humans."

"Not exactly, no. I'm from the Dunamai clan."

Mathias laughed. Ash didn't.

Matthias's eyes narrowed. "That's not possible. They died out centuries ago."

"Most did, yes. But a few of us survived," Ash nodded.

"The Dunamai?" Spiro interrupted. "I've heard stories about them, but they were always shrouded in mystery. Not a single tome ever said what they were."

"Legend has it that long ago, the gods desired champions of great power who would fight for their honor and glory. So, the gods mated with humans and formed the Dunamai clan. Just as the gods intended, their children were incredibly powerful. What the gods did not expect is that they would also be incredibly fruitful. The Dunamai grew from a small band to one of the largest empires in the world. As their power and numbers flourished, none could oppose them. The gods began to fear what they had created. They could not take the power away from the living Dunamai, but they could weaken their offspring. Their goal was to use frailty magic to diminish the power of the children, so that with every generation, the Dunamai would get weaker until they were no different from any other human. They overcorrected. Dunamai children were born so weak that a simple fall could prove fatal. They broke easily and healed slowly. It took less than a generation for the Dunamai empire to fall."

"Then how is he—" Spiro started.

"The gods cast layers and layers of frailty on the Dunamai seed. But every time the child survived a struggle, one of those layers broke. Like a lizard shedding its skin, when a Dunamai gets hurt enough, a layer of the enchantment that weakens them breaks, and they become a little more like the demigods they truly are. What intrigues me is how you survived." Mathias turned his attention back to Ash.

"You see the archer in the green cloak?" Ash gestured to Caelan.

Mathias nodded.

"He found me beat up and near death when we were kids. Growing up on the streets, most people don't take notice, but he did. He nursed me back to health. He was starving, himself, but he shared his food, looked out for me, and whenever trouble came, he was right there with me. Each time, after the fight was over, I was a little different, a little stronger."

"You went from too frail to survive to this?" Matthias chuckled.

"We fought a lot. Before long, I wasn't getting pushed; I was doing the pushing."

"Friends like that are not common."

"No, they are not," Ash agreed.

When their conversation died down, Ash politely excused himself and turned in for the night.

Azalea, Spiro, and Ash spent the days in the warm sun, laughing, relaxing, staring out at the endless sapphire sea. There was something humbling and yet comforting about the vastness of the waters. Caelan lived in the crow's nest, driving the elven sailor mad with his incessant talking. Vale sat on the top deck over the captain's quarters, watching over everyone. Rivik kept sneaking out onto the figurehead, sitting where he could feel the full breeze and the mist of the salt water until one of the crew would find him and scold him until he returned to the main deck.

Grom remained in the room below, finding some comfort in not being able to see the water that surrounded them. Even though he insisted he was a brave troll who would not let the waters stop him, Sera made sure to check on him a few times a day. After a few days, she even tried to encourage him to get some fresh air, but that was a bridge too far.

That night, as the group settled into their bunks, a loud commotion came from above. Elves rushed past their rooms in a frantic, chaotic sprint to get up the stairs. Vale grabbed one of the passing elves.

"What's going on?" he asked.

"Drow. They are on the ship," the elf replied before tugging himself away and rushing up and out of view.

Quickly, they gathered their weapons and followed. Grom excitedly grabbed his axes but then stopped at the door, looking nervous to leave the safety of his room.

"It's ok, big fella, we got this. You stay here," Rivik nodded.

Grom bit his lip and grunted. "Water . . . scary."

"Don't worry, I'll kill plenty of drow for us both."

Grom growled. "Grom . . . no let little man . . . have all fun."

Rivik smiled brightly. "Let's go, then. And don't worry—you get knocked into the water, I'll be right after to get you out," Rivik promised.

Grom nodded and followed them up the stairs.

The moon was bright and full, providing ample light to see the chaos that surrounded them. The sea elves were entangled with the drow attackers. The drow looked remarkably like the elves from their ship. Their skin was darker and their hair was as silver as pure ore but apart from that, they were indistinguishable.

The drow had greater numbers but were not as skilled. Most of the sea elves were successfully repelling three or even four drow at a time. That wouldn't matter as long as the seemingly endless drow forces continued to climb over the side of the ship and join the fray. Caelan climbed quickly from the deck to one of the nests where he could fire his arrows without being harassed.

Rivik ran up one side of the ship, Vale the other, helping cut down drow as they tried to climb aboard. Sera, Ash, Celeste, and Spiro went in different directions, taking on groupings of drow to help support the elves already caught up in the fight.

Grom was so excited he forgot he was on a ship. He charged like a berserker into the largest groupings of drow he could find and sent them flying as his axes whirled and sliced through the air.

Azalea stood near the stairs leading down to the ship below. Bursts of fire launched from her hands. Clusters of magical arrows rained down on groups of drow, magical vines grabbed, winds blew, and drow flew from the ship. They fought hard and effectively. The drow were relentless, the numbers seemingly endless.

Vale cut down drow left and right. For each one he killed, three more appeared. He glanced over the edge of the ship to see its sides covered in drow, climbing from the water toward them. At the front of the ship, he saw Shiv, the captain's knives whirling in silver streaks, slicing through drow with each cut. Vale worked his way toward the elf captain until they stood back-to-back.

"I thought you had this under control." His words rang out like an accusation.

"We did. I have no idea how this happened. You can bet that when it's over, I'm gonna find out," Shiv promised.

"They just keep coming. Got any ideas?" Vale asked.

"If we can get the Mangi powder into the water, the drow still in it will flee."

"And the ones not in the water?"

Shiv shrugged. "They flee or we kill them. Either way, it'll put a stop to this endless wave."

"Break one of the barrels?" Vale confirmed.

"As long as it pours into the sea, it'll work."

Vale ducked down and drove his blade into an attacking drow. He pushed the dark elf back, knocking his body into another drow who had just climbed aboard, sending them both tumbling into the sea. He fought his way alongside the edge of the ship, trying to think of how to get down to the barrels below. He realized that he didn't need to reach them, just puncture one enough that the powder would flow out.

"Azalea!" Vale shouted.

Azalea made her way toward him. It took a minute as she continually had to blast drow out of her path.

"What?" she asked.

"We need to put a hole in the bottom of one of those barrels." Vale pointed at the barrels on the side of the ship below them.

"You called me over here to tell me that?"

"Can you do it?"

Azalea rolled her eyes. "I'm a shape-shifting fire witch who's a vessel designed to hold one of the most powerful beings from the Spirit Realm who wants to use me to become a living god . . . but no, my abilities end just before putting a hole in a wooden barrel."

"Maybe less talking and more doing?" Rivik shouted as he threw a drow over his shoulder and ran him through with his spear.

"I need a knife," Azalea said.

"Take mine." Sera tossed the blade through the air. To Vale's surprise, Azalea caught it.

The red-headed witch jumped over the edge of the ship. Her body was surrounded by a purple light as her form changed into a hawk. She swooped down, dagger held in her claws. She dropped below the barrels before climbing out of her descent. Her wings flapped, and the dagger thumped into the wooden barrel. She tugged it back and flew out of the way as a buttermilk-yellow powder began to spill into the sea below.

The churning of water from the constant stream of drow dissipated. The drow climbing the side of the ship shrieked and dove back into the water, swimming out of view into the dark depths of the sea.

Without the constant waves of reinforcements, many of the drow gave up the fight, diving overboard. The ones that remained didn't last long. After the last drow fell, Matthias led the sea elves in removing their bodies from the ship and taking account of any losses or damage.

Shiv and a group of elven guards walked over to where Vale and the others had gathered.

"Thank ye for your assistance." His tone sounded irritated.

Vale nodded. "Something bothering you?"

"Aye, mate, it is. Something isn't settlin' right. See, we live on the sea. Those barrels are checked by five different crew members every time we dock to make sure they will work properly. All five of them confirmed the barrels were operating before we left the harbor."

"You think someone sabotaged it?" Rivik asked.

Shiv nodded. "I'm quite certain of it, mate. But who and why?"

"Do you have any new crew members?" Vale asked.

"It's not me crew, I can assure you of that. I've known each of them for longer than you lot have been alive. We don't operate that way."

"You think it was one of us?" Sera sounded surprised.

"Be a mighty strange coincidence if not."

"There's no way any one of us would have done that," Vale started.

"I'm thinkin' it was this one." He gestured at Celeste.

"Me?" Celeste gasped in alarm. "I have more invested in this than anyone. I would never! You're a greedy mercenary that cares about nothing but money; how do we know someone didn't pay you to do it?" Her face ran red.

"Oi, that space between your ears just for decoration?" Shiv challenged.

"What?"

"Think, mate. Why on the shinin' blue sea would I sabotage me own ship? If I was gonna take you out, I wouldn't use the drow to do it. I'd just bleedin' toss you into the sea and watch it pull you into its depths."

"It's not Celeste. She wouldn't," Vale started.

"That's funny, cuz me crew saw your girl here leaning over the side of the boat, acting all suspicious like. Care to explain that?"

Chapter 45
Calladun

As the ship disappeared over the horizon, Kade and Dante remained. They stood in silence as they watched, basking in the grandness of the world in front of them. There was something calming, as if the waters had magical relaxation properties. For a moment they enjoyed a brief escape from the weight of their quest.

"It's time." Kade stepped away from the edge of the dock.

"You have not told me anything about where we are going or what we are doing." Dante folded his arms across his chest.

"That's not true. I told you we are going to get the Glyphstone," Kade grinned.

"I need more than that."

"I'll tell you more when we get there."

"That does not work for me. You can tell me more now, or we can stay here. I am not going anywhere until you tell me what we're doing."

A soft, sizzling sound hissed just behind Dante's back. He glanced over his shoulder to see a colorless, magical door with a glowing orange trim. Kade smiled and stepped in front of Dante, placing the Blue Alchemist between himself and the portal.

"No. Do not do it." Dante shook his head.

Kade lifted his hand slowly and waved. Before Dante could react, a burst of energy struck him, knocking him backwards. It wasn't a massive force, just enough to propel him into the air and through the portal.

In an instant, Dante was transported into a dark, damp underground passageway. Water dripped in the distance, the sound echoing down the hallway in measured time. The hallway's cool, undecorated stone walls were broken up periodically by openings covered by iron bars. Mold and chartreuse vegetation were sprinkled down the walls, offering a splash of color in the dull torch light.

"You rotten naiflo, where are we?" Dante protested.

"The only place I know that has a Glyphstone."

"An old dungeon?"

"Not just any old dungeon. This is Calladun."

"Calladun? Are you mad? You brought us to the fortress stronghold of the Order of Dragon Knights?" Dante questioned.

"Unless you know a better way to obtain a Glyphstone."

"Why does a group of dragon knights have a Glyphstone in their dungeon?"

"They don't. It's in the vault on the far side of their stronghold."

"Let me get this straight. Your plan is to walk through the dragon knight's headquarters, in a fortress filled with men and women who have devoted their lives to hunting and killing dragons, which, in fact, you are. Then walk into their vault, where presumably they keep their most valuable treasure under constant watch in order to get this Glyphstone in the hopes that they . . . do not notice you are a dragon?"

"Why do you think I brought you here?" Kade smirked.

Dante furrowed his brow for a moment before it dawned on him. "You want me to glamour you to look like someone else?"

"Not just anyone. Spiro."

"No one would look twice at a dragon knight and a mage walking through the halls." Dante nodded approvingly and reached into his cloak. He pulled out a vial and handed it to Kade who drank it without question.

"How long does it take to kick in?"

"A few minutes. Question: if the Glyphstone is in the vault, why did you bring us to the dungeon?" Dante asked.

"The first rule of teleportation: you can only go where you have first been."

"What were you doing in a dragon knight dungeon?"

"I was a guest here for a season."

"A season?"

"About a decade." Kade's form began to shift. His size, armor, hair, everything, pulsed with light. When the light faded, the man standing before Dante no longer looked like Kade.

"Well?" Kade turned. "Is it done?" Even his voice sounded like Spiro.

Dante nodded. "You certainly look the part. Even still, I imagine they are not just going to hand the Glyphstone over. Do you have a plan to get us out of here?"

Kade pointed behind Dante to the still-open portal. "Once we have the Glyphstone, we need to get back here."

"That will take us back?"

"So long as I can hold it open, yes."

"I thought you couldn't teleport into the Dragon Lands," Dante questioned.

"You can't. You can teleport out, so long as you don't close the portal..."

Kade made his way down the hall toward the stone stairs at the other side. The stronghold was a massive fortress built into the side of a mountain. A single narrow path climbed from the ground below to the front gate at a steep angle. A few fighters could defend the gate without difficulty. With a few siege weapons, which Dante assumed they had, a dozen men could repel an entire army. The walls were lined with more towers than any castle, keep, or barracks Dante had ever seen. Each tower contained a massive ballista, armed and ready to fire. Just inside the gate was a large, open courtyard filled with dragon knight trainees who were practicing their forms while an instructor issued a series of commands and subsequent insults.

Knights holding large halberds, spears, and lances were posted all along the wall, eyes fixed on the skies. Dante didn't notice it at first, but dragon heads were carved into the stone over every doorway. Dragon skulls were used as decorations along the upper walls. Kade turned to the right and led them down an exterior walkway. To their left were open skies broken up by thick arches. To the right was a tall wall littered with occasional doors that provided access to unseen rooms tunneled into the rock of the mountain itself. Kade pulled a pouch from his belt and loosened the thin string. He turned it over, and a fine, gray powder poured out as he walked.

"What is that?" Dante asked quietly.

"Something for later," Kade whispered.

Dante kept quiet, following Kade and trying to draw as little attention as possible. Thankfully, most of the dragon knights seemed preoccupied with other things, allowing them to make their way quickly and undisturbed. The vault was in the back of the fortress, built into the main formation of the mountain. The exterior walkway led them to a large set of double doors big enough to fit a full-grown dragon. As they approached, Dante could see the intricacy of the doors. They were made with wood, reinforced with iron, and inlaid with gold and silver trimming. They looked both solid and regal.

A single guard stood at either side of the impractically massive doors. To one side, Dante saw a single, regular-sized door that blended almost perfectly into the wall. Kade walked to the door without saying a word.

"Halt. What are you doing?" One of the guards turned and stomped over, peering at them through the slits in his helmet.

Kade turned to face him, remaining silent.

"You have failed to identify yourself. State your—"

A blue smoke wafted around the guard, and his body swayed for a moment before going limp. The other guard turned, his long halberd pointing toward them. Another puff of blue smoke rose, and the second guard dropped.

Kade looked at him, and Dante shrugged. "You didn't have an answer for that."

The great hall inside made the impractical size of the doors seem lackluster by comparison. The walls stretched as high as any palace, and entire dragon skeletons were staged and hung as if flying across the ceiling. Murals of knights battling dragons were painted along every wall. The center of the room was a flat walkway with steps leading up to raised floors on either side.

The elevated floors were lined with rows and rows of tables, each surrounded by sturdy wooden chairs.

At the end of the hall was another elevated floor, this one higher than the ones on the sides. Seven chairs lined this platform, one for each of the Dragon Lords. The seven chairs faced the rest of the massive chamber as they looked over the room. On either side of the chairs, along the back wall, was a door.

"Fortunate the hall is empty," Dante remarked. "Which way?"

"The vault is through the door to the right." Kade led as they moved quickly through the massive hall.

Even with a glamour in place, there was something unnerving about being in the center of the Order of Dragon Knights' base of operations. The door at the back was unlocked and unguarded. It opened to a long hallway with several rooms on either side. At the end of the hallway was a staircase leading down. As they walked quietly down the stairs, they could see at the bottom was a wide door in the middle of a thick stone wall. Two guards stood at attention on either side.

Dante retrieved two glass vials from his cloak and tossed them down the steps. Blue smoke filled the air and the guards slumped to the ground in a deep sleep. Unlike the previous door, this one was locked. Careful search of the unconscious guards revealed a key. Inside, they found themselves in a second room, this one with a thick metal door that had a series of dragons painted on its surface. The dragons were laid out like a lineage tree, and each had a hole in the center, making it difficult to tell what sort of dragon it was.

"This must be the vault door, but there is no keyhole." Kade looked around.

"That is not entirely true. There are many keyholes. This appears to be a Araciomatic Seal." Dante wagged his finger in the air.

"A what?"

"It is like an enchanted lock. The key comes from knowing the right combination." Dante pointed to the wall. "See those glowing pegs?"

Kade nodded.

"What is the first thing you notice?"

Kade stared for a moment. "There are a lot of them."

"That, and they just so happen to match the colors of each different type of dragon. It is clever really; a dragon knight vault that can only be accessed by someone who knows the dragon knight hierarchy of dragons. In theory, if we put the pegs in the right places, the door should unlock."

"Good work, wizard." Kade walked over and grabbed a group of the glowing glass pegs. He placed the silver and gold pegs on the top two holes. A loud clicking sound echoed around them, and he could hear unseen gears moving. Kade grabbed another stack, placing them in the second, third, and fourth tiers. When he grabbed the last one, he put it in the final slot. Nothing happened.

"Something is wrong," Kade said.

Dante stared at the wall. "No, that has to be it. What criteria did you use to arrange them?"

"Power—strongest on top, weakest on the bottom. What other way could you organize it?"

Dante rubbed his chin.

"We don't have time for this; I'll just smash the door in."

"If you do that, you might as well announce to the whole keep that we are here, which will make getting back to the portal much more difficult," Dante said.

"We can't just stand here and wait for the guards to wake up."

Every passing second oozed along at a painfully slow pace. From the hall above, they could hear voices echoing.

Dante snapped his fingers. "I've got it. Did you arrange them by actual power or by understood power?"

Kade furrowed his brow. "What do you mean?"

"You are a dragon. You know better than most which dragons are stronger than others. This lock was made by dragon knights. Do they mistakenly believe one type of dragon is stronger or weaker than they are?"

Kade smiled and pulled the green peg out of one spot and switched it with the brown one. Gears clicked, and the door slowly wheeled out of the way, tucking into a groove in the wall.

The vault was not just one big room, it was a series of rooms connected to a long hallway. Each room was labeled and well organized—a testament to the discipline of the dragon knights. One of the rooms bore the label: Magical Stones and Objects. Kade stepped inside it. A moment later, he walked out with a sealed golden box.

"That is it?" Dante asked.

"This is it."

Dante extended his hand. "I will take it."

Kade reluctantly handed it over, and Dante slipped the large stone into his cloak. Kade stared at him, expecting to see his cloak dip or bulge from the weight and size of the Glyphstone. It did neither. They made their way out and back up the stairs into the hall, which was no longer empty. A large group of knights were funneling into the large doors and parting as they made their way to the tables on the upper floors.

"You got this?" Dante asked.

"Need to focus on keeping the portal open," Kade replied.

Dante groaned and reached into his cloak. He pulled out two vials and handed one to Kade. "Drink."

"What is it?"

Dante ignored the question and drank his vial, waiting for Kade to do the same. Time slowed, then came to a stop. The knights filing in were all frozen in place as if they were no more than a painting. The chaotic cacophony of their many simultaneous conversations was suddenly quieted.

Dante walked at a hurried pace. Kade followed suit. The potion made them speed so quickly that time itself seemed to stop. It was very effective, but it would not last long. They managed to squeeze their way through the crowd of knights and made it out the door and back toward the walkway. Not wasting a step, they started back toward the dungeon where their portal was waiting. No sooner did they reach the turn in the walkway than time returned to its normal, unforgiving march. And time was the least of their problems.

At the center of the path leading back to the dungeon, a group of several dragon knights stood in their way. In the middle was a taller knight whose armor looked like much higher quality.

He was clearly a ranking officer of some kind. Dante's mind raced. *Was it better to stop? Turn around? Keep moving and hope the knights wouldn't respond?*

The officer looked at them and walked over. "What are you doing? All dragon knights were instructed to make their way to the hall without delay. You are going in the wrong direction."

"Of course, we just needed to grab something really quickly," Dante started.

The tall dragon knight waved his hand in the air, and a group of other knights rushed behind them, cutting off their escape.

"Do you know who I am?" the knight in regal armor asked.

Dante shook his head.

"I am Dragon Knight Commander Richmond Steele. I am the highest-ranking dragon knight under the seven dragon lords. Yet, I was not informed of any mages visiting our keep. It seems you two have some explaining to do."

Dante and Kade exchanged a glance.

"Commander, I think perhaps—"

"Sorry, why don't you start by explaining to me why you were running away from the hall?" He nodded, and the knights behind them grabbed them, holding their arms back.

"Commander Steele, the mage is with me. I can vouch for him."

"Can you? And who are you?"

"My name is Spiro, sir, I am a dragon—"

"There are no dragon knights by that name, so don't even start." Commander Richmond turned to the knight next to him. "Inform Lord Ludric that I have found the source of our missing items. We've been looking for the thief stealing from our vault for weeks."

"Commander, we are not thieves. I can prove it," Dante pleaded.

"I'm sure you can."

"If we were running, as you suspect, and had stolen something, you would have seen us discard it, right?" Dante asked.

Commander Richmond's eyes narrowed. "What's your point?"

"Search us. If we are thieves, we must have stolen something.

Shadows of the Dark Realm

If we did not discard it, then whatever we stole would still be on our persons."

The Commander nodded again, and the dragon knights spun Kade and Dante around, patting them down. They reached inside Dante's cloak and, to Kade's surprise, found nothing.

"They are clear, Commander."

"Well, you are up to something. I can sense it. Until I figure out what, you won't be going anywhere," Commander Richmond sneered.

A loud screech echoed overhead.

"Dragons!" a voice cried out. A moment later, a loud bell, like a call to arms, rang out.

The sky was filled with dozens of dragons flying toward the fortress. One flew along the outer wall, breathing a wave of fire down. Knights scrambled out of the way; ballistae fired their missiles into the air. Chaos broke out all around the fortress. Several of the knights who'd been holding them let go and charged down the walkway toward the front of the base. Commander Richmond glared at them before grunting and doing the same.

Kade and Dante rushed down the walkway. Lost in the chaos, they moved unimpeded. When they reached the stairway to the dungeon, they veered off, racing down the steps to the still-open portal. They rushed through it without looking back and were returned to the docks in Stormdale. Kade closed the portal immediately before kneeling over to catch his breath.

"The powder?" Dante asked.

"Drakokine."

"You have been walking around this whole time with dragon lure just hanging from your belt?" Dante chuckled.

"Can you think of a better way to divert the attention of a keep full of dragon knights?"

Dante shook his head.

"Give me the Glyphstone," Kade commanded.

Dante reached into his cloak, pulled out the stone, and handed it back to Kade.

"Your cloak . . ."

Dante grinned. "I am honestly surprised it took someone this long to notice."

"Kratimas Cloak?" Kade asked.

Dante nodded again and pulled his cloak open, revealing what appeared to be nothing more than blue fabric. He reached his hand in, and his hand seemed to disappear. Kade stepped in to get a closer look.

"Incredible. How does it work?"

"It is similar to a bag of holding. The pocket is magically linked to my lab. When I reach in, whatever I think of—so long as it is in my lab—will appear in my hand."

"That's why you always seem to have the right item for any situation," Kade confirmed.

"Yes. I spent years brewing different potions and spells to fill my lab so I would be ready for any situation."

"You have powerful magic; why rely so much on concoctions?"

"There is so much untapped potential in humanity. I want to help advance us so that we can continue to thrive. I have devoted my life to the advancement of knowledge. Through potions, I can develop recipes that anyone can replicate. Where I use magic for my own purposes, my creations will endure long after I am gone."

"I see. Head back to the inn. I have something I must attend to before the others return."

Dante peered into Kade's eyes. "Is it what I think it is?"

Kade nodded.

"I am coming with you."

Chapter 46

The Volkili Prismward

Tension was thick in the air as the elves tightened their grips on their harpoons. One wrong move could set off a storm of trouble. Vale slowed his breathing, letting his hand move toward his sword as slowly and smoothly as possible.

Celeste glared, her face red. "Leaning over the edge? That's why you accuse me? And I'm the one with an empty head? You pointy-eared knave! I have never been on a boat before, not to mention spent days with no land in view. The constant rocking makes my stomach turn. So, if you must know, I was throwing up. I didn't want to draw attention to myself, so I tried to be discreet about it. I was leaning over the edge to try and keep your emptos ship clean. Or would you have preferred I just spray it all over your deck?"

Shiv's eyes narrowed as he stared at her suspiciously. "Well, isn't that just—"

"Captain." An elf rushed over, holding something in his hand.

"What is it?" Shiv turned to face the oncoming elf.

"We found what caused the blockage." He held out his hand to reveal a large, dead rat. "Must have made his way down the line, crawled into the hole and gotten stuck."

Shiv picked up the rat and examined it. He closed his eyes and sighed.

"That explains that. Apologies for the assumption." He forced the words out without feeling, making them sound flat and disingenuous.

"How, captain? We've never had rats try to get into the barrels before," the elf asked.

Shiv lifted the rat and moved its fur with his fingers. "Seems some of our friend's regurgitated dinner ended up on the barrel, and the smell lured the rat down." Shiv shook his head and hurled the rat over the edge of the ship. "It was an unfortunate accident, nothing more."

"So now you believe me?" Celeste asked.

"Now that there's evidence to support your claim, yeah, I do," he shrugged.

"Well, aren't you charming?" Celeste growled.

"Charming costs extra, sweetheart. Why don't you get some rest? Sorry for the trouble; it won't happen again."

The group retired without complaint. The next day they learned that eleven of the elven crew had been killed in the drow attack. Their bodies were wrapped in kelp leaves and floated out to sea as the remaining crew sang sweet-sounding melodies in their elvish tongue. Though no one outside of the crew understood the words, the sound of their songs was such a lamenting harmony that it drew the mind towards the deeper thoughts of life.

When the songs were finished, the day passed in somber silence, an honor to the lives of those lost. The soft, blue sky began to darken. Clouds rumbled in the distance. The pattering of rain danced along the deck as a chill washed over them. The cool breeze did nothing to relieve the growing tension that hovered over the ship.

Vale and the others, save Grom, gathered on the quarterdeck. Shiv had informed them they were getting close. Something about his expression was strange. The confident playfulness that normally exuded from his presence had gone cold and grim.

"Storm's coming," Spiro said as he moved closer to the helm.

Shiv stood at the helm, one hand resting lazily on the wheel.

He stared off into the distance, failing to respond or even acknowledge Spiro's presence.

"What is it?" Vale asked, walking up on the other side.

"Something isn't right. I got a bad feeling," Shiv answered.

It was strange for a seasoned sailor to express such a concern. Especially considering that of all the dangers, the journey had been relatively uneventful. They'd seen some merfolk in the distance leaping out of the water as they swam but no monsters. No issues. *What was it that had disturbed the sea elf?* Vale looked around, suddenly feeling uneasy. It was like there was a presence on the wind, something watching them but out of sight.

"What's that?" Spiro pointed into the distance.

"I don't see anything," Vale replied.

"Oh. Must have just been a shadow. Guess the weather got me a little spooked," Spiro answered, waving it off.

"No," Shiv said, turning to Spiro. "There was something there. It was faint, subtle. I barely saw it."

"Oh, well see, there you go. Could you tell what it was?" Spiro asked.

Shiv nodded and turned to face Spiro. "I have questions."

"Questions?"

"Elves live on the sea. I spend more time out here than I do on land. I've been sailing these waters my entire life. I've seen a lot. You know what I've never seen? In all my time, in all my voyages, the one thing I've never seen?" Shiv asked.

Spiro shrugged. "What?"

"A dragon-less sky."

"What do you mean?"

"We are sailing in the Dragon Lands, where there are always dragons in the sky. Yet here we are. We've been sailing for days; I've not seen a one. Strange, don't you think?"

"Yeah, that does sound odd. What do you think it means?" Spiro's voice wavered, making him sound nervous.

"I didn't know what to think until just now when you saw something on the horizon."

"Me? What difference does that make?"

"Aye, you. Ye commented on it without thinking. Then you realized what you'd done."

"What are you talking about? You said you saw it too."

"I did, mate. What I find me-self wondering is, if I could barely see it, how did you see it at all?"

Spiro's voice hung for a moment in a soft, drawn-out groan.

"See, nothin's been quite right about this little voyage. The dragons are off, the drow ambush, your vision—and I can't shake the sense that there is something watching us, and you're hiding something," Shiv replied.

"What would I be hiding?" Spiro asked.

"I haven't the foggiest, but you could start by telling us how your vision is superior to that of the elves."

"You're being ridiculous," Spiro started.

Vale's hand drifted to the hilt of his sword. "Answer the question."

Spiro stepped back. "Are you serious? You're going to draw on me because I have good vision?"

"Good vision is one thing. No human sees that well," Shiv challenged. "How do you?"

"The same way I know that you ate squid yesterday, that there is a small tear in your topsail that whistles in the breeze, and that your crew tapped into the rum barrels last night after you went to sleep. I am a dragon knight."

"Can I shoot him in the face now?" Caelan asked.

"You'll have to explain that," Vale said.

"Oh, come on, let me shoot him. Just a little?"

Spiro rolled his eyes. "Dragons are fast, smart, and powerful. Do you think dragon knights fight them by training with a sword? All dragon knights undergo a ritual of transformation that strengthens our bodies, enhances our senses, speeds up our reactions. That is the only way any of us could contend with a dragon. So yes, I see better than other humans because the blood of dragons runs through my veins, as it does the veins of every dragon knight. Their blood strengthens us so we can take their lives."

"You lot are full of surprises. I hate surprises." Shiv closed his eyes and shook his head. "There is still something suspicious about all of this. If I find out ye got anything to do with it, ye'll be swimming back to Stormdale. Now, if you'll excuse me, I need to think." The elf captain pushed past them and climbed his way up to the crow's nest.

The next day the clouds were so thick that they blocked out the light of the sun so completely, it was difficult to tell it was daytime. The darkness felt unnatural and only seemed to further enhance the growing tension on board. Tension gave way to relief when on the horizon the shadow of an island came into view. The island loomed like a great silhouette, growing larger as they moved closer.

A perfect patch of clear sky encircled the island, untouched by even the thinnest of clouds. The open sky caused the island to appear spotlighted by the sun itself. It was as if the sun broke the tension of distrust that had been growing between them.

"What sorcery is this?" Rivik asked, looking up.

"It's a veil," Shiv answered. "From a distance, the island seems shrouded in darkness. It is only in close proximity that the veil gives way."

"Why?" Ash questioned. "What's the point?"

"Pirates, drow, and a general desire to not have to fend off every ship and sailor who desires their riches or skills. The elves of Salamandri use magic to hide their island from view so that only those who know how to find it, can."

Salamandri's shore contained a large dock and was surrounded by elven fishing huts that ran all along the beach. A path led up to the tiered city, lined with houses and shops, all of which looked over the water. The path up was steep, leading to a large elven palace on one side and an arching elven temple on the other. Shiv guided his ship to the docks with the ease of a well-practiced sailor. When the ship was tied off, he stood on the plank leading to the dock below.

"I've sent one of my men ahead to gather the elven elders. He will send word when they are ready to meet with you. I hope you brought something good, or we came all this way for nothing." Shiv chuckled and moved aside.

Vale and the others gathered just off the docks, taking the opportunity to stretch their legs on solid ground. Grom laid down and extended his arms out, trying to hug the earth itself.

"I don't like it. It's duplicitous," Vale objected.

"Oh, get over yourself!" Celeste folded her arms in front her chest and huffed. "There's nothing moral or noble about letting some archaic code of honor doom an entire kingdom of death. We need it. If this is the best chance to get it, we have no choice."

"It's not just an ethical thing. It's risky," Sera countered.

"What isn't? If we ask and they say no, they will certainly increase their guard, making it that much harder," Rivik pressed.

"Grom . . . love . . . ground," the troll said to himself as he made little sand angels on the shore.

"Ultimately, the question is this: do we believe we can impress on a group of elves the gravity of the situation enough that they will offer us the Volkili Prismward?" Sera's question lingered on the air.

"Looks like we are stealing it," Rivik chuckled. Ash and Spiro agreed.

"So, who's doing what?" Azalea asked.

"Azalea and I will speak with the elders. Caelan, Rivik, and Sera will steal the Prismward once the session has started. Spiro, Celeste, Grom, and Ash—you will be our lookouts. You'll remain at the bottom of the hill. If something goes wrong, you charge in, help get us out, and we fall back to the ship," Vale instructed. "None of this will matter if we aren't prepared to leave. Shiv?"

The elf pirate looked up at the sky. "Sure, we offer expedited escape services. Costs extra though. If yer willing to pay, Shiv will find a way." He smiled brightly and headed back to his ship.

"I think we are forgetting one important thing," Sera started. "Even if we make it to the ship, and the ship is ready, how do we get out of the harbor before the elves are upon us?"

"Why doesn't Shiv just sail out? He can wait offshore; we'll use a couple dinghies to row to the ship and go from there," Celeste suggested.

Sera shook her head. "If Shiv takes the ship away from the dock after having just arrived and with us still being here, it will raise suspicion. That's not to mention the range of the archers or the defensive weapons they have in those towers there." Sera gestured to several towers built up the side of the mountain around beach cover that were certainly equipped with something to fend off hostile ships.

"Leave that to me," Azalea said.

"Care to elaborate?" Sera asked.

"Not really," Azalea smiled.

"Right then. So, Azalea will magically solve the ship problem after we go steal the thing. Here's my question: anyone have any idea what a Vorklali Pagomwap looks like? How do we know if we find it? I assume it's not labeled." Caelan shrugged.

"You've never seen a prismward before?" Azalea laughed.

"Ok, Azalea, you're with Caelan; Celeste, you're with me," Vale smiled.

"Once we have the thing, Azalea will send up a signal so you'll know it's time to go," Caelan added.

After a long period of waiting, two blonde elves with long, braided hair and elegant, flowing robes that were impractically long and obnoxiously ornate, descended the path toward the docks. Their movement looked as effortless as the breeze. They walked with their hands behind their backs and their chins turned up. Caelan immediately hated them.

"Welcome to the Holy City, Salamandir. You are all welcome here, provided you can keep your beast on its best behavior." One of them gestured to Grom. Sera closed her eyes and let out a long slow breath to steel her nerves.

"Grom behave . . . Grom not grab . . . rude little man . . . and use him . . . like toothpick. Troll . . . have . . . better manners . . . than elf." The troll smiled a big, toothy grin.

The pair of elves looked annoyed. They exchanged a glance with each other before moving on. "We have been told you traveled a great distance to make a request of us. It would be rude for us not to hear you out. You may leave your weapons and your pet and follow us."

Vale and Celeste handed their swords to Ash and followed the elves up the hill toward the palace. Once they were out of sight, Caelan, Sera, Azalea, and Rivik snuck around to the outskirts of the town and made their way up the steep slope toward the temple.

Salamandir was a vision. The buildings were carved from a pure white wood. The city looked more like a work of art than a work of construction. Everything from the buildings to the walls, arches, and columns felt like part of the forest, making it difficult to tell where the woods ended and the city began. The whole area appeared organic and alive. Like the frills of a lace garment, intricately carved wooden vines decorated all the structures, giving them a sense of lightness. The details and the craftsmanship were unlike anything Vale had seen. The buildings were beautiful. They appeared both delicate and yet somehow sturdy and well-fortified. Unlike human construction, which used as many walls as possible, Salamandir was open, using walls only when necessary.

"I'm surprised you brought me," Celeste commented under her breath. "Everyone seems to prefer me out of sight and out of mind." There was a pettiness to her tone that agitated Vale.

"You are Royal. For once, I need you to act like it," he whispered. "Elves are an ancient race. I asked for you because I assumed you learned proper court behavior growing up. If you can contain your childishness and put that to use, you could actually help."

They crossed a bridge over a slow-moving stream of water that cascaded down the mountain and wove its way through the town that was built around it, maximizing the enchanting views of the stream. The water was the clearest blue Vale had ever seen. The air felt fresh and sweet. The songbirds sang cheery tunes. This was not a city; it was a dream.

The two elves guided them through the showcase of craftsmanship to a large hall. The hall, like most of the buildings, had no walls and provided a view of the sea from all sides as it looked down over the rest of the city like a watchtower. Beautifully carved columns encircled the space, each one topped with a thick, circular white stone. Whereas most human halls preferred square or rectangular forms, this was a large circle with an open roof that allowed full view of the sky.

Standing in a half circle along the far side of the hall were twelve elves. Each had long hair woven in elaborate braids. They looked regal and dignified as they held their chins high, arms behind their backs in their long, silver, silk robes.

"Greetings, travelers. I am Elder Arathoria, speaker for the council. I will admit your request has our curiosity piqued. It is

Shadows of the Dark Realm

rare that your kind seek out our shores. Rarer still to request an audience with us. Tell us, who are you, and what is your purpose in our city?"

"My name is Vale; I am a knight from Parisia. I am here, along with several of my companions, at the behest of King Alistar. We are Seekers of the Darkstone, on a quest to retrieve an object of power that can save our kingdom from destruction."

The Elder elf's eyes narrowed. "What is it you offer in exchange?"

Silence.

"Surely you have not come all this way to entreat on our good graces. You have no gifts, no offerings, no promises with which to share?" Arathoria sounded increasingly annoyed.

"We did not expect to be here. I am certain, however, if you would agree, that King Alistar would offer great compensation as thanks," Vale stammered. He'd rather face a small army than try to make negotiations.

"You violated the sanctity of our shores and the privacy of our people without invitation. Then you presume to seek our aid? Your lives are so short to be filled with such arrogance. We are aware of what has happened. Draka Mors's theft has put your kingdom in great peril. But I do not see what business this has with my people."

"Without the Darkstone, the veil between the realms will fall, and the Shadow King will return. Surely my noble lords and ladies can see how this affects us all," Vale said.

Arathoria smiled. "I see. Foolish mortals, you believe that the only way for the Darkstone to work is if it is in your possession. Your ignorance is truly profound."

"We have come for—" Vale started.

"My lords and ladies," Celeste interrupted with a warm smile as she bowed her head, her tone urgent, yet pleading. "You have an object that we need to complete our quest. We have risked much to journey here that we may call upon your good graces and beseech you to allow us to use this object."

"You seek the Volkili Prismward?" Arathoria raised an eyebrow. "And you came here, without invitation, because you thought we would just hand over one of our most precious relics to a group of humans because you asked nicely?"

"No. Not because we asked nicely. Even if the Darkstone could keep the Shadow King at bay somewhere else, our kingdom depends on it. Tens, even hundreds of thousands, of lives are at stake. The fate of an entire kingdom may depend on it," Celeste said.

"But not our kingdom."

"No," Celeste's brow furrowed. "Not your kingdom. But helping us costs nothing, while for us it means everything."

"Nothing costs nothing, my dear. To aid you in this quest would place all of Salamandir at risk."

"How exactly is that?" Celeste's formal tone began to slip.

Arathoria grinned an arrogant grin. "You seek the Darkstone but do not understand the stakes? How human of you."

"Perhaps my lady can explain it to us then?" Celeste's tone continued to deteriorate.

"Very well. The Dragon Lands are on the brink of war. Many are fed up with Bag'Thorak's rule. In fact, it has become clear there are more dragons against him than there are who support him. At this point, none would openly challenge the unkillable king of dragons, at least not while he is unkillable."

"What does that have to do with"—

"Draka Mors is not just an elder dragon. He is the usurper who leads a legion of rebel dragons. He seeks to become the king of dragons. Draka Mors plans to use the Darkstone to defeat Bag'Thorak. You see, he didn't just steal the stone to horde it in his roost. He stole it to start a war of dragons. You come here, seeking the means to take back the Darkstone. If we give you that means, we are taking sides. That is not something we can risk."

"But—"

"While you have our sympathy, you will not have our support."

A great emotional weight pressed down on them. What argument could be made? What plea could take hold in the face of such reality? Vale closed his eyes. The diplomatic approach was dead. All they could do now was buy more time.

"My lords and ladies, if you would but—" he started.

"Perhaps you do not understand. We are in the center of the Dragon Lands. Our community is strong and proud, but we are no match for an army of dragons. We survive precisely because we avoid entangling ourselves in their affairs. What you are asking of us is too much. If we give you the Prismward, and Draka Mors finds out, what do you imagine he will do?"

She let her question hang in the air for a moment. "I'll tell you—he will rain down fire upon us until there is nothing left of Salamandir but ash and dust."

"What if he didn't find out? We could put an end to this war, bring peace to the Dragon Lands. When it's done, we can return the Prismward to you, along with the gratitude of a great kingdom," Celeste pleaded.

"That is not an assurance you can offer. In a war of dragons, we are nothing more than insects to be stomped underfoot. Let us not mince words. You are asking not that we help save your kingdom but that we doom ours. I am afraid that even if we desired to help you, we cannot."

"My lady, I urge you to reconsider," Celeste blurted out.

"It will change nothing. Were our roles reversed, I am sure you would understand there is no choice here for us." Arathoria's smile seemed almost genuine.

"Surely there must be something we can do, some arrangement we can make," Vale pressed, more for time than for argument. Though he could sense the growing annoyance of the elves.

Arathoria sighed. "I regret to tell you that your journey here has been for naught. We can offer you our hospitality for the night but must insist you take your leave by morn. Even the presence of Seekers puts our people at risk."

Vale turned as he heard a small popping sound. A purple firework burst in the midday sky. The council of elders glanced up. Arathoria's gaze returned to them, anger flashing in her eyes.

"Guards! Seize them!" She pointed her finger, her voice flush with rage.

A pair of guards rushed in. Celeste darted past one and shoulder-checked the other, sending him toppling down the stone stairs to the floor of the hall below. Vale dodged elven steel meant to strike him down. He drove his fist into the guard's face and grabbed him, throwing his body into another pair of approaching guards.

Dodging where they could, Vale and Celeste rushed down the hill, weaving in and out of buildings as they sprinted down the path. The road was so steep, the faster they moved the harder it was to keep from toppling over and rolling down the hill. Elven guards rushed after them; others charged in from different places to investigate the commotion. Vale knocked over crates, tossed buckets, grabbed anything he could use to slow down the pursuant guards. Chaos enveloped them.

Farther down the hill, Vale could see Azalea's red hair. She was a good distance ahead and moving quickly. Shiv's elves were frantically rushing about the ship, making adjustments and preparing to leave. Grom stood at the edge of the dock, axes in hand, bouncing like an excited child. Arrows whistled by, striking trees, arches, and the ground. Caelan was missing on purpose, firing to give pause to their pursuers. It worked. Each arrow slowed one of the guards chasing them just long enough to keep them out of the elves' reach. The slope began to lessen as the ground leveled. The soft patter of elven boots echoed behind them, but the distance was too great. The ship was already untethered from the dock. Vale saw Azalea, Spiro, and Ash rush up the plank and onto the ship. Rivik waited for Sera to make it up before following. Grom refused to go, waiting until the last moment for the others to make it past him.

Finally, only Vale and Grom remained on the dock.

"Alright, witch, what's your plan?" Celeste shouted.

"Grom, let's go . . ." Vale urged.

Grom lingered for a moment before following Vale up the plank. Once clear, the troll single-handedly pulled the plank up onto the ship. Alarms sounded. Vale could see movement in the defense towers. Elven archers lined the shore, positioning in even rows of perfect order. They drew back as one and held the tension in their bows.

A single elf in silver armor and a white cape stepped forward onto the docks.

"You cannot escape. Surrender yourselves now, return the

Prismward, and the council will show you mercy. Do not, and death will rain down upon you."

"Hey, Azalea, not to tell you how to do your thing or anything, but this would be a really great time to do, you know . . . something," Caelan smirked.

Azalea closed her eyes and extended her arms away from her body. Her feet slowly lifted off the deck. As she rose, the ship lifted out of the water and began to turn in place until it was facing away from the island.

"Fire!" shouted the elven commander in the white cape.

Arrows rose into the sky like a great wave of death. Azalea turned her head, and a great wind suddenly intercepted the arrows, blowing them away so they dropped harmlessly down the shoreline. She turned her head the other way, and the wind changed, this time striking not the arrows but the archers themselves. Elves toppled over one another as the force of the wind sent them tumbling and rolling across the ground.

The ship splashed and bobbed as it sank back down onto the water. A breeze immediately caught its sails. The great ship lurched and then rushed across the water, away from the shore. A large splash echoed around them as sea water sprayed over the deck. The elven catapults had fired, just missing their mark.

Azalea slowly lowered herself to the deck of the ship. A great piercing missile was hurdling toward them. Azalea lifted her arms, and a purple barrier of light engulfed the ship just before the missile crashed into it and deflected into the water with a splash.

"I don't know about you guys, but I knew she had it covered the whole time," Caelan grinned.

A slow clapping echoed from behind them. Sitting on the top of the captain's cabin was a smiling Valron.

"Very well done; I am so impressed."

Chapter 47

Caught

Azalea's hands emitted purple flames that ran up her arms as she turned to face him.

"Azalea," Caelan whispered.

"What?" she snapped.

"That's not a good idea."

"You have no idea what I've been through, what I endured, because of him. Don't try to stop me," Azalea growled.

"No, I just meant fire . . . on a ship made of flammable things and filled with flammable people is probably not the best idea," Caelan responded.

Valron held out his hands. "Whoa, whoa, whoa, why the hostility? What did I ever do to you?" He flashed a wicked grin.

"What do you want?" Vale asked through clenched teeth.

"What a thoughtful question; thank you for asking. I knew you cared." Valron crossed both his hands over his heart. "I'll admit I was frustrated with you, taking the Vas Noomi after I worked so hard to get her. All I want is to see my queen ascend to her throne. You keep getting in my way. But I can see you are guilt-ridden over it, so I will forgive you."

"You killed Aurora," Sera growled.

"Who?" Valron scratched his head. "Oh, you mean that girl from before? They all kind of bleed together after a while."

"I'm going to kill you," Sera glared.

Valron smiled. "It'll be fun to watch you try. Enough pleasantries. You know what I want."

Vale stepped in front of Azalea. "You know what our answer will be."

"Now, now, you haven't even heard my offer."

"I don't need to."

Valron ignored him. "Turn the girl over to me without resistance, and I may let you live."

Vale drew his blade. "You want her? You have to go through me."

"I thought I already did that. How is it you are still alive?"

"Come down here and find out."

"Vale!" Celeste scolded. "She's not worth it."

"Oh, ralk you, you stuck up royal naiflo!" Azalea snapped.

"It's one life against those of an entire kingdom. This is not a choice," Celeste urged.

"It's handing someone over for a fate worse than death. You are right; it's not a choice. As long as I draw breath, it's not happening."

"A simple enough remedy." Valron dropped down to the deck and walked toward Vale.

Vale charged. His sword swirled and danced with years of refined skill and experience. Each swing precise, and each missing its mark as Valron moved and dodged around it. At first, the man in the red and black armor seemed playful, like he was amused by the Black Swordsman's attacks. With each swing, Vale's attacks grew closer, making him work harder, until the amusement on Valron's face was replaced with frustration. He disappeared just as Vale's blade would have pierced his chest.

Valron appeared behind him, grabbing Vale's head, and snapping his neck. Vale's body dropped to the ground in a heap. Valron sighed and dusted his hands off.

"Problem solved. Anyone else want to stand in my way?" he asked with a confident grin.

Elves rushed onto the deck, forming a perfect circle around Valron, harpoons at the ready. Shiv stepped into the circle.

"I am the captain. You boarded my ship without my permission. You will regret this," Shiv started.

"You are for hire, are you not?" Valron turned to Shiv.

"If you can pay, Shiv will find a—"

"Stand down," Vale grunted, snapping his neck back and returning to his feet.

Valron cocked his head, and his jaw dropped open just a little. "How . . . are you—"

Vale grinned. "You're going to have to try harder."

With the elves circled around them, Vale and Valron continued their fight. Valron killed Vale again and again. Azalea watched in horror, her body frozen like a statue. She wanted to fight, to do something. She couldn't move. She could barely breathe. Her mind told her body to act but nothing happened. She just stared, powerless and afraid. Each time Vale died, he got back up and faced Valron. Each time, Valron grew more and more frustrated. Seeing Valron's frustration, Vale began to taunt him.

"Weak," Vale coughed, brushing off the wound in his chest.

Valron struck him down again.

"Honestly, have you ever killed someone before? You're really bad at it." Vale put all of his energy into imagining what Caelan would say. It was working. Valron's rage grew with every word Vale spoke. Vale would never admit it, but it was kind of fun, inciting someone to such fury.

Valron raged and killed him again.

"I'm not trying to criticize you, but it's starting to get embarrassing."

"Why won't you just die?!" Valron shouted.

Vale shrugged. "Performance issues? It happens. Don't beat yourself up about it."

Valron's eyes flashed, and his hands began to glow. Magic coursed through his veins. "I will turn you into dust. Let's see you come back from that."

Valron's hands lifted, and a light began to glow in front of them. Suddenly, his body jerked forward, and the glowing stopped. An arrow pierced his back just behind his shoulder. He grunted and turned.

"I do not know why you people keep making me say it, but nobody kills him but me." Caelan had already pulled back another arrow. He let it loose, and it whistled through the air. Valron snatched it in his hand. He laughed and then winced as the arrow pulled away and returned to Caelan's quiver, cutting his palm.

Sera lunged toward Valron. He stepped back and countered; his fist would have caught her in the chest if Rivik hadn't jumped in the way. Valron's strike sent Rivik flying. His body hit the wooden deck of the ship and slid down the half-wall railing with a thud. Ash grabbed Valron around the shoulders, squeezing him in a grappling hug. None of the others dared to move. Valron drove his head back into Ash's nose, and the big man released him. Valron flung Ash through the air, nearly casting him overboard.

"Cute, but pointless."

A black blade pierced his chest as Vale ran him through from behind. Valron winced. He drove his arm back and knocked Vale to the side. Without removing the blade, Valron grabbed Vale by his head and lifted him off the ground. Vale frantically grabbed at Valron's wrist, trying to break the hold as he screamed and writhed in pain.

"If you won't stay dead, I'll make your life an eternal anguish," Valron grinned.

"Let him go!" Azalea held up her hand and a purple ball of flame appeared in it.

"You think you can hurt me with that cute little fireball?" Valron laughed.

"No." She lifted her hand, placing the flame next to her temple, so close it nearly touched her skin. "But at this range, I could take my head clean off."

Valron's eyes went wide and his whole body visibly tensed.

"All the time, the work, the energy that went into preparing me to be the vessel for your stupid little naiflo queen—I wonder, what happens to all of that if I die? Do you think she needs my head attached for her ascension?" Azalea smiled.

"You wouldn't dare!" Valron's face flushed red with rage.

"The way I see it, I'm dead anyway. Either you take me, and she burns away my soul, or I end it here. At least this way, you lose."

Valron's breathing grew heavy. He opened his hand, and Vale hit the ground and stopped screaming.

"Very good." Azalea's eyes narrowed. "Here's what's going to happen next. You're going to go back to your master and tell her that you failed. Make sure you use your pouty face, so she doesn't get too angry."

"You're making a huge mistake," Valron warned.

"No, the mistake was yours. She picked the wrong vessel. If either of you come after me again—if I even see you again—I'll put a bolt of lightning through my brain so hard, the only thing she'll be able to use her precious little Vas Noomi for will be fertilizing her garden."

"I could stop you," Valron threatened.

"You could try, but what do you think your queen would say if she found out you were responsible for the destruction of the vessel she's waited so long for? I wonder what she would do to you." Azalea let the thought sit for a moment.

Valron didn't respond.

"That's what I thought. Be a good little doggy and run home to your master."

"This . . . is not over," Valron warned before disappearing in a burst of dark smoke.

* * *

When the ship docked at Stormdale, it was late in the evening. The stars were glimmering overhead as the light faded with each passing moment. Vale and the others disembarked, making their way to the Bounty of the Sea Inn to find Kade and Dante. Shiv informed them he would get the ship ready and restocked but that Kade needed to pay the tab before they'd be departing again.

The inn was surprisingly well-maintained and clean for being right off a port. Their rooms were waiting for them with spacious with comfortable beds, especially nice after sleeping on a swinging hammock for their sea journey. Vale was concerned when they discovered that neither Kade nor Dante had checked in yet, but, at the moment, he was too tired to do anything but collapse onto his bed.

"He's just going to sleep? We aren't even going to bother looking for them? What if—" Celeste started.

"I imagine getting killed over and over again can be tiring. Who knew?" Caelan replied.

"We need to find Kade and Dante so we can—"

"We," Caelan emphasized the word, "don't need to do anything. Ship won't be ready for a day or two. Dante is a big boy; he can handle himself and Kade, well . . . Get some sleep princess. You're bad enough when you're well rested; don't make us suffer you tired."

After a bit more protesting, Celeste finally gave it up and huffed off to her room and went to sleep.

It was well into the next day when Vale woke. His body ached, and his mind throbbed as if a legion of dwarves were forging steel inside his skull. He forced himself out of his bed and his room. He was surprised to discover he wasn't the last one up. He made his way down the stairs to a common eating area where the inn served breakfast. No sooner than he sat down did the door to the inn swing open. Shadowed figures stood in the blinding burst of sunlight as it poured in through the open door. Two men stepped inside as Vale's eyes adjusted.

"Good, you've arrived," Kade said as he walked over to the table where Vale was seated.

Vale's eyes jolted as he saw a third figure following behind them. He was small—small enough for Vale to have missed him at first glance. He was nothing more than a boy. Stalky frame, sturdy build, but he seemed short for his age. Vale's eyes grew as realization washed over him.

"Is that—" he started.

"Well, where have you two been? I'm surprised we got back before you." Celeste's boots thumped against the stairs as she descended. Her eyes moved down as she walked over. "Why do you have a kid with you?"

"Varric!" Ash shouted from the top of the stairs. The large man practically leapt from the second floor to the ground below in a single bound. He rushed over and slid on his knees across the floor.

The young boy stood frozen in place as Ash put his massive hand on the boy's back, kneeling in front of him.

"How do you know my name?" the boy asked sheepishly. His voice was so soft it could be chased away by a gentle breeze.

"I was friends with your father."

Varric's expression soured and he looked away.

"I'm sorry to tell you, he—"

"Died? Good. He was no father anyway."

Ash closed his eyes and let out a slow breath. "Listen, I know it's hard. I am sure you have a lot of strong feelings about him, but he loved you. Talked about you all the time. All he wanted to do was get back to you."

"He left me . . . to be sold. Just ran away. Did he tell you that? Did he tell you that I cried out for him as I watched him leave me behind to save himself?"

Ash nodded.

"What kind of father abandons his own son?"

Celeste knelt down, putting her face level with the young dwarf.

"Don't be too hard on him. I was there . . . when he died." She stared into the young half-dwarf's eyes. "He made a mistake. But he was doing everything he could to make it right. He was traveling through the countryside alone, which is very dangerous, going from town to town searching for you."

"He wouldn't have had to search if he hadn't left me." Varric crossed his arms and narrowed his eyes.

"I know. I also know how much he regretted it. He was so ashamed of himself for that. Owen might not have always been brave, but for as long as I knew him, he was trying. He was facing his fears and finding his courage, all because of you. He thought of nothing but you. He wanted to rescue you and be the father you deserved. Nothing would stop him."

Varric's disposition softened as his arms dropped back to his side. "W-w-what happened to him?"

"There was a fight. We found the man who had previously owned you. His thugs attacked us. I took him to safety to keep him out of the fray. We were supposed to hide until it was over. But he wouldn't. He wouldn't sit back with his son still in danger. He rushed ahead into a group of thugs with no weapon and no plan. He wanted to save you, to be brave for you. So, he almost got himself killed in a fight he had no hope of winning."

"Almost?" Caelan repeated quietly as his eyes narrowed.

Celeste looked back at him and glared before returning her attention to Varric. "He gave me a message for you."

Varric looked into Celeste's eyes as pools formed in the edges of his own. "W-what did he say?"

"He said, 'Tell my son . . . I didn't run away.' He made a mistake when he ran from you, but he died running back to you. That says it all, doesn't it?" Celeste smiled softly and patted Varric's shoulder.

"Why did you say—" Caelan started.

Celeste looked over at him, her eyes widening for a moment, then turning into a scowl. "It's not the time for your comments, Caelan. I'm trying to offer comfort to a boy who just lost his father," she stated, glaring.

Caelan shook his head. "Just a weird thing to say."

"Shut up about it!" Celeste let out a loud exacerbated exhale and stormed off, out of the inn and out of sight.

"What is wrong with her?" Dante asked.

Caelan shrugged. "Ralk if I know. She's going to be a problem."

"Sir?" Varric turned to Kade. "What happens to me now?"

"Why'd you do it? Don't take this wrong, but you don't seem the type to go out of your way to help some mortal you hardly know," Caelan interrupted.

"I'm surprised you have to ask. A half-breed boy, left alone in a world that despises him for what he is? There are not many who I can relate to, but that . . . " Kade shrugged.

"Still . . . "

"You can't change the past. Sometimes life gives you the opportunity to stop it from repeating itself."

"Philosophical dragon. What do you plan to do with the boy now? It's not like we can take him with us," Caelan pressed.

"We can't leave him here alone, either." Ash stood up.

"My attendant, Ammonia, will take him to one of my holdings in Taggoron where he will be safe until our quest is complete," Kade answered. "From there, the boy can determine his own fate."

Ammonia arrived a little later and took Varric with him. By that time, everyone had gathered downstairs.

"The ship should be ready by tomorrow. Take the day. Gather what supplies you need. Rest up. We will convene tonight to go over the plan and make any final preparations. Ready yourselves; tomorrow, we sail for the Darkstone," Vale said.

* * *

That night they sat around a long rectangular table discussing the plan for stealing the Darkstone from Draka Mors. Everyone had their own idea about how they should approach it and what they should do. Kade stood behind Vale, leaning against a wall away from the table, trying to keep himself out of the discussion.

"Once we discover the location of the Darkstone, we will need to approach carefully. We can't risk Draka Mors discovering our presence while we search for a way into his lair," Vale started.

"I really hope the next step isn't, 'Caelan finds the Darkstone and steals it,'" Caelan said.

"That is your job," Celeste snapped.

"I get it. I'm the thief, but it's a huge dragon lair. Wouldn't it be better if we split up and had multiple people looking?"

"More people means more risk of discovery. You're the thief; act like it," Vale replied.

"Thief or not, I'm not wandering around the place by my lone self, hoping I stumble upon the Darkstone before the dragon."

"We have no idea what to look for," Vale started.

"Dragons all horde in the same way," Kade interrupted. "There will be a large inner room mounded with treasure like hills of gold and precious jewels. The Darkstone is no ordinary treasure. It will be the prize of his collection. As such, he will display it proudly. You can be certain the Darkstone will be positioned on a ledge, someplace prominent and easy to see from anywhere in the main cavern. If you can't find it, you are not much of a thief."

"Great, and how exactly am I supposed to get into this little cavern of dreams?" Caelan asked.

"The primary entrance point will be from above, that's how Draka Mors gets in and out. There are, however, usually tunnels —small access points that are hard to reach and harder to find, unless you know where to look."

"Access tunnels?" Vale asked.

"Dragons use them as vents to create a cross-breeze. We will use them to dispense the Slumbaspice to ensure Draka Mors is fast asleep," Kade said.

"They leave these tunnels unguarded?" Vale seemed surprised.

"Dragons are arrogant. They protect their treasure from other dragons. They'd never even consider lowly humans a threat to sneak in and steal from them," Kade answered.

Vale stood as an idea formed in his head. "Here's the plan. We will use the Glyphstone to find Draka Mors's lair. Once we have a location, Kade will travel ahead and mark the tunnel entrances. Ash, Rivik, Sera, Spiro, Dante, and I will pair up."

"Wait." Dante interrupted.

Vale raised an eyebrow.

"I must ask a question before we continue," Dante turned to Spiro.

"Tell me, dragon knight from the keep at Calladun, why would the commander there tell us there was not a knight named Spiro among any of their ranks?" Dante's tone was thick with accusation. The eyes of everyone at the table shifted to Spiro.

"You went to Calladun?" Spiro's shock was evident.

"Do not bid for time," Kade warned. "I will not suffer your posturing. Answer."

Spiro shook his head, "The commander wouldn't know my name, nor would he the name of any other dragon knight."

It was Dante's turn to look confused. "This does not make sense."

Spiro smiled. "It does when you understand how the order works. Dragon knights aren't trained. We are forged. Like steel, what we were goes into the fire, is melted down, and formed into a weapon against our enemy. When our transformation is complete, we are each given new names. These are the names we use amongst our brothers, the names we are known by."

"Spiro is not your dragon knight name?" Dante asked.

"It is my birth name. It would only be known to the keeper of records."

"Why did you not give us your new name?"

"You are not dragon knights. I decided my birthname might be more relatable to you. It was not an intentional deception, I merely chose one as I did not think the other so relevant."

Vale looked between Kade, Dante, and Spiro. "We good?"

When they all nodded in agreement, Vale turned back to the map.

"As I was saying, we split into teams. Each team will take a portion of Slumbaspice to a designated tunnel. Once done, we head back to the ship where Celeste, Kade, Grom, and Azalea will be waiting. Meanwhile, Caelan will sneak in, find the Darkstone, retrieve it, and meet us back at the ship. Once back, we will return to Stormdale on the Moonlit Maiden. From there, Kade will teleport us back to Parisia."

"Wait, why not just teleport us right away?" Rivik asked.

"It's too risky. Opening a portal that close to a dragon's roost, in the heart of the Dragon Lands, there would be no way to ensure other dragons wouldn't follow," Kade explained.

"A portal out would be a last resort. If everything goes according to plan, we won't need it anyway," Vale said.

The group nodded in agreement.

"Any questions?" Vale asked.

"There's one thing that's bothering me," Caelan said. "When Celeste was talking to Varric, she mentioned that Owen charged at the thugs, and it almost cost him his life."

Celeste rolled her eyes and huffed. "Not this again; I misspoke, get over it."

Caelan held out his hands to keep anyone from moving on. "I considered that. But the thing is, people rarely misspeak by adding an inaccurate detail. That sounded more like a slip of the tongue," he accused.

"What are you suggesting?" Vale asked.

"In the alley where Owen died, did you see the thugs' weapons?" Caelan looked at Kade and then Ash.

The two exchanged a confused glance but neither replied.

"What's this have to do with anything? You're wasting time!" Celeste snapped.

"You fought them, princess; what were they carrying?"

"I don't remember," Celeste said.

"It wasn't long ago. You fought and killed three men in an alley, and you're telling me you don't remember what weapons they had?"

"It was pretty chaotic." Celeste shook her head.

"Must be that Royal privilege." Caelan shrugged. "I still remember what the first few people I killed where wielding. To this day, I can picture it in my mind, clear as if it was right in front of me. Maybe that's just because I didn't grow up in some posh palace where mommy and daddy took care of everything for me. Details don't matter to you, spoiled girl."

"One had a spiked club, one had a crudely-made, curved sword, and the other had a long dagger. There, you happy now?" Celeste's eyes narrowed.

"You coming to a point, Caelan?" Vale asked.

"You want to tell them, or should I?" Caelan asked, looking at Kade.

"I am not sure what you wish for me to say here," Kade replied.

"You saw the wound, right? The one that killed Owen?"

"I did," Kade nodded.

"Could an axe or club have caused it?" Caelan asked.

"No," Kade shook his head. "It was a thin puncture wound."

"Ok, so we've established that it was the one with the dagger, great," Celeste interjected.

Caelan reached behind his back and pulled out a long, curved knife and tossed it to Kade.

"This is . . . ?" Kade stared at the blade.

"I felt like I was missing something the whole time, so when I saw Owen's body, I checked the wound. Any chance that could have caused the wound you saw?" Caelan asked.

Kade shook his head. "No. The wound was small, caused by a thin weapon."

"Great, so that's not the knife he used. Can we move on now?" Celeste scowled.

"That, princess, was the only knife in the alley. I checked all the bodies. None of the weapons matched the wound. Unless, of course, it vaporized after use."

Caelan walked to Celeste, standing behind her. In one swift motion, he drew her sword and tossed it across the table. Celeste stood up and whirled around, but she was too late.

"What about that? Could that have caused the wound?" Caelan asked.

Kade looked at the blade and then at Celeste. "Yes. It would be a weapon exactly like this," he confirmed.

The room went silent for a moment.

"I checked all the bodies. They were all killed with the same weapon. Yours," Caelan accused.

Ash practically leapt over the table, grabbing for Celeste's neck. Spiro tried to pull him back but was unable to do so. Kade set down the sword and darted over, helping pull Ash back.

"Why?!" Ash demanded, his face red, the vein at his temple throbbing as he pushed and squirmed, trying to get past Kade.

"You don't know what you are talking about." Celeste straightened her shirt and glared.

"What is wrong with you? He did nothing! All he wanted was to find his son and you killed him?" Ash accused.

"I don't have to explain myself to a common Taggoronian thug!"

"You're a monster!" Ash snapped, still struggling to free himself from Kade and Spiro's restraining hold.

"A monster? Is that what I am? You were going to risk the lives of hundreds of thousands of innocent people. Mothers, fathers, children, all of them in peril while you were gallivanting around trying to save one boy. You call me a monster? That's fine. When we return the Darkstone, they will call me a hero. What do I care what you think?"

"Heroes don't kill defenseless, innocent people," Ash snapped back.

"You think I wanted to do that? You think I feel good about it? I didn't have a choice. Owen had you wrapped around his little finger. Every step took us farther from our goal. You weren't going to stop. You'd have gone to the end of the continent and beyond if needed. I'm sorry your feeble mind can't understand that sometimes you have to make hard choices. Some of us don't have the luxury of doing whatever we want. I have a responsibility to my people. He was taking precious time we didn't have."

"We had time. We were so close," Ash grumbled.

"You didn't know that. You didn't even know if he'd actually be at the next town. You were so focused on the little problem in front of you that you all lost sight of the big one that hangs over us. If I didn't do something, by the time we retrieved the Darkstone, it would have been too late. I am not going to fail because you can't make a tough call. I'm not letting my kingdom fall because of one sad story. We have more important—"

Sera's fist slammed into Celeste's face, cutting off her words.

"Shut your mouth. Or I will shut it for you," she demanded.

"I did what I had to do," Celeste sneered, wiping blood from her lip and spitting a bit more of it onto the ground.

"Ralk this." Caelan pulled his dagger from behind his back.

"Take a breath, Caelan." Vale stepped between them.

"No. She's doesn't get to live after what she's done," Caelan protested.

"She will face judgment when we return to Parisia," Vale stated.

"Judgment? You mean from her uncle, the king? Don't be a rooki. We don't need her," Caelan grunted.

"Actually, you do. My family spent the last century layering enchantments on the Darkstone to bind the magic to our bloodline. If you want access to the power of the Darkstone, you need my blood."

"Your blood. At this point, I'd rather spill it than use it," Caelan glared.

Celeste laughed. "I get it now. To think, when all this started, I looked up to you. You were so confident and capable.

You had experienced so much life where I had known so little. I wanted to learn, to see the way you did. Now I see it; you're nothing more than a gershwa."

"What did you say?" Caelan growled.

"Have you forgotten? You were ready to kill Azalea when you found out she was possessed by the Red Empress. You said sometimes you have to make hard choices. Sometimes you have to make sacrifices for the greater good. That's what you said. You didn't want to do it, but it needed to be done. The difference between you and me is that I actually did it. I did what you said, and now you want to paint me as the villain? Hate me if you want; I did this for you. I did it for everyone. They may have just been words to you, but to me, they were life. I just did what you couldn't."

"You can keep your ralking stone; I'm going to kill you." Ash's rage renewed and pulled against Spiro and Kade's grips. Spiro's gave way; Kade's did not.

"That is it," Dante muttered.

"What is?" Vale asked.

"That is why Draka Mors stole the Darkstone," Dante commented.

Caelan turned to Dante. "What are you talking about?"

"I wondered why he would go through all the trouble of stealing the Darkstone when, surely, he would have known he would not be able to use it."

"And?" Caelan pressed.

"He did not take it for himself," Dante said.

Rivik shook his head. "You lost me."

"We have been treating the Red Empress and the stolen Darkstone like two separate threats. What if they are not? What if they are linked?"

"How do you mean?" Vale asked.

"Think about it. The elves told you that Draka Mors is leading a rebellion against Bag'Thorak. If he is unkillable, they wouldn't dare resist him, even if they had a majority. It would be suicide. Dragons may be overconfident, but they are not stupid. No one would move against him, or even plot against him, unless they had a way to stop him."

"Such as?"

"What is a dragon's primary weakness?"

"Spirit Magic," Kade answered.

Dante nodded. "Like the magic the Red Empress possesses."

"You're saying Draka Mors stole the Darkstone so he could give it to the Red Empress in exchange for killing my father?" Kade questioned.

"It is more than that. When the stone was taken, our concern was that the veil would weaken, and the Shadow King would return. Perhaps that was never the intention. Perhaps the purpose of taking the stone was to weaken the veil so the Red Empress could return."

Caelan ran his hands through his hair. "Ralk . . . "

Chapter 48

The Lair of Draka Mors

The room was a picture frozen in time. No one moved. No one spoke. Minutes passed before Vale finally rubbed his temples and let out a long, slow grunt.

"I say we take her out to sea and throw her owa overboard. Let the water swallow her into its depths where she belongs," Sera said. The idea caused Grom to shiver.

"No," Kade replied. "She's coming."

"You sure about that, dragon boy?" Caelan pulled one of the arrows from his quiver.

"Careful. I need her. I do not need you," Kade warned, flames flashing in his eyes.

Blue plates like circular shields formed around Dante's hands and expanded larger and larger. "Watch yourself," he warned.

"Enough!" Vale stepped between Dante and Kade. "This isn't helping. I don't like it any more than you do. What choice do we have?"

Caelan started pacing back and forth. "This isn't going to work, Vale. Ain't none of us going to trust her."

"You don't have to. I'm not asking you to trust her or to like her. I'm asking for your help to finish what we started. We all took up this quest for different reasons. We have different motives and different goals. I don't think any of us knew what to expect when we started. What we did know was the price of failure.

"Now we are here, so close to the goal. Thousands of Seekers, and we are the only ones who remain. Everything has been stacked against us, yet here we are. We must steel our nerves. We must press on. The weight of a kingdom, of perhaps the realm, may rest on what we do right now. The lives of everyone you know, of every person you care about, hang in the balance.

"Whatever differences or concerns you may have, bury them. Until we have returned the stone, they can wait. I'm asking you to put aside your differences for a few more days, that we might save the world. After that, she's all yours."

The room returned to a brief silence. Caelan and Ash exchanged a look. Ash slowly nodded.

"Fine. Until it's done," Caelan agreed.

"Oh, so I'm just supposed to help all of you get what you want—use the stone to get your wishes—so you can discard me when I'm no longer useful to you?" Celeste folded her arms and huffed. "I think I'll pass."

Kade turned and grabbed her by the throat. He lifted her off the ground and pinned her back to the wall behind them. The flames in his eyes grew wilder.

"Silence your tongue. After what you did, you are lucky to be drawing breath."

She tried to wiggle free but was unable to do so. "Un . . . hand . . . me," she grunted out.

Kade dropped her to the ground. Celeste collapsed to her knees, gasping for air. After she caught her breath, she stood up tall and ironed her clothes with her palms.

"You don't seem to get it. I am the one who can wield the Darkstone. I am the one who can activate its power. I am not about to help you just so you can kill me."

"There are many ways to die—some slower and more painful than others," Kade grinned.

"You can't kill me. I am the niece of the king! You hurt me and he will hunt you to the very edge of the world. You will never again know peace."

"That's only if he finds out, though, isn't it?" Sera said.

"He already knows," Celeste grinned proudly.

"What are you going on about?" Ash asked.

"That's the ralker you've been talkin' to at night, isn't it?" Caelan snapped his fingers.

"Caelan?" Vale asked.

"I noticed it a while back. We were at an inn; everyone else was asleep. I came back to see a glowing blue light under her door. I heard her talking to someone. I knew I recognized the voice, but I couldn't place where I'd heard it before. That's it. It was the king," Caelan explained.

"Where did you hear the king's voice?" Dante asked.

"From that spell he used to talk to you and Vale when you snuck out for a secret chat back in Wellar."

Vale's eyes widened. "You heard that?"

Caelan smirked. "Course I did. That's hardly the point now. She," he pointed at Celeste, "has something that lets her talk to the king."

"Our meeting was not an accident, was it?" Dante asked.

"My uncle asked me to do whatever it took to get onto your Seeker team. I agreed. This was my chance to get out from under my father's thumb and prove myself. Not even my father could deny the king. So, we concocted a plan. He would demand that you lead a team of Seekers. Then I would make sure you picked me to be a part of that team. You were surprisingly easy to convince," Celeste grinned.

"She's been spying and reporting back this whole time," Caelan said.

Celeste lifted her chin. "And the king will expect regular reports, so if you don't do as I say—"

Caelan stepped right in front of her, leaning in close to Celeste and whispering in her ear. "I swear to you by the gods below, before this is all over, one of my arrows will pierce your shriveled, deformed heart."

Celeste grunted and pushed him away. "Enough with your petty threats. We have work to do." She stopped talking and her hands moved up her sides as she started patting herself down.

"Looking for this?" Caelan tossed a glass orb slightly larger than an orange into the air and caught it. The orb was a murky translucent blue. The color swirled around inside it like the rolling of storm clouds.

"Give me that!" Celeste lunged forward.

Dante stared at the object. "That is a phorasee orb."

"A what?" Rivik asked.

"It is a magical means of communication. It lets two people talk from anywhere in the world like they were standing right next to each other. They are extremely rare and quite valuable," Dante explained.

"Really? It's a such a shame this one is broken." Caelan drew his arm back and threw the orb against the floor as hard as he could.

Celeste screamed as the orb shattered on the ground, the glowing fog contained inside dissipating before completely disappearing in the large room. Celeste dropped to her knees, picking up some of the shattered pieces.

"You rooki piece of gwar!" She lunged forward, driving her fist at Caelan's face.

He dodged it with ease and swung his hand around, backhanding her so hard across the face that she lost her balance and fell onto the floor with a thud.

Caelan knelt down over her. "I feel sorry for you, Celeste. We have to put up with you for a little while longer. You have to live with yourself every day."

"We're done here," Vale said. "Rest. Do what you need to do. Tomorrow, we save the world."

"Aww, what an epic and inspirational speech. I always knew you were the hero of this story," Caelan jested.

"I swear, you are the absolute worst," Vale replied as the group began to file out of the room.

"Whaatt? It was a compliment."

Vale groaned.

"See? You're warming up to me."

***

The next morning, they loaded their supplies on board the Moonlit Maiden. Grom made his way immediately below deck while the others stayed above. Kade positioned himself near the helm, using the Glyphstone to provide navigational instructions to Shiv as the sea elf steered the ship. Spiro became Kade's shadow. He seemed fascinated with the Glyphstone and how it worked.

The Glyphstone was a golden box with a hollowed-out circle in the middle. The square-framed box was carved with all sorts of strange symbols. Three thick rings of gold following different paths were layered on top of each other, constantly revolving as the outer layer was fixed to the inside of the hollowed-out hole in the box. Inside the three rotating rings was a pulsing black sphere that glistened as if perpetually wet. A melodic humming sound came from the sphere as a lavender light hovered around it like mist rolling over a lake in the cool of the early morning. As the rings moved, a faint, glowing purple triangle appeared above them. As they moved, the triangle would turn. When it did, Kade would instruct Shiv to turn the ship to keep the triangle facing straight ahead.

"How do you know this is leading us to the Darkstone?" Spiro asked, mesmerized as he watched the rings turn.

"It tracks magical power. The arrow points toward the most powerful object in its range," Kade answered flatly.

"But couldn't there be something more powerful than the Darkstone?"

"There is not. The Darkstone is one of the most powerful objects in this realm, and the objects that are more powerful are not in the Dragon Lands."

"Where did these Glyphstones—" Spiro started.

"Be silent or be gone. I am busy," Kade cut him off.

Days became weeks as the Glyphstone guided them farther and farther from the continent. The group became restless; Grom especially was almost as tired of waiting as he was of being on the water.

Finally, on the horizon they saw it—a tall, shadowed spire climbing like a great rocky tower into the sky. A thick, unnatural, gray fog seemed to seep around the rocks. Silver veins wrapped up the black rock, pulsing with an ominous light, giving the dragon's roost the appearance of having endless bolts of lightning all around it.

"Why the ralk wouldn't the Darkstone be there? That looks like what a nightmare has nightmares about." Caelan shook his head. "Are you serious with this place?"

"I didn't pick the location," Kade said.

"Course you didn't; you're not the one about to go wandering about inside it either," Caelan replied.

"There." Vale pointed to a tall rock jutting out from the sea. "That should keep the ship hidden. From there, we row in and hide the boat while we wait for Kade to return with the location of the tunnel entrances."

Shiv steered the ship impressively close to the large rock, effectively hiding it in the rock's shadow. Kade pocketed the Glyphstone, flew off the ship, and began circling around the spiraling rock dragon roost. Azalea, Celeste, and Grom remained on the ship while the others got in a small boat. Six brown packs were loaded into the back of the boat after them. Each pack had a long, white wick that was pulled out of the top seam and tied into a loose bow. Matthias and his crew helped lower them down to the water, and they rowed their way toward the small, rocky beach that surrounded the black rock home of Draka Mors.

The water was rough, making the rowing process an exhausting endeavor. When they finally reached the shore, they pulled the little boat up onto the rocky beach. There was no plant life or visible caves that they could use to hide the boat, so they concealed it as best they could along a path of larger rocks.

Kade flew next to them not long after.

"Come with me," he motioned and started walking around the beach.

After about thirty paces, he stopped. He pointed to the spire. "Tunnel entrance is straight up here. Easy climb, lots of ledges, just mind your footing. I marked it with a small, glowing orange stone."

"Alright, see you back at the boat." Sera walked over to the ledge of rocks, joined by Rivik.

"You go first; I want to enjoy the view," Rivik grinned.

Sera punched him on the arm and then climbed up ahead of him.

At the next stop, the highest tunnel, Spiro and Vale paired up, leaving Dante and Ash to climb to the last one. Once the teams were on their way, Kade lead Caelan to a small opening at the bottom of the spire. It was so well hidden in the shadow of the rocks, he could have sat down in front of it and never known it was there. They waited in silence until Kade sniffed.

"That's the signal," Kade said.

"I didn't see anything. How can you tell?"

"I'm feeling sleepy," Kade answered.

Caelan nodded. "Here we go."

"Follow the path upward and to the right. Use this." Kade reached down and picked up a palm-sized, oval stone. He closed his eyes, and the stone began to glow with a dim orange light.

"Count the passages as you walk. The first three have sudden drops that will kill you on impact. The fourth leads to a large spider you'd be good to avoid. The fifth opening on your right side will take you to a path that circles upwards and into the main cavern. Make sure you take that one. If you miss it, the sixth opening will drop you straight onto where Draka Mors will be sleeping."

"You saw all that flying around?" Caelan asked.

"No, I used a spell to map the tunnels. The Slumbaspice will put him to sleep, but if you make too much noise, it won't keep him that way."

"Great, and you thought now would be a good time to spring that on me?"

Kade smiled. "Don't make noise, and it won't be a problem."

Caelan sighed. "Anything else you should have told me a long time ago that I should know before I go?"

"When you find the stone, be careful that you don't touch it."

"Are you serious?"

"If the enchantments work the way I suspect, if you touch the stone without having contact with someone of Royal blood, it will likely kill you."

"Gods below, this keeps getting better and better. How am I supposed to retrieve the stone without touching it?"

Kade handed Caelan the Volkili Prismward. "Use this. One more thing."

"Of course, there is."

"As a last resort, if things go badly, there's a small hole, barely bigger than you are, in the back corner of the room. It will effectively let you back down and out of the spire. It should be wide enough to fit you all the way though."

"Should? As in, might not be?"

Kade shrugged. "That's why it's a last resort. Good luck. Don't ralk it up."

"Don't ralk it up," Caelan mimicked after stepping inside the tunnel and starting up the narrow path. "I'm Kade, I'm a grumpy, know-it-all, part-dragon, magic-wielding jerk with a ridiculous jaw line who's just going to sit back on a ship and relax while Caelan gets to wander around through some creepy dragon tunnels to steal the most important object in the realm. Oh yeah, and there's a giant ralkin' spider. How fun!" He whispered to himself as he made his way up the cavern path.

He carefully counted the number of openings, wanting to ensure he didn't end up accidentally bumping into a giant spider. The glowing stone Kade gave him proved helpful in lighting just enough of the path for him to see where he was going. He passed a small gap in the rock.

"Ralk . . . does this count?" He peaked his head inside it. The small hole opened up into a fairly large space. He stepped carefully inside. There was no clear path through. There was an upper ledge he could climb to, but he didn't see the point. This was clearly not a path and shouldn't be counted. The light he carried was too dim to see the movement on the ledge above him.

He passed the fourth opening and then reached the fifth. He turned to the right as Kade had instructed and followed the path upward. The slope grew suddenly steeper. The path was smooth enough that Caelan had to grip the sides of the walls with one hand to pull himself up. He deposited the glowing stone in his pocket as he could see light coming from an opening. It must be the main cavern. He was close. He grabbed a hold of the stone wall and pulled himself up. The path beneath him flattened, and a few paces ahead, he could see the entrance to the main cavern. This was it. Even from inside the tunnel, he could see mounds of gold, rubies, sapphires, emeralds, and every other kind of treasure imaginable.

He lifted his head up and saw the large tail of a silver-scaled dragon. He took a step closer and found no footing. The rock was wet, the path slick and steep. He lost his balance and slid, his shoulder hitting the rock and his body shooting through the opening and into the bright room. Caelan reached for the walls, trying to grab hold of something to stop himself, slow himself down even. The walls widened out of reach as he slid helplessly faster. The path below him might as well have been a slide.

He passed the opening and any hope to catch himself. As his body slid faster, everything seemed to slow down. Realization struck him like an icy dagger to the heart. Kade had counted that little cavern, and he'd gone past the path he was supposed to take. This was going to spit him out right on top of the sleeping dragon. He could see the slope, the trajectory; he would ramp off the edge into the air and land on Draka Mors. No way the Slumbaspice would keep him asleep through that.

Here lies Caelan—couldn't count. Got eaten by a dragon. Ralked it up just like Kade said not to. Well, I showed him, Caelan thought to himself. Then he saw it, at the very end of the path—a small lip that would act like a ramp at his current speed of descent. An idea struck like lightning. He reached back and pulled free his knife. He spread his legs, aiming the heels of his boots for the edges of the stone lip. He slammed his knife into the path, trying to bury it in the stone. It didn't sink in but did help slow him down. His feet caught the edge of the rise, but he was going too fast to stop. His body lifted, momentum pushing him forward. He let go of his knife and spun around as he went over the edge. He reached out, fingers just catching the lip of the stone slide.

"Gods below, Caelan, what are you doing hanging from a ledge in a dragon's lair? Well, that stupid man-dragon counted an opening as a passage. Openings are not passages, are they? No, they are not. Openings are open. Passages . . . allow passage.

Emptos bloody dragon-man," Caelan whispered to himself. "Better believe if I die here, I'm haunting his owa."

He strained to lift himself up. Then he saw it—sitting on the ledge directly below him was a small pedestal. Centered on the pedestal was a round, deep violet stone that seemed to pulse a light that shifted between purple and green. It was the Darkstone.

The ledge below didn't stick out as far as the one he was holding onto, but the path he'd slid down was too steep to try and climb back up. If he could swing himself enough, he might be able to make the landing and grab the stone. If he missed, well, it would be no different than any of his other alternatives, which all seemed to end in being dinner for an elder dragon.

He gripped the rock as hard as he could and kicked his body away, waiting for the momentum to swing in the right direction. He'd have to time his release perfectly. His fingers started to slip as his body swung. It was too soon. He grunted as he held, pressing his fingers down, digging them into the stone until he thought they would snap. He closed his eyes and felt it, felt the swing of his body. He visualized the angle, and he let go.

Chapter 49

The Showdown

His feet struck rock, and he instinctively tucked his body into a roll. He wasn't entirely sure how wide the ledge was, but he hadn't much choice. His back struck the rock hard, causing a burning, tingling pain to shoot up his spine. He shook his head and slowly opened his eyes. He half-expected to see the maw of a great dragon chomping down on him. Instead, he saw the ledge in front of him. He'd hit it and managed to roll alongside it into the side wall of the room. At the end of the outcropping of rock, there it was. After all this time, the Darkstone was right in front of him. Caelan forgot about the pain in his limbs as he stood and walked over to the stone.

It wasn't shiny like the typical treasure desired by dragons, but it was quite exquisite. The stone gave off an aura of power that drew him in. Caelan pulled out the Volkili Prismward that Vale had entrusted to him, and he carefully, without touching the stone, closed the Prismward around it. Stuffing the box into his pocket, he looked around for a way down. The ledge he was on opened to a tunnel leading away from the main room. Caelan smirked. When he recounted this story later, he planned to make his exit sound much more difficult and adventurous.

He stepped into the tunnel and froze. A chill crawled up his spine to his neck as every muscle in his body tensed involuntarily. A faint, scraping sound —a soft almost-hiss. He pulled the glowing stone Kade had given him from his pocket and held it up. He covered his mouth with his other hand to stifle his gasp as the entire hallway was filled with a massive, hairy, black spider. The spider was moving closer, though recoiling slightly at the light from the stone. Caelan held the stone out, trying to keep the creature away as he backed up, returning to the inner chamber. With its eight legs pushing off walls and allowing it to alter direction quickly, the spider grew closer. The light held it back, but it wouldn't be enough to stop it. The spider-monster was nearly upon him. Caelan turned and dove for the entrance, tucking and rolling out onto the ledge as the spider lunged, its fangs landing right where he had just been.

The spider stopped at the entrance, not daring to move inside the open room. Caelan sighed in relief a moment too soon. The massive spider's legs reached out after him, Caelan hopped back to avoid them, his feet slipping over the edge. His back arched as it struck against a pile of gold coins, causing a hailstorm of clattering coins to bounce and clang down to the floor. Caelan turned his head to see where he was. Sprawled out on his back, he had landed on a hill of gold right next to the sleeping Draka Mors's massive head. He froze in place as if the damage wasn't already done. The dragon moved, adjusting its position, but still appeared to be sleeping. Caelan sighed; that was too close.

Suddenly, the great silver eyelid peeled back, and Caelan was staring into the glowing blue eye of an elder dragon. The eye was as big as he was. Caelan rolled over and dove, riding the pile of gold down to the floor below. His eyes scanned the horizon, looking for the hole Kade had mentioned.

"Be nice if you'd told me which wall was the back one," he muttered to himself.

"Whhaatt . . . issss . . . thissss?" Draka Mors's voice boomed so loud it shook every coin in the room. Caelan slowly turned around to see the silver dragon rise up on his legs, his long, scaled neck stretching into the air, his eyes never leaving Caelan.

"Well . . . ralk." Caelan turned and sprinted toward a wall, hoping that he'd get lucky, and it would be the right one.

It was not. Draka Mors roared in rage, and the massive dragon's silver tail hurled toward Caelan. The piles of gold coins interfered with the motion, allowing Caelan time to dodge the attack. Coins flew like debris from an explosion, crashing into him. He winced as he protected his face from the projectile currency. Caelan slid up against the wall. As his back pressed against the stone, he saw it—the last resort Kade mentioned. It was a small hole. Caelan was not sure he'd fit.

"Of course, why wouldn't it be the opposite wall?" he muttered to himself.

"Youuu dareee enter myyyy rooooost?" Draka Mors opened his massive jaw and silver flames sprayed toward him. Caelan ran, not away but toward the flames, sliding his body along the floor as low as he could. The flames poured over him. He could feel their heat as he slid under them and out of their path. Pushing up into a dead sprint, he rushed toward the far wall. A large, silver dragon foot stomped down in front of him. He altered his path, weaving around it, and pressed on.

"Ruuun . . . ruuun, little mouse . . . There is nowhere for youuu to goooo," Draka Mors threatened.

The dragon was remarkably quick for a creature its size. It moved right in front of Caelan's path, the great dragon's head rearing back and preparing another burst of flame. Caelan dove between the creature's legs, his body skidded roughly on some loose coins as he slid toward the wall. He lined his slide up with the small hole and couldn't bring himself to look.

Caelan closed his eyes and braced himself. He didn't hit anything; rather, his body felt like it was rushing, almost falling, but with more restraint as he whooshed and swirled around the cool, smooth, stone tunnel like an enclosed slide. He tightened every muscle in his body, trying to make himself as small as possible. He knew if he got stuck in this tunnel, it would be the end. No help would come. He would die, slowly, stuck in the tunnel of a dragon's lair. He shivered at the thought and tried to push the horror of it from his mind.

"I do not enjoy small spaces," he muttered to himself as he slid.

Every little bump or catch made his heart thud and nearly burst in his chest until, suddenly, the hole gave out, and he felt himself falling completely unchecked. He opened his eyes. He wasn't in the spire anymore. He was free-falling straight toward the ocean below.

The water was cold as he sank under it, sinking below the surface and feeling the current slowly tugging against him. He immediately started swimming up toward the light, his head cresting out of the water as he gasped for air. It took him a moment to get his bearings and catch his breath. He looked around frantically as little waves crashed over his head, the salt of the water burning his eyes.

In the distance, he saw the others rushing toward him, carrying the boat between them as they moved it out into the water. After a minute of treading water, they reached him and pulled him inside.

"Did you get it?" Vale asked.

"Your concern for my well-being is touching. I can't even express to you what it means."

"Did you get it?" Vale asked, louder and more forcefully.

Caelan pulled out the Prismward and nodded. There was a collective sigh of relief that swept over the boat.

Caelan broke the silence,"We might want to move quicker."

"Why?" Dante started.

"Draka Mors is awake," Caelan shrugged.

"Awake? How? The Slumbaspice was supposed to take care of him," Rivik protested.

Caelan shrugged. "I guess it doesn't work for long."

Dante turned to see the silver dragon rising into the sky. It hovered above its spire and roared. A burst of light illuminated the sky, and the boom of thunder echoed in its wake. They rowed hard and fast, ignoring the burning pain that seared through their muscles. The little boat moved quickly through the water but not quickly enough. The silver dragon spotted them and flapped its mighty wings, flying toward them in a frenzy of rage.

"That's Draka Mors?" Rivik glared, his body tightening as his hand instinctively reached for his spear."

"That's what he called himself," Caelan confirmed.

"That is the dragon who burned our home." Rivik's face burned with rage.

"Revenge later. Row now," Vale called out.

Silver flames burst from the dragon's maw, beaming toward them in a constant stream as it dove down, gliding just above the water. Caelan grabbed his bow and fired one of the arrows Kade had given him. It hit Draka Mors in the shoulder, causing the dragon to flinch. The motion altered his path just enough for the flames to run wide and miss their little boat completely.

"That was close," Sera sighed in relief.

"That's not going to work for long," Rivik said.

"I'm open to ideas," Caelan replied as Draka Mors circled around.

"We aren't exactly in a great position to fight a dragon," Sera noted.

Draka Mors was flying right toward them, a trail of silver flame spraying down and moving closer and closer.

"Hold on!" Dante shouted.

A glowing blue rope appeared in his hands and he swung it out around a nearby rock, pulling hard. The rope crackled and pulled them, jerking the boat to the side, suddenly moving it out of the path of the flame. Dante whirled around, and the rope disappeared.

"Cheeaap triicks woon't save yoou for loong!" Draka Mors called out.

"Keep rowing; Caelan and I will do what we can." Dante closed his eyes and focused all of his magical energy.

He cast a spherical shield around the boat that absorbed the next wave of Draka Mors's flames but shattered after. Caelan fired arrow after arrow, but they did little to slow the massive dragon down. They were getting closer to the ship, but with each pass they had to strain a little harder, and the flames got a little closer.

"Caelan, give the Darkstone to Rivik!" Sera instructed.

"Why?" Caelan asked, firing an arrow at the approaching dragon.

"We aren't going to make it, but he can. He's like a fish in the water," she explained.

"No way, I'm not leaving you behind," Rivik protested, his

hand sliding into his pocket and feeling the ring Missanja had given to him.

"She's right. You have to!" Vale commanded. "The Darkstone is too important."

"I'm not going. I don't care what you say."

Caelan turned and stuffed the box containing the Darkstone into Rivik's tunic.

"Sorry," he said, sliding his foot behind Rivik and pushing him overboard. Rivik splashed into the water and immediately reached up to pull himself back in.

"Dante!" Vale shouted.

Dante turned and closed his eyes. A surge of energy swelled and lifted Rivik up and pulled him away from the boat. The water shaped into a giant hand wrapped around Rivik's body as it tugged him through the water toward the Moonlit Maiden and away from their boat. Rivik yelled and reached against the force of the enchanted wave, but it did no good. Draka Mors's flames moved steadily closer.

"It has been an honor." Vale stood, letting go of the oar and looking to the others.

The silver flame grew larger and closer. Vale instinctively covered his eyes with his arm as the flames were about to consume them. The fire wasn't as hot as he expected, or perhaps it was so hot he couldn't feel a thing. It was odd. He'd expected something, but he felt nothing. He slowly pulled his arm down and opened his eyes. The silver flames were being blocked by a glowing orange half circle that deflected them out of the way. Between them and the dragon flame was Kade, hovering above the water.

"Get back to the ship; I'll deal with him."

Kade flew around, attacking and distracting Draka Mors, keeping the large silver dragon occupied as they rowed to the ship. By the time they reached it, Rivik was already on board. He helped the elves rope the boat and pull it up. He glared at Caelan as he tugged the archer out of the boat and onto the ship. Once everyone was onboard, Shiv gave instructions to his crew, and they were off.

"You have a plan?" Dante asked.

"A plan? Mate, ya didn't tell me you were robbin' a bloody elder dragon. There ain't no plan for that," Shiv replied.

"What about those big harpoon guns?" Sera asked.

"They ain't gonna stop him. Might slow him down, but it's a long way to sail with a dragon on our tail."

"So, what, we just wait to die?" Celeste asked.

"I didn't say that. Matthias, load the dragnet," Shiv called out.

Matthias nodded and rushed off, gathering a few other elves and heading below deck.

"Dragnet?" Dante asked.

"Aye, watch and learn."

Kade was holding his own against the great elder dragon, but despite his best efforts, Draka Mors was advancing. Caelan tried to help, firing at Draka Mors when he could do so without the risk of hitting Kade. Dante used his magic, but neither had much effect.

"Guide him behind the ship!" Shiv called out.

Kade attempted to maneuver the elder dragon, but it was Dante's magic that ended up moving Draka Mors into place.

"Fire!" Shiv shouted.

Kade dropped down, nearly smashing into the water to avoid the large net as it stretched out and wrapped around the silver dragon. Draka Mors roared as his wings were suddenly pinned to his side. The dragon hit the water with a great splash, disappearing from view underneath the surface of the sea.

"That was . . . effective." Dante nodded as Kade landed on the deck of the ship, appearing exhausted.

"Don't get too excited, mate. It won't hold him forever, and when he breaks free, he's gonna be extra fiery," Shiv said.

"Can we get far enough away so he won't be able to find us?" Sera asked.

Shiv laughed and shook his head. "Trust the process, girl. We've got this."

Elves rushed around the deck, carrying a large, thin, shimmering fabric. They moved quickly, unfolding it again and again. Several of the elves began climbing up the ropes, tugging the ends of the fabric behind them as they moved up to the top of the ship. They moved in perfect harmony, seamlessly opening and raising the fabric up.

"What is that?" Dante asked.

"Mirror silk," Shiv replied. "They drape it around the ship, and it will make us invisible. We draw in the sails and stay still. Your dragon friend can fly overhead all he wants; he'll never find us. Then we just wait until he gives up. Easy as floating in a bathtub."

"I thought you said you didn't have a plan," Sera accused.

Shiv smirked. "Aye, well, I may have pulled your leg a little. We live in the Dragon Lands; we always have plans for dragons."

"How long does it take to get up?"

"The mirror silk? Couple of minutes is all. Then we just relax, keep quiet, and wait him out."

Kade turned to Rivik. "The Darkstone. Now."

Rivik raised his eyebrow. "Now?"

"Yes, now. Celeste, come here," Kade commanded.

"I thought we were waiting until we got to Parisia," Rivik objected.

Dante shrugged. "It seems rushed. Perhaps we should let things settle down before—"

"I am not asking. The Darkstone—now," Kade demanded.

Rivik reluctantly pulled the Volkili Prismward from his pocket. He held the box out and clicked it open, so the stone was in view. Kade grasped Celeste's hand and motioned for her to grab the stone. She hesitated before reaching out and placing her fingers on the smooth stone. Once she had, Kade did the same. He stared into her face.

"Close your eyes. Focus your thoughts on that which you desire most," Kade commanded.

"This is not the time or place," Celeste protested, but the pressure from his squeezing on her hands led her to follow his instructions.

The Darkstone pulsed as its unique tune waned in and out before a burst of smoke sprayed into the air. A warm, tingling sensation rushed through their bodies. Celeste opened her eyes and looked around.

"Is that it? How do you know if—"

"It worked." Kade smiled and took a deep breath, taking in the fresh air.

"How do you know?" Ash asked.

"When you use it, you will know," Kade smiled. "After all these years, the time has finally come."

A loud splash echoed behind them, and Draka Mors burst from beneath the sea, flying high up into the sky overhead.

Shiv's confident expression turned to terror as he stared up at the rising dragon.

"That's . . . not possible. It's too quick . . . we aren't—"

Draka Mors descended, hovering just above the ship, his mighty wings creating enough wind to make the ship lean in the water.

"Raatss on a sshhip . . . yooou ssssteal from meee, the greaaat Draka Morssss? I will burn yoooou to asssssh and scatter your remaaaains toooo the wind."

"I have an idea. Rivik, get your spear ready. I need time," Azalea whispered.

"I'll give you one chance to live, Draka Mors, before I—" Kade stepped forward and extended his arms.

"Kaaade . . . the abomination spaaawn of Bag'Thorak? What aaare yoooou doooing here?"

"My business is my own. I won't say it again. Leave here or die—badly."

"Suuuuch arrrrrogance from the dragon weeeeelp. I am noooo lesser dragon to be scaaaared by your hollooooow words," Draka Mors laughed.

"Perhaps you should be," Kade warned.

"Yoooou have taaaaken something ooof mine. I waaaaant it back."

"I am curious; why did you steal the Darkstone? It has no natural lure for a dragon," Kade asked.

"I neeeeed it," Draka Mors answered.

"For what purpose?" Dante interrupted.

Draka Mors turned his head and looked curiously at the man in blue.

"Myyyy people have diminishhhhed. We haaaave been weakened toooo the point of forrrrrming pacts with ratsssss like

Shadows of the Dark Realm

yourselves. For millennia, dragons have suffffered under Bag'Thorak. It is time for a new kingggg of the dragons. A kingggg who can restore ussss to our rightful place as rrrrrrulers of this realllllm."

"You have had the Darkstone for some time but still have not used it. Surely by now you have realized that you cannot. The Darkstone has no value or use to you. What need could you have for it?" Dante objected.

"I doooon't need to usssse it. It is a giffffft," Draka Mors explained.

"Looks like you were right," Kade whispered to Dante.

"Keep him talking," Dante whispered back.

"That explains it. You aren't smart enough or brave enough to go against my father without someone backing you up. Who is it?"

Draka Mors glared. "Nooo dragon can opppoose the unkillable Bag'Thorak. But I fooound someone who caaaaan. Someone whose powwwwer can kill even an unkillable dragon. The suunnn is setting on Bag'Thorak. The time for the rise of Draka Mors has come."

"The Red Empress," Dante called out.

"Ahhhhh, a clever raaat you are. Yessss. In exchange for the Darkstone, ssshhheee will kill the king of dragons, and I willll ascend to his throoon."

"And then what?" Dante questioned.

"Shhhe will rule the sooouth and I the nooorth. Together, this reaaaalm will be ourssss."

"She gets a stone, you get a throne. Quite the deal," Dante smirked. "At least until she decides to take that too."

Draka Mors flapped his wings harder, glaring down at Dante. "Explaaain yoursseellllf, little rat mannn."

"Surely, as powerful and wise as you are, you do not need me to spell it out. Vespera does not share power. She will offer it when it benefits her to do so. Sooner or later, she will betray you and take the throne from you," Dante explained.

"Liessss!"

"Think, you dim, scale-brained beast! What's to stop her from taking the stone and then killing you once she has it? If

Vespera is strong enough to bring down my father, then she's more than capable of destroying you." Kade posited.

"Good point. Draka Mors will forccce her to kill Bag'Thorak firssst. Then, when sssshe comessss to cccclaim the ssstone, l will usssse it to desssstroy her as well," Draka Mors growled.

"Wait, those are two different dragons?" Caelan said.

Draka Mors's eyes narrowed. "Careful, rat thief. I will not sssssuffer your inssssults."

Caelan held up his hands. "It's just . . . your names all sound alike to me."

"Sssilence!"

"It doesn't matter what you do. You're not getting the stone," Kade said.

"Whhhhy do resisssst me Kade? We share the sssssame goal, the sssssame enemy. We should worrrrrk together."

"You'd align yourself with a half-breed abomination?" Kade asked.

Draka Mors grinned a toothy, menacing grin. "It isssss your father's law that half-breeds are to beeee hunted down and kkkkkilled, not minnnnne. He says half-breeds ddddilute our bloodlines and make usss weak. Clearly, thissss is a lie. I've seen your ppppower, your resourcefulnesssss. Join me and we can cccchange the way our people seeee you. We can fffforge a new era together."

Vale looked nervously between Draka Mors and Kade. The offer had to be tempting—to be accepted by his own kind, to finally have a place in the world. If Kade took it, things were going to get very difficult.

"That is as intriguing as it is tempting. But I've waited too long for this. No one kills my father but me," Kade nodded.

"I sssssee you have inherited your mmmmother's foolishness."

Azalea glanced at Rivik and nodded.

"Wellar," Rivik said.

"Is that ssssupposed to mean sssssomething to me?" Draka Mors asked.

"Not yet, but it will. Wellar was my home until you burned it down for no reason, killing my friends, my family," Rivik said.

Draka Mors turned his head slightly. "Did I?"

"Vengeance is mine!" Rivik spun, lifting his spear. Azalea extended her hands and purple light encased it as Rivik drew his arm back to launch the spear at Draka Mors.

"Do it! Kill the dragon!" Spiro yelled, drawing his sword enthusiastically as Rivik stepped into his throw. He was standing too close, and his shoulder bumped into Rivik as he moved. The spear launched through the air, hurling at the silver dragon. The lightning enchantment from the dragon soul made the spear move too quickly for Draka Mors to dodge. The bump from Spiro altered the spear's course ever so slightly. The green shaft pierced through the dragon's shoulder, missing his heart.

Draka Mors roared in pain as he tilted his head back, his cry echoing loudly around them. That's when they saw it. Dragons circling overhead, too numerous to count. They were hiding above the clouds, staying out of view. With Draka Mors's scream, they started to dive.

"Time to go," Kade said, pushing the group together.

"I thought you said teleportation from the Dragon Lands was dangerous," Dante objected.

"It's less dangerous than fighting off a horde of angry dragons." Kade created a portal trimmed in orange light. "Go now!"

One by one, they rushed through the portal, leaving Kade alone on the ship with the elves.

"Come with us?" he asked the elf captain.

Shiv shook his head. "Nah, we don't leave the ship. We got a few tricks to fend 'em off. Plus, once ye go, their reason for being here goes with you. I'm sure we can sort it out."

"They will likely kill you."

"Well, better to die on sea, mate, than to end up surrounded by land," Shiv shivered.

"You willlll not escape mmmeee!" Draka Mors cried out, diving down toward the ship.

Kade stepped into the portal, and as soon as he felt the ground beneath his feet, he closed it.

"Land . . . Grom love land!" The troll jumped and dashed around with glee, feeling the ground beneath his large troll feet.

Dante looked around. The grass was so green, sky so blue,

crops so plentiful, there was only one place they could be—Parisia. Behind them was the massive stone wall that separated the prosperous kingdom from the world around it.

"We did it!" Celeste covered her mouth with her hands. "We did it!" The glee in her voice was undeniable.

"Rrrrreturn . . . the . . . sttttoonnnne," came a booming, echoing voice from above them, the unmistakable voice of Draka Mors.

Chapter 50

Retribution

The silver dragon winced as he flapped his wings, Rivik's spear still stuck in his shoulder.

"You don't look so good," Kade said.

"Whaaaat . . . is this . . . whaaat have you . . . done to me?" he groaned.

"The Red Empress, who you joined forces with, kidnapped me, tortured me, and tried to kill me. She wants to use my body as her vessel. You have been helping her. So as a token of my gratitude for the pain and suffering you put me through, I cast a spell on Rivik's spear. Right now, it's pumping spirit magic into you. Your kind doesn't like spirit magic, do they? I imagine that hurts really good," Azalea smirked.

"You foooolish rats still don't seeee it, do you?" Draka Mors bit the shaft of the spear in his shoulder and tugged it free, spitting it to the ground below. "Yoooou think I didn't knoooow what you were doing? Yoooooou didn't steal the Darkstone. I let yooooou take it."

"The ralk you did," Caelan protested.

"He's telling the truth," a voice came from behind them.

Azalea turned to see the sinister, smiling Valron.

"I warned you what would happen if I saw you again." Azalea lifted her hand, but before her finger could reach her head, red vines burst from the ground, wrapping her up and binding her arms to her side.

"And I told you it wasn't over," he smirked. "You caught me off guard before. It won't happen again."

Dante turned. "Rivik, the Darkstone; get with Celeste. Use it."

Rivik nodded and pulled the box from his coat. He lifted the box free, and his arm froze. He looked down at the box to see blood splatter over it, a large sword protruding through his chest.

"Ughh, that's . . . not good," he grunted out before falling to his knees.

Standing behind him, holding the sword that ran him through, was Spiro. The dragon knight snickered, reached over Rivik's shoulder, and grabbed the Darkstone in its container.

"Well, that was easy," he grinned.

Sera screamed and slid across the ground, catching Rivik's body as he collapsed forward. Tears streamed down her face as she held his head in her lap.

"Sorry, love . . . looks like . . . I messed this one up," he groaned.

"Shh—shh. —shh . . . don't say that . . . you'll be fine. You'll—" she protested.

"Pretty sure the heart isn't just a flesh wound," Rivik chuckled and coughed up blood.

"Spiro, what are you doing? Why would you betray us?" Celeste's face sank in confusion.

"Betray you?" he laughed. "I was never with you. I am serving my master, the glorious Draka Mors."

"Serving? But . . . you told us . . . your village—" Celeste protested.

"You mean the little village of horrors? Yes, most people would see a paradise filled with smiling faces because most people don't look past the surface. It was a small village and yet, somehow, I was invisible—or worse. The other kids—they laughed at me, mocked me, sometimes they'd even pretend to include me in games only to gang up on me and beat me."

"What about your brothers? Your sister?" Ash asked.

Spiro laughed. "My brothers? They were the worst. Every night when I'd lay down to sleep, they'd find some way to torture me. Bugs on my pillow, a snake in my bed—they would wait until I fell asleep and tie me to the bed with a gag in my mouth. They thought it was so funny to pick on me. Made my life miserable. And my sister, she treated me like I was a living, breathing plague. The only person in that gods-forsaken town worth remembering was sweet Leana. She made life bearable—until she fell in love with my older brother, and I went back to be nothing."

"It was all a lie?" Dante questioned.

"No, it was true. Except that when the dragon came, I wasn't afraid, I was delighted. My whole life I'd been weak and invisible, and here was this majestic creature, so powerful no one would ever overlook them. I heard my master's voice in my head. He offered me power, immortality—a new life."

"And what did you have to give him in return?" Vale glared.

"Nothing I wasn't eager to give. After I proved myself to him, he allowed me to bind my life to his, and I became his thrall."

"Proved?" Vale asked.

"When I found out my master was being hunted by foolish dragon knights, I saw my opportunity. I set a trap to lure the knights in. Told them a story. While their eyes were fixed on me, my master ambushed them. He even let me help kill them," Spiro laughed.

"Your village—that was the trap?" Caelan asked.

"Yes. It wasn't the dragons who burned down my village, it was me. I killed them all. I bathed in their blood, and through it, I was reborn. I took the armor of one of those foolish knights and have been using it ever since."

"But you were fighting him—we saw you at Wellar," Azalea protested, still tugging unsuccessfully against the vines that bound her.

"What better way to gain your trust? And gain it I did. You were quick to turn to me. The whole way, I was working against you, and you never even noticed. I convinced the death dragon to attack you. I sabotaged the drow repellant on the ship. I bumped his throw on purpose. It was all me. And you never even suspected. Did you ever wonder how Valron always knew where you were and where you were going? It was me."

"He found us even when you were not with us," Dante said.

"The necklace I gave to Rivik is enchanted. It allowed Valron to track you," Spiro smirked. "I made up the story about the dragon knight customs."

"You and Valron . . . know each other?" Azalea looked confused.

"We've been watching you for a long time. My master wanted me, his most dedicated thrall, to keep watch. I did so much more. Now, he will be king of dragons, all thanks to me! To me!" Spiro laughed.

"You've done very well, Spiro. You shall be rewarded. Now give me the Darkstone." Valron extended his hand.

Spiro tightened his grip around the box. "You will keep your promise? Make me into a dragon, that I can be like my master?"

Valron nodded. "I will make you just like your master."

Spiro tossed the box to Valron, who caught it with a grin.

"You think—" Caelan gripped his stomach and shook his head, laughing so hard his eyes welled with tears. "You think he's going to—" he shook his head again. "You think he's going to turn you into a dragon?"

Spiro glared. "Shut your mouth and die with dignity. I will not be mocked by the likes of you!"

Caelan straightened up and smiled brightly. "I'm not mocking you. I'm distracting you."

Spiro turned to see Sera's face in front of his. She stared straight into his eyes, as if peering into his soul. Her knife buried into his stomach. He groaned, and she sneered, slowly twisting the blade. She released the handle and then gripped it again to twist it farther and farther, ensuring his wound would not seal. She pulled her blade free and stepped back, spitting on the ground at his feet.

Spiro coughed up blood as pain filled his body. He stumbled toward Draka Mors, clutching his wound.

"Master . . . help me," he pleaded.

Shadows of the Dark Realm

The great silver dragon cocked his head to the side and grunted. "Why?"

Tears filled Spiro's eyes. "I have . . . devoted my life . . . to you . . . I am your loyal servant . . . I—"

"You're riiiiight . . . " Draka Mors reached his tail out, curling it so Spiro could lean on it. The dragon knight wrapped his arms over the dragon's tail, using it to hold himself up.

"Thank you . . . master . . . I knew you wouldn't let me . . . die . . . " Spiro's words grew softer.

Draka Mors flicked his tail, and Spiro's body flew through the air, bouncing on the ground and crunching into the stone guardrail at the edge of a nearby road. He grunted as his head struck the stone, and he slumped lifelessly to the ground.

"Disgusting creaturrrrre, you outlived yooour usefulness."

"I will return once my queen has taken possession of the Vas Noomi." Valron walked over to stand next to Draka Mors.

"I don't think so," Vale said, lifting his sword.

Valron rolled his eyes. "How boring. We've done this dance. You can't even—"

Dante fired a blast of magical energy at Valron. Draka Mors roared and sprayed his silver flames at the group, forcing them to dive back.

Kade exhaled and his body began to glow and then grow. The orange light pulsed until he stood in his massive dragon form. He dove for Draka Mors, who flew up into the sky. Kade flew after him, and the two battled back and forth, striking and slashing, flames bursting wildly as they struggled in their aerial wrestling match.

The others attacked Valron, coordinating their strikes but finding no success. Valron caught Grom by the arms and threw the troll effortlessly, sending him bouncing and rolling down a hill. Caelan's arrows bounced off some invisible barrier that surrounded Valron. Ash managed to strike him in the jaw, to which Valron responded by hitting him so hard in the chest he slumped forward, and then striking his head so hard, Ash fell to the ground unconscious.

Valron caught the tip of Celeste's sword in his fingers and snapped the thin blade. He sent a burst of magical energy into her. Had it not been for the Shield of Argon given to her by Kade, she would have been killed.

Sera was trying to cut the vines that bound Azalea when Valron sent a current of electricity through her body so hard she shook and convulsed before slumping to the ground. Dante and Caelan continued to work together, but to no avail. Valron teleported out of the way of one of Caelan's arrows before striking him again and again, hitting him fast and hard. Caelan gasped and struggled to breathe as his vision blurred.

Valron let his body fall to the ground, Caelan groaning and gasping for air as Valron chuckled.

"This is almost entertaining."

Dante fired a blast of energy at Valron's head. Valron extended his hand, catching it and sending it back, knocking Dante away and leaving only Vale between him and Azalea.

"Are you dim? You did see what I just did to your friends. You really think standing in my way is a good idea?" Valron taunted.

"Good idea. Bad idea. It makes no difference. You're not taking her." Vale tightened his grip on his sword.

His blade swirled forward surprisingly fast. Valron ducked back, barely avoiding it. Vale swung and thrust. Valron dodged. He was backing up to where Dante was struggling to get back to his feet.

"We've done this dance. It's so predictable," Valron scoffed.

"Let's try something new." Vale spun, holding his blade with one hand as he sliced at Valron's throat. Valron leaned back, narrowly avoiding the strike. As he spun, Vale pulled a dagger from behind his back with his other hand, stabbing it at Valron's head. Valron's hand shot up instinctively. He gasped as the dagger pierced his hand. Vale smirked as he readied his sword again.

Valron sneered and pulled the knife from his hand, dropping it to the ground. He looked at the blood and slowly licked the wound. He held his hand out and Vale watched as the skin closed up, healing almost instantly.

"You see, now, how futile your efforts are?" Valron chuckled.

"Mine may be. But hers . . . " Vale gestured over his shoulder.

Shadows of the Dark Realm

Azalea tilted her head back and screamed, the red vines holding her shattering into dust. Her body glowed as she levitated off the ground. Chest rising and falling, breathing heavy, she glared down at Valron.

"Cute, but your power is no match for mine," Valron smirked.

"It is . . . not just her power," Dante grunted as he got to his feet. "You began the Nomasyncha process. Now she can draw not only her power but that of Vespera as well."

Valron's eyes widened. "Th-that's not—"

Valron reached his hand out and red energy fired from it. It bounced away from Azalea without her even flinching. She floated slowly closer to him. He attacked again and again, slinging magic wildly. For all his effort, not a single strike even slowed her down. He started to sweat as he stepped back, trying to distance himself from her. He closed his eyes and let out a long, slow breath. A glowing ring of lighting surrounded his body and surged with power. Azalea stopped, hovering in place, looking down at him.

"That's right, you know what this is. The Soul Wave may not hurt you, but your friends . . . " Valron extended his arms. "They will all die."

"He has the Darkstone, Azalea; you have to stop him, even if it costs us our lives," Vale cried out.

"Hey," Caelan replied, pushing himself up. "I mean, yeah, but . . . at least feel bad about it, for a while."

Valron turned the pulsing red ring expanding around his waist. "Surrender yourself and they live. Resist and they die. What's it going to be? Your life or theirs? You have but a moment to decide."

"Neither," Dante shouted as he charged forward.

The ring of red lighting struck him, and he grunted but pushed through it. The energy pierced his body and pulsed around him like lightning striking repeatedly in the same spot. He groaned and pressed forward, wrapping his arms around Valron.

"What . . . how are you . . . get off," Valron grunted.

"That is an attack you can only use once," Dante chuckled and closed his eyes.

He summoned a large, blue dome that encased himself and Valron. Valron cried out as the energy of his spirit wave spell flashed out, hitting Dante's dome and ricocheting back in. Light and smoke filled the air until the dome finally faded. Dante's cloak was covered in burns, his body charred. His grip released as he slumped to the ground.

Valron looked at him in annoyance. "Fool, you accomplished nothing," he grunted as his body lifted off the ground, encased in a purple light.

"I see you now. I see your power, your fear." Azalea's voice sounded ethereal as she lifted her hand, raising Valron higher. "All you have belongs to me." She squeezed her fist, and a glowing ball of energy drew from Valron's chest and into hers. She dropped him to the ground.

Valron tapped his chest, breathing heavily. He extended his hand. Nothing happened. He grunted and tried again. Still nothing.

"You're mortal now. You have no magic. No link to the Spirit Realm. No power at all," Azalea said.

"W-wait . . .n-no . . . you can't do that . . . please, I," he pleaded.

"Hey, ralk-face," Caelan called out.

Valron looked over in time to see the arrow as it struck him between the eyes, knocking his head back. He was dead before his body hit the ground.

Azalea floated down until she was standing on the ground, and the haze around her disappeared. She rushed over to Dante. Vale was already leaning over him, clutching his hand.

"What did you do?" Vale shook his head.

"Sorry, I know dying for everyone else . . . is kind of your thing. Thought I would give it a try." Dante's words were slow and breathy.

"What happened to not being the one to make the sacrifice? All the knowledge you have?" Vale protested.

"Turns out . . . I am just a gershwa . . . "

"You saved us all."

"Not yet." Dante's hand trembled as he reached into his cloak and pulled out the orange-red feather and pushed it into Vale's palm.

"Wait, is that what I think it is?"

Dante nodded. "Place it on the wound . . . and hold your hand over it. The feather will do the rest."

Vale nodded and started to move Dante's arm out of the way. Dante pulled it back and shook his head.

"Not mine. Rivik. Give it to Rivik."

Vale stared at him. "No, not now. She told you how to make the potion, to fix your heart. You can—"

"Vale . . . fixing . . . my heart . . . will not bring back . . . my daughter. I thought . . . I thought I needed . . . to live . . . to be the warehouse . . . of knowledge . . . to preserve it—" He coughed and chucked. "Having traveled . . . with all of you . . . let me do this."

"But—"

"I have lived too long. I am weary. I just want to rest. Please . . . my friend . . . let me go . . . let me have peace."

"It should have been me." Vale gripped Dante's hand tighter.

Dante chucked and then groaned. "I hope . . . you find your peace. To me . . . you will always be . . . a man of honor."

Caelan, Ash, and Azalea were standing over Dante as his eyes closed and his body went limp. Vale gripped the feather tightly and walked toward Sera, who was still holding Rivik, weeping as Grom knelt over her.

"What do we do about them?" Caelan asked.

Vale glanced up to see that the sky battle between Draka Mors and Kade was still ongoing. They were high enough that even Caelan's arrows couldn't reach them. Celeste stood behind the others at a distance, keeping herself out of the fray as her focus shifted between Kade's fight and what Vale was doing.

"Nothing we can do right now. It's up to Kade," Vale said, kneeling down next to Rivik.

"He's cold," Sera wept, rocking Rivik's body in her lap. "Why is he so cold?"

Sera looked confused as Vale gently moved her hands out of the way and pressed the orange phoenix feather against Rivik's chest. The feather glowed as if being consumed by flame, fizzling and sparking as it disappeared into a burst of orange flakes that sank into the blood on Rivik's chest. Light pulsed and the skin parted by steel closed back up. It looked similar to how Valron had healed but a bit slower and with a lot more glowing. The skin of his chest knit together, and a long, thick scar formed where the two pieces of flesh reunited. Then, nothing. For an eternal moment in which no one even breathed, there was nothing.

Suddenly, Rivik gasped and sat up, his hand clutching his chest. He blinked and shook his head.

"W-what happened?" he asked, sounding confused.

Sera gasped and punched him in the arm before wrapping him up and smothering him in kisses.

"What . . . what did I do?" He looked sincerely confused.

"You emptos goraum, you died!" she said before kissing him again. Rivik leaned his head back.

"Died? What do you mean died?"

"What part has you confused? Spiro killed you. Then we used a magical feather Dante had in his pocket to bring you back to life. Try to keep up," Caelan smirked.

A loud boom interrupted them as the ground beneath them shook. Dust and debris filled the air, making it impossible to see. When the dust settled, Draka Mors was standing on top of Kade, pinning the orange dragon to the ground with his hind feet and roaring triumphantly. Kade, in his dragon form, was struggling, but his effort was minimal, and his resistance weak.

"Slaying soooome younglings does not mmmmean you can sssstand before the might of an eeeeelder dragon!" Draka Mors snickered proudly.

He lifted his head, preparing to sink his fangs into Kade's exposed neck. An arrow pierced his scales, causing Draka Mors to flinch. He roared and bore his fangs.

"You have meeeeeeddled in the affairs of draggggggons. You shall rrrregret it," Draka Mors roared.

"Grom . . . kill . . . dragon." Grom's axes slammed into Draka Mors's hind leg. The axes shook and vibrated as they deflected off the dragon's hard scales. He pulled his hands back, looking confused.

"No . . . fair . . . Grom crush." He lifted his arms up again. Draka Mors turned his neck to snap at the troll. Celeste stood as if ready to fight, but she made no move toward the dragon.

Vale pushed her out of the way as he crossed the gap and nearly reached Kade. For a moment, Draka Mors was off balance, trying to determine which of his attackers to deal with first. When Vale tried to pull Kade free, the silver dragon turned all his attention to him.

"I am gooooing to enjoy . . . killllling you," his voice rumbled.

He lifted his head back, flames forming in his throat. Kade, still in dragon form, was too weak to move on his own and too heavy to drag. If Vale leapt aside, he could spare himself but would doom Kade to the fire. He thrust his blade into the dragon's chest, the black metal piercing the dragon's scales. Draka Mors groaned in surprise as the force kept him reared back. Rivik, who had retrieved his spear, hurled it at the dragon. The metal shaft whistled as it cut through the air, piercing into the silver dragon's side. Draka Mors howled in pain as his weight shifted.

"I willllll burn you allllll!" His wings started to flap; heat pulsed from his body.

"No," Azalea replied, her body lifting off the ground again as she closed her eyes, holding her palms up and arms out.

"You will burn in Lamera." A great purple beam shot from her chest into the silver dragon, piercing its scales and bursting out the other side.

Draka Mors blinked, a gaping hole in his chest. Rivik tugged his spear out of the dragon's side and whirled it around as he moved in front of the silver-scaled beast. Draka Mors stumbled and slouched to the ground, looking confused. His gaze shifted down to see Rivik standing in front of him. His body trembled, and for the first time in thousands of years, he felt fear.

"I ammmm the ancient of days . . . the eternal . . . unnnending. I have survived . . . eons of mennnn. I will not be . . . felled by aaaa . . . " His words were slow and clumsy as he tried to hold on.

"You were dead the moment you burned my village, you piece of gwar." Rivik's spear thrust into the open hole caused by Azalea's magic.

He shoved the spear deep into the dragon's chest until it pierced the dragon's heart.

Draka Mors's eyes closed, his long neck curling in on itself as he slumped to the ground with a thunderous crash that made the earth around them tremble.

Chapter 51

The Legend of the Seekers

Before they left, Vale retrieved the Darkstone from Valron's body. Grom carried Dante over his shoulder, while Ash carried Kade after he'd shifted back into his human form. They made their way to the nearest town, Elysia. While the city looked the same as it had the last time they were here, it felt very different. Once they checked Kade into a room, the others went out to bury Dante and offer their last respects. They took a few days to recover and prepare for the journey back to the palace. Celeste was overly eager, constantly trying to rush them back. The others just ignored her.

Finally, with Kade recovered, they decided it was time to leave. They started down the road to a private place where they would not be disturbed.

"Our quest is not over. We need to get the Darkstone back straightaway," Celeste demanded. "Kade, can you open a portal?"

"About that," Rivik started.

"You're not coming," Vale finished.

"I have done what I set out to do. My village will no longer be Vagra. Our honor is restored. What else do I need?" Rivik grinned.

"Really? After all that? There's nothing you would wish for? Surely, there has to be something," Caelan asked.

"There is plenty I would wish for. Nothing obtained that way has any value to me. I don't trust things earned by magic. I'll keep my fate in my own hands. I have no wish, only a request: that I may take the head of Draka Mors to complete our custom and honor our traditions."

"It is yours," Vale spoke for everyone. "What will you do now?"

Rivik shrugged. "I'm not sure. My village will need some rebuilding. After that, who knows? Perhaps I will hunt down that Death Dragon and get revenge for Rinar."

"Don't be emptos," Sera punched him in the shoulder.

"Me? You're the emptos one!" he snapped back.

Sera put her hands on her hips. "Excuse me?"

Rivik shrugged. "Look at your taste in men."

Sera rolled her eyes as Rivik chuckled to himself. "You've got a point there."

"Let's get going," Rivik nudged her.

"You too?" Caelan asked in surprise.

"Yeah, as ridiculous as my man is, he's often right about these sorts of things. Just don't tell him I said that."

"I'm standing right here," Rivik protested.

Sera put her hand on his cheek softly. "And you're looking good doing it. Now be quiet."

"Grom . . . go, too."

"Of course, Grom, you're part of the family now," Rivik said.

The troll smiled brightly. Grom, Sera, and Rivik went around the group, hugging, shaking hands, saying their goodbyes as they wished the others well.

"If you all ever end up in Rag'amor again, don't be strangers," Sera smiled sweetly.

"If ever you need anything . . . " Vale said as the three started toward the wall.

Rivik looked over his shoulder. "We know. And you."

"I know," Vale nodded.

"Before you go." Kade reached out. Dangling from his hand were three small amulets.

"You're giving us jewelry?" Rivik grinned. "I didn't think you were the type."

Kade grunted, "These are Amulets of Calling. I got them from an elven tinkerer. Each is bound together. If you press the stone, the other amulets will pulse with a glowing energy."

"If you find yourself in need." Kade glanced away as they took the amulets.

"We press the stone, and everyone comes running?" Rivik grinned.

Kade nodded. "It would alert the rest of us that you were in trouble and help us find you. It uses tracer magic so if you activate it, the other amulets will lightly tug on the wearer in your direction."

"Kade, that is a very thoughtful gift. Thank you." Sera hugged him. Kade stood rigid for a moment before returning the embrace.

"Grom . . . like . . . shiny. Stone . . . purple—"

"Don't touch it; it will set the thing off," Rivik warned.

Grom scowled. "Grom know . . . little man be silent,"

Sera and Rivik made their rounds, saying final farewells. Sera took a moment to speak to each person, offering them a parting message. Rivik said less but nodded in agreement as she spoke. After she finished her farewells, she gave each person a hug, with the exception of Celeste, who she nodded to but did not embrace. Grom followed in her wake, imitating the goodbye process. It was clear trolls didn't express such sentiments often as he seemed to have no idea what to do. One by one, Grom picked up each of them, lifting them off the ground with what was too firm a squeeze to be considered a hug.

With their farewells said, the three headed off. Vale, Azalea, Caelan, Ash, Kade, and Celeste watched in silence for a moment until their friends become little more than silhouettes on the horizon. It was a strange feeling. They hadn't known each other all that long, but their departure left a sense of loneliness hanging over the group. The silence that ensued was heavy.

Kade reached into his pack and pulled out several more amulets, giving them to everyone in the group except Celeste. She seemed offended by the slight but said nothing.

"My father's death is long overdue. It's time I take my leave as well."

"Wait, can you at least teleport us to the palace before you go?" Celeste sounded annoyed, as if it was absurd for him not to offer.

"Hold on princess," Caelan interrupted. "We're not going back until we've made our wishes."

"That can wait. After we return the Darkstone, my uncle will—"

"Yeah, no. I'm not putting my hope in a Royal who ordered my death not that long ago. We do the wishes, then we take the stone back," Caelan said.

"Agreed," voiced the others in unanimous support.

"One thing you should know about the Darkstone before you use it," Kade started. "I explained to Dante that the power that holds the veil is Inherent. The wishes are source magic. All source magic comes from somewhere. The Darkstone's wish-granting power comes from the soul of a djinn. It is limitless because it draws from exchange. The greater the wish, the greater the cost."

"What do you mean, 'an exchange?'" Caelan asked.

"If you change the past to save someone who was supposed to die, the magic will take the life of someone who was supposed to live in their place. If you make one kingdom prosper, another will fall to ruin. The exchange is that the stone will keep all things in balance. Your wish can control what the magic gives, but there is only one way to control what it takes."

"Which is?" Vale asked.

"A sacrifice."

"A sacrifice of what?"

"It could be anything. The greater the sacrifice, the more potent the magic. The most powerful sacrifice is that of life."

"You mean like—" Vale started.

"Yes. Without a sacrifice—an acceptable exchange—the wish will take its price at random. Either way, no wish is ever granted without equal loss being enacted. I thought you'd want to know before using it."

"You already made a wish," Caelan pointed out.

Kade nodded. "I will pay the price of it soon. Once my father is dead."

"What did you sacrifice?" Vale asked.

"That is my business," Kade answered.

"You're sure you won't come with us? At least to the palace?" Vale urged.

Kade shook his head. "I've been waiting for this for a thousand years. It's finally time. I'm going to go track down my father and kill him."

"Any idea where he is, your father?" Vale asked.

"North of the Sapphire Sea. Far beyond our journey together. His roost is in the northern-most reaches of the Dragon Lands where few ever venture."

Caelan grasped Kade's shoulder and squeezed. "You know, when we first met, I really didn't like you. I thought of a hundred ways to kill you."

"There aren't that many ways to kill me," Kade smirked.

Caelan shrugged. "Maybe not, but now I'm rooting for you. Good luck killing your father."

"We couldn't have done it without you," Vale said, shaking Kade's hand.

"I know," Kade smiled.

"Thanks to you, for the first time, I have a chance to get justice for my mother. In all my years, I've never had reason to say thank you to anyone for anything, but thank you. I'll open the portal so you can go."

"You're gonna leave, just like that? No goodbye roll in the hay? Not so much as a kiss? Here I was thinking we'd had a special moment, and now you're going to fly off to the edge of the world to never be seen again? Talk about blowing a girl off," Azalea grinned.

"Something tells me, this isn't the last I will see of you, Azalea." Kade bowed his head.

"You should be so lucky," she replied.

"It's strange, I haven't felt like this in centuries. I think I might actually miss you," Kade said to the others.

"Now you're just embarrassing yourself. Get out of here while we still have some respect for you," Caelan teased.

Kade chuckled and turned his attention. "One last thing before I go."

He reached out in a flash and grabbed Celeste by the throat, lifting her off the ground. He pulled her close as she gasped and choked. Orange flames danced in his eyes. Celeste struggled, pulling at his wrists to no avail.

"If they did not need you to complete their wishes, I would fly you above the clouds and drop you. You may have saved your kingdom, but you are no hero. You are nothing. Once my father is dead and their wishes are complete, I want you to know that, if somehow you are still alive, I will come for you. I will kill you. You won't know when. You won't know how. But there is no world where you get to live on after what you did."

Celeste's face turned bright red as she gargled desperately. Kade tossed her back. She landed on her back, gasping for air and clutching her throat.

Kade extended his arm and a portal trimmed with orange light appeared behind the group. "The portal will take you to the gate just outside the capital. I'll hold it open for as long as I can, but once I'm far enough away, the magic will fade. I wouldn't waste too much time."

He gave one last goodbye nod and flew into the air, disappearing behind the clouds.

"Ok, let's make our wishes and go," Caelan suggested.

"Seriously? After what Kade just told us? You want to risk it? No! We need to get the Darkstone back to my uncle. Once we have saved the kingdom, then you can worry about your wishes," Celeste protested.

"And what—trust that the king, who no longer needs us, will, out of his immense gratitude, allow us to make our wishes freely?" Caelan laughed.

"Yes. King Alistar is a man of honor."

"I wouldn't trust a Royal to do anything that didn't suit their own interest."

Celeste crossed her arms in front of her chest. "And if I refuse?"

Caelan grinned and motioned to Ash. "We let Ash tear you apart slowly for what you did to Owen."

"Fine, but we don't have a lot of time. If you want my help,

Shadows of the Dark Realm

we do it all at once. I'll activate the stone, you make your wishes, and we go," Celeste declared.

"Can we do that?" Azalea asked.

"It's this or nothing. Torture me, kill me, I don't care. I will not risk the fall of Parisia to another unnecessary delay."

They gathered around and put their hands on the stone. Each of them closed their eyes, and the Darkstone began to pulse as it had when Kade used it. When they opened their eyes, Celeste had moved to the edge of the portal. She held the stone in her hand and stepped through it without a word.

The group moved quickly, following her through the portal. As they stepped into it, they were whisked away. In a flash, they were standing just outside the gates to the capital city of Parisia.

"Did it work?" Azalea asked, sliding her hands down her stomach and sides. "I don't feel any different."

"Kade said we would know. But how?" Ash asked.

The rumble of hooves echoed around them, growing louder as riders approached them with great haste. Celeste was already walking toward the approaching soldiers.

"Celeste, what did you do?" Vale asked.

She turned and smiled. "What I always do, I protected you from yourselves. You knew the cost and yet were so determined to make your wishes. I must say, I'm disappointed in each of you."

"What ... did ... you ... do?" Azalea repeated the question.

"I put limits on your wishes. Since you can't be trusted to do what is right, I did what was necessary—again. Nothing that could take life, cause significant damage, or bring harm to innocent people. In gratitude for your service, I allowed the Darkstone to grant as much of your wish as possible within those parameters," Celeste grinned.

"You don't even know what our wishes were," Caelan started.

"I'm done talking about it. If you'd like to join me, I expect there is a parade in our future."

Caelan pulled back an arrow, aiming it at Celeste's head. "Not in yours."

"Caelan . . . don't," Vale nodded as knights swarmed around them, spears at the ready.

"Oh, no. It looks like you missed your shot," Celeste smiled.

"Everything ok, Lady Celeste?" one of the knights on horseback asked.

"Yes, commander, my friend here was just dramatically reenacting a part of our adventure. Please take us to my uncle. I have what he's been waiting for."

The guard escorted them through the city streets. Knights in exquisite armor marched in perfect unison on either side of the group. Horsemen rode behind them, and three rows of knights marched like a moving wall in front of them. People gathered, gates and doors swung up as the entourage guided them straight into the throne room.

"Celeste! My beloved niece, you have returned!" King Alistar stood from his chair and clasped his hands together. "I was wrought with worry."

"Not only have I returned, uncle, I have succeeded. I did what no other seeker could. I retrieved for you, the Darkstone." She lifted her hand and opened it, revealing the black stone orb.

The room gasped and cheered. The king descended the stairs and embraced Celeste with a warm hug. He shook the hand of each of the others, congratulating them on their success. A group of mages collected the Darkstone from Celeste and rushed off to return it to its place.

"Parisia owes you all an incredible debt," he announced in a booming voice as he ascended back to his throne. "As I have promised, you will each be awarded land, titles, wealth, and whatever else you desire that is within my power to grant. My counselor will meet with each of you separately to determine what reward can best express the gratitude of our kingdom for your heroic service. For now, I am sure you need rest. Please, be my guests here in the palace. My staff will wait on you and tend to your every desire. Welcome home, lords, champions, heroes of Parisia!"

Before anything else could be said they were whisked away, put up in a private wing of the palace reserved for the king's special guests. They spent the first few days eating, resting,

Shadows of the Dark Realm

soaking in all that had happened. Then the parades. The king had them marched all around the empire to celebrations of joy so the whole kingdom could see its heroes. His hope was to encourage future generations to answer his call, should Parisia ever be in need again.

With the Darkstone returned, the monsters and troubles that had been growing faded back into the darkness. The kingdom was once again at peace in the blissful joys of its squalor.

* * *

Celeste knelt before the king; a few counselors and guards were the only others in the room.

"The law does not even allow for—" King Alistar said.

"You are the king—change it. Need I remind you that without me, there would be no law, because this kingdom would be in ruin."

"I can't just snap my fingers and change the law."

"You have no idea what I sacrificed, what I had to do to ensure that the Darkstone was returned as soon as possible. You pushed me. You told me it necessary, so I did it. I gave up too much for this to have you go back on your word." Celeste glared up at the king.

"It's a big ask, Celeste."

"I'm not asking. You will change the law, and you will make the announcement today that in view of my achievements, you can think of no greater or more deserved reward than to name me your heir."

King Alistar glared. "You dare instruct me? Who do you think you are?"

"Or should I tell the kingdom how you power the Darkstone? I wonder, how would your beloved people respond if they knew their king was stealing their children to ensure the prosperity of your reign."

"Guards, seize her! Take her to the dungeon!"

Celeste grinned. "You know, arresting me after parading us around as the saviors of the kingdom is going to lead to some difficult questions."

"I can deal with questions; I will not deal with this treason."

"Perhaps, you could. However, I left instructions with several associates that, should something happen to me, they may uncover some evidence that would be more difficult to deal with."

"You would destroy your own family over this?" King Alistar challenged.

"You would see your kingdom fall, all to avoid naming me your heir? That's all it takes, and all of this goes away."

After a moment of staring, King Alistar agreed.

"Thank you, your majesty. It's been a pleasure." Celeste bowed.

"Get out of my sight before I change my mind and lock you in a dungeon so deep, you'll forget what light looks like." He scowled and sank into his throne.

Papers were drawn up, the laws were changed, and the king sent heralds to every corner of the kingdom to announce Celeste would be his heir.

That night, King Alistar retired to his quarters. He lived on the highest floor of the palace. Guards were posted at the top and bottom of the stairs that provided the only access to his floor, giving him both protection and privacy.

The king removed his crown and royal garments, replacing them with a blue robe made of the finest silk as he retired to the far corner of his bedchamber.

His room had a balcony looking out over the city below, giving him an unhindered view of the clear night sky. The light of the moon made the waters around the palace sparkle like glistening diamonds. The cloudless night sky was peacefully serene and calm.

King Alistar leaned over the railing of his balcony and took a deep breath. The Darkstone was finally back where it belonged. His kingdom and his legacy were secure. He should rest and enjoy the victory, but Celeste was pestering his mind. He was already formulating a plan to rid himself of his troublesome niece—a tragic accident that claimed the life of one of Parisia's greatest heroes. He played it out in his mind, and a smile formed on his face. There was no way *that girl* would ever inherit his kingdom.

"Lovely night," a voice came from behind him.

King Alistar whirled around, heart pounding in his chest. "Who said that? Who's there?"

Vale stepped out from behind the wall he'd been leaning against and into the light cast by the torches set along the balcony exterior.

Alistar's hand clutched his chest. "Oh, Vale, it's you. You gave me quite the fright. You know, you really shouldn't be up here. Entering the king's private residence without permission is an act of treason and punishable by death. How did you get here, anyway?"

"Friend of mine," the Black Swordsman gestured, and a second man stepped into view. This one was wearing a green, hooded cloak and had a bow strapped over his back. He smiled warmly and waved.

"Who is this?"

"You remember Caelan, the man you ordered me to kill? The terrorist, Caelan."

King Alistar's eyes grew wide. "Guards!"

"Do you remember when we first met?" Vale lifted the black blade in his hand, pointing it at the king and causing him to go quiet. Vale paced back and forth menacingly.

King Alistar swallowed. "Well, yes, you were . . . just a-a boy."

"I thought Fortuo himself had blessed me. A king rescuing me, a lowly slave boy, setting me free, bringing me to this paradise. I was so grateful that when you came back, asking me to wield my sword to protect all you had given me, I didn't hesitate. I carried out every order without question. I knew the king who rescued me from war would never command something evil. I trusted you, bled for you, killed for you," Vale said, all while staring into his blade.

"You . . . were a loyal and faithful knight. Until you led your men to—"

"It's funny that you should mention that, Your Majesty," Vale interrupted the king's jab. "You stripped me of my rank, position, and title. You made me the disgraced knight for killing my entire unit after they went mad. Yet still I assumed you were right, that my shame was what I deserved. Who was I to question the judgment of such a noble king?"

"Well . . . that is true, you are right to—"

"Imagine my surprise when I learned it was all a lie. That the massacre that haunted my dreams and caused my curse was orchestrated by you." Vale turned to face the king.

"What?! How dare you!"

Vale pulled a ruby-studded dagger with a golden hilt from behind his back. "I'd buried it after the massacre. Now I know what it is—the dagger of Arran Groaul."

"You are mistaken. Someone has bewitched you, turned you against me."

"There's an easy way to be sure. I give this to your guards at the door, tell them it's a gift for their exceptional service, then leave you be."

The king's eyes widened as terror washed over him. He reached his arms out. "Wait . . . d-don't do that . . . I-I can explain. You just need to listen to me. You have to understand the burden I carry. Ruling demands hard choices—choices I would never desire to—"

"I trusted you. You betrayed me. You are a disgrace to the crown you wear."

"W-w-what are you going to do? You can't kill me. I am your king. You swore an oath. You are honor bound to—"

"Honor? Let me show you what honor demands."

"Y-y-your archer . . . stop him . . . I'll give you anything. Money . . . power . . . name it. I'll give it to you."

"Save your breath o' king. That village you had wiped out was my home. I wouldn't stop him for all the gold in your vaults."

"P-p-please . . . you don't have to do this—" The king's voice caught as Vale's sword pierced his chest.

"Don't worry, this won't kill you. This is to purify my blade from all the blood it shed for you," Vale said, staring the king in his face.

King Alistar grabbed onto Vale, desperately trying to hold

himself up as tears filled his eyes. His other hand clutched his wound as blood oozed between his fingers. He opened his mouth to speak, but his words caught in his throat.

"It's the fall that will kill you."

Alistar looked up, realization striking him as Vale shoved him hard. He felt his back hit the railing, slowing his momentum. Vale reached down and lifted his feet, sending Alistar's weight back and casting him over the railing. The king reached up, desperately trying to grab hold of the ledge, watching as it got farther and farther away. The breeze was cool and refreshing as his body plummeted downward. For a moment, it felt nice. He hit the ground with a loud crack.

Caelan leaned over the railing next to Vale to get a look at the king's body.

"Oh, that's gonna be a fun mess to clean up. Some poor servant is in for a long night."

"Time to go," Vale cut him off. They made their way around the balcony to the other side of the upper floor where they'd left the rope they used to climb up.

"How did you know to bury the knife? And when did you retrieve it?" Caelan asked.

"What? Oh, this?" Vale pulled out the dagger he'd showed the king. "This is a vanity blade made by a local craftsman. I knew he wouldn't look closely enough to notice. He just needed to see something."

"That was a bluff?" Caelan shook his head and grinned.

Vale smirked.

"I'm a good influence on you."

"Keep talking, there's a nice clean spot next to the king," Vale warned.

They took turns sliding down the rope to the floor below. Quickly, they made their way inside, down the stairs and out of the palace as the clamor of rushing guards grew louder.

They made it outside the palace itself without incident, crossed the courtyard, and made it through the palace gates, which were still open. They moved quickly away from the palace, trying to cover as much ground as possible before the guards could coordinate a response. Time was on their side for the moment, but with every passing second it would start to turn against them.

Caelan grabbed Vale's arm and pulled him against the stone wall of a nearby building as a group of soldiers charged by.

"What's happened?" they could hear one of them asking.

"Someone in the palace must have been attacked," another answered.

Good, Vale thought. The guards were still responding to the alarm. That meant they wouldn't move to secure the outer wall yet. If they could reach the outer wall of the castle and make it into the capital itself before the signal fires were lit, things would be much easier.

Vale kept his hand on the hilt of his sword as they ran. The chaos was greater than he expected. Their response times were slower than they should be. Parisian soldiers had grown undisciplined over years of complacency. Under normal circumstances, Vale would have found this irritating. Today was not a normal day.

They hurried, walking at a rapid pace, careful not to run so as to draw unwanted attention. They needed to look busy, not suspicious. One wrong move, a single shout from a passerby, and they'd be ralked.

Two guards stood between them and a clear path to freedom. Vale walked toward the gate. Caelan caught his arm, leaning over to catch his breath.

"How are you tired? We've been walking."

"Quickly walking and a lot of it; just give me a second to breath," Caelan protested.

"You can breathe when we reach the tavern," Vale answered.

"You're the worst." Caelan stood up and nodded, walking more slowly toward the gate.

The guards stepped together, closing off the open space.

"Hold it there," one of them shouted. Vale tightened his grip on his sword hilt. If they had to fight their way out, things would get much more difficult.

"Lovely evening, isn't it, gents?" Caelan flashed his easy smile.

"Where you coming from?" one of the guards asked.

"The smith up the hill." Caelan gestured in the direction from which they had come.

"At this hour?"

Caelan chuckled. "Not by choice. I had to drop off some parts for him."

"Supplies?"

He was asking too many questions. Vale exhaled slowly, preparing himself for an altercation.

"I may have had too much to drink the other night. Got up on a table. It broke. Apparently, it had sentimental value. Now the owner's got me running all around, picking up parts the smithy will need to fix it. Finally done—just need to get back and let him know before he sends someone to rough me up."

The guard peered at him for a moment. A long, agonizing moment. "You hear what's going on at the palace?"

Caelan shook his head, "Not a clue. Just trying to get out of the way for whatever it is, you know?"

The two guards exchanged a glance and stepped apart.

"Have a good night," one of them said as Vale and Caelan passed by.

Azalea and Ash were waiting for them at the tavern at the edge of the capital, near the gates. They looked up as the two men entered. Vale and Caelan kept their heads down as they moved over to the table in the back corner of the room.

"Is it done?" Ash asked.

Vale nodded. "We can't stay long. They will be hunting us now."

"What next?" Azalea asked.

"That's up to you. Whatever you decide, I don't recommend remaining in Parisia. We could travel to the wall together, and then go our separate ways," Vale suggested.

"After all that, we are just going to part ways?" Azalea sounded disappointed.

Vale nodded. "We had a mission. It's over. Time we got back to our lives."

"Don't go getting all soft on us," Caelan jested.

"I'm not telling you what to do. If you want to stay together, that's your choice," Vale answered.

"Time for me to head back to Maylor," Ash said.

"To that cesspool?" Caelan smirked.

"You say cesspool. I say home. There's a lot left for me to do there. What about you, Vale?"

"I think it's time I tracked down some witches," Vale answered.

The door behind them opened, causing tension to rush through the group. Two rough-looking drunks stumbled their way in, laughing loudly as they made their way to the bar.

"We should go," Vale said.

"Surely they wouldn't be looking for us yet," Ash countered.

"Probably not, but I will sleep better when we are out of Parisia."

They traveled at night, finding secluded places to sleep during the day when patrols would be more active. The journey was quiet for the most part with only the occasional encounter with farmers or travelers along the way. With the Darkstone back in place, Parisia's lands were returned to their former tranquility. No monsters. No bandits. Nothing but green grass and blue skies as they walked. They spent their time remembering and mostly laughing about their adventures together. There was a melancholy that hovered around them. Their adventure had bonded them in a way that none could explain or even express. They knew this was probably the last time they would see each other. The weight of that felt oddly heavy. Kade was gone. Rivik and Sera had returned to their home. The Seekers who had fought side by side to save the realm were disbanding piece by piece.

They seemed to be ahead of any troops from the capital, but they didn't want to risk carelessness. They were careful to avoid entering towns or cities as a group. When they needed supplies, Caelan would slip in, acquire what they needed, and meet them on the other side. They stopped at the last town before Elysia as they got closer to the wall. Caelan returned with four posters. He handed them to Vale.

"Now we're really famous," he said.

Each poster contained a semi-accurate sketch of one of them, along with their name and REWARD written in big, bold letters.

"Oh, I'm gonna burn some people for this. Why did they make my nose crooked like that? It's just insulting," Azalea protested.

"Read the bottom," Caelan said.

Ash examined his page. "'For the crime of regicide, these four traitors are sentenced to death. Beware, they are armed, dangerous, and ruthless. Reward offered for any or all, dead or alive.' Seriously? We weren't even there," he chuckled.

"Not that part." Caelan pointed to the very bottom of the page.

"By order of Queen Celeste DeLalouche," Vale read. "They made her queen?"

"Ralk," Ash crumbled his paper.

"Can we kill her now?" Caelan asked.

"Two rulers in one week? That seems a little much, don't you think?" Ash jested.

"Just let me kill her a little," Caelan shrugged.

"Leave her be; she's not worth it," Vale replied.

They made their way to the gate. After waiting for nightfall, Azalea transformed into an owl and flew over the wall, waiting for them on the other side.

Caelan shook his head as he watched. "That feels like cheating."

"The guards are looking for a party of four. Three will be less suspicious," Ash said.

"The gate is sealed and guarded. We don't have a writ of passage like last time. They won't just let us out because we ask nice. If I were a gambling man, which I am, I would bet on us having to fight our way out,"

"No. There's another way. The wall has a small access gate, well hidden, invisible from the other side. The Phoenix Legion would use it to sneak out undetected," Vale offered.

"Well, isn't that fun? Could have told us that sooner," Caelan said.

Vale ignored him. He led them around the barracks, past an outcropping of rocks hidden from the view of the watchtower.

He peaked around the rocks. Along the wall was a small door. The door was made to look like stone, blending it in so that it would be hard to spot for anyone who didn't already know it was there. Standing around the gate were three guards.

"Three of us, three of them." Caelan pointed, "One, two, and three. We can each take one, and then we're home free."

"I've got number two," Ash said quickly.

"One," Vale added.

Caelan sighed. "Really, you're going to leave the one that looks like a hairless bear?"

"You should have claimed the one you wanted faster." Ash waved as he rushed off, circling around out of view to make his way behind the guard Caelan had labeled number two.

Caelan turned to Vale, who shrugged, "Hard to argue with that. See you at the gate."

Caelan rolled his eyes, "Typical. Leave all the hard work to Caelan. Been carrying your lazy owa this whole time; why change it up now?"

He walked up to the over-sized guard, acting casual like he was just coming over to ask a question. He could see the guard's attention settle on him. Caelan smiled. Out of the corner of his eye he saw Ash grab and subdue guard two. The ease with which he completed it was annoying.

The guard Caelan was approaching looked even bigger the closer he got. He was holding a giant double-sided battle axe, just to add to his menacing demeanor. The guard eyed Caelan as he approached. Caelan smiled, trying to look as nonthreatening as possible.

"You lost?" The guard's voice was as intimidating as his demeanor.

Caelan nodded. "Is it that obvious? I'm looking for . . . " He used his words to try and draw the guard in. As he got close, he struck. He kicked at the guard's knee, then swung around, wrapping his arm across the guard's neck and trying to choke him. The guard grabbed Caelan's arm, pulled it away from his neck, and threw him.

Hitting the ground knocked the wind out of him. He grunted and blinked through the pain. Before he could move, the guard

Shadows of the Dark Realm

grabbed him, lifted him up, and slammed him back onto the ground. Caelan felt the air leave his lungs. This was great. Had he really survived so much only to die at the hands of an oversized guard?

Caelan felt his feet leave the ground as a hand clutched his throat so tight, he could hardly breathe. He struggled and flailed, trying to kick at the man holding him. He could see the shadowed vignettes growing in his vision. If he didn't do something, he would pass out. Just as he felt himself slipping into the black void of unconsciousness, the pressure on his throat vanished, and his feet hit the ground.

The guard toppled over. Behind him stood Vale.

Caelan coughed and gasped for air. Vale grinned.

"Quit playing around, let's go." He helped Caelan up, and they made their way to the small stone door. It was barred shut. They moved two heavy wooden beams and pushed the stone door open, revealing a dark hallway that led through the wall. Vale led them through it to a small, hidden door on the other side.

He pushed it open, and they stepped outside. The door swung closed and latched behind them with a loud click. They let out a collective sigh of relief. They had done it. With Parisia behind them, they were free. Azalea came walking out of the woods on the other side of the wall.

"Took you long enough," she smirked.

"We had to stop and ask for directions," Caelan replied.

"Let's keep moving," Vale interrupted.

They travelled the rest of the night to put some space between themselves and Parisia. The next morning, after sharing breakfast, it was time to go their separate ways. Ash was the first to go. He stood up from the embers of the morning fire, put his hands on his hips, and announced, "This is where I leave you. It was good to see you again, Caelan. If you ever end up in Maylor again, come find me. But consider my debt to you paid." He smiled and embraced his friend.

"Vale, you are an honorable man. It was my pleasure to stand with you."

Vale nodded in reply.

"Azalea," Ash's tone changed. He hugged her and held on.

"That's enough of that," Caelan interrupted. "Get out of here before I get tired of looking at you."

Ash headed off, back to Maylor.

"I've decided," Azalea brushed her hands over her stomach gently, "I need to figure out who I am, what this power inside me can do, and how I can keep that red naiflo out."

"You have a plan?" Vale asked.

She shook her head. "Just head north for now. I've heard Taggoron has some great mages and some wise sages. Maybe I can find someone who can help me."

"I'll go with you, make sure you—"

Azalea shook her head. "No. I need to do this alone. Besides, you have your own problems to worry about."

"They aren't going anywhere," Vale countered.

"You've put it off long enough. Go. Remove your curse. Be free. Then, if you want, come find me. We can see where the road takes us." She gave him a wink. "And if you need me, just use the amulet. I'll come rescue you, I promise."

Vale chuckled. "My hero."

And then there were two.

"This is it," Vale said.

"Is it? You really think I'm going to leave you alone?" Caelan answered.

Vale shook his head. "Go live your life, Caelan."

"I intend to—right after we kill those witches who murdered your family and cursed you."

"You don't have any reason to help me," Vale started to protest.

"True. You're still the worst."

Vale grumbled, "This is not your fight."

"You can keep talking all you want. I'm coming. Might as well just accept that," Caelan grinned. "Let's go end your curse."

Vale sighed, accepting his fate, even if he didn't like it.

With that, the two set out on a new journey together.

THE END

Afterword

I hope you enjoyed Shadows of the Dark Realm!

Ratings and reviews on sites like Amazon and Goodreads as well as posting on social media makes a huge difference for Indie authors like myself. Thanks for reading!

Reapers of the Dark Realm

Coming soon - Book 2 of the Dark Realm

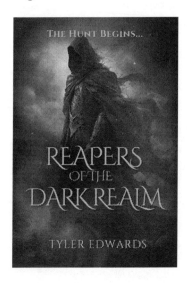

The Outlands Trilogy

With his make-shift family of "Undesirables", Jett Lasting struggles to find his place in a world where drawing attention to yourself can get you killed. His very existence is considered a crime. To survive, he must avoid guards, beggar gangs, and an ever-growing tension that could drag the whole city into chaos. His choices could lead to freedom or the death of everyone he's ever known or cared about.

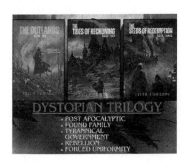

Also by Tyler Edwards

Just scan the QR code with your phone

Stay in the loop: sign up for my newsletter at: https://authortyleredwards.wordpress.com/

Glossary

- NAIFLO – a distasteful and disgusting woman of questionable morals and inappropriate behavior
- GORAUM – idiotic
- LEAKS – intense anger
- PLEK – a rude term for a person that behaves in a cruel or rude manner
- EMPTOS - stupid
- ANTILYTE - Pagan / outsider
- MEMORA - a magical spell that allows people to enter the memories of others
- LAMERA – A place of eternal punishment and suffering considered by many religious groups to be the destiny for those who live wicked lives
- BAVASO - Someone born outside of a marriage
- GWAR – feces
- GERSHWA - a hypocrite
- RALK – A word so rude it is frown upon by polite society. It is an expression of intense emotional, usually anger
- CHUG - suck

Glossary

- Rooki – a fool
- Dim - Dumb
- Owa - A reference to the butt or a person behaving like one
- Siochaol Agreement – (Taggoronian for Peace) pact between dragons and the kingdoms outside of Parisia
- Mionogaol – (Taggoronian) an oath kin
- Dimea vol selio – a sort of dimensional sphere that prevents the people in side from affecting anything outside of the sphere.
- Potemania – the effect of an object of power on the mind. Typically driving them to obsessive behavior or anger
- Vas Noomi – spirit vessel
- Maldiactia- (dragon speech) cursed one
- Naus Menalius – (elven) men of the sea
- Vagra - Taggoronian for 'cursed to wander' like ronin
- Sygenis for sygenis – Taggoronian for "kin for kin"

Acknowledgments

I'd like to take this opportunity to thank a few key people who helped make this book a reality:

My wife Erica who is more supportive of my writing than my skill may deserve.

Momma Mountain who is always offering her insights and encouragements.

Kirra Antrobus for her incredibly thoughtful edits and notes to help improve the final draft to what it is.

To the Street and Arc team members who have been such an encouragement and support for my writing (including one who has threatened me with figurative violence if her name were to be used).

Made in the USA
Middletown, DE
26 August 2024